DEVIOUS LITTLE LIARS

SAINT VIEW HIGH #1

ELLE THORPE

WWW.ELLETHORPE.COM

*For my friend and fellow bully romance author, Sara Massery.
Thanks for the shove to write this book.*

1

LACEY

I was about to be arrested.

That was my first thought when a flash of movement outside the window caught my attention.

Extreme overreaction?

Perhaps.

But when you'd illegally let yourself into your school on a Sunday, these were the worries that plagued a girl.

Acting on instinct, I hurled myself off the piano stool and onto the floor, scuttling to the windows overlooking the quad. Maybe they hadn't seen me yet. The late afternoon sun was sinking, and perhaps, if I was lucky, the glare would temporarily blind them. I could make my escape out one of the back doors. There was an exit in the administration hall. Others in the math and history wings. Of course, not one anywhere near the music rooms. Helpful.

Ever so carefully, I lifted to peer out the window, and yelped at the face on the other side. I ducked down again, though there was no chance he hadn't seen me, what with his nose an inch from the glass.

I was totally busted. But at least it wasn't the police.

Lawson's laughter on the other side of the window made me realize how ridiculous I was being. I stood, embarrassment heating my face.

"You want to let me in?" he yelled.

I squeezed my eyes closed but nodded. "I'll meet you at the door."

Scrambling down the hall, I tried to come up with a plausible story that would result in the least amount of trouble. I still had nothing by the time I pulled open the heavy, ancient oak doors of Providence School for Girls.

My uncle stood on the other side, boxes of his work balanced precariously in his arms. He shifted beneath their weight, sending a USB stick and a pile of papers sliding off the top. They fluttered down around our ankles.

I knelt hastily, tucking the USB stick into my pocket and gathering up the runaway pages. I glanced up at his familiar face. "Before you say anything, just remember, I'm your favorite niece."

"You're my only niece," he grumbled, but there was still a hint of laughter in his voice.

I put the papers back on top, then took the box from him, lightening his load. "Which means you won't have me arrested?"

He kicked the doors closed behind him. "Well, that depends on how quickly you start explaining why you're at school on a Sunday night, instead of at Meredith's, which is where you said you were going. How did you even get in here without tripping the alarm? If you broke a window, I won't be impressed." He walked toward his office.

I hurried to keep up. "No, no. All windows are intact. I used the code."

"What? How do you even know it?"

I snorted, then remembered I was probably about to be

grounded until I turned eighteen. Which, admittedly, was only a couple of weeks away. But still. I tried to force my expression into something more suitably chastised. "Sorry. But you've been driving me to school and unlocking that door in front of me for the past three years. The code is my birthday. Just like all your passwords."

That resulted in a withering look, but I knew he wasn't really angry at me. We wove through the administration offices until we reached Lawson's, his gold-plated Principal nameplate on the door. He unlocked it, and we both dumped our boxes on the table.

Then he turned to me, folding his arms across his chest, giving me his best principal's glare. "How long have you been sneaking in here for?"

No point lying about it now. "Months."

His mouth dropped open. "To do what? Please don't say drugs. If you say drugs, I swear, I'm going to take you down to that police station myself."

I sniggered. "No. Something much worse."

"Sex? Booze? What could be worse?" He narrowed his eyes, but they crinkled at the corners. He was trying not to laugh. "Are you running some sort of illegal cock fighting ring out of the gym?"

I raised an eyebrow. "No, but wow. Thanks for the ideas. If college doesn't work out for me, I'll be sure to consider those options. I've just been practicing in the music rooms. All alone. No sex, drugs, or farmyard animals of any kind."

My uncle frowned and grumbled. I'd won him over. He knew how important music was to me. "So. No police?"

His expression morphed into fatherly affection. He put his arm around my shoulders and kissed the top of my head. "What do you think? I'm hardly going to call the police when I'd be the one to pay your bail. I've got work to do. Go on, go do your thing. But set your alarm and meet me back here in two hours. You know how you lose track of time when you play."

I breathed a sigh of relief. He so rarely lost his temper, and almost never at me. I couldn't have stood it if he were angry. I kissed his stubbled cheek. "Love you..."

Not for the first time, the word 'Dad' formed on my lips. But at the last moment, I swallowed it down. Instead, I gave him a grateful wave and hurried back to the music rooms.

When I got there, I shut the door behind me and made a beeline for the piano, running my palm over its gleaming black surface. This was my happy place. And it filled something inside me in a way that nothing else did.

Pulling my phone from my pocket, I set the alarm so I wouldn't be late.

Then I pressed my fingers to the keys and closed my eyes, the first lilting notes lifting to the air. Time ceased to exist until a blaring alarm cut through my bubble.

I lost focus, hit the wrong key, and the entire song unraveled. "Dammit!" I slammed the keys hard.

I glanced at my phone and silenced the obnoxious beeping. In the blink of an eye, two hours had passed, and the real world came rushing back in. The sun had set, leaving me in near darkness, and I hadn't even noticed. Patting the top of the piano like it was a dog who'd just completed a new trick, I murmured, "Until next time."

In the corridor, I stopped dead as I caught a whiff of something unpleasant. "What the hell..." I murmured, wrinkling my nose. I took a few more steps, then froze.

Smoke.

I peered into the darkness, trying to remain calm while my brain scrambled to find logical conclusions. It was nearing the end of summer. People could be having barbecues nearby, and the smoke might have just blown in on the breeze. Or perhaps a wildfire had started. The smoke alarms weren't going off. Nor were the sprinklers. I picked up the pace, heading for the admin offices. The entire time, I scrabbled with my thoughts, fighting against the obvious. Pushing myself to believe those excuses, because what was right in front of my eyes was too scary to comprehend. I rounded a corner and stopped dead.

There was no denying it anymore.

The building was filling with thick, acrid smoke.

Something instinctual pushed me forward, and my feet went with it, instead of listening to the panicked voice in my head screaming to turn and run in the opposite direction. I fumbled for my phone, pulled it out, and dialed nine-one-one. Smoke invaded my chest and eyes. I coughed, trying to clear it while fear clawed its way up my spine.

"Fire!" I gasped when the operator answered. "Providence School for Girls." Racking coughs took over. I hung up, but the farther I got, the thicker the smoke became, until it didn't matter if I spoke or not. I held my arm over my mouth and nose, trying to keep it out, but it was a losing battle. My lungs protested, but I moved on, my pace increasing until I was running. I skidded around the corner, bashing my hipbone on the wall. The darkness was disorienting. The visibility next to nothing. I couldn't see farther than a few steps ahead of me.

"Lawson!" I yelled, immediately regretting it when smoke filled my mouth and nose. It got thicker with every step. I coughed again and ran my hands over the wall where I thought the light switch should be. I came up empty, my nails scratching over nothing but drywall.

I spun around, confused now at exactly where I was. I needed to get to my uncle. I knew, that if there was a fire, he would have come for me. Called me. He knew where I was. And there was only one way to get there. We couldn't have missed each other. I pushed my legs harder, not certain that I was even heading in the right direction, but I had to try.

Suddenly, the room around me opened up, and I nearly wept with relief as I recognized the foyer. But there was no time for that.

I'd found the source of the smoke.

Flames licked the walls.

"Lawson!" I yelled again, tasting ash. Panic surged, adrenaline kicking in and powering my movements. My brain short-circuited, whether from lack of air or fear, I didn't know. The one thing I was certain of was that I couldn't lose another parent. I couldn't add my uncle to the broken part of me that had existed ever since my birth parents' disappearance. He was the only father I really remembered. And he wouldn't have left without me. I knew that without a doubt. He wouldn't have left me there to die.

Which meant he was still inside.

I ran in a crouch toward the flames. They grew with every second that passed. "Laws—" I couldn't even get his name out this time before the lack of air stole my voice. I held my breath and rushed toward his office, throwing open doors as I went and dodging the deadly heat.

I skidded to a stop at the glass window of the principal's office. A scream curled up my throat but came out silently.

Lawson's still form lay facedown on the floorboards.

Flames billowed up around him, higher in here than anywhere else. They crawled across the ceiling, like slithering beasts of orange fury. I bashed on the window so hard it should have broken, desperately yelping my uncle's name between racking bouts of coughing.

Overhead, a beam cracked.

Sparks flew and I flinched away. I tried again, lunging for the door, but the heat drove me back. Tears streamed down my face. "Help," I croaked.

I couldn't save him alone. He was right there, the flames getting ever closer, and I couldn't reach him. I stumbled back the way I'd come, dropping to my knees and crawling when my feet wouldn't take another step. My eyes stung. My gaze flitted around the smoke-filled room, but my head grew cloudy.

With a sudden certainty, I realized we were both going to die.

There was no way out.

I closed my eyes. At least the last thing I'd done was something I loved. I remembered the way it felt to have my fingers flying over the piano keys, the song soaring, not only in my ears but in my heart. When the flames took me, that's where I'd be in my head. In the place I was happiest. The only place I had true peace.

Something grabbed me.

Not something, someone.

I dragged myself back into the present. There was somebody else here. Someone who could help. Hope surged within me.

"My uncle," I choked out.

Startled by hands on my bare skin, and my body being lifted from the floor, I tried to force my stinging eyes open. But my vision was so blurred I couldn't make out a face. I turned into the person's chest, and my gaze focused instead on the thing closest to me. Letters floated across my vision, a mere inch from my nose.

The man—it had to be a man, his body had none of the softer curves of a woman—didn't say anything, but gripped me tighter while he moved through the crumbling building.

Heat seared at my legs, my arms, my face. I couldn't do a thing but fist my fingers into the material of his shirt and hold on. The embroidered feel of the letters scratched, in contrast with the softness of the fabric.

He muttered something that sounded like, "Hold on, Lacey."

A thought floated through my head, but it was too hard to grasp. I wanted to chase it, grab it, and force it to make sense. But I was too tired. I watched it go, disappearing into a smoke tendril.

My body jolted against his with each step. I wanted him to run. I wanted him to get me out of this place, but it all just seemed impossible now. Everything hurt. My lungs screamed in pain. It was too hard to hold on. My grip on his shirt loosened.

"Lacey!" he yelled, but his voice was far away.

I closed my eyes and let the darkness take me.

2

LACEY

*I*f the size of my uncle's wake was anything to go by, he was the most popular man in town.

I leaned against the wall, in a corner of my house, a tall potted palm doing a bad job of obscuring me from the room full of people. The champagne flute in my hand was almost empty, so I ditched it and grabbed another from a passing waiter.

"Lacey," a woman cried, grasping my free hand and squeezing tightly. Her wrinkled skin was thin as tissue paper and dotted with age. "Your uncle was a great man. Much too young." Her voice dripped with fake sincerity.

I tried to force my lips to move, knowing I should thank her.

I couldn't.

The woman's concerned look disappeared, only to be replaced with an expression of mild disapproval. She tutted beneath her breath, dropped my hand, and moved on to the next group of people.

I watched her go, not caring I'd been rude. I didn't even know who she was.

"How you doing, Lace?" Meredith appeared beside me. She propped one stiletto heel up on the wall.

Owen sidled up next to her, casting a worried eye over me.

"I don't even know who most of these people are. Like those girls over there." I jerked my head in the direction of a group dressed in pretty blue and green tones. "Have I even met them before?"

Owen eyed the girls, his lip lifting in a sneer of disgust. "Freshman bimbos. Probably just here to gossip."

I sighed, wanting this entire thing to be over. Waiters in white shirts and black ties circled the room with canapés on their trays as if this were a party, the same as the hundreds my aunt had thrown in the past. Selina had a wine glass stem firmly clutched between her perfectly manicured fingernails, while she held court in the center of the room, surrounded by her tennis buddies, her hairdresser, and her nosy best friend. Her over-Botoxed expression didn't betray any real emotion.

She had her mask firmly in place.

I'd lived in fear of losing mine every day since the fire. It was easier to live behind fake smiles than to allow myself to think about my uncle, the man who'd been my father for thirteen years, being gone.

Fire was all I thought about now. That, and my aunt. She'd lost the love of her life. The man she'd woken up next to every day for twenty years. She was hurting, and I hated I couldn't do anything to make it better for her.

"I had to talk to the police again," I said quietly to my friends. "That's three times now. I think they're trying to trip me up in my story."

Meredith frowned. "You think they don't believe you?"

I lifted one shoulder as I twisted to face her. Her pretty

blonde curls had been tamed back into a sleek bun that better matched her black knee-length dress. A single strand of pearls around her neck set off the Audrey Hepburn look. She even had oversized sunglasses perched on her head. "They can't find any footage from the security cameras that corroborates my version of that night. Apparently, the security cameras were all switched off. Along with the smoke detectors and the sprinkler system. I don't think they believe me when I say a man carried me from the flames."

Meredith's eyes widened. "But you were found barely conscious on the quad! And your burn! You were in such bad shape, they can't seriously think you walked out of there by yourself?"

"That seems to be exactly what they think." The burn on my leg throbbed beneath its bandages.

Meredith threw up her hands in frustration. "That's ridiculous. Ugh! They make me so mad with their uselessness. Do they even have to do an entrance exam? Or do they just accept those plastic badges you get in the cereal box?"

I couldn't agree more. The police in our town had never had a reputation for being particularly adept. I, more than anyone, knew that firsthand.

"They don't suspect you, though. Right?" Owen chewed his bottom lip, gaze darting between me and the rest of the room, as if he were on the lookout for any sign of danger.

Something about it reminded me of a meerkat, the thought so amusing I almost smiled. Maybe I would have if he hadn't been kind of annoying. He'd been smothering me with his concern ever since last weekend, and it was beginning to get a little ridiculous. It wasn't like another fire was just going to spontaneously ignite.

I hoped.

"I don't know," I answered his question. The same

thought had plagued me ever since I'd woken up in the hospital. The way the cops had taken my story had felt more like an interrogation than an interview. "My story hasn't changed. Someone carried me from that building before it collapsed. His shirt had the letters SVHF. And he knew my name."

"That's the part that freaks me out the most," Meredith nibbled at a fingernail distractedly. "That means you know him."

"Or at least, he knows me." I gazed around the room full of people I'd never met. But all of them knew me because of who my uncle was. Was it someone in this room? It had definitely been a man. I remembered the hardness of his chest. Tall and strong. Big enough to pick up my five-six frame from a dead slump on the floor and carry me out through the back of the school building. That's where I'd been found by the firefighters who had arrived too late. Laid out on the grass, barely conscious, and gasping for breath. I'd been lucky, they'd said. A few hours on oxygen had cleared the smoke from my lungs, and my burns were superficial. They'd scar, but not badly, and should heal quickly. But I didn't feel lucky. To the depths of my soul, I was gutted. My entire world had been ripped from my hands.

Again.

"Did you hear we're all being moved to Edgely Academy?" Meredith asked, changing the subject. She twisted and looked in the direction of the bar. "I hope he goes there. Owen, do you know him?"

I followed her line of sight. The 'he' in question worked behind the makeshift bar, set up off one side of our spacious living room. My aunt had brought in our usual caterers, but if he'd worked our parties before, I hadn't noticed. Blond hair flopped in his eye as he poured a drink of something bubbly and passed it into the waiting hands of an older woman. She flashed him a smile, her mouth full of teeth so perfect they couldn't have been real. He grinned back at her. He was tall, and broad-shouldered, a deep tan coloring his face and hands. Handsome for sure. I could see why he'd caught Meredith's eye.

Owen squinted at him. "Never seen him before, but Edgely is a big school."

"He seems young but he's working a bar," I noted. "Gotta be at least twenty-one."

Meredith straightened, pulling back her shoulders and sticking her tits out. "Even better."

The man's attention drifted in our direction, and I waited for it. For his gaze to sweep her. For hunger to flare in his eyes. Meredith was hot. There was no denying that, with her long legs, big doe eyes, and a natural D cup that suited her taller frame. I was pretty. I was vain enough to admit that. But I was girl next door in comparison to Meredith's Hollywood.

But he barely hovered on Meredith a second before he switched to me. His eyes locked with mine, and the corner of his mouth tipped up adorably. Distracted by one of his colleagues thrusting an empty drink tray into his hands, he finally turned away.

Meredith nudged me. "You're looking at that man like you want him to devour you."

I grinned at her, not hating the way that smile had stirred something inside me. "Nothing like a good devouring when you're feeling down, right?"

Meredith elbowed me, and we both giggled.

Owen groaned. "And that's my cue to go get a drink." He walked away, the tips of his ears reddening.

Meredith acted like Owen hadn't even spoken. "Get over

there!" she encouraged me. "Go get you some. That boy is down for it, for sure. And I sure as hell am not going to talk you out of a little distraction. You need it. Go get your pussy munched."

I burst out laughing, attracting confused looks from the rest of the room. My aunt was one of them. Her gaze darted to Meredith, a disapproving frown flickering over her features before it smoothed back into place.

I got it. My laughter was out of place amongst the low murmur of polite conversation. Normally I was better behaved, but the champagne was going to my head.

"You're so inappropriate," I hissed to Meredith. "This is a wake." But the edge of a smile told her I didn't really mean it.

"Yeah, but I got you smiling. And as your best friend, that's my job. But your aunt is gesturing for you to go to her, and since I'm a bad influence, I should probably go find someone else to talk to. Or make out with. I wonder if your cutie has a friend..."

I didn't bother mentioning that one moment of mutual eye appreciation did not make the cutie mine.

I found my aunt in the crowd, and she immediately put her arm around me. I resisted the urge to lay my head on her shoulder like I had as a child. My aunt wasn't perfect. I hated the way she had little ambition, beyond being a lady of luxury. Her life centered around her appearance.

But she was also warm and caring. She'd taken me in when I was barely five years old and had never treated me as anything other than her daughter. She'd stuck Band-Aids on my scrapes, wiped my forehead when I was sick, hugged me tight when boys preferred Meredith to me.

I put my arm around her waist and squeezed her right back. We'd get through this. Together. Somehow.

I hovered around, keeping an eye on her as the afternoon dragged, turning into evening. The house slowly emptied out, and for the first time all day, there was enough room to breathe.

"Sweetheart," my aunt said, taking me by the elbow and tugging me into the hallway that led to the back of the house. Tension pulled her perfect eyebrows together in lines I knew she'd be horrified by if she could have seen them.

"Headache?"

She squeezed my fingers. "I'm sorry. I just need to lie down for a little while. Almost everyone has left anyway. Do you mind?"

"I'll take care of it. Go rest."

She leaned in, her lips brushing over my cheek then she hurried up the stairs, her long black dress billowing out behind her.

I wandered back to the main room, and for a moment, watched the staff bustling around, packing up chairs and rounding up stray wine glasses.

I wasn't needed here. What I needed was some fresh air and time alone.

As often happened when I wasn't distracted by other things, the memories of that night played in my head. I'd thought the alcohol might help with that, but I was pretty buzzed, and yet the memories were still sharp as tacks. I drifted outside, skirting the sparkling blue pool and following the slope of the land that descended into a grassed area. Tall trees rimmed our property, providing privacy from the neighbors. My uncle had always been on the gardeners to keep the trees healthy, fearing one sick plant would infect the lot and he'd lose the mini forest that kept prying eyes from our business. I'd once heard him joke about the trees allowing my aunt to sunbathe nude, and she'd laughed and swatted his arm. I'd been embarrassed and slunk away, pretending not to hear.

Now, I'd give anything to hear him say it again.

Give anything to have him back.

"Sorry for your loss."

I jumped at the deep voice that seemed to come out of nowhere. I spun around, searching for the owner in the disappearing light. He leaned against a wide trunk, cigarette dangling from his lips.

The bartender from earlier.

Hell. He really was attractive.

It took me a moment to draw my gaze away from his mouth and up to his eyes. Were they blue? Green? Something light-colored for sure.

"Thanks." I shoved my hands in the pockets of my dress, studying him.

He pulled a lighter from the pocket of his black dress pants and sparked it. A small orange flame erupted, sending a chill rolling down my spine. He brought it to the end of his cigarette, dragging hard to light it. When he straightened, he blew a lazy cloud of smoke out the corner of his mouth, his gaze trained on me the entire time.

After the shitty day I'd had, I liked the way he looked at me.

He didn't look at me like I was the poor little rich girl who'd lost the only father she'd ever known.

He didn't look at me in suspicion, like the police did every time I met with them.

The only thing his look held was the promise of a good time.

He pulled the cigarette from his lips, holding it between two fingers, and offered it to me. "Smoke?"

I shook my head. "Not my thing."

But something about the relaxed expression on his face as he inhaled made me want to try it.

Fuck it. I inched closer to him, eyeing the cigarette. He passed it to me, our fingers brushing in the exchange. I drew in a breath at the thrill that one tiny touch sent through my body.

I grasped the cigarette with unpracticed fingers and brought it to my lips. I sucked on it, smoke filling my mouth and lungs. My head spun, flashing back to the moment I'd dropped to my knees outside my uncle's office, overcome by the smoke and flames. I coughed at the invasion, my chest constricting, fighting the foreign feeling.

The man plucked it from my hand with a chuckle, while my tarred lungs tried to haul in fresh air. I carried on with the deep breaths, longer than my lungs actually needed, just to give myself time to drag my head back to the present.

"Well, that was a mistake," I gasped out.

"First time?"

I managed to cough up a yes.

He grinned, his eyes twinkling with mischief. "It's like sex. It gets better the more you do it."

I wouldn't know. But I wasn't about to tell him that. Not even Meredith knew that I was still holding on to my V card.

"What's your name, sad eyes?" He took another hit but this time didn't offer it to me.

I was glad. Once was enough.

"Lacey," I answered.

"Banjo."

I raised an eyebrow. "Interesting name."

"Interesting parents. Apparently, they were hippies. But I rock it."

It wasn't false confidence. Then name suited him. He had a laid-back vibe that seemed to fit with hippie parents.

"What do you mean, apparently? You don't know for sure?"

He tilted his head back, letting his hair rest against the bark of the tree, and blew smoke rings into the sky. "Kind of a personal question, don't you think? Considering I've only known your name three seconds."

Heat crept into my cheeks. "Sorry. Blame the dead father figure for my lack of tact."

He nudged me with his foot. "I'm messing with you. They took off when I was a kid. Ended up in foster care for a while, until my brother aged out and took custody of me. I barely remember them."

"We've something in common then. Mine disappeared when I was five."

"Disappeared?"

"Apparently." I mimicked the word he'd used. "Cops determined they were dead or didn't want to be found."

His gaze shifted to the mansion looming over us at the top of the hill. "This place doesn't seem like a foster house."

I smiled ruefully. "No, I was lucky. My aunt and uncle adopted me after my parents were declared legally dead."

"Can't even imagine what growing up here must have been like. Servants to wipe your ass?"

I laughed. "Monday to Friday. We give them weekends off."

He chuckled, darting a glance at me from beneath his flop of blond hair. "You're cute."

I bit my lip, not sure what to say. Thanks? You're cute, too? My aunt would probably have a conniption if she knew I was hiding in the back garden, talking to a man I didn't know. Especially one who obviously wasn't from around here. The guys in Providence weren't waiters. If they had summer jobs, it was with their fathers' law firms. Not serving drinks at parties. I loved my aunt to pieces, but she was a snob. She wouldn't have given Banjo a second look. Handsome as he was, she wouldn't have even noticed him. Her eyes would have glossed right over him as if he didn't exist.

But Banjo was a nice distraction after a shitty day. My eyes weren't doing any sort of glossing over him. More like studying every inch of him, wondering what he'd look like with that tie loosened and his hair mussed up.

"I should probably go," I said eventually, pretending he hadn't said anything. "I'm supposed to be saying goodbye to people and making sure the caterers are packing up." I eyed him. "Which they're obviously not, since you're down here smoking."

"They'll be fine without us."

I drew in a deep breath and willed myself to push off the tree and put some space between us. "They might not notice you're gone, but I was kind of in the spotlight today."

I started to walk away, but his hand shot out, circling my wrist, pulling me back. I smiled as tingles shot up my arm. I stared up at him through my eyelashes.

"Don't go," he said, voice husky. He dropped his cigarette, putting it out with one scuffed boot, without breaking eye contact for a second.

"Why not?"

"I like talking to you. And I think you liked talking to me."

"What makes you think that?" I shot back.

"Your eyes were a little less sad and a little more..."

I waited.

"Interested."

"I didn't come out here to talk," I admitted.

He inched closer. "Why did you then?"

"To find something to take my mind off everything up there." I jerked my head in the direction of the house.

His gaze turned curious. "Something, or someone?"

The light pressure of his fingers encouraged me to step into him. I could have moved back but I didn't want to. I stepped closer. Closer than was polite. So close my nipples touched his chest. They hardened instantly.

"Someone," I whispered.

Banjo's fingers grasped my chin and tilted it up. He leaned in. "You want me to kiss you, sad eyes? Because the way you're staring at me says you do."

I did. I really did. I wanted to close my eyes and lose myself in his lips. I wanted to inhale his scent that was an intoxicating combination of cigarette, coconut, and something distinctly man.

His lips brushed over the corner of my mouth, the barest of touches, but it sent a jolt of good feelings through my entire body.

I wanted more.

His mouth floated across my skin, to the sensitive spot beneath my ear.

"Go out with me," he said huskily.

Good feelings gone.

I blinked, jerking back. "Excuse me?"

His lazy gaze rolled over me. "Like I said before, you're cute. And your sad eyes intrigue me. So, I'm asking if you'll go out with me?"

"Are you joking?"

He cocked his head to one side. "Why would I joke about something like that? You're fucking gorgeous, Lacey. So yeah, I want to go out with you."

I breathed out a sigh of relief. He thought I was hot. Okay, that was good. Great even. I thought he was hot, too.

He'd caught me off guard by asking me on an actual date, like he might have wanted something more than just sex. A date was not on the table. Sex? Totally on the table. And on the bed. Hell, if he kept checking me out with those half-lidded eyes, I'd do him just about anywhere. V-card be damned. I'd been wanting to get rid of it for a year now anyway. "Why go out? We're both here right now, aren't we?"

He studied me for a second, and obviously what I wanted was written all over my face. He barked out a laugh. "Well, shit. Didn't expect that. You seem so sweet and innocent."

I edged closer and tilted my head back to look up at him. "I'm not in the mood to beat around the bush. It's been a shit day. I just want someone who will make me forget that for a little while."

"And I'll do?"

I shrugged. "That bother you?"

Something flickered in his eyes, but it disappeared as quickly as it had appeared. "That you want to use me for sex? No, sad eyes. You wouldn't be the first."

Though the statement intrigued me, I was more interested in other things he could offer me. It wasn't worth my time delving into his personal problems when all I wanted to do was fool around and forget that this day, and the last few weeks had existed. "Come on, let's go upstairs."

I towed him back up the hill and through the glass doors. He threw a wink at one of his work colleagues, who just shook his head. My aunt would have died a thousand deaths if she'd realized her niece was about to take the hired help upstairs for more than just cleaning. But she was in bed, and the only people left downstairs were Banjo's coworkers. None of my aunt's friends to tattle on me. Though in that moment, I might not have cared.

All I knew was that Banjo's hand in mine felt warm and alive. And I wanted more of that. Warmth to replace the cold dead feeling that had been slowly devouring me.

The front door opened right as my foot hit the bottom stair.

"Lacey Knight? Stop, please."

I twisted at the unfamiliar voice and glanced past our maid, Angelique, to the uniformed officer on the doorstep.

"We need you and your guardian to come down to the station with us. Immediately."

Banjo shifted slightly, so he was between me and the officers. "What for?"

The officer cast his gaze over Banjo, and I knew instantly what he was seeing. Banjo's too-long hair. His waiter's uniform. A tattoo peeking out from beneath his collar.

The officer's lip curled slightly, distaste in his gaze. "Who are you?"

I stepped in front of Banjo. "Not important. How about you tell me why you want me to come to the station? Again. I've already told you everything I know about the fire."

The officer's steely gaze landed squarely on me. "Perhaps. But either way, you can come willingly, or I can arrest you right here."

My anger boiled. The officer looked at me with the same contempt he'd looked at Banjo. He knew then. Knew exactly who I was. Who I'd been, and what had happened in my past. Judgement rolled off him.

"Bartholomew Johns, is that you?" My aunt's voice from the top of the stairs held a barely constrained anger. "You did not just waltz into my house and threaten to arrest my niece, did you?"

I glanced up in surprise, meeting her eyes. She swept down the stairs without a hair out of place or a wrinkle in her clothing. Nobody would have ever guessed she'd just been trying to sleep off a migraine. Her hand found the small of my back at the same time she noticed Banjo beside me. She frowned but ignored him, nudging me forward.

I dropped his hand.

The officer went a little pink around the cheeks, but he didn't apologize. "New facts about your husband's death have come to light, Mrs. Knight. You both need to come to the station. Don't make this harder than it has to be."

Selina took her purse from a coatrack by the door and stared the man down. "Try using your manners next time then, perhaps?"

The officer bit his lip and spun on his heel, disappearing from the doorway.

Selina sighed. "Let's just get this over with, okay? I know you don't like the police, but the sooner we get this done, the sooner you can get back to..." She cast a glance over her shoulder at Banjo, who hadn't moved. "Whatever you were doing."

Banjo's sharp gaze darted to my aunt but quickly came back to me. I lifted my shoulder an inch and followed my aunt's lead, picking up my purse and heading for the door.

"Lacey," he called.

I stopped.

Banjo had his hands shoved into the pockets of his work pants. "See you around."

I nodded. But I sincerely doubted it.

3

LACEY

*S*elina shifted on the hard plastic seats, clutching her purse on her lap. She hadn't touched the desk in front of us, or the plastic cups of water the police officers had left for us. She cast her gaze around the dingy room, her nose wrinkled in distaste.

"This is ridiculous," she muttered, not for the first time this evening.

I agreed, but I didn't reply. Complaining about it wasn't going to get us anywhere. The fact they'd put us in an interrogation room couldn't mean anything good. The last few chats had been more informal. I'd given a statement. Then repeated it a few days later. Then answered some more questions. But that had all been in the hospital, our home, or the captain's office. Today was different. There'd been a more serious vibe when the officers had come to our door. And there'd been no one here to greet us as we'd arrived at the station. We'd been left to wait, though why, I couldn't work out.

The door swung open, and Detective Appin strode in. Another detective behind him, one I didn't recognize, shut the door quietly. They took the empty seats on the opposite side of the grimy-looking table.

"Finally." Selina shot a glare at the detective we were familiar with. He'd been the one who'd come to the hospital to take my initial statement, the day after the fire.

"We apologize for keeping you waiting, Mrs. Knight. But new information about your husband's case has come in. We wanted to be sure we had all the facts before we discussed them with you."

Selina sighed. "Fine, but can we make this snappy? We have a meeting at my niece's new school tomorrow, and I don't want her exhausted for it."

It wasn't late. Most ten-year-olds probably had later bedtimes, but nobody argued with Selina about it.

The detective turned to me. "Ah, that's right. Orientation at Edgely Academy. That'll be a big change for you all. Never in a million years would have thought they'd be turning the boys school co-ed. I hear they're already building new wings to accommodate you all."

I didn't answer. I wasn't in the mood for idle chitchat. And starting a new school year at Edgely Academy didn't exactly thrill me with joy. Especially because we all knew the reason nobody could go back to our old school.

Appin seemed to get the idea I wasn't interested and opened a folder on the table. "Right. Well, we've asked you both down here tonight because Lawson's autopsy results came back."

"Yes? So? We already know he died in the fire. This isn't news."

Appin grimaced. "Actually, he didn't. The autopsy results found he was already dead before the fire started."

My aunt let out a gasp, but my brain worked quicker. "How?" I demanded. "A heart attack? Stroke?"

The detective cocked his head to the side. "Stab wound."

"What?" I choked out. "No, that can't be right. I would have seen the blood..." Wouldn't I? I tried to think back, but all I could remember were flames and heat. The floorboards in Lawson's office were dark. Could I have missed that he was lying there, bleeding to death? Bile rose in my throat as I realized I couldn't recall paying any attention to the floor. Why would I have? The walls being eaten up by flames had been kind of distracting.

Selina let out a cry of pain that ripped me in half.

I tugged my chair closer to hers and stretched my arms around her narrow shoulders. "Sssh, Sel. It'll be okay."

She trembled beneath my touch but then hugged me back hard. "Why?" she whispered. "He was a good man. There was no reason for anyone to hurt him." She choked on the last words, but I grabbed her hand and squeezed it. She swallowed hard, her throat bobbing.

"That's what we now have to work out." He turned to me, his calculating gaze sweeping my body. My skin crawled.

"Don't even think about accusing my niece." Selina's voice sharpened into steel. "Lawson was the only father she knows and she nearly died in that fire herself. There's no way she did this."

The detective folded his arms across his burly chest. "And you, Mrs. Knight?"

If this situation hadn't been so bleak, I would have laughed. My aunt was three inches shorter than me, making her a full foot shorter than my uncle had been. She barely ate and probably weighed one hundred and twenty pounds on a fat day. But besides all that, the woman wouldn't hurt a fly. She might have been a bit of a snob, and too focused on her looks, but she was also the woman who put milk out each night for a too-skinny neighborhood cat. And the woman who'd shooed the help away when my friends came over, because she wanted to make sandwiches for us herself. But most of all, she was the woman who worshipped the ground her husband had walked on. While her friends all slept with their gardeners, and men from their gyms, my aunt's attention had never swayed. She'd met Lawson at the door every night, ready to kiss him and ask him about his day.

Selina's gaze narrowed. "I was at home with a headache, and my entire staff can vouch for me. Don't you people talk to each other? I've already told you this." She pushed to her feet, hauling me up with her. "If you want to talk to us further, contact our lawyers. And in the meantime, how about you do your job?"

She dragged me toward the door, and the detectives made no move to stop her. But in the doorway, I put on the brakes.

"The man who pulled me from the fire. What do you know about him? Did you even investigate him?"

"We still have no proof there was anyone else there that night, but—"

My blood boiled. "Why do you need proof? I'm telling you someone was there. That makes me a witness!"

The detective held his hand up. "Stop. You didn't let me finish. I was going to say, while we have found no proof of another person being in the building that night, we are taking your accusations seriously. We researched the letters you told us about. The ones you say were on the man's shirt."

I froze. "SVHF. You found out what they mean?"

The detective leafed through his papers. "We believe so.

There were a few options, but we believe the most likely is Saint View High Football."

"Saint View High?" my aunt asked. "You think one of the thugs from that God-awful hellhole of a town killed my husband?"

I mulled the idea over in my head. Saint View, despite its pleasant-sounding name, was anything but. Saint View was the wrong side of the tracks so to speak. Inside the Providence estate where we lived, there wasn't a house worth less than two million dollars. The developers had bought out a huge area of old buildings and bulldozed as much as they could. The school and the church had been the only things left, and only for the fact they were heritage listed and the local politicians wouldn't allow them to be torn down. But just fifteen minutes across town, outside the gates of our community, the suburb of Saint View sat, an ugly blip on the radar. Mostly full of low-income housing, it was a notorious hot spot for criminals, drugs, and violence.

"We have no suspects at this stage. Just...interests." He narrowed his eyes at me when he said it.

I wasn't intimidated. I had nothing to hide. I took two steps back into the room and placed my hands on the table, leaning down so I was eye height with the detective. Amusement sparkled in his eye.

"You can suspect me all you want, Detective. But you're wasting your time. I suggest you look elsewhere. Before you botch up yet another investigation."

I shoved the table, hard enough for it to push into Appin's belly, but he didn't comment. He knew what I was talking about. He'd been the detective on my parents' case years ago.

He'd failed then. But I wasn't a helpless five-year-old anymore. I wasn't going to take his ineptitude lying down this time. I'd be down here at his office every damn day until he worked out who'd murdered my uncle.

———

*S*elina and I were both quiet on the drive home. She stared out the window and clenched her fingers around the strap of her bag in an attempt to keep them from trembling. I drove, eyes trained to the road, apart from the odd glance to the passenger seat to make sure my aunt was okay.

"I can't believe this," she whispered eventually. She seemed smaller, her slight frame hunched in on itself. "Why would someone want to do this to him? He was a good man. Everybody liked him."

I stopped at a traffic light and tried to keep my fingers from tapping on the wheel impatiently. "Did he know anyone from Saint View High? The principal? Their football coach?"

She shook her head, dark hair falling around her face gently. Even this upset, she was still beautiful. "I don't think so? I can't imagine why he'd have anything to do with the principal of a school like that. And he didn't even like football. Maybe they got in, hoping for money?"

"In a school? How much money would be kept on the grounds on a Sunday night?"

She mulled that over. "Perhaps for the computers and equipment, then? But surely someone would have seen something if that were the case. A truck or van leaving the premises."

"I don't think this was a random attack. The man knew my name."

My aunt darted a worried glance at me. "Are you sure he

said your name? You were so out of it that night, sweetheart..."

I shot her a look as the light went green and I let the car roll forward. "Please don't say you don't believe me either."

She reached across the gearshift and gripped my arm, squeezing it reassuringly. "Of course I believe you. Always. It's just that none of this makes sense."

"I know." I swallowed hard. "Appin thinks I'm lying, doesn't he? You've known him a long time."

She nodded. "It doesn't matter what he thinks."

"But it does. He's going to waste all his time investigating you, and me, and not paying attention to the facts. I don't want him on this case. Ask for someone else."

Selina sighed. "Who, though, Lace? He's the most senior detective they have. And I have no pull with the police department. Even if I did somehow manage to persuade them to give the case to someone else, you think he wouldn't have his nose all in it? It would just make things worse. He'd be embarrassed in front of his colleagues and he'd come after us twice as hard."

Frustration rose inside me, and I gripped the wheel tighter. "So what? We just let him fuck this whole thing up like he did with my parents' case?"

A dark shadow crossed her face. "Language. But, no. Not like that. That can't happen again. I can't stand the not knowing."

An idea bubbled to the surface, and I pondered it in the silence that fell over us. My aunt would never go for it. I knew she'd be horrified, even by the thought. I'd seen the way she'd wrinkled her nose at the mere mention of Saint View. But the more I thought it over, the more it seemed like the only way. I had a chance now to do something I hadn't when I was a kid.

I had a chance to make this right.

If the police weren't going to investigate properly, then I would.

"Enroll me at Saint View High."

My aunt's head snapped in my direction. "What?"

Her eyes were huge, as if I'd just punched her in the gut. But surprise I could work with. It was better than an outright refusal.

"Seriously, Selina. SVHF. Saint View High Football. Doesn't it make sense that someone there might know Uncle Lawson? Maybe someone he worked with? Or went to college with even?"

"I suppose," she said slowly. "But what are you suggesting? That someone held a grudge since his college days?"

I shrugged. "I don't know. But I want to find out."

"By enrolling at the school?"

I went quiet. We were almost home before I answered. "I can't just do nothing. Not again. Please. I'd rather do this with your blessing, but I'm nearly eighteen and I can enroll myself If I have to."

Selina sucked in a deep breath, and I knew why. I'd always been a good kid. Perhaps it was the fact that my aunt and uncle weren't my biological parents, and I therefore still subconsciously felt like I always had to do the right thing in case they decided to give me up. I never stayed out past curfew. I did all my homework and got good grades. I had a perfect attendance record. But this wasn't some insignificant thing, like getting another award at school. This was something I had to do. "Please, Selina. I have to."

I pulled the car into the driveway and hit the beeper for the electric doors on the garage. They rolled open agonizingly slowly, while Selina pondered my request. I didn't dare glance her way. I was full of bravado. I might have been able to enroll myself if I'd wanted to, but the fact was, Selina could find other ways to stop me. Take my car, so I couldn't get there. Or worse, kick me out entirely for going against her wishes. I didn't want either of those things. I loved my aunt. I had a nice home with her, and I didn't want to lose it, right after losing Lawson.

But I had to do something.

"You've got that look in your eye," Selina said with a sigh.

"What look? I don't have a look."

She laughed. "Oh, but, sweetheart, you do. You look just like your mother. Full of fire and determination."

My heart squeezed. I barely remembered my mother. I'd blocked out so much of my early life, it was like a black hole. I remembered the way she'd made me feel, more than her appearance. And deep in my heart, I still knew that she hadn't just disappeared of her own free will. She'd loved me. She wouldn't have just abandoned me.

My eyes filled with tears. She'd been stolen from me. Just like my dad. And my uncle. I kept losing people, and I didn't know why.

Selina leaned across and pulled me into an awkward hug. She sighed. "So, what does one wear on their first day of public school?"

4

LACEY

*S*aint View High had all the charm of a prison block.

Kids streamed from all directions, headed for the stairs that led up the squat, bare cement building, looking as thrilled as if they were headed to a funeral.

So many nameless faces. There wasn't a single soul I recognized.

My attention caught on a couple, making their way across the patchy grass of the quad. She was a cute blonde, with athletic legs, shown off by a skirt so short it was little more than underwear. The guy she hung off was tall, his broad shoulders tapering down to a narrow waist. She talked animatedly about something I was too far away to hear, while he appeared bored, his gaze wandering around the crowd, as if he were searching for someone. Or perhaps searching for an escape from his girlfriend. His gaze caught mine, and I looked down quickly, embarrassed at being caught staring.

My cell buzzed in my backpack, the ringtone lost to the crowd of teenagers forced to divert around me. I fished it out and answered the call without checking the caller ID, just grateful I had something to do to busy my hands.

"Girl! Where are you? I thought we were meeting on the steps, but it's five to, and you're a no-show. Are you in the parking lot or did you sleep in?"

Shit. Meredith. Orientation at Edgely Academy. We'd organized to meet beforehand, and I'd completely forgotten. I cringed. "Actually, neither. I'm standing in front of Saint View High."

There was a moment of surprised silence, then, "Uh, okay. But why?"

I sighed. "Too long to get into right now. It all happened last night. I'll call you tonight and explain, but I'm not coming to orientation today."

"Okay, I'll get your schedule for you."

"No need. I'm not coming at all."

"What?"

"I promise, I'll call you tonight. Love you." I hung up before she could ask any more questions.

Someone rammed into me, catching me off guard. I stumbled sideways a few steps, dropping my phone in the process. It clattered to the ground. I glanced over my shoulder, annoyed.

The cute little blonde was a whole lot less cute when she was scowling.

"What are you doing, standing in the middle of the path like you own it?" she snarled. Her ice-blue gaze rolled down my body, taking in my skirt and cardigan set. "You're in everyone's way."

She was probably right, but she didn't need to be a bitch about it. There was plenty of room to walk around me.

Ignoring her, I knelt to grab my phone from the ground, only to find it sticking out from beneath a scuffed black shitkicker. The laces were so loose I wasn't sure how the owner walked in them. I lifted my head, taking in black jeans and a white T-shirt. Broad shoulders were barely contained by the tight fabric. From across the quad, I hadn't really noticed his face. But up close, holy shit. He was beautiful. His jaw strong and clean-shaven, his cheekbones high. He did a double take as our gazes clashed.

I fought not to drown in eyes so dark I could barely see where the pupils began. They drew me in, holding me in place, refusing to release me from their grip. He was vaguely familiar. Like I'd seen him on a movie. Or as if he looked like somebody I knew. We hadn't met before. I was sure of that. There was no forgetting someone who left you without the ability to speak.

The girl laughed, the sound cruel. "I think the princess is checking you out, Colt."

His expression changed in an instant. His eyes narrowed, turning hard and cold. The corner of his mouth tipped up as if he were amused, but his eyes held no warmth. There was no sign of laughter in those dark-brown depths, despite what his mouth might have been doing. A shiver ran down my spine. I wasn't sure if I found him insanely attractive. Or if I was terrified just by looking at him. Probably both.

His gaze swept over me, and despite the impenetrable expression of his eyes, heat rushed through me. Okay, so yeah. Maybe more attraction than fear.

"Actually," I spoke up, irritation rising at being called a princess when this girl had no idea who I was, or where I was from. "I'm waiting for him to move so I can get my phone back." My knee twinged with pain from kneeling on the concrete path. Well, that was something at least. I'd regained feeling since I'd stopped staring at him.

He squatted so we were eye height, then leaned so far in

I caught a whiff of something delicious-smelling. Cologne? Deodorant? Soap? I had no idea, but it was intoxicating. I fought to keep from him like he was a pie I'd like to take a bite out of.

Colt's gaze pinned me in place. And then he opened his mouth.

"If I'd known it would be so easy to get the new girl on her knees, maybe I wouldn't have fucked Gillian in the parking lot just now."

I blinked.

The girl, Gillian, laughed, but it didn't meet her eyes. She ran her hand through his hair. It might have appeared affectionate to anyone watching from a distance, but there was no mistaking the possessiveness in the action.

"Yeah, you would have," Gillian said. "You know how those preppy rich kids are, baby. She's probably saving it for marriage. That right, princess? You forbidden fruit?"

I ignored her and focused on Colt. "Get off my phone."

He didn't take his eyes off me for a second. Just slowly moved his foot. I grabbed my phone and straightened. He stood slowly, his gaze raking over my legs, my belly, my breasts, before he stood to full height. I felt every inch of his gaze as it rolled up me.

"You don't belong here," he said.

Gillian pressed herself against Colt's side. "No, she definitely doesn't. I'm bored. Let's go find the others. She won't last a day."

She dragged Colt away. He walked backward for a few steps, watching me then turned around and slung his arm over Gillian's shoulders. She glanced back at me, throwing me a triumphant glare as if she'd won some battle I wasn't even aware of.

Whatever. I hadn't exactly expected a warm welcome.

There never was one anytime a group of kids from Providence came across a group from Saint View High. It happened from time to time, mostly on the beach. I'd hoped to blend in a little longer than five minutes, though. I'd tried to dress down. Selina and I had riffled through my wardrobe, trying to find the least expensive skirt and top I owned. I realized now, though, just by gazing around, that nothing I owned would have worked. I stuck out like a sore thumb. The kids around me rocked an array of tight ripped jeans, midriff tops, band T-shirts, baseball caps, and skirts so short underwear was on display. A far cry from the knee-length, pleated skirt and white button-down shirt I'd worn each day at Providence School for Girls. A long cry from even my weekend wardrobe. I didn't own anything with holes in it, deliberate or otherwise. Dammit. This was not my plan. I needed to fly under the radar, not draw attention to myself.

Adding 'shop for clothes' to the top of my to-do list, I tucked my phone into my backpack and strode down then path toward the doors of Saint View High. A few short steps had me at the entranceway, the crowd petering into two lines in order to enter the gloomy building.

"No cutting in. Back of the line, princess," a voice said.

I spun around but didn't see Colt anywhere. I couldn't work out who had spoken, but judging from the stares of the students waiting in line, I was the princess in question. Was that a thing already? How? It had to be a coincidence. I wandered to the back of the line and didn't say anything to the people in front of me while we shuffled along. I strained to see ahead, to work out what the holdup was, but the glass doors had some sort of tint or reflective coating that made them impossible to see through.

I tapped my foot impatiently, worried I wasn't going to

get enrolled before first period started. I had severely under-estimated how many kids attended this school. They continued to stream in from the road and came in droves from the carpark. Others pushed bicycles or got off the buses rolling to a stop outside the gates. They all joined the lines I was currently in.

Finally, I reached the top and followed the girl in front of me inside.

A burly man with 'security' printed across his tight black T-shirt stopped me. I blinked in surprise, no idea what I was being stopped for.

"Do you have any weapons on you today, miss?"

Weapons? Did the compass in my geometry set count? Jesus Christ.

I squeaked out an answer.

"Hold your arms out, please, and put your backpack on the table."

I did as I was told because what else was I supposed to do?

The man ran a wand type instrument around my arms and legs, while another viciously went through my backpack, shoving aside folders and pens and my wallet.

"Do you think you could be a little careful with that, please?" I asked.

He snorted on a laugh as he handed it back to me. He didn't even bother answering. I snatched the bag from his grip and clutched it to my chest feeling somehow violated. The school's website hadn't warned there'd be metal detectors and bag checks on the way in. I supposed I should be grateful there wasn't a cavity search.

I shouldn't have been surprised. The interior of Saint View High was no less prison-like than the outside. There was no grand entranceway like there'd been at Providence.

Just one long hall that ran farther than I could see, hundreds of grubby white lockers lining both sides, only interrupted by doors that I assumed led to classrooms or other, similarly icky hallways.

I wandered, pushed along by the crowd who all seemed to know where they were going. They yelled greetings to each other, and every now and then I picked up a little conversation. "How amazing was that party?" and "Oh my God, I was so drunk that night." I hovered when a familiar name caught my attention. "Fuck, did Colt get even hotter over the summer? I'm wet just looking at him."

I wrinkled my nose in the direction of the girl who'd spoken. It wasn't Gillian. But it didn't surprise me that Colt was the object of more than one woman's desires. I'd bet Gillian had her hands full, keeping hold of that one. He could have had any girl he wanted.

Including you.

I shook my head slightly. Not including me. He might be beautiful, but with a school this large, there'd be a plethora of hot boys to choose from. If I wanted to date, that was. If the metal detectors were anything to go by, dating the boys here might not be in my best interests.

I stumbled across the administration office, and after explaining who I was and why I was there to the harried woman behind the desk, I was given a bunch of forms to fill out. I did so hastily and shoved them back across the desk. In return, the woman passed me a freshly printed piece of paper with my schedule on it.

"It's just temporary," she warned. She added another piece of paper to my hands—a school map. "You'll be able to choose your elective subjects with the guidance counselor later in the week."

I nodded and studied the timetable. "Wait, all-school

assembly?" It was the first thing listed under Monday mornings.

The woman peered over at my paper. "Yes, every week. In the gymnasium. You'd best hustle. Principal Simmons doesn't appreciate latecomers."

"No, I do not."

I swiveled on my heel. The tall man behind me, Principal Simmons I guessed, seemed out of place with his neat navy suit pants and a button-down shirt tucked into an expensive belt. His shoes shone, and a gold watch gleamed on his wrist.

He peered past me to his secretary. "New student?"

I stuck my hand out before she could answer. "Lacey Knight."

He took my hand, his smooth cool fingers wrapping around mine. "Ah, Lacey. I believe I was just speaking with your aunt."

Well, that was just great. I'd kill her when I got home.

Selina had tried to convince me all morning to let her come down to enroll me, but I instinctively knew that would be a nail in my social coffin at a school like this. At Providence, and Edgely Academy, parents were often alumni and present at all events the school held. They were like mini high school reunions, and few of the parents missed an opportunity to check out who was doing what. Or doing who. Selina had been set to take me to orientation this morning, and it hadn't bothered me the least. But I'd talked her out of driving me to Saint View, though she'd only let me get in my car after I promised to pack Mace into my bag.

Apparently, I should have been more specific with my demands. No calling the principal obviously should have been top of the list.

"She speaks very highly of you. Top of your junior year, I'm told."

I smiled politely.

Simmons cocked his head to the side, as if trying to figure me out. He was pretty hot for an old guy. I'd bet he was buff beneath his preppy clothes. His eyes were a pale blue, set off by his dark hair. It was flecked with gray, but it was attractive in a George Clooney sort of way. My aunt's friends probably would have thrown themselves at him if they'd seen him out around town or at the beach...until they realized he was the principal of a public school and probably made chump change.

"Come along, then. The first bell is about to go, and I don't make a habit of being late to my own assemblies. I'll show you to the gym."

I nodded and trailed along, a few steps behind him, hoping the other students wouldn't realize I was being escorted.

We exited through doors at the back of the school, briefly walking through the sunshine, and followed the swarm of students inside a huge gym, completely detached from the main building.

I wrinkled my nose. It was a cavernous space, with a high ceiling and bleacher-style seating down the long sides of the rectangle. But it had a vague musty sweat smell that hung in the air, despite the fact this was the first day of school and the building probably hadn't been used all summer. A basketball court was painted on the floor, and each end held ratty basketball nets. They were ripped and torn and I wondered if this school was so poor that they couldn't even afford to replace something so minor. That one little thing, so insignificant, hit me hard. This was a whole different world to where I came from, yet it was just fifteen minutes away? When we'd run into groups of Saint View kids at the beach, I'd really had no idea. I knew the area was rough. But I'd never considered what that really meant.

Principal Simmons stopped in the middle of the floor, and as if out of nowhere, a boy appeared and handed him a microphone. Simmons turned to me. "Just go sit on over there at the bottom of the bleachers. After this is done, I'll find someone to show you around the school."

I shook my head and held up the crappily printed map. Admittedly, I'd probably need a magnifying glass and a detective's license to work it out, but that was fine. Better than being someone's tagalong. "No need. I'm good."

He shooed me away. "Nonsense. I like to make sure my new students feel welcomed."

I somehow doubted I was the only new student. And I didn't see him foisting his 'help' on anyone else. Not wanting to make a scene, I wandered to the nearest seats. Unsurprisingly, most of the top ones were full of kids talking and jostling. A few couples used the spare minutes to make out. I took the first step, not wanting to be the only one sitting close to the principal.

Simmons had either ideas. "Just there, Lacey."

I flashed him a forced smile, ignoring the titters of laughter from the upper levels. Great. Nothing like a little awkward embarrassment on your first day. I perched on the lowest seat of the bleachers, all alone. But then the bell rang, and students poured through the multiple open doorways that led in from outside. It was like a tidal wave of human bodies. Within two minutes, the bleachers were full, and I no longer felt so on display. I found myself wedged between a tall blond boy with glasses and a severe case of acne. And a short red-haired girl who chatted animatedly with someone on the other side of her. Neither seemed interested in the new girl. Suited me. I wasn't here to make friends. Just to find out information. Then I could get the hell out of here and back to school with Meredith and my other friends.

Principal Simmons started the assembly with the usual beginning-of-the-year speech all principals seemed to make. I trust you had a great summer. This year will be the best ever. Yadda yadda. I tuned out and let my gaze wander over the crowd across from me, searching for guys who fit the profile of the one who'd carried me out of the fire. I'd scanned the back three rows, left to right before I caught on that I was perhaps actually looking for someone in particular, rather than just casually observing. The memory of Colt's dark eyes was hard to forget so quickly.

"...new student, Lacey Knight. Come up here, please, Lacey."

I snapped my attention to the center of the room and Principal Simmons who was smiling broadly, and gesturing for me to join him in the center of the gym.

My stomach sank. For fuck's sake. Why was he trying to torture me?

I pushed to my feet, trying to ignore the stares of what had to be six hundred students. The room fell into a hushed silence as I slunk my way to the principal's side.

"I'm sure you all heard about the recent fire at Providence School for Girls. Lacey was the top of her class junior year, and we're incredibly pleased to have her continuing her education at Saint View. I'm sure all of you in the senior class especially put your best foot forward and endeavor to show Miss Knight that Saint View is the same high-quality school she's used to."

Kill. Me. Now. Simmons beamed at me, like his words

weren't currently painting a bull's-eye on my back. What fresh hell was this? Some sort of passive-aggressive bullshit? He was deluded if he thought Saint View offered the same sort of education Providence did. Hell, I'd had to promise Selina I'd do extension work with a private tutor before she'd even considered allowing me to enroll here. Providence had brought in teachers from all over the world, paying astronomically high wages in order to attract and retain the best. A teaching position at Providence set a person up for life. There was nothing higher than that for educators. Except, of course, for the principal's position, but my uncle had held that for longer than most could remember. His job had kept my aunt in the lavish lifestyle she'd grown up in.

I didn't have to see the faces of my fellow classmates to know each and every one of them were right now hating my guts. I couldn't blame them. I was completely out of place in Jimmy Choo sandals that probably cost the same as some of their cars.

But I wasn't going to stand here, shriveling like a wallflower either. I wouldn't give anyone that sort of power over me. So I kept my head held high and my shoulders pushed back. I looked around the room while Simmons droned on, digging my social grave even deeper, meeting the gazes of those who tried to stare me down.

My gaze caught on Colt's dead black stare. His mouth lifted in the corners, like this entire situation amused him. I didn't see how. Gillian sat next to him, her piercing eyes forcing me to take a little internal step backward. What was her problem? She hadn't seemed like she'd cared about what Colt had said earlier. About not fucking her if he'd known...well. Yeah. I would have been pissed off if I'd been her. He'd been an asshole. But she'd acted like he couldn't have possibly been serious and hadn't given the comment any weight at all. But the hate shining in her eyes right now told a different story. It was enough to wilt even the strongest of characters, and it made me want to curl into a ball. I wouldn't show it externally, but I'd obviously somehow managed to make an enemy before I even got to first period. Great.

There were two more boys on the other side of Colt, facing each other in conversation. One had dark hair, shorter than the other and artfully tousled. Black-rimmed glasses sat on the bridge of his nose. He was cute from what I could tell. The glasses suited him. The other boy...I frowned at his profile. Blond flop of hair. Tanned skin. Beaded wood necklace around his neck and a surfer logo on his T-shirt. He turned to face the front again, and recognition jolted through me as our gazes met.

My mouth dropped open.

"Banjo?" I mouthed unconsciously. What the hell was he doing sitting up there with the students? My head spun in dizzying circles as I tried to make sense of what was happening here. His face split into a wide grin, and my heart fluttered, but at the same time, my brain caught up. He was either the dumbest twenty-one-year-old in the history of forever and had repeated senior year multiple times.

Or he wasn't twenty-one.

His cheeks blushed pink, and he shrugged sheepishly. I couldn't help it. I smiled and shook my head at him, just a tiny bit. Damn. He was cute. For a liar. If he lied about his age, who knew what else he lied about.

Colt elbowed him sharply, and Banjo broke his stare-off with me in order to shoot him a dirty look. I couldn't hear them from where I stood, but Banjo seemed to ask what Colt's problem was, and Colt argued back.

"...okay, then. That'll do for this morning. Rafe, can I see you, please? Everyone else, happy first day of school. Make it a good one." Principal Simmons switched off the microphone and gestured toward the main exit.

Groans rang out around me, echoing my internal one that grumped that this had been a stupid idea. I kind of agreed with it right now. I shifted my backpack to my shoulders. Kids streamed down the bleachers, but I kept my attention glued to Colt and Banjo. They loped down the stairs, both taller and broader than most around them. I didn't know if it was solely the fact that they were both big guys, or perhaps the fact Colt seemed ready to burn you alive if you got too close to him, but people gave them a wide berth. They paused at the bottom, slapped hands, and went in different directions, presumably to their first class of the day. Banjo shot me a look, and mouthed, "Later."

I bit my lip to fight from smiling. He might be a liar, but it wouldn't be the worst thing in the world if I had a friend. Could I consider someone I'd barely met but considered giving my virginity to a friend? Surely that made us friend-ish? My attention snared on Colt as he strode by me, closer than he really had to. His intoxicating scent washed over me once more, and something low in my belly clenched.

He walked with such confidence it would probably be called swagger. Like he owned the school.

And knew it.

"Lacey, this is Rafe," Simmons said, interrupting my drooling over Colt.

The third guy, the one who'd been talking with Banjo, stood by the principal's side. Whoa. His profile had not done the guy justice. He stood with his arms crossed over his chest, his shoulders filling out a T-shirt nicely. His red-and-black Converse sneakers matched a pair I had at home. I wished I'd worn them today. Not that they went with my outfit.

"Hi." I stuck my hand out.

He took my hand and smiled, but it didn't really reach his eyes. "Nice to meet you."

Simmons beamed. "Look at you two getting along so nicely already." He clapped his hands. "Rafe will be your guide. He'll show you around, introduce you to students and teachers. I'm sure he'd be happy to sit with you at lunch, too, right, Rafe?"

Rafe seemed like he'd rather watch paint dry than do any of that. "Sure. Yeah. Whatever. Can I go?"

Principal Simmons nodded.

Rafe walked off without another word, leaving me to chase after him. But I refused to be a follower. His long legs had a good few inches on mine, but I lengthened my stride and hurried my gait in order to walk side by side with him as we burst out into the sunshine again. He didn't say anything, just strode on like a man on a mission.

"Don't you want to know what my first class is?" I asked, confused because we seemed to be walking in the complete wrong direction to all the other students. Instead of joining the tail end of the teenagers streaming back into the school, we were headed toward the back of the gym.

A wooded area loomed beyond the school grounds. Or at least I assumed it was beyond the school grounds. There were no fences to mark a boundary. Perhaps the school used the woods for cross-country running or archery practice.

"Are there classrooms out here?" I asked, half-running to keep up.

My God. Their gym was ginormous. We followed the long side of the brick building, each step taking us farther and farther away from everybody else.

Rafe took a sharp right when we ran out of wall to follow and led me behind the gym.

I stopped abruptly. "There's nothing here."

"Exactly," he answered.

I probably should have been concerned by the situation I'd gotten myself into. I was alone with a guy I didn't know, well away from the school buildings, which held the people who wouldn't hear me scream. But oddly, I wasn't scared. Rafe's attitude was full of disinterest, but he wasn't remotely threatening.

He pulled a lighter and a hand-rolled cigarette from his pocket and lit up. He took a long drag, and as he blew out the smoke, I realized I'd been wrong. Not a cigarette. A joint.

"Seriously, dude? It's not even ten." I folded my arms across my chest.

"Don't know what the rules were in your last fancy-ass school, but round here, there's no rules on what time we can get high."

I somehow doubted, even at a school like Saint View, you were allowed to get high on school property. "You couldn't wait until you'd delivered me to my first class? I really don't want to get kicked out of school on my first day because you wanted to smoke a joint."

He held it out to me. "Relax. You look like you need this more than I do."

I shook my head stubbornly.

He shrugged. "If you change your mind, you know where I am. Trust me, Saint View is a lot easier to deal with if you're a little baked."

"Ain't that the truth."

I spun around at the feminine voice behind me. A girl, about the same height as me, but in a short, tight denim skirt and a top that showed a sliver of her toned stomach joined us. Her long hair fell down her back, a deep crimson that looked fresh out of a packet of cheap hair dye. But it suited her. I kind of wished I had the lady balls to try a color that bright. My hair looked downright mousy in comparison, even though I'd paid two hundred dollars at my last salon appointment.

The girl plucked the joint from Rafe's fingers, inhaled, and blew the smoke in his face.

Rafe didn't seem to mind. Just took the joint back from her without a word.

I eyed her carefully, a little on edge after Gillian's hostility this morning, and at being caught out here alone with Rafe. Was he her boyfriend? That'd be all I need. Another girl hating my guts because of something her boyfriend did.

But the girl's red lipsticked lips stretched into a wide smile when she turned in my direction. It lit up her entire face, her dark eyes gleaming. "New girl. Right? Stacey?"

"Lacey," I corrected. I stuck my hand out for her to shake.

She ignored it, and to my surprise, hugged me instead. I breathed in her perfume, an unfamiliar scent. Or perhaps it was just the fact it was mixed with the smell of pot smoke. It wasn't unpleasant, though. She squeezed me tight, while I stood awkwardly, not exactly sure what to do with my hands.

"You're scaring her, Jag," Rafe drawled, leaning back on the brick wall of the gym. "Go easy."

"Oops, sorry! I'm Jagger. And I'm a hugger. But it's better you know that upfront anyway, since we're going to be friends."

I shook my head, pulling out of the hug. "We are?" I asked before I could think about it. My head spun. And I was a little suspicious after Colt and Gillian had been so icy this morning. Were they setting me up? But then I looked into Jagger's smiling face, and either she was a terrific actress or she was sincere. I wanted to believe the latter.

She hooked her arm through mine and steered me away, throwing a wave at Rafe over her shoulder. "Of course. I've just been waiting for someone interesting to come along. There's only so much of Gillian and her crew I can handle. And everyone else is as dull as dirt. Come with me, Rafe is a useless guide. And anyway, Banjo sent me to rescue you. He said you're a good one, so that's enough for me."

"He did?" I asked.

What the hell? Banjo and I had barely spent thirty minutes together. He couldn't know if I was a good or bad anything. This entire morning had been overwhelming. I needed a minute to catch my breath and perhaps take some notes. Colt, Gillian, Banjo, Rafe, Jagger. At least I remembered their names. Five out of a school of hundreds. It was a start. I was suddenly regretting not taking a hit from that joint. It probably would have calmed my nerves.

"Yep. So let's get you to your first class, because you strike me as the type who doesn't like to be late. Am I right?"

I couldn't deny that.

Jagger put her hand out. "Schedule?"

I riffled through my backpack and fished out the now slightly crumpled piece of paper and handed it over.

Jagger paused to squint at it and then looked back to me. "You've got math in the D block. It's at the other end of the school. Come on, I'll take you there." She set off at a brisk pace.

I jogged a few steps to catch up. "Don't you need to get to your own class?"

She shrugged. "Already late. And, hey, wouldn't want to

set my new teachers up for anything other than disappointment on the first day. Best they know now that I'm perpetu-
ally late for everything."

I smiled at that. We couldn't have been more different,
and just knowing I was already late for class made my skin
itch. But there wasn't much I could do about it, and I would
have been a whole lot later if I was still waiting for Rafe, so I
was grateful.

We walked along the now empty halls, passing classrooms with teenagers lolling at desks. I peeked into each
open door as we went, but it all looked much the same as
Providence. Students all barely paying attention to their
teachers. I guess money didn't change that.

"So, you don't get high?" Jagger asked.

I shook my head. "No. Never really felt the urge to try it."
I eyed her sideways, wondering if she'd give me a hard time
about it. There were plenty at my old school who liked to
party. Though I'd never seen anyone smoking a joint at
school, first thing on a Monday morning. That would have
been risking expulsion. And getting expelled from Providence...I couldn't even imagine the uproar that would have
created.

"That's cool. I don't normally at school either. But Rafe
always has good weed."

"Does he do that a lot?"

She shrugged. "Define a lot?"

I chuckled. "Sounds like a yes then."

"Probably."

"Has he ever been caught? It's not exactly an original
hiding spot he has there. You seemed to know exactly where
to find him."

Jagger took a sharp left into a new corridor, and I tried to memorize the path we were taking. This school was humongous.

"Oh, all the teachers know. But Rafe is an Untouchable."

"A what now? Is that a club?"

Jagger stopped abruptly and faced me. "Sort of? I mean, not officially. It's just what most of us here call them."

"Them?" I hated to sound like a parrot, but my interest had been piqued, and my need to get to class on time died. My whole reason for being here was to find out who had been at the fire that night. And learning about the students and staff was the best way to do that. If Jagger was a gossip, all the better for me.

"Yeah. The boys who can do no wrong. Or rather, do everything wrong, but everyone turns a blind eye. Rafe's surname is Simmons. That's what gives him membership."

It only took me a second to catch on. "As in, Principal Simmons?"

Jagger beamed like I was a puppy who'd just learned a new trick. "They're father and son."

I blinked. "Oh wow."

"Kinda hot, huh? Principal Simmons is a fox. And Rafe is just the younger, faster, sleeker version. Though he probably wouldn't appreciate me calling him fast. Not exactly a complimentary term for most guys. If you know what I mean."

I'd have to be pretty sheltered not to. I grinned. "So, Rafe is untouchable because his dad is principal. Got it."

"And because he's on the football team."

My heart thudded, and I was suddenly considering Rafe in a whole new light. "Football players are Untouchables, too? Or just him?"

"All of them, really."

"Who else is on the football team?"

She raised one eyebrow. "You want me to rattle off the entire list? Girl, I ain't got all day, and we're hella late for class."

"Right, of course. Sorry. Where is my class again?"

Jagger pointed to the room across the hall. I nodded and thanked her. I'd taken two steps toward the closed door of my classroom when curiosity got the best of me. "Wait, Jagger?"

She'd already started walking to her own class, but she spun around. "Yeah?"

"Banjo? Is he an Untouchable?"

She nodded. "He's their star quarterback."

I rushed on before she tried to leave again. "Colt?"

"You know Colt, too?"

I shook my head. "Sort of. Not really. We met this morning." If you could call him keeping my phone hostage and sexual innuendo a meeting.

"No, he's not on the team."

I frowned. "Oh. Okay." I wasn't sure why that bothered me.

"He is an Untouchable, though. I've never really been sure why. Maybe because he and Rafe and Banjo have been best friends for a million years?"

"Or maybe because he's just scary intimidating." It wouldn't have surprised me if all the teachers were as wary about Colt's dark eyes as I was.

She cocked her head to one side. "You think?"

"You don't?"

She shrugged. "He's not so bad. He's actually kind of nice when you get to know him. Sometimes, anyway."

I'd barely met the guy, but somehow 'nice guy' just didn't fit his vibe. "Are we talking about the same Colt?"

"Tall. Hot. Always has a snarky blond hanging off him?"

"Sounds about right."

"Definitely an Untouchable."

I'd apparently run out of questions, so I didn't stop Jagger when she continued on her way. Instead, I turned to my own class and cringed as the teacher gave me a disapproving glare and told me to stay behind after class.

Seemed I wasn't an Untouchable. What a pity.

5

LACEY

I managed to find my second class on time, and, to my relief, the teacher didn't ask me to introduce myself. I supposed it was unnecessary after Principal Simmons had given me such an over-the-top welcome in front of the entire school. My biology teacher, a middle-aged woman with stress lines creasing her forehead, just pointed me to a seat in the front row and started with her lesson. It was work I'd done two years earlier and knew I could do in my sleep. So I tuned out and let my mind wander over the idea of Untouchables.

I was called to see the guidance counselor during lunch, which was a relief since it meant I didn't have to face the embarrassment of having no one to sit with. The counselor —short, dumpy, and definitely not capable of carrying me out of a burning building—talked me through my class options and asked what I wanted to do with my future. He seemed surprised when I laid out plans centering around music, but he steered me in the right direction, and I was actually looking forward to the classes I'd chosen. Anything had to be better than the boring biology and math classes I'd endured today.

Gym was my last class of the day, where I spent the entire time studying the other students and trying to narrow down my suspect pool. But it seemed like Saint View had an overwhelming amount of big, muscled seniors. There were half a dozen in this class alone that could bench press me if they'd wanted to. I'd slipped out right as the bell rang, hurrying for the school gates, ready to get back on my home ground and relax for the night. I hadn't anticipated how tiring a new school and playing detective would be. Mentally tiring, that was. I hadn't exactly exerted myself during gym class.

"Lacey!"

I stopped and waited for Jagger to catch up. She hugged me, and I was a little less stiff this time, managing to hug her back.

"Girl, what happened to you at lunch? I searched for you everywhere!"

"You did?"

"Of course. I wasn't going to let you eat alone. Meet me out front of the cafeteria tomorrow, okay? I'll introduce you to everyone." She slung me a sidelong look. "Everyone you don't already know, anyway. You already met all the hotties, apparently."

"I'm sure there's more than three hotties, but thank you, that would be great."

"Where's your ride?"

"Oh, it's just..." I glanced across the huge parking lot to where my bright-red convertible sat gleaming in the afternoon sun.

A group of kids stood around, admiring it. Or gossiping about the owner maybe. I was uncomfortable at the thought, realizing it was another faux pas. I should have parked a few blocks away and walked. Or caught a bus, not that I knew how. Did buses even run through my neighborhood? I couldn't recall ever seeing one, now that I thought about it. While the school lot was filled with cars and a handful motorcycles, only a few seemed new. And even those that still shone with all their paint still intact, were cheap models. My convertible had been a gift from my aunt and uncle when I'd turned sixteen. I'd put a few dents and scratches on it while I'd been learning, but all I'd had to do was tell my uncle, and the next day it had magically been fixed. This lot was full of cars with dents and scratches and mismatched panels. Some of these cars were older than I was. A lot older.

Heat flushed my face.

"Did you walk?" Jagger made a beeline for an old green Dodge with rust spots on the bumper. "Jump in, I'll give you a ride."

Oh Lord, no. That would be worse. I didn't want to completely alienate my only new friend by bringing her to my massive house. I doubted the guards on the gates of our community would even let us pass in that car, though it hurt me to think about how downright snobby that was. Reluctantly, I pointed to my car. "No, it's okay. Mine is down there. The red one."

Jagger raised an eyebrow as her gaze followed my finger. "Damn, girl. I take that back. You can give me a ride."

Without bothering to lock her car again, she grabbed my hand and pulled me toward the convertible, grinning ear to ear.

"Out of the way," she said to the kids standing around gawking. "We got places to be." She trailed her fingers over the perfect paintwork and grinned at me over the roof. "Open it already! This is the hottest thing I've ever seen."

"You like cars?" I asked, hitting a button on my keys. The locks slid down without a noise.

"I like this car!" she practically sang. She slipped into the passenger seat as I got behind the wheel and started the engine.

Jagger's eyes were huge. "Leather seats! Oh my God, they're so soft. Put the top down!"

That was the last thing I wanted to do, but I was also kind of digging her excitement. She'd been so kind to me today. It was a kick to see someone enjoy this car in a way I never had. I'd never thought about how nice the seats were. Or how it was pretty cool to be able to take the top down and let the late summer breeze blow through my hair. I hit another button, and the roof cranked to life, folding back above our heads.

Jagger bounced excitedly on her seat, like a toddler, impatient to go to McDonald's.

I laughed at her, then pulled the gearshift into reverse and glanced over my shoulder to check it was safe to back out.

A large body landed in my back seat, and I yelped, slamming my foot down on the brake automatically.

Banjo gave me a lopsided grin. "Told you I'd see you around. This wasn't exactly what I meant, but hey, I'll take it. Man, these seats are like butter."

My brain short-circuited while I tried to form words. Eventually, I stuttered, "Wh...what are you doing?" I couldn't quite look him in the eye. Not after last night when I'd practically thrown myself at him. That was suddenly mortifyingly embarrassing.

"Getting a lift?" he asked cheekily.

"Could have asked!"

"But you would have said no."

"You don't know that." He was right. I would have, to save myself further embarrassment. Being this close to him was stirring things inside me that I needed to keep a lid on. Especially since we weren't alone.

"Lacey, can I get a lift in your sexy-as-fuck car?"

"No!"

"See?" He grinned. "That's why I didn't ask!"

It was hard to keep a straight face. He was so cute with all that blond hair flopping in his eye, his smile full of mischief.

I guided the gearshift back into park. "Banjo. Get out of my car."

"Lacey. Go out with me."

Jagger let out a gasp from the passenger seat and then clapped her hands with glee. "Well, this just got interesting!"

I shot her a glare. "Not interesting. He's joking."

"No, I'm not."

Jagger slapped me on the arm. "What are you doing?" she hissed. "He's the hottest guy in school and the freaking quarterback. If he asks, you say yes!"

Banjo was like a rooster preening in the sun.

"Oh, for fuck's sake," another voice said. Rafe appeared on Jagger's side of the car. "Look at you right now, Banjo. You're fucking ridiculous. Your ego is so big I could stroke it from out here."

Banjo grinned at him. "Come on, we all know it's not my ego you want to stroke."

My eyes widened. But Rafe just dumped his backpack on the ground and hoisted himself over the side of the car. He landed beside Banjo, and the two of them launched into a full-blown tussle.

"Oh my God, stop!" I yelled. How the hell had I gone from wanting nobody to see my car, to three people inside it, two who seemed to be about to launch into a fistfight? I leaned as far away from the rumbling guys as I could. "Should we get someone?" I yelped to Jagger.

She waved her hand, like it was no big deal. "Got my money on Rafe!"

Banjo paused. "Hey!"

She shrugged. "What?"

"I don't understand what's happening right now," I squealed, cringing away from the two boys to avoid a wayward elbow.

The two guys eventually settled down, shoving each other into opposite corners of the car, matching grins on their faces, both breathing a little harder than they had been.

"You two done now?" I asked.

Banjo gave me an impish grin. "Sorry, pretty girl. We got carried away. I wasn't hurting him."

Rafe rolled his eyes while he straightened his shirt. "Like you could."

"What the fuck is going on here?"

All four of us flinched, and when I looked in the direction of the voice, I fully expected to see a teacher standing there. That's how much authority that statement had held. Though in hindsight, the use of 'fuck' probably should have given it away. This might have been Saint View, but I still doubted teachers were in the habit of dropping F-bombs. Even if it was after hours.

Colt's black eyes raked over the scene, taking in Jagger in the front seat, Banjo and Rafe in the back. Finally, his gaze landed on me. I didn't think it possible, but I could have sworn his eyes hardened further.

"Quit fucking around and let's go," he said to Banjo and Rafe. "Leave the princess alone."

I bristled at his tone. "I'm not a princess."

He raised one dark eyebrow. "No? Do you see anyone else around here driving a seventy-five thousand dollar car?"

"Colt—" Banjo started.

Colt cut him off. "I said, let's go."

There was a shuffle from the back seat, and Rafe got out, grabbing his backpack from the ground.

Banjo followed more reluctantly. "What the fuck is up your ass today?"

Colt didn't answer. A shiver rolled down my spine. There was a power in him that I found intriguing.

But it also pissed me off that he thought so highly of himself. My fingers clenched around the steering wheel. "You don't get to judge me."

Jagger sucked in a tiny breath beside me. She shook her head ever so slightly.

"Untouchable," she said beneath her breath.

Colt bent down, leaning in until we were eye to eye. "You should listen to your friend there, princess. I do whatever I want around here. If I want to judge you, then there isn't a thing you can do about it. Is there?"

Then he ran one finger down the side of my face, starting at my temple and tracing his way along my jaw.

I knew a power play when I saw one. He expected me to back down. To flinch away.

I wouldn't. Not now, on day one. Not ever. It took more than a handsome face who overestimated his importance to intimidate me.

So instead, I got closer. I got so close our faces were less than an inch apart. If I'd been across the parking lot and seen a guy and a girl this close, I would have assumed they were going in for a kiss. My body flushed with heat at the thought, even as I fought to keep my anger under control.

I knew what he expected.

I wasn't going to give it to him.

"The pauper bows to the princess, Colt. You'd do well to remember that."

And with that, I threw the car into reverse once more, slammed my foot on the gas, and shot us out of the parking space. The three guys scrambled to get out of my way, but my gaze never left Colt's. I put the car into drive and high-tailed it out of the parking lot, tires screeching, back end fishtailing, leaving the three boys behind in a cloud of black smoke.

6

LACEY

*M*y fingers still trembled with anger when I pulled into my driveway. Jagger had said little as I'd dropped her back at a modest-looking house in the middle of Saint View's suburban area. The house had white peeling paint but neatly tended gardens, with a few flowers, wilted from the heat of summer. I vaguely remembered promising to pick her up for school in the morning, since we'd left her car there and she'd have no ride, but the rest of the drive home had been a blur. Louis, the guard at the gate, had asked me something, and I hadn't even answered him. I'd just driven through.

"Shit," I muttered. The automatic doors on the garage opened, and I guided the car inside. I felt like a right royal asshole for ignoring Louis. He was a nice man, with three small kids—James, Ally, and Kendra— plus a wife who I'd made a chocolate cake for at Christmas, because Louis had told me that her birthday was December twenty-fifth, and she hated her birthday cake was always leftover dessert from Christmas Day. They were good, kind people.

A voice in the back of my mind whispered that perhaps

that wasn't the only reason I felt like a jerk right now. What I'd done with Colt...played on the fact I had money and he didn't...

I clenched the steering wheel tighter. No. I wasn't going to feel bad about that. He'd been the one to call me a princess. I'd just played into it.

Yeah. Like that really made me a hero.

Groaning, I got out of the car and opened the internal door that led to the bottom level of our house. I trudged up the stairs, my limbs heavy with guilt. That wasn't who I was. I knew what it was like to have nothing and no one. I might not have remembered much about the years before my aunt and uncle had adopted me. But I'd gathered together enough bits and pieces of conversations to know we'd been dirt poor. My aunt and uncle often told the story about how when I arrived on their doorstep, I had nothing but the clothes on my back and a ratty teddy bear.

"Selina?" I called out. But no reply came. I didn't call out again. Her car had been in the garage, so she was likely in bed with a migraine. I sighed. That sucked. I wanted to unload some of my day onto someone. Not all of it, obviously. I wasn't planning on telling anyone about Colt and the shitty things we'd said to each other. Or about how I knew Banjo, and how he'd asked me out twice now. Or how Rafe had offered me drugs, not even an hour into my first day. Yeah. I wasn't about to tell Selina any of that. It was probably better that she was asleep. At least I'd have a chance to process my feelings before I spoke to her.

I opened my bedroom door.

"Hi!"

"Oh fuck!" I yelped, jumping near out of my skin. I put my hand over my heart to calm it, while Meredith laughed at me.

"You goose," she said from her position, sprawled out on my bed. She threw her phone down onto the mattress.

"I didn't see your car outside."

"I had our driver drop me off after orientation."

"How did that go?" I cast an eye over her gray skirt and starched white shirt with the Edgely Academy logo embroidered on the pocket. "Nice uniform."

She pushed off the bed and went to stand in front of my floor-to-ceiling mirror. She smoothed down her skirt and twisted to the left, then to the right. Eventually she wrinkled her nose. "It's awful, isn't it? That said..." Her gaze caught mine in the mirror. "What on earth are you wearing?"

"Seriously, does no one like this outfit?" I muttered.

Meredith grabbed my hand and pulled me toward the padded window seat. Our maid, Angelique, had opened the gauzy white curtains, and late afternoon sun streamed through the spotless window. Meredith perched on the edge of the seat, and I sat heavily beside her.

"Start talking, Lacey-Lou. I'm pretty sure this morning I heard you say you were enrolling in Saint View High."

"I did."

"Are you on drugs? Is this a cry for help?"

I snickered. "No. I'm fine."

"You're not fine if you willingly enrolling in that school. I heard they have to have armed security guards because a kid was stabbed there. Rumor is, he bled out on a classroom floor."

I hadn't noticed if the security guards were armed, but it wouldn't surprise me. As for a kid being murdered there... The dark expression in Colt's eyes flashed in my mind. Who knew? I couldn't rule it out for sure. He'd looked like he wanted to kill me as I'd peeled out of the parking lot. "While that might very well be true—"

Meredith gasped.

I ignored her. "I had to."

She squeezed my hand so tight I yelped. "Had to? No, you did not have to. What you do have to do is burn that awful outfit. And perhaps take a decontamination shower. Who knows what you've picked up there. What do lice look like?" She cringed away like she could see something crawling on me.

Which was ridiculous. But I scratched absently at my head. "Someone there killed my uncle."

Meredith's mouth dropped open. "Back up. What now?"

"Long story. Short version is the man who carried me out was wearing a Saint View High Football shirt. And my uncle didn't die in the fire. He was murdered first."

Meredith froze. Then a bunch of different emotions flickered across her face, too fast for me to grasp any of them. "Are you serious?"

"Deadly."

Her face went white.

"Sorry," I said, not really knowing why I was apologizing, when I was the one who should be traumatized by the word. But it was in bad taste, and Meredith had always been more sensitive than me.

"So, your plan is to just go all high school detective like you're Veronica Mars or something?"

"Do you have to say it like that? You make it sound…"

"Ridiculous?"

Heat rose in my cheeks. "What am I supposed to do, then, Mer?"

She sighed. "Okay, fine. So say I'm on board for this… whatever this is. Sting operation?"

I snorted.

"Whatever. This plan then. What exactly *is* your plan?

You're just going to start asking people if they're killers in their spare time? You're going to conduct interviews in the cafeteria?" She wrinkled her nose. "Ew, you didn't eat the food there, did you?" Her eyes went wide. "Maybe that was their weapon of choice! Deadly high school meals!"

I glared at her, but we both dissolved into laughter. It felt morbid to joke about this, but it kept me from crying.

"Seriously. If you're doing this, you need a plan."

I leaned back on the windowpane and tucked my feet up beneath me. "Truthfully? I hadn't really thought that far ahead. Get into the school was my number one goal. It seemed like a good idea at the time. But now..." Now it all seemed hopeless and impulsive.

She strode across the room to my desk, opened the top drawer, and pulled out a legal pad. She grabbed a pen from the cup on the desk and then plonked herself down in my desk chair. "Enough of the wishy-washy attitude. You've committed. Let's at least see what you can find out. Number one suspect is the football team. Right?"

I nodded. "Right."

"How many guys is that?"

"Not a clue."

She glanced over her shoulder at me. "You were there an entire day and you didn't even find that out?"

I shrugged.

"Christ almighty, lucky you have me." She switched on my laptop, and after waiting for it to boot up, she brought up Saint View High's website. "Bingo!"

I got up and stood behind her. Right there on the main page was a photo of last year's football team.

"Trust a public school to put sports on the front page of their website," Meredith muttered. "No names on this photo, though."

I squinted, then stabbed a finger at the screen. "That's Rafe. Principal's son. And that—"

"Holy shit, is that the bartender you were making fuck-me eyes at?"

My jaw dropped open. "Excuse me? I was not making fuck-me eyes at him." I didn't mention the fact I'd been set to take him up to my bedroom before the police had arrived last night. Hell, how had that only been last night? It felt like a lifetime ago.

"Oh, right. Maybe that was me then." She flashed me a grin.

Jealousy surged through me. Just the tiniest bit. But it was there. I pushed it away. "His name is Banjo."

Meredith wrote it down on the pad. "Right, know any of these other guys?"

I shook my head.

"What about the coach's name?"

"You think it could have been the coach?"

Meredith squinted at the screen. "I don't think you can assume it was a student. Coaches would have team shirts. Probably half the school does, actually. If they support the team. Or like to socialize on a Friday night."

I groaned. This had been a stupid, stupid idea.

"But let's not get overwhelmed. Your task for this week. Find out the names of everyone in this photo." Meredith pointed at the computer screen, jabbing her finger into each guy's face a little too viciously for my liking. My poor monitor.

"Okay. And then what, oh fearless leader?"

She grinned. "That's the easy bit. We're going to stalk them."

7

BANJO

he faded red paint on Colt's front door was as familiar to me as breathing. I twisted the handle and let myself in without knocking. I'd been doing that for almost half my life. Ever since Augie, my brother, had pulled me from the foster care system. We had a place next door—practically identical in layout to Colt's. All the houses on this street were. They were all government housing. The rents were subsidized, which was the only way Augie had been able to afford a place of his own and raise me until I was old enough to contribute to the monthly payments.

Willa, Colt's mom, looked up from flipping through a Walmart brochure when I wandered into her kitchen. At her warm smile, I detoured to her side, and put my arms around her tiny frame, engulfing her in a hug that lifted her off the floor. She yelped but hugged me back. I set her down and leaned on the kitchen counter, picking at the chipped countertop.

"How are you, B? Everything good?"

She'd been asking me that question for eight years now. When I'd first moved here, and started playing with Colt out on the street, Willa had been a good head taller than me. I'd long since towered over her, though she still liked to fuss as if we were still those ten-year-olds with scraped knees. She never failed to ask how I was or if I needed anything.

Though there were some problems even Willa couldn't help me with. And some I wouldn't tell her, solely for the fact I loved her like a mother, and I didn't want her worrying about me. So, instead, I laughed a little too loudly and made my posture as casual as possible. "Everything is great. Football training is about to start up in earnest, though. Reckon you can tell Coach to go easy on us this year?"

She elbowed me. "Like he'd listen. You'll thank him when you make the playoffs this year, though. Last chance before you go off to play college ball."

The smile slid off my face, and I turned away, pulling open the refrigerator door so she wouldn't notice. "You got anything to eat?" I asked, avoiding her comments about college. "I'm starving."

She pushed me out of the way and closed the door. "Rafe and Colt already cleaned me out. They're upstairs in his room. If you're quick, they might not have devoured the lot."

I bent and kissed her cheek, then loped toward the stairs and thundered up them. Music poured out from Colt's bedroom in the attic, but a different noise caught my attention. I frowned and detoured to my left, knocking quietly on the door. The noise from within stopped abruptly.

"Aria?" I asked, without opening the door. "You okay?"

There was a moment of silence, then, "Go away, Banjo."

Nope. That wasn't going to do. I clapped a hand over my eyes and turned the door handle, letting myself inside. "If you're not decent, get a robe on or something because you've got ten seconds before I move my hand. Ten...nine...

Something hard bounced off my head. I moved my hand to rub what was probably going to be a bruise. "Shit, Ari. That hurt!" I complained.

Aria, Colt's younger sister, glared at me. "Good! It was supposed to. Get out of my room."

"Not until you tell me why you're crying."

"I wasn't!"

Tearstains streaked her cheeks, her eyes bloodshot.

"I call bullshit."

"I mean it, Banjo. Leave me alone. It's none of your business."

"Boy drama?"

She rolled her eyes. "Do you really think I'd be crying over a boy?"

I shrugged. "Isn't that what girls do?"

"Only the dumb ones," she muttered.

"Wow. Harsh. We boys mean so little, huh?"

She softened. "I'd cry over you, B. You know, if you got a raging case of gonorrhea and died or something. I'd miss my brother's annoying best friend barging into my room whenever he feels like it."

I winced at the thought of my headstone saying I'd died from an out-of-control STD. Was that even possible? My hands subconsciously drifted to cover my junk.

Ari's mouth lifted at the corners.

A relief settled over me. She wasn't just Colt's younger sister. I'd always thought of her as mine, too, and even though we liked to give each other a hard time, I knew she'd been crying and I hated it.

But I also knew all about not wanting to share your secrets with the world. And I wasn't going to try to pry Ari's from her if she wasn't ready to share them on her own. I pulled the door closed a little, but at the last moment, before she disappeared from sight, I added, "I'm right next door whenever you want to talk about it. Okay?"

Her smile turned sad, but she nodded. "My brother is probably waiting for you. And judging by the music he's been blasting since he got home from school, he's in a mood. Good luck with that."

Yeah. Great. I closed the door and took the final set of stairs to Colt's bedroom. The music grew louder with every step and then hit me square in the face when I let myself in. Rafe sat by an open window, blowing smoke out of it, while Colt thrashed an electric guitar, playing a song I didn't recognize. Rafe lifted his joint in greeting and held it out to me, but I shook my head and instead flopped down on Colt's bed, kicking off my shoes and making myself comfortable on his pillows.

The room was large, which was why Willa had let Colt have it. It had space for my drum kit, which lived here permanently so Colt and I could practice together. My brother had claimed the attic in our house, running his business from it. Our bedrooms on the second level, like Aria's, were small and cramped. Definitely not big enough for two guys and the mess of thrift shop instruments they'd taught themselves how to play over the years.

Colt didn't even look up from his guitar. He had his eyes closed, his fingers all over the fret, pulling sounds from the guitar that I'd never been capable of. Eventually, when he showed no signs of stopping, I went over to my drums and took up a beat.

The stress left me as I played. Every hit of my sticks against the top head released a little more of the pent-up frustration I constantly carried.

"That's hot," Rafe yelled from his perch by the window.

"I hope you can remember whatever you two are playing. That could be something."

Colt slammed his open palm over the strings, an off-key screech filling the room. I winced and stopped playing, too. Colt glared at Rafe.

"What?" Rafe asked.

"You killed my flow."

Rafe rolled his eyes. "You obviously weren't really in it if you even heard what I said. So shut up."

Colt glared at him.

Rafe didn't back down.

I sighed. "Seriously, knock it off, both of you. Colt, you want to tell us what's up your ass today?"

He shoved his guitar, none too gently, into its stand. Then sank down on his bed. "Nothing. I'm fine. Move on."

I eyed him warily. "Man, you need to call Gillian to come suck your dick or something."

"She's exactly what I don't need right now."

I shot a glance at Rafe. He shrugged.

I turned back to Colt. "Don't tell me Mommy and Daddy are on the rocks?"

Colt shrugged. "No, we're fine. I'm just not in the mood for her shit this afternoon, and she's been blowing up my phone. I can't deal, and I don't want to fucking talk about it. Change the subject."

"Fine. Let's talk about the new girl. I call dibs." I gave them both a shit-eating grin. "You know that girl I was telling you about from my gig in Providence last night? It's her."

"What?" Rafe and Colt said in unison.

I nodded. "Yeah, small fucking world, huh? She lives in that big-ass mansion, and then she turns up at Saint View. Crazy."

Rafe was shaking his head. "Great story, but you ain't calling dibs. She's fine. And my dad actually seems to like her."

I scoffed. "You want to date her because your dad approves?"

Rafe reached over and shoved me in the arm, sending my stool sliding on its wheels. "No, I want to date her because I can't stop thinking about how hot her legs looked in that skirt."

I grinned to show him I didn't mean anything by the teasing. We all knew Rafe's dad was a dick and made his life impossible at every opportunity. But that didn't mean I was letting Rafe have a crack at Lacey. Not when I'd spent all night thinking about her, trying to work out how I could get her phone number. She'd rushed off with the police, leaving me standing by her front door, wondering what the hell had happened. One minute we'd been going upstairs, her soft hand wrapped around mine and her citrus scent making me wild. Then next minute I was staring at her front door and she was gone. If my lips hadn't still tingled from the tiniest of kisses we'd shared, I would have thought I'd imagined her.

"Can you both fucking shut up about her? Neither of you are doing anything with her."

I raised an eyebrow in Colt's direction, ready to make a crack about Gillian not being enough for him, and that if he wanted Lacey, too, he'd have to get in line. But the laughter fell from my lips when my gaze met his.

"You're serious?"

"As a fucking heart attack. Leave her alone."

Rafe frowned. "I know your dark and mysterious thing works on girls, but I've known you since kindergarten. So you're gonna have to give me more than that."

Colt shook his head. "She isn't going to be around for long. You saw her today. She doesn't belong here. And I'm going to make sure she goes back where she came from."

"What exactly did she do that's got your panties in a bunch?" I asked.

"Nothing."

"So you've just decided to hate her and run her out of school for sport?" Rafe seemed confused. "You're a prick, but not normally to this degree."

None of this made any fucking sense.

"I'm going to do whatever I have to do. And you two are as well."

I held up my hands. "Nah, Colt. I'm not. Whatever you've got against her, you're going to have to get over. I like her."

Colt scoffed. "You like her tits."

"True," I admitted. "But she didn't talk to me like I was beneath her at the funeral. There's something between us. And I know she was feeling it, too. I'm not playing when I say I want to get to know her."

Colt paused for a moment, but then a flash of pain twisted his features. He got it under control quick, but I'd seen it. And judging by the expression on Rafe's face, he'd seen it, too. He crossed the room and sat next to Colt on his bed. "We aren't just going to run a girl out of school for no reason. You gotta give us something."

When Colt lifted his head, his eyes were glassy. I recoiled. I'd known Colt since just before our tenth birth-days. And the only time I'd ever seen him cry was when he'd told us his dad was dying from cancer.

"Fuck," I swore under my breath. I abandoned the drums and sat on the floor in front of the other two. "What the fuck happened? Who is this girl to get you like this?"

Colt shook his head. "It's not my place to say. I swear, if I could tell you, I would."

"Since when do we have secrets from each other?" I asked, a little hurt. "We're brothers."

Colt swallowed hard and met both our gazes before he said anything. "I've never asked you guys for anything, have I? I've been there for you, keeping your secrets about your brother—" he looked at me, and a flush crawled up the back of my neck. He turned to Rafe. "And about your dad?"

We both nodded.

His gaze hardened. "Lacey needs to go back where she came from. For all of our sakes."

8

LACEY

*J*agger chatted happily all the way to school the next morning, but I was too in my head to hear any of it. I was still replaying yesterday afternoon in my mind. Making an enemy of Colt was stupid. I'd tossed and turned last night, unable to sleep over it.

I couldn't change it. And I wasn't going to apologize. But we'd obviously gotten off on the wrong foot, and maybe I could do something to steer us back in the right direction. I didn't know what but hoped an opportunity might present itself.

Jagger and I parted ways in the main hall when the first bell rang, and the morning was nothing out of the ordinary. I had all the same subjects as yesterday, and I disguised myself in each classroom, sinking into seats in back rows and corners wherever possible, and paying next to no attention to the teacher.

My education really was going to suffer, but that was a problem I could deal with once I'd done what I came here to do.

When the bell rang for lunch, I hurried from math,

down the crowded hall toward the cafeteria where I was supposed to meet Jagger. I'd somehow managed to not bump into her all day. Also noticeably missing were Banjo, Rafe, and Colt. Rafe was in my math class, so I guessed he was absent today. Or maybe he just hadn't bothered showing up and was getting stoned behind the gym again.

A gleam of gold in my peripheral vision had me putting on the brakes before I got to the cafeteria doors. I hadn't come down this far yesterday, after my lunch break got swallowed up by the guidance counselor. If I had, there's no way I would have missed the gigantic glassed-in trophy cabinet. The thing was huge, standing floor to ceiling and several feet wide. Every shelf was filled with sporting memorabilia. Trophies, banners, certificates, awards, photos...it was a mishmash, completely unappealing to the eye, most things obviously just shoved in haphazardly, but I was a little surprised by how much there was. This school might not have been up there in the academic stakes, but judging by the sheer number of trophies, sports was where they excelled. Football, cheerleading, lacrosse, basketball... I let my gaze flick over each one until my eye snagged on a familiar photo.

Last year's football team. The same photo from the website. But this copy had the entire team's names printed beneath it in tiny white writing, on a maroon-colored background. Bingo. Exactly what I needed so Meredith and I could get our stalk on. I pulled my phone out and through the grubby glass, snapped a photo. I tapped the screen to enlarge it. "Yep, that'll do," I murmured after ensuring I could read the writing. Someone really needed to clean that glass more often, though. Gross.

"What are you doing?" Jagger asked, coming up behind me.

I hit the home button on my phone, making the photo disappear, but I obviously wasn't quick enough.

She side-eyed me. "Don't tell me you have a thing for jocks?"

"Oh." I shoved the phone in the pocket of my jeans. Designer jeans, but I hoped most of the kids wouldn't notice that. "Um, yeah." I tried to think quick. I really didn't have a thing for jocks. I'd always gone for musicians in the past, but how else could I explain taking photos of the football team? I smiled at her and shrugged, like I was a bit embarrassed about being busted checking them out. "I guess I kind of do."

Jagger gave an exaggerated sigh. Her crimson hair had streaks of purple in it today, which matched the violet liner she'd liberally applied around her eyes. "I can admit that there are some hotties on the team. But most of them date the cheerleaders." She narrowed her eyes at me. "Please tell me you aren't a cheerleader. I don't know if we can still be friends if you are."

I shook my head. "God, no. We didn't even have a cheerleading squad at my old school."

"Really?"

I shook my head. "Nope. Providence School for Girls wasn't big on sports like football."

"You didn't have a girls' team?"

I tried to imagine Meredith or any of my other old friends wanting to play football...and just couldn't. Even getting them to their mandatory gym class had been met with complaints about broken nails and running makeup. There'd even been a petition, at one point, to cancel gym altogether and half the alumni had signed it, putting pressure on my uncle. Eventually, he'd worked with the gym teachers, and gym had changed from running laps, rope climbs, and shooting hoops, to yoga, Pilates, and yogalates... whatever the hell that was. That had pacified the masses.

"No, definitely not. We went to watch Edgely play a few times, though."

Jagger wrinkled her nose. "Edgely Academy?"

I raised an eyebrow. "Why do you say that like it tastes bad?"

"Because they probably do?" She snorted at her own joke. "They're notorious for cheating and playing dirty. I just assume they're nasty all round. But maybe you'd know for sure?"

I shrugged.

"Ooooh, there's a story there! Come on, tell me over lunch."

I let myself be pulled along and contemplated exactly how much to tell Jagger about my life. I didn't want to lie. I'd dated a few guys from Edgely. Made out with a couple, even. But it had never gone further than that. The interest just hadn't been there on my behalf.

But it had been with Banjo. Would I have slept with him if we hadn't been interrupted? I didn't know. All I knew was I'd wanted to throw caution to the wind and just live in the moment. I didn't know if that was because of him or if I would have felt the same with any guy who had been available that day.

It was probably better we hadn't. I could only imagine how awkward that would have made school. It was awkward enough, just after sharing that one, sort-of-almost kiss. Plus, he was on the football team, which made him one of my suspects. No. Definitely better that we'd been interrupted.

"Have you seen Banjo today?" I asked as we pushed through the swinging doors. A weird aroma wrinkled my nose. Probably the slop that was being served up on plates.

Great. Not only was I going to end up with a half-baked education, but I was probably going to end up with food poisoning, too. I vowed to bring a packed lunch tomorrow.

I scanned the room, my gaze coming to rest on one familiar face. Banjo's lazy gaze rolled over my body, a slow grin pulling at the corners of his mouth. My heart fluttered. He sat at a table in the center of the crowded room, entirely by himself, looking completely at ease about it.

"I guess I don't need to answer that question, then?" Jagger said, tugging me toward the food line. "Come on, quit making eyes at that boy and let's get some food."

I followed her along, but it was hard to keep my attention on the lumpy brown stew that landed on my tray when I could literally feel Banjo's gaze on me. A flush crawled up the back of my neck as we moved along the line, waiting to get our drinks.

"So, you going to tell him yes?" Jagger asked.

"Tell who yes?"

"Banjo asked you out yesterday. Quit dodging the topic. Judging by the way you two were just eye-fucking, you want to say yes."

Shit. In all the Colt drama, then the Meredith distraction when I'd gotten home, I'd completely forgotten that Banjo had asked me out. Again. That was twice now.

But somebody had killed my uncle and started a fire to cover it up. A fire that had nearly killed me before I'd been carried out. They could have left me for dead. Hell, they should have. I was now potentially somebody who could identify them. Would Banjo honestly ask me out if he'd been the one to do it? I doubted it. Being the starting quarterback probably meant he knew the guys on the team well. He was exactly what I needed. Somebody to spill all the inside details.

My heart rate picked up at the thought of going out with him. If I said yes, it wouldn't be solely because I was playing sleuth. There was something more between us. I'd noticed it from the very first moment we'd met. It might have only been attraction, but it was a powerful one.

"Yeah," I said slowly. "I think I'd like that."

Jagger's eyes lit up. "Let's go tell him."

"Whoa, no. In the middle of the lunchroom?"

"Hell yes, before one of these skanks tries to get their grimy claws into your man."

I jostled my tray into one arm so I could pick up a drink, passing a bottle of water back to Jagger. "Bit soon to call him my man."

She shook her head like I was completely hopeless and annoying, took her water, and marched across the lunch-room. I followed after her, cringing a little when I realized she was making a beeline for Banjo. I caught him watching me and bit my lip, holding in a smile.

Jagger stopped in front of him, dumping her tray on the table. She grabbed my arm, propelling me forward until Banjo and I were face-to-face.

"Uh, hi," I said, awkward as fuck.

"Hi to you, too." His green eyes sparkled with a mischief that I found incredibly appealing.

I could only imagine where he'd take me on a date. It wouldn't be dinner and a movie. No way. He'd be a bonfire on the beach. Or he'd try to teach me to skateboard, which would probably be a disaster, since I was one of the girls at Providence who was wholly uncoordinated thanks to the lack of gym class, and was probably better off sticking to yoga.

Jagger cleared her throat and shot a look at me. I ignored her.

"About what you said yesterday—"

I got cut off by a scraping noise that was as painful to listen to as fingernails down a chalkboard. It was so loud, the entire room stopped their conversation and watched while Colt spun the chair next to Banjo. It clattered back onto all four legs, and he straddled it backward, folding his arms on top of the backrest. Colt's eyes narrowed on me. He was pissed. And it seemed to be my fault, judging from the way his anger practically radiated like laser beams.

All thoughts of turning over a new leaf with him flew out of my head. I glared, not expecting he'd back down but sure as hell not willing to be the first to turn away either.

"Uh, Lacey?"

I jolted out of my Colt stare off and focused back on Banjo. Back where my gaze should have been all along. Colt wasn't worth the effort.

"I'd love to go out with you," I said to Banjo, firmly.

Banjo's smiled faltered. He shot Colt a look, and shook his head slightly, but whatever Banjo was trying to convey didn't get across.

Colt was too busy laughing his ass off. "Oh, this is rich. Yesterday, you were too good for us. Today you want to date him?"

Ugh, I wanted to punch this guy. "I said I was too good for you, jackass. Not him." More words I'd probably feel bad about later, but something about Colt brought out the worst in me. And in that moment, I didn't care.

I turned back to Banjo, but my stomach sank at the expression on his face.

He stood and pulled me aside, a few steps. His hand was warm on my arm, sending a pleasant tingling feeling across my skin. "Listen, something's happened...I'm really sorry..."

I almost felt sorry for him. His cheeks were pink with embarrassment, and he looked genuinely apologetic.

"Dumped on your second day of school," Colt said, loud enough for all the kids at the tables around us to titter.

"Colt, shut up, man" Banjo complained. He turned back to me. "Lacey..."

I was trying my best to keep my emotions in check, but that was being made more difficult by his expression. True disappointment burned behind my eyes. But then it turned into anger as a thought popped into my head.

"Was asking me out yesterday just some sort of prank between the two of you?"

"Yep," Colt said.

"No!" Banjo said at the same time. "Seriously, Colt, fuck off. I'm doing what you want, don't make it worse."

A tiny part of me wanted to know what he meant by that, but a much bigger part wanted to save face. Which meant getting out of Colt's firing range. "Come on," I said to Jagger. "I'm over this."

"Damn straight." She smacked Banjo on the back of the head as we walked past.

"Hey!" he complained, rubbing the spot where Jagger's palm had made contact with his skull.

"You deserved that. And you," she rounded on Colt. "You're a dick."

He didn't comment.

Jagger and I walked out of the cafeteria with our heads held high, even though I was dying on the inside.

9

LACEY

*J*agger and I took our lunches outside in the sunshine of the quad and found a rickety-looking bench away from other people. We both picked at our crappy, sloppy food, then simultaneously dumped it in a nearby trashcan.

"I'm really sorry about before," Jagger said, settling back on the seat with her bottle of water. "I feel like I pushed you into that and it blew up royally in your face. I don't know what their problem is today."

"They're jerks?" I asked. I took a long swallow of my drink to push down the lump that had been stuck in my throat. I gave myself a mental scolding over how ridiculous it was to be upset about what had just happened. Colt was a dick. That was fine. But Banjo...I didn't understand what had happened there.

"Thing is, they're not normally. They're super popular."

"I can't imagine why."

Jagger sighed. "I'm struggling to remember myself right now. Maybe something happened over the summer."

I snapped my head in her direction. "Do you think?"

Something like murdering a man in cold blood and setting a building on fire, perhaps? Not that I could say that to Jagger. She'd think I was crazy.

Jagger kicked at the patch of grass beneath our feet. "Who knows? Maybe Gillian just isn't putting out, and Banjo's surf this morning was ruined by flat waves. It's not worth worrying about." She clapped her hands together and I jumped at the sudden noise. "There's a party this weekend. You're coming."

"I haven't been invited to any parties..."

Jagger patted my head while she laughed. "Oh, sweet Lacey. Were you expecting a written invitation hand delivered in a glossy envelope by a servant with a silver tray?"

I shrugged. "Maybe not the silver tray, but..."

"Oh Lord, you rich kids are something else. You're gonna sit at home every weekend if you're waiting to be officially invited to parties. Around here, if you hear about a party, you can go."

"Okay, so where's the party?"

"One of the guys on the football team has a house to himself this weekend. His mom is away for work or something. I don't know. But all the team will be there. Perfect place for you to find yourself a new man to shove in Banjo's face."

I shook my head. "I don't need to shove anything in his face."

"Pft. You may not need to. But it will be fun. And you said you liked jocks. It will be jock city at this party. Come on, please? Entertain me. And meet some people. Make some friends. It'll be good for you."

I wasn't exactly sure about that. But I did need to get closer to the football team. And if that wasn't going to be through Banjo, then I had to find another way. "Okay, sure. I'll go. On one condition."

Jagger bounced on her seat with excitement. "Yes! Anything, name it."

"You take me shopping. Because I have no idea about the dress code for a Saint View High party."

Jagger's eyes lit up. "You're talking my love language, sister. Done deal."

I left Jagger a few minutes before the bell rang signaling the end of lunch. She'd stared at me like I'd grown a second head when I'd told her I wanted to get to class early, but I'd been looking forward to this class all day.

My music elective was in a building so far to the edge of the school, it was as if the sounds of teenagers practicing instruments were offensive and needed to be well out of hearing distance from anyone else.

The teacher, a young blonde woman, glanced up as I entered the room.

I lifted my hand in a half wave. "Hi, sorry. I know the bell hasn't gone yet, but I'm Lacey."

The woman stood from her desk and crossed the room, long skirt swishing around her ankles. It was an explosion of color, and she'd matched it with a plain white tank top, which calmed the crazy skirt a little. Big hoops hung from her ears, giving her a bit of a boho vibe. She held her hand out for me to shake, and I took it with a smile, instantly liking her vibe. Or perhaps it was just that any room where music was played left me at ease.

"Lacey. Lovely to meet you. I'm Miss Halten. Principal Simmons tells me you're quite the musical prodigy."

I shook my head. "That might be a bit of a stretch. But I do love it. It's my whole life."

She gave my hand a little squeeze. "Good for you. Enthusiasm is more important than some preconceived notion of a God-given talent anyway. You can learn almost anything if you're willing to practice."

"I agree."

"Good. Then we'll get along just fine. Grab a seat anywhere. The bell is about to go."

I dropped my backpack where I stood and slid into a seat in the front row. I couldn't have cared less about impressing teachers in my other classes, but music was special. And I hoped Miss Halten might actually be able to help me improve. Hell, may as well make the most of my time here. I didn't want to waste my entire senior year.

The bell rang, and Miss Halten went back to her desk, picking up a pen and scribbling something on a sheet of paper. I stared off into space, glad to have a few minutes alone while everyone wandered over from the cafeteria. I was still riled up by what had happened with Colt and Banjo, but the best way for me to get over anything I was angry or upset about was to play. And I was itching to get my fingers on the acoustic guitar standing to the side of Miss Halten's desk.

"Oh, the princess is in our class. Great. Should we bow? Curtsey? I'm not sure of the protocol."

I didn't even have to lift my head to recognize Gillian's voice, sharp and vicious. I looked over in her direction, deliberately slowly, as if I were bored with her statement. "That's because you have no class, sweetie." The words dripped with fake sugar and sarcasm. I'd never used the term sweetie in my life. But Gillian irked me. She'd taken an instant dislike, with absolutely no reason behind it, and I wasn't about to take her shit lying down.

She folded her arms beneath her breasts, which only thrust them higher than the push-up bra peeking from the low cut of her top. If she wasn't careful, one of them would pop right out and give the class a hell of a show, but I somehow got the impression that wouldn't have bothered her in the least.

Gillian's overflowing D cup didn't hold my attention long, though. Colt's infuriating smirk drew my gaze like a magnet. I hated that I found it so sexy. His lips were full, and when they turned up the way they were now, they were hard not to stare at. I wanted to reach out and trace the curve of his mouth.

Preferably with my tongue.

Watching him like this wasn't comfortable. It was as if I'd been stripped naked and exposed. Like he could read all my thoughts. But I couldn't drag my eyes away either.

Until Gillian stepped between us. She spun around to face him, lifted up on her toes, and put her mouth to his ear. His smirk turned into a grin, and he put his arm around her as they headed for the back row of seats.

I tensed when his big body moved past mine. His free hand trailed over my desk, on a collision course with the bare skin of my arm. I jolted out of the way before he could make contact.

He tilted his head in amusement. "Keep digging your hole, princess. You starting a war with Gillian, just means she runs you out of school before I do."

Something inside me snapped. I shot my hand out and grabbed his arm.

Shit. Bad move.

Sparks shot up my arm as if I'd been electrocuted.

Colt stopped and looked down at my hand in surprise, which quickly morphed to amusement.

That only pissed me off more. "What exactly is your problem with me?"

His eyes narrowed, and his voice lowered. "If you don't know, it's not worth explaining."

He shook my hand off and took his seat at the back of the room. Gillian gave me a smile that could rival a shark's.

If you don't know, it's not worth explaining.

What the hell did that mean?

I twisted back in my seat only to find Banjo entering the room. I slunk down. While I was perfectly happy to go head-to-head with Colt, Banjo was different. Heat flushed my cheeks when his gaze landed on me. He hurried to my desk, and I shot a glance at the teacher, hoping she'd save me from the embarrassment of having to talk to him again. But alas, she still had her nose buried in whatever paper she was marking.

"Banjo."

Banjo ignored Colt's command. His mouth pressed into a straight line. "Can we talk?" he asked me.

"Banjo!" Colt said again.

"You'd better go. Your king is calling."

"He's not my king," Banjo muttered.

"Could have fooled me," I said quietly. There was no malice in my voice this time, though.

Banjo's shoulders slumped, and he took his seat right as Miss Halten stood and introduced herself to the class.

The teacher's voice became a drone while I tried to ignore the sensation that someone was staring at my back. I had no idea which of the three it was. But I hoped it was

Banjo. I hadn't quite given up on him yet, even though he'd wounded my pride.

Colt and Gillian could both go to hell.

"So, this is senior year," Miss Halten said, finally capturing my attention. "Right off the bat, I'm setting your first assignment. There'll be a concert at the end of semester. Time will be limited, as the other performing arts classes will also be involved. Therefore, this semester's assignment is to work in pairs. I want you to find a song that suits both partners' strengths, because you'll be marked together. So don't go hogging the limelight for yourself. If you don't share the weight, you both fail."

It might have been my imagination, but I could have sworn Miss Halten turned in Gillian's direction when she said that. It didn't surprise me. It was already obvious to me that Gillian liked being the center of attention. She was probably back there fuming over not getting to do a solo. The class buzzed with excited chatter, and Miss Halten held up one hand in a stop motion until everyone quieted.

"Additionally, I'll be choosing one person to do a solo."

"How will that person be chosen?" Gillian called out. "Will there be auditions?"

Well, that confirmed it. Gillian's eagerness could have been heard by a deaf person.

"No. The spot will be given to the student who has the highest marks the week before the concert. So I suggest you all practice a piece and have it ready to go in case you're chosen. Any other questions?"

I raised my hand tentatively. "Are partners assigned?"

"Why? Worried no one will pick you, princess?" Gillian said snidely.

Miss Halten shot her a dirty look, then turned back to

me. "Since you're new, Lacey, you can pick your partner first. Stand up, face the class."

I did as I was told and studied the classroom of about thirty kids. I didn't know any of their names bar the three in the back row. My gaze landed on Gillian who appeared to be trying to burn me on the spot with the fire in her eyes. I switched to Colt, who wasn't paying attention, too busy chatting quietly with Banjo. When I looked back at Gillian, she was ready to explode.

Oh, wouldn't that be fun. To pick her boyfriend. It was on the tip of my tongue to say his name, just to spite her, but then the thought of having to actually put up with Colt for the next few months made me reconsider. I tried to think fast, because I was well aware that an entire classroom was waiting on me to make a decision. I needed to be smart about this. This was a chance to get one-on-one time with someone. Perhaps gain their trust. I needed to choose someone from the football team. My gaze flitted around the room, but none of the faces were even remotely familiar.

"Miss Halten, if she can't make a decision, I'd be happy to go first," Gillian said.

"I choose Banjo."

Banjo and Colt both snapped their heads forward. Colt narrowed his eyes.

Miss Halten clapped her hands together. "Excellent! Our first matchup. You two move your desks together, and once everyone has chosen a partner, you can start discussing your potential song choices."

Banjo stood slowly and picked his way to the front of the room, taking the empty desk beside mine then pulling it over so close they touched. "What are you doing?" he murmured as we both sat. "You're making this worse for yourself. Colt is going to go after you harder, just for picking me."

"I picked a music partner. That's it. If you don't want to work with me, then you'd best take it up with Miss Halten."

He shot me a sidelong glance. "I want to work with you, Lacey." His voice dropped so only I would hear it. "I want to do a lot of things with you."

My breath stuttered in my lungs. "What?" I whispered. Though there was no denying the sexual undercurrent of his words. It was the same one that had been there that night after my uncle's funeral, when I'd very nearly fallen into bed with him. "You're the one who said you didn't want to go out with me. Make up your mind, Banjo. I don't play games."

He sighed. "I'm not playing anything. But it's complicated."

"I don't do complicated either." Then I forced out words I didn't really mean. "So just forget it. I only chose you because I didn't know anyone else's name. Can we just talk about what song we want to do?"

Banjo appeared wounded by that, and I tried to keep myself from apologizing. He deserved a little of his own medicine, even if I did feel bad.

"If that's what you want."

That was what I wanted. For now, anyway.

10

LACEY

I'd never been to the mall in Saint View. I gawked around at the different stores, food courts, and the Saturday morning crowd like a little kid who'd never seen the ocean.

Jagger thought it was hilarious. "How much of a bubble do you rich kids live in that you've never been to the mall?" she asked, dragging me along a tiled floor toward her favorite store, where she'd assured me I'd be able to buy an entirely new wardrobe full of clothes for less than a few hundred bucks.

I was trying super hard not be skeptical about that. I knew Meredith would have been horrified. Which was exactly why I'd lied to her when she'd asked me what I was doing this morning, and I told her I had a study session with my new tutor before I went to the party tonight. She'd sounded a bit miffed, but I'd promised to pick her up first thing Sunday morning for breakfast. First thing meaning ten, because Meredith didn't do early mornings.

"I've been to a mall," I said to Jagger. "Just not this mall."

She shot me an incredulous look. "By mall, do you mean

you walked down Woodline Avenue, where all the designer boutiques are?"

I grinned. "Okay, I'm a snob. But I swear it isn't my fault. I didn't even know this place existed. I actually like it."

Jagger hooked her arm through mine. "Me, too. Well, I like it when I have money to spend. Spending other people's money is a second best. Here we are." She took a sharp left into the nearest clothing store, and I blinked in the sudden change of lighting. The store was much darker than the rest of the mall, and colored strobe lights flashed across the painted black ceiling. Spotlights lit up the racks of clothes, and music blasted through a sound system, loud enough that I had to raise my voice in order for Jagger to hear me.

"It's like a nightclub in here!"

Jagger's hips swayed in time with the beat. "I know! Isn't it great? And the clothes are awesome. Hey, Maya!" She waved to the tattooed girl behind the counter, who waved back.

"How often do you come here?" I asked curiously.

"It's my home away from home. I like to come at least once a week. Check out anything new. They normally restock on Thursdays, in time for the weekend rush."

"They should give you a job."

"I wish. I'd love a job where I got to work with clothes."

"You'd be a great designer. I love the outfits you put together. That's why I made you come with me today."

Jagger picked up a slinky green dress and ran her hand over the sparkly fabric longingly. I recognized that move. It was the same thing I did with musical instruments I desperately wanted to play. She gently put it back on the rack, tucking it between other dresses, and instead chose a short, tight, black one. She held it out in front of me. "Nah, you just asked me because I'm the only one in school who isn't scared by this little war that Gillian and Colt have declared on you."

I cringed. "War? That's a bit extreme. We had a few jabs at each other, yeah. But that's not exactly a war."

The rest of the school week hadn't been much better than my first two days. I'd managed to avoid any further run-ins with Colt and Gillian, but other than Jagger, nobody made an effort to speak to me. I'd tried a few times to introduce myself to the kids I sat next to in my classes. At best, I'd received an awkward smile and a polite dismissal.

Jagger shot a worried glance in my direction.

"What?" I asked.

She sighed. "It's a war. They put a blast out on Instagram."

"What? Show me."

Jagger shook her head. "Babe, no. Don't worry about them. I don't. Colt and Gillian are so full of shit. They think they own the school and that the rest of us are their minions. I'm not. I'm sure there's others who feel the same."

"Jagger!" She was stalling. No doubt about that. "Show me what they did!"

Her lips pressed together, making one long purple lipstick line. But she reluctantly pulled her phone from the back pocket of her ripped up jeans.

I crowded in on her, trying to peer over her shoulder. She brought up the Instagram app and scrolled until she found what she wanted. Then she thrust it into my hand.

"They share an Instagram account?" I scoffed, taking in the username. Gillyncolt. "Jeez, co-dependent much?"

Jagger sniggered.

I tapped on the first post on their profile. It was a stock photo by the looks of things. A golden crown against a bright-pink background. But someone had drawn a circle in thick black ink, with a diagonal cross through the middle.

"How artistic," I said sarcastically. "But this could be about anything."

"That's optimistic of you. Read the caption."

"There might be a new princess in town, but Saint View High already has a king and queen. This is one throne you won't ever get to sit on."

I passed the phone back to Jagger and rolled my eyes. "Seriously? You're worried by this?"

Her eyes were wide. "You should be, too. Did you see how many followers they have?"

I shrugged. "So they paid some click farm to look extra popular."

"Or they just are that popular. Seriously, Lacey. I told you about the Untouchables. There aren't going to be too many who will go against whatever Gillian and Colt are putting out there. This is something to be worried about."

I bit my lip. This wasn't at all what I'd envisioned when I'd enrolled in this school. I'd imagined waltzing in, flying under the radar, and just casually poking around for information. I imagined watching from afar, taking notes, maybe even sitting in my car and taking photos from a safe distance. Yet somehow, in the space of a week, I'd managed to put myself right into the middle of some sort of popularity contest for an imaginary throne I didn't even want any part of?

I pulled my shoulders back and took another too-short dress from the rack in front of me, holding it up for Jagger's approval. She nodded enthusiastically and towed me toward the back of the store where the changing rooms were.

"Yes! Try that on. You'd slay in that at the party tonight."

I let myself be tugged along and slid the thick curtain

across the changing room to give myself some privacy. It was only then I let out a shaky breath and wondered what the hell I'd gotten myself into.

———

*M*any hours and sore feet later, Jagger and I emerged into the sunshine of the ginormous parking lot that served the mall. We trudged back to my car, arms laden with more bags than I think I'd ever held at one time. Jagger sure knew how to shop. We'd bought enough clothes to last me almost a year, and her eyes had gotten big when I'd pulled out a black AMEX card and charged the lot.

I dumped everything into the back seat. All except one bag. "Here," I said, thrusting it into Jagger's hands. "For you."

"What?"

"Just open it."

She did, pulling out the shimmery green dress I'd seen her eyeing. I'd snuck it beneath a pile of my own clothes when she'd been trying on sunglasses and making faces at herself in the store mirror.

"You like it, right?"

She nodded but bit her lip. "I didn't need you to buy me this, though." She pushed it back at me and dropped her hands to her sides.

"I know," I said. "But you gave up your Saturday morning to come shopping with me, and you're the only person at school who has been nice to me. So consider it a thank-you present."

She crinkled up her face, and I could practically see the thoughts whirling around her mind. She didn't want my charity. But she really wanted the dress.

"Jagger. Seriously. If you don't take that dress, I'm going to use it to change my oil."

Jagger's eyes went huge, and her lips formed a tiny O. "You wouldn't!"

I just looked at her.

"Oh my God, you're a beast." She snatched the dress from my hand, then wrapped her arms around me in a tight hug. "Thank you."

I hugged her back. "That dress was made for you. You're going to have guys passing out as you walk by them tonight."

"I hope not. A roomful of unconscious men doesn't sound like much of a party. They kind of need to be awake to be any fun."

I giggled. "True."

Movement across the parking lot caught my eye. Two guys talked by a dark green sedan. It had probably once been a nice car, but now it was in need of some serious TLC. One of the guys looked older, his blond hair cropped close to his head and light stubble across his jaw. His shoulders were broad, his chest thick beneath a tight white T-shirt. He passed a small package to the other guy, who tucked it into his pocket.

"Ah fuck," Jagger said.

I glanced over at her. "What?"

She nodded in the direction of the two guys. They slapped hands and parted ways. The blond guy got back in his car, while the other turned around.

"Is that Rafe?" I hissed. "And was that what I think it was?"

"Did you think it was a drug deal? If so, yeah. I wonder if Banjo knows."

I frowned. "What's it got to do with Banjo?"

She folded her arms across her chest, and we watched

Rafe quietly thread his way through the parking lot, toward us. "That was Banjo's brother he just scored from."

The green car reversed slowly out of its spot, Banjo's brother's tanned brown arm resting on the open window.

"Banjo's brother deals?"

She didn't answer. Just scowled at Rafe as he approached.

He was busy shaking his head at Jagger, so I let myself check him out. Yep. Still as cute as he'd been at school. Brown shorts that showed off athletic calves. A white button-down rolled up at the elbows. Dark hair artfully slicked and the same black-framed glasses he'd worn at school. He was more dressed up than most of the guys at the mall had been. Was that so nobody expected he was here to score? Or maybe he was on his way somewhere? Rafe's clothes made me think his family might have been a little better off than most of the families in Saint View. I wondered what his mother did for work. I couldn't imagine that a public school principal would earn all that much money.

"Don't give me that look, Jagger," he complained, stopping in front of us. His gaze strayed to me, wandering over my features, and then lower before drifting back up to my face. He shook his head slightly, like I'd somehow disappointed him just by standing there. He turned back to Jagger without even a hello to me.

"You want to kill your brain with drugs, go at it. But do you really think that scoring in the middle of the day, from Banjo's brother, of all people, is a good idea?"

He sighed. "Just don't say anything, all right?"

She softened a little. "I know you've got your problems."

He snorted on a laugh. "Babe, you knew my problems when we were fourteen. You've got no idea."

She frowned. "Then tell me."

"What for?"

"Because I care about you."

"Like a brother."

She stared him down, while I wondered what the hell was going on.

"I still care," she said.

"Well, I don't. Just promise me you won't say anything to Banjo."

She ground her teeth together. "Fine, asshole. I won't say anything."

"Good. Because it's really not your business anymore."

Jagger seemed like she wanted to argue about that. But then she nodded. "I guess not. See you around, Rafe."

He walked off without saying goodbye or glancing in my direction again. Jagger got in the car and slammed the door. I followed suit, getting in behind the steering wheel.

"Okayyyy," I drawled, letting out a long breath. "Do you want to tell me what the hell all that was?"

She pinched the bridge of her nose like she had a sudden headache. "Old history with a sad ending. Can I tell you later, though? It's a downer, and we've got a party to get ready for."

I desperately wanted to know what had gone on with the two of them, but I respected her enough to not want to pry either. It's not like I'd told her all my secrets either. So I just nodded and got us back on the road to Jagger's house.

My first Saint View High party was only hours away. I didn't have to ask to know there'd be alcohol. Alcohol meant loose lips, and another chance to find out more about who killed my uncle.

11

LACEY

*T*he pounding bass line greeted us the minute we stepped out of Jagger's car. It boomed through the entire suburban neighborhood. I was sure if I put my hand against the wall of the house we were parked in front of, it would be vibrating.

Jagger locked her car and came around to my side, straightening the shiny green dress I'd bought her earlier. It really did suit her, skimming over her hips and ass, the neckline plunging between her breasts.

In comparison, my dress was tame. But it was shorter and tighter than anything I'd ever worn before, the material black and slinky. If a breeze picked up, I was gonna feel it on my backside. Especially since Jagger had talked me into wearing a thong. My aunt would have had a fit and compared the dress to something a two-dollar hooker would wear. Okay, perhaps she wouldn't have said it in those exact words, but I could easily imagine her horror. Which exactly why we'd gotten ready at Jagger's place. Jagger's mom was young—like, actually young, not full of Botox young—and she'd said our dresses were hot. That was it. No, be home by midnight. No, be responsible.

I didn't know what to make of that.

We joined the stream of people crossing the patchy lawn leading to a single-story house. Nobody stopped us at the door. In fact, nobody even knocked. They just let themselves inside like they owned the place. Jagger had called it the nice side of town as we'd driven in, and now, I tried to check my privilege. While the house wasn't completely ghetto, it wasn't what I would have described as nice either.

"Are you sure we're not overdressed?" I asked, eyeing the jeans on the girl ahead of us and tugging my hemline down.

"Hell no. We look fine. And just wait. You'll see. There'll be plenty of booty shorts and miniskirts."

I followed Jagger through the unfamiliar house, trying to catch a glimpse at the photos on the walls as we passed. There was a heavy football theme to most of them. Individual photos of a little kid in pads that were too big for him, right through to what had to be last year's photo. He smiled widely, his football helmet tucked under one arm, and right by it, was that photo of the team from last year.

Tate Masters, I realized with a start. I'd spent all week trying to memorize the names of the team and match them with their photos. I was semi-proud of myself for remembering.

Jagger's hips swayed in time with the beat, and she nudged me playfully. "Loosen up!"

"I'm loose!" I yelled back over the music.

The look she gave me said I was anything but. "Okay, I'm scared if this is you loose. Let's get a drink."

I shook my head. "No, I'm good. You go ahead, though."

We found the kitchen, and Jagger ignored my protests, filling a red Solo cup from the huge keg and passing it to me.

Truthfully, I wanted a drink. Butterflies rioted around my stomach, and my gaze flitted from person to person, trying to take in the scene. I wasn't sure if I was dressed okay. I wasn't sure if I should be here at all, though I now understood that invitations weren't the done thing around here. Mostly, I was worried about who I might bump into tonight. And what I might find out.

I took the drink from Jagger and swallowed, the beer sliding down the back of my throat. It wasn't particularly nice, but at least it was cold. I surveyed the array of alcohol bottles on the counter and watched other kids mix drinks with a complete lack of skill or finesse that even a brand-new bartender would have. I winced as one kid filled her cup almost all the way to the top with vodka, adding a splash of soda at the end. I recognized her from my English class. I mentally vowed to check on her before we left and make sure she wasn't passed out somewhere.

"Where did they get all this alcohol from?" I asked Jagger.

She took a sip of her beer then we were on the move again. I was grateful to get out of the crowded kitchen.

"It's a football party. It was probably donated."

My mouth dropped open. "Seriously?"

"Seriously. Not officially, of course, since they're underage. But it's not hard to get a backdoor delivery when you're one of the Untouchables."

I took another sip of donated beer and pondered a town that held high school football players in such high regard.

"Ah shit," Jagger said, stopping so abruptly I near spilled my drink all down her back. "I can't watch that."

She turned around to face me and held her cup to her mouth, chugging down her beer. Past her, Rafe sprawled on the couch, legs spread wide, a blonde girl straddled across his lap. One hand gripped the back of her head while they kissed, the other held a lit joint.

I tilted my head, studying Jagger. "How long did you two date for?"

She glanced back over her shoulder. "I don't know. A year, maybe? We were fourteen."

Wow. That was a lifetime for a high school relationship. I'd never dated anyone close to that long. I'd never really dated anyone actually. I went out. With friends, and with guys, but nothing had ever turned into a real relationship. "What happened?"

"I broke up with him."

I tried to ignore the warmth settling low in my stomach as I watched Rafe kiss the girl on his lap. His fingers were tangled in her hair, and the kiss was slow and drugging and...hot. A tiny flare of jealousy sparked inside me. I hadn't ever been kissed like that. The two of them looked like they'd forgotten there were other people in the room. "You broke up with him?"

She nodded. "Is that hard to believe? I know he's hot but—"

I grabbed her arm and dug my fingernails in a little bit. "Don't be stupid. That's not what I meant. Just, why?" Because he was hot. Insanely so. And smart, from what I could work out. He was in all the top classes at school. On the football team. There wasn't much of a downside if you asked me. "Is it the drugs that bother you?"

She shook her head. "No, he wasn't even doing them when we were together. That started after. And I'd be a bit of a hypocrite, considering I'm not averse to taking the odd hit myself."

"Why then?"

"I just don't feel like that about him. We were young. He was more like my brother. Who I had sex with occasionally."

My eyes went wide. "You were having sex with him at fourteen?"

"You weren't having sex at fourteen?" She seemed honestly surprised.

"No! Of course not!"

She blinked. "How old were you then?"

I went quiet.

Her mouth dropped open. "You are not a—"

"What are you doing here?"

Jagger and I both jumped at the intrusion.

Rafe glared at me, eyes tinged with red. If I hadn't already seen him with a joint, his bloodshot eyes would have given away that he'd been smoking.

"Me?" I asked in a squeak, though it was obvious he wasn't talking to Jagger.

He'd stepped right between us, and his ice-blue gaze pinned me to the spot. Smoke clung to his skin and clothes, invading my nose.

"Yeah, you, princess. You weren't invited."

Heat flushed my cheeks, and I hoped the thick makeup Jagger had plastered all over my face hid my blush. This was exactly what I'd been worried about. But Jagger had said nobody had invitations. So I decided to call his bluff. "Where's your invitation, then?"

Rafe's eyes narrowed, like he was pissed I'd dared to speak back to him. It made him look mean. Nothing like the chilled-out boy who'd taken me behind the gym on my first day of school. He might not have been interested in being my guide, but he hadn't been cruel about it. Not like he was now.

"This is a football party. I'm on the football team. Last I checked, they didn't let girls play."

I rolled my eyes, like he bored me to tears, even though what I was really thinking of doing was running for the door. This had been a huge mistake. I was too awkward and out of place to blend in. "What's your problem? This room is full of girls. You stay over there, getting high, and letting random girls dry hump you. I'll stay over here and dance with my friend. How about that?" I didn't wait for him to reply. "Come on, Jagger."

I went to reach around him for Jagger, but he cut me off with a deft step that brought our chests together hard. I gasped at the sudden contact and had to tilt my head back to maintain eye contact with him. His hand brushed over my hip, ever so slightly, and then around to press on my lower back.

To my surprise, I let him. Later, I might call it shock that held me immobile. But in that moment, I knew the truth. His fingers skated over the cut out of my dress that left my lower back on display. His fingers were warm, calloused, and when his palm flattened against my skin, the reason I didn't move was because I liked it.

He leaned in, and when he lowered his voice, some of the sharp edges had softened. "Colt will lose it if he sees you here. You really want to piss him off some more?"

I stared into his eyes. The malice had gone. It had disappeared so quickly I wondered if he'd ever really meant it. And what was left behind sounded more like concern.

"I just want to have a good time with my friend. I'm not here to start anything." Despite my flippant words, I was powerless to look away. It was all I could do to hold myself rigid and not sink into him further, like a sudden surge of hormones begged me to do.

The hand at my back disappeared and his eyes hardened again. "Your funeral."

Air rushed my lungs as he walked backwards to where his girlfriend of the night sat pouting at him, her lip gloss smudged from their earlier efforts. An odd sense of disappointment washed over me. He sank into the couch and pulled her onto his lap. And that was that. His tongue was back down her throat, and I was left standing there like a fool.

Jagger sidled up next to me, nabbing my attention.

"You okay?" she asked, brows furrowed together. "That was...intense."

I nodded. "Fine."

"We can go if you want. I'm really sorry. Maybe I shouldn't have brought you."

"No. He doesn't intimidate me. None of them do. I have as much right to be here as every other person who didn't receive an invitation, right?" I forced a laugh.

Jagger grinned. "Right. Dance?"

"Definitely."

We polished off our now warm beers and weaved through the tight crowd to the covered outdoor area that had been turned into a makeshift dance floor. Cheap plastic chairs and a matching table had been pushed to one side, to make way for writhing bodies and flailing limbs. There seemed to be no in-between. You either jumped around like you'd been mildly electrocuted, jerking your body and waving your arms in time with the beat, or you found yourself a partner to grind against.

I glanced over at Jagger. We didn't need to say anything. We were already in tune with each other. Simultaneously, we both threw caution to the wind and joined the dancers.

Laughter fell from my lips at Jagger's antics. She whipped her long ponytail around like a stripper, and I raised my hands in the air, shaking my ass and gyrating my hips like I was dancing in a cage at a strip club. Minute by minute, song after song, I loosened up. I shook off Rafe's warning. I quit pondering which look he'd meant. The mean one, where he'd called me a princess and told me to leave. Or the kinder one, where he'd warned me away from Colt. I forgot about it all and just let the beat course through me.

A few songs in, a guy I didn't recognize moved in behind Jagger. He was cute, with dark-brown skin and his hair shaved close to his scalp. His eyes sparkled above a wide, friendly smile.

"Incoming!" I said, dragging Jagger in so she could hear me. I nodded over her shoulder, and she craned her neck to see.

"Aaron!" She threw her arms around his neck, and he squeezed her close.

"Dance with me?" he asked.

She pulled away and motioned toward me. "Lacey, this is Aaron. Aaron, Lacey."

I waved a hand tentatively but didn't wait for him to respond. I was happy for the first time all night and I didn't want to be brought down if he was one of Gillian and Colt's minions. "You two should dance," I said to Jagger. "I'm going to get some air."

She ducked her head. We were pretty similar heights normally, but her stilettos were a good few inches taller than mine. "You sure? I don't have to."

Judging by the way she hadn't batted Aarons hands off her hips, she wanted to stay. And I didn't want to kill her vibe by being a third wheel. Plus, it really was hot in the middle of a throng of people, and some cooler air sounded great. "You two have fun. I'll find you later, okay?"

She kissed my cheek. "Thanks. Come find me if you get lonely. And remember, fuck everyone else. You're fabulous, and if they can't see that, then their loss."

I hugged her tight and then left her with Aaron. She put her arms around his neck, and they joined the rest of the couples without an inch of space between them.

I pushed my way out of the crowd and found myself in the backyard. A few other people had the same idea and had found spots on the grass to stand around and talk. One couple made out against the corrugated iron wall of a small shed. There were no fences in this neighborhood, but a thicket of trees seemed to form a natural barrier at the back of the property. I wandered as far from the party as I could, the darkness engulfing me, though a dim glow from the house left enough light to see. I sucked in deep lungfuls of fresh night air and let the light breeze cool my heated skin. I was surprised to find I was actually having a good time. This wasn't entirely different from the parties I usually attended. Sure, I wouldn't normally have worn heels this high or a dress that showed this much skin. I would have been labelled a cheap slut if I'd rocked up at a Providence party with a hemline that barely covered my ass. But I liked the way I looked. Who got to determine what was slutty anyway? This dress showed off my legs and made the most of the modest cleavage I couldn't do much about unless I was willing to get a boob job. Which I wasn't. Providence parties might have had bodyguards and servants to handle the food. But there was also generally a stash of liquor that someone had scored with a fake ID. There was still dancing and making out. At the heart of it, though we might have been different on the outside, teenagers were all much the same. We all just wanted to fit in. Have a good time. Have people like us, whether that be romantically or in a friend-ship capacity.

At least I'd found one of those with Jagger. I watched the crowd, searching for a glimpse of her, and when I found her, I smiled. She had her arms around Aaron's neck and was smiling up at him, while he talked animatedly. They were cute together. I made a mental note to quiz her about him on the drive home.

A soft moan off to my left caught my attention. I twisted, peering into the darkness, trying to find the source of the noise. Maybe someone had too much to drink and was back here, sick.

That thought was quickly annihilated when my eyes focused.

The moan came again, a soft, "ohhh," that fell from the girl's lips. Her head tilted back, resting against a tree, just barely within the thicket. Her bright red dress was hiked up around her waist, showing off long legs and naked thighs. She seemed wholly unaware of anything but the rhythmic thrust of the guy pumping into her.

But his eyes locked with mine. Dark, black, bottomless eyes, so familiar they'd already graced my dreams once this week. I froze. My brain screamed for me to turn around and get back to the party. Leave these two to their business and mind my own. Embarrassment flushed my cheeks. But Colt's gaze was magnetic. And once he had you in his sights, it was near impossible to move.

With one hand, he gripped Gillian's milky-white thigh, his tanned skin contrasting with hers. His fingertips pressed to her flesh while his hips pulsed against hers, slow and rhythmic. His free hand wrapped around her exposed neck, then trailed slowly down across her chest.

But the entire time, it was me he watched.

And I watched him.

My nipples hardened beneath my dress, and heat shifted from my face to between my legs.

This was wrong. I should turn. Walk away. What the hell was I doing, standing here, watching him fuck her?

He reached inside Gillian's dress, pushing aside the material and exposing her breast. He pinched her nipple, hard. My own nipples ached, jealous they were untouched. Gillian cried out, her fingers digging into his shoulders and her hips urging him on, faster and faster.

I couldn't get away. Not until he let me go.

His lips tipped up in a mocking smile, like he knew exactly the power he had over me.

And how to use it against me.

He grabbed Gillian's chin, forcing her head, and then took her mouth roughly with his own. With one last look at me, he closed his eyes.

The spell broke.

I stumbled away, back toward the party, knowing I needed to get out of there immediately. What the fuck had I just done? Stood there, like a statue, staring at him and Gillian having sex?

I pushed through the crowd, texting Jagger to say I was leaving while tears built behind my eyes. I was hot. Too hot. Every part of me was flushed and feverish, and I just wanted to get out of there. I burst through the front door and out onto the street again, only to remember I'd come with Jagger.

"Shit," I muttered.

I didn't even know the address. Dammit, I was going to have to walk to the end of the road, check the street sign, and call an Uber.

"Need a lift?" a voice said behind me.

I spun around, half-expecting it to be Colt. But relief crashed over me when it was Banjo, leaning on a car, smoking a cigarette.

"You drunk?" I asked.

"Nope. Not high either."

I pulled my heels off and walked over to his side. "Then yes. I just want to get the hell out of here."

12

LACEY

*B*anjo stubbed his cigarette out on the pavement, and I didn't even bother to scold him for not picking it up. Right now, saving the environment seemed far away from the top of my priority list. He walked down the road a little, and I followed. We stopped at a familiar dark green car.

"What's wrong? Get in, I'll drive you home. You look like you've seen a ghost."

"I..."

He waited.

"Is this your car?"

He let out a chuckle that was deep and throaty. "You think I'm gonna steal us a ride?"

I shook my head. "No, I just...I saw your brother in this car earlier today."

Banjo's eyebrows furrowed, and I rushed to clarify. "Jagger told me it was your brother, anyway."

"Probably was. It's his car. I borrow it a lot. He knows, if that's what you're worried about."

That wasn't what I was worried about. I bit the bullet. "Are there drugs in the car?"

Banjo's eyebrows shot up.

"It's just I've heard all the stories, you know? Young girl gets in a car with a guy she barely knows. Cops pull them over and she ends up in jail when they find a trunk full of cocaine."

Banjo stared at me. Then burst into laughter.

I folded my arms across my chest. "Why are you laughing? It's not funny. My aunt would kill me if I landed myself in jail."

Banjo shook his head and took a few steps around the car. To my surprise, he picked up my hand as he passed me, and I followed him to the back end. He used a key to unlock the trunk and then popped it open.

"There's nothing but sweaty gym clothes and a baseball bat in the back of this car, see?"

"What's the baseball bat for? Taking out your pound of flesh on people who owe you money?"

Banjo shut the trunk and leaned on it. But didn't let go of my hand. And I didn't mind that. It felt nice. Like an anchor.

"The bat is for playing baseball, Lacey. That's it. My brother and I have both played for years."

"Oh." I sank back against the car next to him.

His thumb stroked over my hand, and I looked down at our intertwined fingers. There was something inherently safe about Banjo. Maybe it was that I'd met him before I started at Saint View High, so he seemed somehow removed from that world. Even if he did have a questionable choice of friends.

"I'm not going to let anything happen to you. I promise."

I peered up into his green eyes. He seemed earnest, but

that wasn't what he'd said during the week. "Who exactly are you protecting me from? Just the police? Or Colt?"

He ran his hand through his blond hair. "What happened between you two? Why does he hate you so much?"

My mouth dropped open. "You think I have any idea? I really don't. I'd never even met him before the first day of school. Gillian took an instant dislike to me, and Colt followed suit."

His eyebrows drew together. "That can't be it. Colt wouldn't warn me away from you, just because Gillian doesn't like you. Gillian doesn't like any pretty girl who might draw Colt's attention."

I wasn't sure which part of that statement to focus on. The fact Gillian was so insecure about her relationship with Colt. The fact Banjo had called me pretty. Or... "Colt warned you away from me? And you listened? What is he, your owner?" Anger swirled in my stomach, replacing the warmth that had been there a moment ago. "That's such bullshit. You and I were...we had...shit, I don't know. But we were something before I even met Colt." I dropped Banjo's hand. I didn't want to be holding it if he was just Colt's little puppet.

But he grabbed my hand and squeezed it. "It's not like that. Colt's not just my friend. He's more like my brother. We're family, even if we aren't blood related. Yeah, he told me to stay away from you. And yeah, I'd do anything for him. I've got good reason for that. But he'd do anything for me, too."

"Then why aren't you staying away from me? Why are you out here with me right now, offering to drive me home, and holding my hand?" I peered up into his eyes, really wanting to know.

He lifted a hand and brushed a strand of hair back from my face. "Honestly?"

I nodded.

"Because I can't. I nearly didn't come at all tonight because I knew you'd be here. That's why I'm so late. But then I get here, determined to ignore you, and you're fleeing the party like Cinderella at midnight. And here I am, with a waiting carriage. I can't ignore you, Lacey. Not when I can't stop thinking about that night we met. What we were going to do..."

A tingle ran down my spine. We'd been well on our way, up to my bedroom. I'd been so out of it that night, so wanting to forget myself that I'd been willing to lose myself in someone else.

"I still want to do that. Nothing has changed for me, Lacey. I still want to take you upstairs and make you feel good."

Oh shit.

My knees buckled as heat warmed through my body. This wasn't what I'd come here for tonight. But there were still things, stuck inside my head that wouldn't remove themselves. And now the images of Rafe dry humping that girl on the couch, and Colt and Gillian fucking in the garden, were added to the list of things I was better off forgetting.

"Okay," I whispered.

Banjo froze. "Fuck. Really?" His words were barely more than a breath. He rounded on me, standing in front of me now, while my ass rested on the back of the car. "I didn't think you'd give me another chance..." He shifted in, slowly, inch by inch, giving me the chance to change my mind if I wanted to.

But I didn't want to.

His hands skated down the sides of my face, my neck, across my shoulders, and down my arms, sending electric pulses through my skin. He stopped at my hips. Then with one quick movement, he lifted me as if I weighed nothing, and my ass hit the top of the trunk, the car shifting ever so slightly on its tires at the sudden addition of my weight.

Not for one second did either of us break eye contact. His green eyes were lit only by a nearby streetlight, and when he pushed my knees apart, I let him. I knew I was flashing him the tiny thong panties Jagger had insisted I wear "just in case." I was glad for that now. His eyes were trained on mine anyway, but when he stepped between my legs, I slid my ass to the very edge of the trunk, not caring that my dress hiked right up around my thighs. I ran my hands up his chest, fisting my fingers in the material and tugging him down, sick of waiting.

He paused, his lips hovering right over mine, and let out a shuddering breath. "You sure?" he murmured. "I was a dick..."

"Then make it up to me," I said on a breath.

His lips touched down on mine, hungry and demanding. One hand slid into my hair, the other found my lower back. Banjo pulled me tight, lips against lips, chest against chest. His erection, covered by his jeans, but still so evident nudging my panties.

He groaned into my mouth, forcing out the thoughts of Rafe and the girl on his lap.

He kissed my neck, wiping out the memory of Colt's stare while he fucked someone else.

My head spun in dizzying circles while I grabbed at him, wanting more. Wanting everything.

Banjo's cock pressed hard to my core, and I let out a

whimper of need. I'd never felt like this when I'd kissed other boys. Never forgotten about the world around us. I suddenly realized why Gillian had let Colt fuck her in the garden, with an entire party full of people just feet away.

Because Banjo made me feel the same way.

Anyone could walk out of the house at any minute and see everything we were doing. I wasn't sure I cared.

Banjo seemed to come to the same conclusion at the same time. Because suddenly he was lifting me from the back of the car. I clung to him, my lips to his neck. I eyed the house, but no one appeared, and then Banjo had the car door open and was putting me down on the back seat. I scrambled to the far side and he followed me in, closing the door behind him.

We stared at each other for a moment, both of us breathing hard. Then a slow smile spread across his face.

Damn if it wasn't contagious.

"Get over here, Lacey," he groaned. "Fuck, get over here right now."

I grinned and straddled his lap, wetness building between my legs as his straining erection pressed to my core once more. I wanted to reach down and unbutton his jeans, slide my fingers inside and circle them around his cock. But that was a move that required more courage than I had in that moment. I had very little experience with men. And though I knew exactly where I wanted it, my body complaining loudly it wasn't already there, I didn't have the guts to initiate it.

Our mouths fused together once more, the kiss hot and searing. I rocked on him, acting more on instinct that anything else, feeding the maddening sensation building inside me. Banjo's hands landed on my thighs, dragging upward along my skin, gathering up the skirt of my dress. It bunched around my waist, leaving my ass on display, bare in its thong, but it was dark and there was no one around. The party was still in full swing in the backyard, and not one person had come out in the entire time we'd been out here. He took two handfuls of my ass cheeks, squeezed, and I forgot all about any last shreds of modesty.

His mouth trailed off mine, finding the sensitive spot beneath my ear, sucking and biting his way down my neck.

Oh damn. That felt entirely too good. His fingers gripped the lacy thong, and my clit throbbed, the soaked material rubbing on it. He moved one hand between us, shifting the tiny scrap of lace to one side. I gasped.

He pulled back, eyes studying me. "You okay?"

I nodded, my mind whirling. Is this where I should tell him exactly how little experience I had? But his fingers were so close to where I wanted them. "I'm good," I whispered.

The first touch of his fingers was light. He brushed over my bare mound. Then his big fingers were parting me and slicking through the wetness between. His fingers slid back and forth easily, gliding over my clit. "Banjo," I panted.

Tell him, my brain urged. *Tell him you've never had a guy's fingers there before and you're the tiniest bit scared even though you're so damn horny at the same time. Tell him to be gentle.* But then Jagger's comments about losing her virginity at fourteen and her shock I hadn't stopped me.

"Yeah?" he murmured into my neck. "Fuck, Lacey. You're so wet. That's so hot."

I moaned.

"You like when I talk like that?"

My cheeks heated.

He chuckled. "Yeah, baby. You do."

I really did. It was a huge turn-on.

His big finger circled my nub, and sparks ignited in my core. His finger slid lower, finding my entrance. And I braced myself for the invasion of his fingers inside me. But it didn't come. He prodded me gently, then moved back to my clit before returning. His fingertip entered me this time, but then he was straight back to my clit. The sensation drove me nuts. He did it over and over, teasing my clit, then my entrance, his finger barely moving inside me each time, until I was panting and desperate to be filled, the ache inside me intense.

"Banjo," I moaned. "Please. More."

He slipped back again, and this time I ground down, taking his full finger. "Oh," I cried out. It felt good. I'd expected a little pain, but there was none.

"You want more?" he whispered.

I didn't say anything.

"Tell me, Lacey. It'll be better with two, but I won't if you aren't okay with it. Is this enough for you?"

I shook my head.

"That's my girl."

A second finger pushed inside me, stretching me deliciously. He was right. It was so much better with two. His mouth found mine again, his kisses hungry and demanding while he worked me in a slow, thrusting rhythm that had my hips rolling.

I gyrated on his fingers while our mouths devoured each other. Pleasure built inside me, foreign, but damn, it was so good. "Don't stop," I whispered.

"Not a chance. I want to watch you come."

My nipples tightened, and I rotated my hips faster. Banjo's fingers met me with well-timed flicks of his wrist until I was on the verge of orgasm.

"Oh, God," I moaned, digging my fingers into his

shoulders.

He'd probably have little crescent-shaped bruises in the morning, but I was lost to the feeling inside me. He pumped his fingers hard, one last time, and it was all too much. Something inside me burst, and pleasure soared through my system.

Banjo's lips swallowed my cries as I pulsed around his fingers, riding it out, thighs shaking. He slowed his pace and the sensations became all too much. I shuddered in his arms.

He kissed me softly while I floated on cloud nine. It gave me a chance to catch my breath before he withdrew his fingers.

Ever so slowly, he raised them to his mouth, sucking them inside.

Holy hell.

He grinned, removing them. "Don't look so embarrassed. I want to put my mouth on you so bad right now, but there's just not enough room in this car."

I dropped my gaze, suddenly awkward as fuck but imagining what that might be like.

His lips came to my ear. "You taste amazing, Lacey."

I lifted my eyes to meet his once more. He seemed to be waiting for some sort of response. "Um. Thanks?" I choked on a laugh. I obviously had no game whatsoever. No witty comebacks. Definitely nothing dirty to throw back at him. I should have admitted to Jagger I was a virgin. Maybe she could have given me some tips on what the hell you were supposed to do with a guy like Banjo, who had obviously done this a time or two before.

He tilted his head to one side, studying me. "You a virgin, princess?"

I groaned. "Why is everyone in this school so obsessed with that?"

He shook his head. "Not obsessed. Just want to know so I don't go too far. Tonight, anyway."

A tremble of anticipation rolled down my spine. There was a promise in his words that I liked. "Yes," I said quietly. "That was the first time I've even..."

His eyes widened. "Had you kissed anyone before me?"

I nodded quickly. "Yeah, sure. I'm not a total prude, you know. I just haven't found anyone I wanted to do more with."

Banjo grinned at that. "You've got nothing to be embarrassed about. You know that, right? The fact you're still a virgin is smoking hot."

"You think?"

He kissed me again. "You kidding? I love it."

I reached for the button on his fly, a bit more relaxed now. Whether that was from the orgasm or the fact I'd come clean about my lack of experience I didn't know. But I was ready to learn some more. I wanted to make him feel as good as I did. "Did you bring a condom?"

He caught me by the wrist and then leaned in and kissed me hard. "For tonight, this is enough, okay? We can work up to more. There's no rush."

My shoulders slumped. I wanted more. I wanted to see him and touch him and learn what made him feel good. But he was right. I was already a little tender, in a good way.

"Chin up, babe," he said, lifting me off his lap. "You know what you need after every good orgasm?"

I shook my head.

"Food. The greasier the better. Burgers, fries, and shakes are my go-to. You in?"

I grinned. "I don't think that's how this is supposed to

work. I offer to touch your dick, and you instead decide to feed me?"

He scrubbed his hands over his face and groaned. "Come on. Let's go get that food before my dick realizes what I've done."

13

LACEY

*M*eredith sent me a text message early the next morning, saying she had a few errands to run and she'd be thirty minutes late for brunch. That suited me. I wandered out of bed, got dressed slowly, and put on my makeup, all with a big smile on my face. I had Banjo on my mind. Last night, after fooling around in his car, we'd gotten food and slid into a booth, sitting closer than necessary, considering it was made for at least six people. I'd picked at my fries while he wolfed down his burgers. Plural. And then he'd driven me back to Jagger's place to pick up my car. I'd wanted to kiss him again. Badly. But he'd just brushed his lips against my cheek sweetly and said he'd see me at school on Monday.

He'd left me wanting more. And I couldn't wait to see him again. I had no delusions we were a couple now. Hell, that wasn't what I wanted anyway. I knew he wasn't going to walk right up to me first thing Monday morning and plant his lips on mine in front of everyone. Not with the way Colt and Gillian were carrying on. But I knew what we'd done together. And there'd been a promise in his goodbye that made me antsy for his next move. I didn't want everyone at school knowing our business, and the thought of sneaking around with Banjo behind Colt's back gave me a secret little thrill.

Colt could stick it in his pipe and smoke it.

"You look awfully happy this morning," Selina said.

I dropped onto a stool at the breakfast bar. "Do I?"

Selina's smile was soft. She put down the glass of orange juice she'd been drinking. "Want to tell me why? Perhaps over eggs? Bacon? What do you feel like?" She moved toward the cupboards we stored the frying pans in, her silky white satin robe trailing behind her.

"No, nothing for me. I'm meeting Meredith soon. But you should eat." I frowned at my aunt. "I'm sorry I haven't been around much this week. Can we have dinner together tonight?"

Her sad eyes brightened, increasing my guild tenfold. I'd been so preoccupied this week with the new school, shopping, and then the party. I'd barely seen Selina.

"That would be lovely. I'll cook."

"Or we could just order Chinese?"

She cocked her head to one side. "Are you implying my cooking is bad?"

I cracked a smile. "Maybe. Or maybe I just really like Chinese food. I'll leave it up to you to decide." I slid from the stool and went to her side, putting my arm around her.

"It's different around here now," she said quietly.

"Yeah." I knew exactly what she meant. My uncle had been a loud man. Always full of life, and big stories and loud conversation. He'd think nothing of bellowing for me from the bottom of the stairs. Or riding his dirt bike through the trees at the back of our house, the loud engine drowning out my aunt's tinkling yoga music. His school papers had never seemed to be contained to his office. They were often spread across the dining room table or haphazardly discarded to the side of the couch.

There was none of that anymore. All the papers had been put away. The dirt bike sat idle in the garage. He was never going to yell my name from the bottom of the stairs again.

A tear dripped silently down my cheek, and I brushed it away quickly.

But then a sob burst through the silence, and Selina's shoulders shook beneath my arm. "I miss him," she choked out.

That was all it took to break the walls I'd erected around myself. They crashed down around me, and the grief rolled in, heavy and painful.

It hurt. God, it hurt. Lawson was never going to kiss the top of my head or be the first one on his feet to give me a standing ovation at a recital. That had all gone up in the flames with him, and the entire thing felt like my fault. Maybe if I hadn't left him that night. If I'd fought harder to get to him, maybe I could have saved him.

If someone had taken a dagger to my chest and ripped it open wide, I was certain it couldn't have hurt more. I couldn't stop the tears. They became an out-of-control flood that threatened to consume me whole. Selina and I clutched at each other, holding the other up while we both broke down.

"It's not fair," I said eventually, pulling away slightly. "I don't understand why this happened."

Selina stroked my hair like she had when I was a child. "Me neither, baby. Me neither. Have you heard anything around school yet?"

I shook my head, ashamed I had so little to report after

being there an entire week. I'd spent more time worrying about what Colt, Banjo, Rafe, and Gillian were doing, than I had actually digging up any dirt on them. My stomach churned at the thought of digging up dirt on Banjo. How would it feel if he turned out to be the one who'd done it? I'd let him...

I swallowed hard. We shouldn't have taken things as far as we had. Not until I was one-hundred-percent sure Banjo wasn't a suspect. Surely I could keep it in my panties until I found some evidence that cleared him from my list. I had such fuzzy memories of that night. The guy who rescued me hadn't had a distinctive voice. It had been deep and masculine. Banjo's voice fit the bill, but so did any number of guys. Hopefully Meredith would have some good ideas at brunch today. I had a list of the football team names at least, like she'd told me to get, so I was ready to hear her great plan on how we were going to stalk them. I just prayed it didn't involve peeping into any bedroom windows. I wouldn't have put it past Meredith to have ulterior motives that included catching a glimpse of the football team in their underwear.

"You know you can change your mind at any time, honey?" Selina ran her fingers beneath her eyes, dashing away her tears. "You just say the word, and we'll get you right over to Edgely."

I shook my head. "No, I've started it. I want to finish."

She looked worried but didn't say anything more.

I picked up my keys and purse and headed for the door. "See you tonight for dinner, okay? You're too thin. I'm going to order us at least six different dishes, and you're going to eat all of them. Deal?"

She gave a laugh, but her smile didn't reach her eyes. "My trainer might not be too impressed with that, but I like your style. See you tonight."

She was humoring me, but I'd hold her to it. She might have an obsession with being thin and looking young, but I wasn't going to let her waste away to nothing. I needed her too much to lose her to her grief.

I drove into the main street of Providence where there was a strip of cafés and five-star restaurants, vowing I'd be around more for Selina. I was lost in a mental list of things we could do together when I hit the doorway of Archer's café. A tiny bell rang over my head as I entered, and I paused, looking around for Meredith. I spotted her quickly, her golden mane of Afro curls springing out wildly around her head. She had her head down, scrolling through something on her phone, so I didn't bother waving. A waitress came over to assist me, and I pointed in Meredith's direction then threaded my way through the packed tables, all full of Sunday morning couples and families, digging into granola, bacon, and pancakes. My mouth watered just from the delicious smells wafting from the other diners' plates.

"I'm starving," I announced, pulling out the chair opposite Meredith. "Please tell me you already ordered for us."

Meredith's head snapped up, and her thumb dove for the home button on her phone. Whatever she'd been reading disappeared before I got a chance to see it.

I raised an eyebrow. "Wow, what were you looking up? Porn? I've never seen anyone shut down a browser so fast." Then I narrowed my eyes. Something was wrong.

Her eyes were glassy with unshed tears, but she pasted on a fake smile. "Yep, just thought I'd get my porn fix, at eleven in the morning, in the middle of a café. You know how us porn addicts are."

I ignored her words because the expression on her face betrayed her joking tone. "You seem like you're about to burst into tears."

Meredith waved her hand around and sniffed. "No, I'm fine. This is just allergies. Hay fever or something. I need an antihistamine."

I somehow doubted it. "You sure that's all it is?"

She nodded hard.

I riffled through my purse and produced a packet of antihistamines. "Here. I still have these from last spring."

"Thank you." She took them from my outstretched hand and busied herself with the foil backing, popping two tablets free. She threw them into her mouth and took a large swallow from her glass of water. "Okay, so did you get all the names of the football team?"

I found the printed version of the photo I'd taken during the week and put it on the table. "Here. Now are you going to tell me how exactly you plan to stalk them? There's two of us and a whole team full of them. Plus, I don't know any of their addresses. Except for Tate." I point a finger at Tate's handsome face in the back row of the photo. "I was at his place last night."

Meredith glanced up. "Excuse me now?"

I rolled my eyes. "For the party. Remember? It was at his place. Lots of other people there. It wasn't a party for two." I didn't mention the party for two Banjo and I had in his brother's car. Heat crept into my cheeks at the mere thought of what we'd done on that back seat. I clenched my thighs together.

I should have known better than to think I could get anything past Meredith. Her sharp gaze caught mine and held me pinned.

A smile tipped up the corner of my mouth. I couldn't help it.

"Spill it! What happened at that party last night? Something hot and dirty if that smile is anything to go by."

"You're like a bloodhound, you know that? Perhaps I should have sent you to Saint View High. You can sniff out a secret like no one else."

Meredith seemed quite proud of that. "I can sniff out a sex secret, sure. I don't know about a murder secret. But that's beside the point right now. Who did you do the nasty with? And was it nasty? I don't know about those boys from Saint View, Lace. They look kind of...brutal."

"Brutally hot?"

She shrugged. "If the 'just out of prison' vibe is your thing, then yeah, sure, I guess?"

I giggled. "Well, it's not my thing. And the guy I did the nasty with was someone you sort of know. And just for the record, there was nothing nasty about it."

Meredith's eyebrows furrowed, but then realization widened her eyes. "The hottie from last weekend?"

I nodded.

"Oh, you dirty ho bag. Tell me everything."

I shook my head. "There's honestly not that much to say. Other than he's got some talented fingers."

"Just his fingers?"

"Trust me, that was enough to do the job."

"Where? At the party?"

"Back of his car."

Meredith snorted on a laugh. "Oh, if that isn't so Saint View High!"

"Please," I scoffed. "Like you didn't go all the way in the back seat of Scott Amerson's car after junior prom."

Meredith laughed. "It wasn't all the way. Just..."

"Third base?" I supplied helpfully. "Well, same. So you're as big a ho bag as I am."

"And that's why we're friends."

Relief settled over me. This was the Meredith I knew

and loved. I hated seeing her upset. Or, as she put it, with allergies. But I wasn't going to push her to talk about whatever it was. She'd tell me when she was ready to talk. That's what best friends did, and Meredith and I had been best friends since the second day of our freshman year.

I tapped my fingers on the table, ready to get this conversation back on track. "Okay, so first things first. Do we have food coming?"

"I ordered you the pancakes you always like."

"Side of bacon?"

"Of course. I wouldn't be much of a best friend if I didn't know your order now, would I?"

"Gold star for you. Now, earn yourself another one and tell me what we're doing about these guys?" I nudged the crumpled piece of paper across the table to her.

"Aha." She picked up the photo and squinted at the names. Then picked up her phone.

"You got a crew of private investigators on speed dial?"

"Nope. Better. I've got Instagram. Scoot your chair over here."

I did, so I could see over her shoulder.

She touched the app to open it and brought up the search bar. "Let's start with your party host from last night, shall we? Tate...Masters."

She typed in the name. "Bingo." She tapped on the profile pic of Tate in his football uniform. His profile loaded instantly.

"Hello, hottie!" Meredith elbowed me. "Okay, as soon as we clear this guy from your list of suspects, I want an introduction."

"I thought the boys at Saint View were too 'just out of prison' for your liking."

"Yeah, well, that was before I saw Tate's abs. Damn. Who

knew it was possible to have more than a six-pack?" She opened up a photo Tate had posted over the summer and zoomed in. It was one of those photos that was supposed to look all natural. Yet it somehow showed off Tate's abs and the definition in his arms, while he not so casually threw a Frisbee on the beach. Totally posed if you asked me. Which Meredith should know, since she was the queen of the posed Instagram photos.

"Concentrate for a second here, okay?" I complained.

"Right. What date was the fire again?"

"Sunday the twenty-second."

"Okay, well, let's just see what Tate was doing that day, shall we?" She scrolled down slowly, checking the dates on each picture.

"Boy posts too many photos of himself," I muttered when we had to scroll quite far down to find a date from just a few weeks earlier.

"Yeah, but that's good for us. Because now we know exactly where he was at the time of the fire. See?" She thrust the phone into my hands.

"He was at a bonfire at the beach." The photo appeared to have been taken around dusk, the sky pinks and oranges behind Tate and another guy I vaguely recognized. Both stood with their arms around each other, hair dripping from the surf, a bonfire already lit behind them. "This could have been taken days or weeks before and just posted late."

"True," Meredith said. "But this guy he's with…"

"I think it's Nathaniel Lyons." I pointed him out on the football team photo.

"Let's see what he posted that day… Tate was kind enough to tag him for us and everything." Meredith switched to Nathaniel's profile. It was just as jam-packed with shirtless boy photos as Tate's was.

"Don't these people have any concept of a private account?" I asked.

Meredith scoffed. "Lacey, I know you don't really get Instagram, since you have all of three photos on your profile and they're from when we were fifteen, but nobody has a private profile. How would you end up with thousands of followers? How would you judge your own popularity? How would you have potential hookups sliding into your DMs? Speaking of which, I might just slide into Nathaniel's...is the entire football team this hot? I'm reconsidering my school choices right now."

"Stop it. Find the twenty-second and see what he posted."

Meredith did as told with a pout. I had no doubt she'd be in Nathaniel or Tate's DMs before the day was out.

"Oh, bingo. A group photo. This wasn't just a couple of friends hanging out at the beach. This was a party."

I zoomed in on the photo. "Not just any party. A football party. Give me a pen."

Meredith pulled a pen from her purse and handed it to me. I put the phone down on the table. "Okay, I'm crossing out Tate and Nathaniel. And that's Jerome." I tapped the pen against the screen. "Thomas, Wiley, Jordan..." The list rolled on.

Our food arrived, but neither of us did more than take a solitary bite. We were both too engrossed in searching through all the names of the kids who were tagged, looking at their photos of that night.

"Bet it was a good party," Meredith mused. "They're all so happy."

They were. The fifteen or so accounts we checked told the complete story of that night. From the girls getting ready, to a barbecue on the beach, but the ones I was most interested in were the ones after the sunset. A roaring bonfire featured in many of the photos. Couples kissing. Guys with their arms around each other, grins ear to ear. I felt a twinge of jealousy. These kids might not have had fancy cars or expensive houses, but they had true friendships. It made me think about what Banjo had said about him and Colt being more like brothers than friends.

I peered down at the photo of the football team. I'd crossed out three-quarters of the players. But there were two players I recognized instantly, who still remained unaccounted for.

"Banjo isn't in any of these photos," Meredith said.

"And there's nothing posted on his account that day. Nothing on Rafe's either."

Meredith locked her phone and put it facedown on the table. "They're still on the list of suspects then."

I sighed. "I guess so."

I didn't like how that realization felt.

14

LACEY

*M*y history class seemed designed to send me to sleep. I'd spent the previous forty minutes doodling in the margins of my page, while Mr. Sliden droned on and on about trench warfare. I'd started out drawing random shapes, which had morphed into flowers, and then abruptly shut my folder when I realized I'd doodled Banjo's name. I hadn't seen him yet today. Hadn't heard from him at all since the night of the party. It was an odd feeling, walking around on eggshells this morning, wondering if I'd run into him. I was a little more at ease this week, in clothes that didn't immediately tell everyone around me I didn't belong. And now that I knew where all my classes were, I didn't feel quite so lost.

A knock at the door five minutes before the end of class stopped Mr. Sliden's rant about the Nazis. A young-looking redheaded girl stood in the doorway, staring right at me. I frowned.

"Yes?" Sliden asked her, impatience rolling off him like this girl was seriously killing his mojo. The teach was really into Hitler's life story, apparently.

"Principal Simmons wants to see Lacey Knight in his office immediately."

A chorus of "oooohhhs" rang out around me. Someone muttered something about the new girl being in trouble already.

What on earth did I do?

"Okay, okay. That's enough. Lacey, off you go. The rest of you, get back to work."

I stood slowly, gathering my things, dread rising in my gut. I hadn't done anything wrong, that I knew of. I'd stuck to all the rules. Sure, I'd been late to a class or two, but that was only because I'd gotten lost. Surely Principal Simmons wouldn't hold that against me.

I met the girl at the door and followed her down an empty corridor. "Do you know what this is about?" I asked her, but she simply shook her head and kept on walking, her head down, obviously avoiding further conversation.

The classrooms we passed all had their doors open, and I caught snatches of lessons. A few curious eyes diverted in our direction, but I ignored them. Until one familiar set made my steps falter. I tripped on nothing but thin air, stumbling a little, but unable to take my eyes off Colt. He sat back in his seat, folding his arms across his muscled chest, a satisfied expression on his face.

A sudden thought occurred to me. Colt had said he was going to get rid of me. Was that what this was? I narrowed my eyes at him, but he just did that annoying half smirk that had my fingers itching to slap him.

"Are you okay?" the girl beside me asked.

"What?" I said, snapping out of my Colt trance. I shook my head. "Yeah, sure. I'm fine."

"Can we keep walking, then? Principal Simmons is waiting."

I hadn't even realized I'd come to a dead stop. Shit. No wonder Colt was smirking at me. I'd just given him pure proof that one look from him was enough to stop me in my tracks.

For fuck's sake. Rookie mistake in a game of cat and mouse. I'd just given him the upper hand.

Vowing not to do that again, I nodded to my young escort, and we made it to the office without any further instances of me losing my head over a guy who hated my guts.

"What are you doing here?" Rafe snapped as soon as we entered the administration office.

I might have spoken too soon. I'd found the only other ridiculously hot guy who hated my guts. Lucky me. "Well, hi to you, too. Thanks so much for the warm greeting."

He scowled. "Fine. Hi, Lacey. What are you doing here? Better?" His voice dripped with sarcasm.

"Your father wanted to see me."

"Yeah, well, me, too. So get in line."

Figuring the seat beside him was the line, I sat down.

He stiffened. "There's a whole row of seats right here, and you take the one closest to me?"

"That bother you?" I asked.

"In more ways than I care to explain."

I wasn't sure if he meant that in a good way or a bad way. So I just ignored it. I had a chance to talk to him alone, away from Colt, away from parties. He seemed sober today, too. If Principal Simmons just stayed in his office for a few more minutes, I might be able to get some information out of him.

"Some party the other night, huh?" I asked.

"Same as all the others."

"You go to all the football parties then?"

Rafe nodded. "Sure. Everyone does."

"What about the bonfire at the beach a few weeks ago?"

Rafe twisted so we were facing each other. "How do you even know about that? You weren't a student here then."

I shrugged, trying to play it cool. "I heard about it from some other people. Apparently, it was the party of the summer."

Rafe shrugged. "I wouldn't know. Didn't go."

"You didn't go to the party of the summer? How come?"

"I had other things to do. Are you always this nosy?"

I twisted back to face the office door. "Just trying to be friendly."

Rafe ran a hand through his hair, then dropped it onto his lap. "I wish you wouldn't."

"Wouldn't be friendly?"

"Yeah."

"You'd prefer me to be...what? Rude? Ignore you completely?"

"Maybe."

"You some sort of masochist? You get off on people being mean to you?"

He cracked a smile, and I couldn't help smiling back. He was awfully cute. His teeth were so perfectly straight and white, his lips soft-looking.

"No, Lacey. It would just make my life easier if you were a bitch."

Understanding dawned on me. "Because of the target Colt and Gillian have drawn on my back?"

"Something like that."

I shook my head. "I kind of thought you were too smart for their bullshit. Guess I was wrong."

"Lacey..."

The office door opened, and Principal Simmons stuck his head out. Despite the fact Rafe had been there first, I shot out of my seat and stepped toward the older man. "You wanted to see me, sir?"

He peered past me to his son. "I wanted to see both of you actually. Together. Come on in."

He pushed the door open, and I took a seat opposite his desk. Rafe sat beside me. We both put our arms on the armrest at the same time. A spark of energy crackled over my skin when it made contact with his. His head snapped in my direction, and I snatched my arm back.

Rafe didn't say anything. But judging from the way I could see him staring at me from the corner of my eye, he'd felt something, too.

Principal Simmons steepled his hands together, his elbows resting on the desk. He smiled brightly, his gaze flicking between the two of us. "So. How are you settling in, Lacey? Rafe has been a good tour guide, I hope?"

I fought back a snort of derision. Rafe had done nothing but give me a tour of his preferred smoking spot and then told me off for going to a party he and Colt didn't want me at. Other than that, he'd completely left me to wander the school alone. If Jagger hadn't adopted me, I'd probably still be searching for my first class.

Rafe shot a worried look at me. Which was a little insulting. Did he really think I was going to rat him out to his father? I could be the bigger person. "He's been a great host. Very...accommodating."

Principal Simmons' smiled widened, and I wondered why he even cared. He was genuinely thrilled by what I'd said. "Wonderful. I'm so happy the two of you are getting along well." He pulled a manila folder from his in tray and opened it. He produced two sheets of paper and passed them across the desk to us.

"What's this?" Rafe asked, sounding bored.

I glanced down at the piece of paper. "Donor dinner speech? What's that?"

Rafe groaned, and Principal Simmons glowered.

Rafe pulled his shoulders back and sat a little straighter, but he still didn't look happy about it.

Principal Simmons addressed his comments to me, since Rafe obviously already knew all about whatever a donor dinner speech was. "The donor dinner is an annual event, held at the beginning of every school year. You're probably aware that schools like Saint View don't require our students to pay a fee to attend. We, of course, get some government funding, but if we want our students to have all the opportunities kids from other schools have, we have to fundraise. This dinner is our major source of yearly funding."

"And each year, he forces me to get up on stage, dressed in a uniform that nobody here even wears, and beg a bunch of rich snobs for their money." Rafe made no effort to hide his disgust.

I frowned at the 'rich snob' part. "Not everyone with money is a snob, you know."

Rafe snorted like the notion was ridiculous. It somehow felt personal. Even though he hadn't said my name directly, he knew the school I'd come from. He'd seen my car, and I'd bet Banjo had told him about my house. He was talking about me when he talked about rich snobs.

"Of course not," Principal Simmons said after shooting a glare in Rafe's direction. "Which is why I'd like the two of you to do the speech from the students. You might know some of the donors perhaps, Lacey. And we've invited your aunt."

"Excuse me, sir. I understand why Rafe would do the speech. He's probably top of our class, right?"

Principal Simmons nodded. "Top of his junior year. Just like you were at Providence."

I smiled stiffly. "Right. But why are you asking me, then? Isn't there a student body president or someone better qualified for this role? I've only been a student at this school for a week."

Rafe threw a bored look in my direction. "He wants you because you're one of them, not one of us."

"Rafe!" Principal Simmons' gaze was steely. His expression held a distinct warning. It softened when he turned in my direction, though I doubted the sincerity.

I was pretty sure Rafe had nailed it on the head.

"I'll give you extra credit for it," Principal Simmons stated.

I shook my head. "There's no need for that. I'll do it." I didn't exactly need his extra credit. But keeping the principal on my good side was more important than losing a single Friday night of my life. Plus, I'd bet it would be my music class on the chopping block if the school didn't get enough funding. It was the only subject I enjoyed. "Will other teachers be going?" I asked.

The principal nodded vigorously. "Oh yes. All the nonessential class teachers will be there to discuss their programs with our donors. All the arts teachers and the sports coaches."

Of course the football coach would be there. Searching Mr. Tontine on Instagram and Facebook and numerous other social media sites had led Meredith and I to a dead end. But a dinner, where hopefully he'd be drinking, would be a better place to meet him and perhaps gently prod him over his whereabouts the night of the fire. If I could cross him off my list of suspects, that was one less person to worry about.

I still hadn't worked out a way of crossing Rafe off my list, but perhaps something would come up during the dinner. There was no downside here that I could see.

I pasted on a smile for Simmons. "I'm can't wait."

pumping into hers. The slow, sensual roll of his hips that did weird things to my insides.

"Take a photo, princess. It'll last longer," Gillian snapped, coming up behind Colt and putting her hand into the back pocket of his jeans.

Colt raised an eyebrow in my direction. "Oh, Lacey likes to watch. Don't you?"

A choking sound came from the back of my throat. I knew exactly what Colt was talking about. Gillian let out a cackle of a laugh. Had he told her? I was certain she hadn't seen me, she was so busy riding Colt's dick. Did it matter if he had? It shouldn't. I didn't give a shit what Gillian thought of me. And no one else had seen me out there. I'd deny it if he called me on it. Because no way was I going to admit that watching Colt screw someone else had stopped me in my tracks and held me mesmerized, wondering what it would be like to be with him like that.

The two of them took their seats, and Banjo leaned again. "What did he mean by that?"

I shook my head. "I don't know. Does it matter? He's an asshole."

Banjo teeth bit into his bottom lip. "Actually, there's something you should know. Colt lives right next door to me."

"You're serious?"

Banjo nodded. "That's why we're so tight. We've lived in each other's pockets since we were kids."

"That's...nice." For them. "Perhaps I shouldn't come over tonight then? Colt is the last person I want to see outside of school."

Banjo's eyebrows furrowed. "Yeah, I was just thinking that. Colt...I can't tell him about us. It'll just make him worse. If he knows what we did, he'd use it against you." He glanced over his shoulder, then gave my hand a quick squeeze. "But I want to see you, Lacey. Out of school. Out of a cramped back seat. We could go somewhere else? Your place?"

I shook my head. "My aunt..."

"Wouldn't approve?"

Fuck. It was the truth, but I hated it. Banjo didn't need me to say it. It was written all over my face.

Banjo swore low under his breath. "She wouldn't let you date me?"

I shook my head slowly. "I don't know. Maybe she'd surprise me. But I don't want to put you in a shitty situation like that. Where I just spring it on her and she's rude to you. You don't deserve that. Just give me some time. Let's just hang out. See what this is. And if it's something, I'll talk to my aunt."

He sat back and ran his hands through his shaggy blond hair. "And I'll talk to Colt."

I glanced over at him, right as Miss Halten called the class to attention.

I lowered my voice to barely a whisper. "So tonight..."

Banjo thought that over for a second. "Tonight you're coming to my house. Even if I have to sneak you in through the back door."

*J*ust before darkness fell that evening, I found myself parked on a side street in the middle of the worst area of Saint View. Around me, identical houses all stood in a row, each one in a state of disrepair. One had broken steps, the wood so old and rotted someone's foot had gone right through the boards. Most had peeling and flaked paint. Rusted shells of cars seemed a popular lawn decoration, and a firepit had cheap plastic chairs circling it, beer bottles scattered on the grass in between.

Bringing my car here had been a very bad idea. I pushed the locks down as a group of young guys passed by on the other side of the road, all four of them staring at me and my car like the abnormality we were. I pulled my thin black scarf up over my hair and turned away, like that would somehow protect me from them.

I jumped a mile when there was a tap on my window. My heart immediately went into double-time, until I realized it was Banjo. "Shit," I said, rolling down the window. "You scared the hell out of me."

"Did you think I was a car jacker?"

I cringed. "Maybe?"

He leaned through the window and popped the lock on my door before opening for me. "Don't stress. See that guy over there?"

He pointed to the nearest derelict house. A huge white guy with arms like tree trunks and decorated with crude black tattoos stepped out of the shadows.

"Yeah, I see him." Now. I certainly hadn't a minute ago. Had he been there the entire time? Just watching me? My fingers trembled. The guy was scary with a capital S.

Banjo took my fingers and squeezed them. "He's a friend. He'll keep an eye on your car. No one will touch it while it's parked here. You don't even need to lock it."

I made sure the windows were all up and that I hadn't left anything of value on the front seat, then hit the central locking button. "All the same, I think I'll lock. Just for shits and giggles."

Banjo slung an arm around me and steered me toward a

bicycle that lay abandoned on the cracked footpath. I stopped and stared at it. Then at him.

"You rode? How far is your house?" I asked.

"A couple of blocks, why?"

"Oh, okay. So we can walk then."

"We could..." Banjo winked at me as he picked the bike up off the ground. "Or you could jump on the handlebars and we'll get there twice as quick."

I snorted on a laugh. "You're kidding, right?"

He slung one leg over the seat of his bike and patted the handlebars. "Jump on."

"How?"

"Have you never done this before?"

"No! Why would I have?"

Banjo looked puzzled. "You rich kids are weird. Didn't you ever ride your bikes around the neighborhood, just for fun?"

I couldn't remember a time where I had ever done that. Uncle Lawson had taught me to ride a bike when I'd been six, but I couldn't remember riding one much after that time. "No, I guess not."

"Then you're in for a treat."

Before I knew what was happening, Banjo had his fingers digging into my hips and then my butt was planted on the handlebars. I squealed. And slipped straight off.

Banjo cracked up laughing. "That's not what was supposed to happen."

I shoved him in the shoulder. "Well, you gave me no warning. Do it again."

His fingers grasped my hips again, and I grinned at his touch. But I wouldn't let it distract me. I was determined to prove to him I wasn't some hopeless rich kid. I could ride on his handlebars, dammit. How hard could it be?

This time, I managed to balance there, even if it was with white knuckles.

"Hey, you're doing it. Now, hold on, and I'll get us back to my place in minutes."

I grit my teeth as Banjo pushed off and pedaled down the sidewalk. I squealed like a kid when he wobbled slightly, but he just laughed and pedaled faster. I thought that would be worse, but it somehow wasn't. The cooling evening air whipped through my hair, and a bubble of happiness burst inside me. My laugh surprised me.

"I can't remember the last time I rode a bike!" I yelled back to him over the air rushing past us.

"Sounds like you might be enjoying it!"

I nodded, then squealed when the movement wobbled the bike. My arms ached, but it was worth it. Banjo peddled hard and fast, and we cruised down a hill that took my breath away.

Yet somehow, I wasn't scared. At any moment, we could have hit a pothole and gone tumbling. Neither of us had a helmet on, and I could only imagine the scrapes and bruises or even broken bones we'd suffer if we came off at this sort of speed. But Banjo hooted and hollered behind me, and that gave me confidence. He wasn't scared. And when I was with him, neither was I.

"Left turn!" he yelled, and I leaned with him. He diverted off the path and into a patch of trees.

The bike bumped along, and I yelped, ass bouncing on the unforgiving metal of the handlebars. "No padded seat, remember!"

But then we were stopping, and I slid from the handlebars. "Ow," I complained, rubbing my backside. "Could have warned me about the off-roading."

He dropped the bike and came around to stand in front

of me. His arms snaked around my waist, then dipped lower, his hands cupping my butt cheeks. "I just wanted an excuse to make sure your ass was okay. Is it?"

I shoved him away, but the truth was, I liked having his hands there. Though I probably would have a bruise tomorrow.

"You protest, but you liked that, didn't you?"

"Maybe."

"Good. Because now we have to go work on our assignment. And that probably won't be fun at all. Neither will sneaking past Colt. That's his house just there."

We were at the back fence of a row of two-story houses. Banjo grabbed my hand and let himself in the back gate of the house next to the one he'd pointed out as Colt's.

"Is he home?" I whispered.

"Yeah, Gillian's car was out the front when I left. So hopefully they're up there, too busy having sex to notice what we're doing down here."

I gazed up at the house again. "Which bedroom is his?" I asked. Then bit my lip. I shouldn't have asked that. It had slipped out without me even really thinking about it.

But Banjo answered easily. "Very top one. His bedroom is in the attic."

Banjo tugged my hand, and then we were running across his backyard, giggling like two naughty kids who were about to get caught. Right as we hit the back porch, I took one last look up at Colt's tiny bedroom window. But it was empty. I supposed it would be if he and Gillian were in bed together, like Banjo assumed they would be.

I pushed Colt out of my mind and followed Banjo through his unlocked back door. As soon as we were inside, he guided me toward the living room.

"Wow," I said, allowing myself to be towed along.

"Not what you were expecting?"

I squinted at him. "Truthfully? When you said it was just you and your brother, I kind of expected it to be a pigsty. Beer cans, pizza boxes, funky smells..."

"You're surprised we know where the trash can is?"

The place was sparkling clean. Nothing was particularly new, but everything had a place, and the room, though small, smelled fresh. Like windows were opened daily. It was obvious Banjo and his brother knew their way around a mop and a bottle of disinfectant. It didn't look like the drug den I'd kind of been expecting.

"It's great," I said.

Banjo flopped down on the couch, the springs squeaking beneath him. I sat beside him, twisting so we were facing each other.

For a long moment, we just stared. His dirty-blond hair fell over his forehead, carelessly shoved to one side. Around his neck he had his wooden bead necklace, and now that it wasn't dark, I noticed the freckles across the bridge of his nose.

"You're staring at me, Lacey."

I smiled. "You're staring at me, too."

"Because you're beautiful. I feel like I'm always staring at you, even though I know I shouldn't be."

My insides went gooey. "You're a sweet-talker."

He shook his head. "I mean it."

I believed him. I felt beautiful with his gaze drifting over me like it was right now. His eyes drank me in, until the expression there changed from playful to something hotter.

"We've got until December to do that assignment..." I mused out loud.

Banjo grinned. "Exactly what I was thinking. Get over here."

He didn't need to tell me twice. I straddled his lap, bringing my hands up to cup his face. Our lips hovered a few inches from each other. "You're really cute, you know that?"

He raised an eyebrow. "Cute?"

"Mmm-hmm," I murmured, gaze dropping to his lips. "Cute."

He grinned, his white teeth sparkling, then brought one hand to the back of my head and pulled me down. "Not as cute as you, princess."

I didn't even mind that name when it fell from his lips. From Colt and even Rafe, it sounded harsh. From Banjo, it sounded like a pet name. His lips pressed to mine, and I forgot all about anything but him.

Our kisses turned sensual, dragging out, driving me mad. Ever so slowly, my hips ground over his lap, like they had a mind of their own. Slow, rocking movements that brought the center of me directly against his dick, hard beneath his shorts. It only served to build the growing need inside me. It was as if no time had passed between Saturday night and now. Except now I had more clothes on.

That was rapidly becoming a problem I wanted to fix.

"Is your brother home?" I asked between kisses.

Banjo's lips were slightly swollen and shiny from my lip gloss. Without even waiting for him to answer, I leaned in and kissed him again. His lips were a magnet I couldn't seem to drag myself away from. I just wanted to keep going back for more.

Banjo groaned and flipped me down on my back, the cushions breaking my fall. He reared over me. "He's not home. Shouldn't be back for a while. We've got time..."

I grabbed his shirt. "How much time?"

"Time to do our assignment?" He chuckled at himself.

I shook my head. "Wrong answer."

"Time to do what I wanted to do Saturday night?"

"What was that?"

I had no idea why I kept asking him stupid questions when I could just be getting him naked. I vowed to keep my babbling to myself and dragged his shirt over his head.

He chuckled. "Here I am, trying to be a gentleman, and—"

"Here I am trying to make it hard for you?" I supplied, a teasing question in my voice.

He ground his pelvis against mine, heat flaring in his eyes. "No problem in that department. I'm always hard when you're around."

"Even in music class?" I asked, nipping at his lips playfully. There I went again with the questions. I couldn't seem to stop. At least that one had come out flirty.

"Especially in music class. Do you know how hard it is to sit that close to you and not be able to touch you?"

"You can touch me now."

"Can I? How much? I need to know what you've done before, so I know how slow I need to go with you."

I shook my head. "You don't need to go slow."

He sat back on his knees, drawing in a ragged breath, uncertainty written all over his face.

I couldn't even reassure him. I was too distracted by my first proper glimpse of Banjo without a shirt on.

I was a sucker for abs. And Banjo had them for days. His long, lean body was tanned to golden perfection, his shoulders broad, biceps toned. A light-colored trail of hair ran below his belly button and made a line between the delicious V of muscle either side of his hips. It all pointed straight down, toward the impressive bulge of an erection straining behind his shorts.

I sat up, too, and ran my hand down his chest, marveling at the way he trembled when I touched him. I trailed my finger lower, over his abs, and to the waistband of his shorts. I flicked the button, and his eyes flared. But when I went for the zipper, his big hands covered mine.

"Lacey," he warned.

I stared up at him through hooded eyes.

"Tell me what you've done. With other guys."

"Tell me what you like," I countered. I went for his zipper again, and this time he groaned when I lowered the pull.

"What are you doing to me?"

I grinned. "It's my turn."

"That's not how this works."

I ignored him. I might not have had much experience with anything beyond kissing. But I knew what guys liked. I tugged his shorts off.

"Commando sort of guy, huh?"

"Went surfing this afternoon. Hadn't gotten changed yet."

I stroked my hand experimentally over his thick length, fighting down a surge of apprehension. He was big. Bigger than I'd expected, though I had little to compare with. But I doubted he had anything to worry about in the locker room. If that had been my dick, I would have been happily swinging it around, showing it off to anyone who would pay attention.

"You okay?" he asked quietly.

I reached up to smooth out the wrinkles creasing his forehead. "For a guy getting a hand job, you look awfully worried."

"I don't want to scare you off."

"Does your dick often scare people?" I said with a laugh.

The worry was replaced with a smile. "Well..."

I ran my hand over him again and liked the way he sucked in a breath.

"You don't scare me, Banjo. Giant cock and all."

I circled my fingers around the base of him and then stroked upward to his tip. "I don't know what you like," I whispered, though there was no one else in the room.

Banjo watched my hand roll over his erection. "You're perfect."

I didn't really believe him. I knew there was something he'd like more. Something I'd been thinking about doing ever since he'd talked about putting his mouth on me.

I dipped my head and darted my tongue out to lick the head of his cock.

Banjo's eyes widened, and his hand came up to the side of my face. "Hey..."

"I want to," I whispered, feeling brave. "Show me what to do."

Banjo eyed me. "You sure?"

I licked him again.

"Fuck," he groaned. "Open your mouth, Lacey."

Heat bloomed between my legs. Muscles low in my belly clenched, and I opened my mouth for him. Leaning in, I closed my lips around his tip, tasting the salt from his earlier swim still clinging to his skin. I rolled my tongue down his length, taking as much of him as I could, before pulling back, licking as I went. Gentle pressure on the back of my head guided me, but I trusted him, so it only turned me on more. I gazed up at him through half-lidded eyes, feeling sexy and wanted. I liked the effect I had on him. His fingers fisted in my hair, and his body shook with the force of holding himself back.

"Are you sure you haven't done this before?" he asked, his breaths turning into pants. "Your mouth...so good."

A flush of pleasure roared through me. I wanted it to be good for him. I wanted him to feel what I had on Saturday night. I held him in place with one hand but dropped the other to work in time with my mouth. In unison, I licked and stroked him, watching in fascination as his hips rolled.

"Lacey," he groaned. "Fuck. Too good—"

"What the fuck is going on here?"

I jerked, scrambling to get away from Banjo's dick, a yelp of surprise escaping me in the process. I whirled around, cheeks flaming. For some reason, in that one tiny second, I'd assumed the barked question had come from Colt. I knew he was just next door. And he and Banjo were so tight, it wouldn't have surprised me if Colt had felt comfortable enough to waltz in without so much as a knock. That was all we needed. Colt finding me sucking Banjo's dick would have been a swift end to whatever Banjo and I were.

But my relief at seeing Banjo's brother glaring at us from the doorway was short-lived. It quickly turned into mortifying embarrassment. Time to leave. I scrambled around the floor for my purse.

Banjo swore low under his breath and shot his brother a death look. Only then did he casually pick up a pillow to hold over his erection. "Fuck, Augie. What are you? Some kind of stealth ninja?" Banjo scowled at his brother, then turned to me. "Lace, stop. It's all right."

It was anything but all right. It was downright mortifying, is what it was. I just wanted the earth to open up and swallow me whole. Oh God. Swallow. Not a good time to be thinking about swallowing. Fuck! And I couldn't even just leave. I didn't even know where we'd left my car or how to get back there. It was fully dark outside now. I'd be lost in seconds.

"Can you take me back to my car?" I whispered to Banjo. I couldn't even look at Augie. Not after the position he'd caught us in. It was too mortifying.

"Stop. Sit down, both of you." Augie's tone didn't leave any room for argument.

I sat next to Banjo. I couldn't help noticing he hadn't even bothered putting his shorts back on. He just sat butt naked on the couch beside me, with the cushion in his lap. I couldn't help it. I snorted on a laugh. Banjo grinned at me.

"Want to introduce me to your friend, little brother? Now that her mouth isn't wrapped around your dick?"

Annnnd, I was back to mortified.

"Lacey, Augie. Augie, Lacey."

I raised my head to meet Augie's eyes. He wasn't impressed. I hadn't realized how big a guy he was when we'd seen him at the mall, but up close, Banjo's brother was huge. Tattoos peeked out beneath his shirt sleeves, and his body had the solid appearance of a man who spent a lot of time in the gym. He stared at me now with an expression of pure annoyance. I wanted to shrivel beneath it. Even Colt's black gaze had nothing on Augie right now. While Colt was intimidating, Augie looked...dangerous.

I shifted a little closer to Banjo, and when he put his arm around me, I was grateful. I liked the safety he provided.

Augie's gaze didn't linger on me for long. It snapped back to his brother. "You know I don't care which random skanks you hook up with. But don't be doing it here, in the middle of the fucking living room, when I've got a client coming over. What if I'd had someone with me? You think they would have stuck around after seeing your little underage sex show?"

Banjo's expression reeked of boredom.

Augie sighed. "Whatever. Get it out of your system now. You know once you hit eighteen—"

Banjo's expression hardened. "Will you quit bringing that up? It's not happening." He pushed off the couch and thrust the cushion at his brother. "It's my house, too. And she's not a random skank. So don't ever fucking call her that again. Got it? We'll be in my room."

With that, he grabbed my hand, pulled me up from the couch, and dragged me up the stairs. Still completely buck-ass naked.

He opened the first door after we hit the second-floor landing and guided me inside, slamming the door behind him. "Fuck him," Banjo muttered. "He can go to hell."

He dropped my hand and stalked to a chest of drawers, yanking out the middle one with so much force I was shocked it didn't fly right off the runners. He snatched up a pair of black sports shorts and drew them up over his ass.

I leaned back on the door. "Well, that was mortifying."

Banjo strode across the small room and pinned me in, cupping my face with both hands. I expected him to kiss me. And kiss me hard. But instead, he paused, lips hovering just over mine.

"I'm sorry," he whispered. His voice got a little louder. "That was really bad, wasn't it?"

"It wasn't the best," I agreed.

He stared at me.

I stared at him.

Slowly, a grin tugged at his lips.

Damn him, it was infectious. I slapped his chest. "Stop it. It's not funny!"

"It's a bit funny!"

"Your brother caught us while I was giving you a blow

job, Banjo. Like, your dick was actually in my mouth. He saw that! Can I curl into a ball and die now, please?"

He gathered me up in his arms and kissed my forehead. "How do you think I feel? He interrupted before you got to finish. My balls are blue right now!"

We both choked on our laughter. He led me over to the bed, and we sat side by side on the narrow single mattress. His room was painted blue and decorated with surfing photos, mostly big waves in tropical locations I doubted he'd ever been to. Magazines sat piled up on his bedside table. A small flat-screen TV was attached to one wall, Play-Station cords dangling down. Typical teen boy bedroom, except the bed was neatly made and there weren't dirty socks on the floor.

I picked up a framed photo of Augie and Banjo and ran my thumb along the frame. "Is he going to be super mad at you?"

Banjo shrugged. "I don't care. I'm not happy with him either. Sorry about what he said. You aren't a skank. He's just an asshole."

"Has he caught you with a lot of girls? Like that, I mean?" I bit my lip, almost wanting to take the words back. I suddenly wasn't sure I wanted to know the answer.

But Banjo put his hand on my leg and squeezed it. "I can promise you, you're the first he's ever caught in that position."

That was somehow worse. I groaned loudly and buried my face in my hands. "Kill me now."

He pried my fingers away and traced a finger over the ring on my index finger. "Who gives a shit what he thinks?"

"He's your brother."

"He's a bastard."

We both went quiet.

Then I remembered something. "What did he mean by you only have until you're eighteen? He's not going to kick you out, is he?"

"I wish. No. He wants me to go into business with him after my birthday."

I paused. "His drug business?"

Banjo shook his head. "No. He does some other stuff, on the side." He pushed to his feet. "Honestly, it's not anything I really like thinking about. How about I take you home? Or back to your car, anyway."

I nodded, standing as well.

Banjo opened his arms, and I stepped into them for a hug. It wasn't anything sexual. Just a mutual assurance that everything was going to be all right. But Banjo's vagueness about his brother's business bothered me. Something wasn't on the up and up.

"Maybe we can pick up where we left off another night?" Banjo asked.

I buried my face in is shoulder, breathing him in. Who knew how long it would be before we got to do this again. "That could possibly be arranged. If you're lucky."

"Am I pushing that luck if I ask you out for Friday then?" he asked.

I opened my mouth to agree, but then I shook my head. "Actually, I can't. I have plans."

"Oh? Something with your aunt?"

I moved back so I could see his face better. "Something with Rafe and my aunt actually."

"Rafe?" He seemed interested but not concerned. He linked his fingers through mine and led me toward the door.

"We're doing a speech at this donor dinner thing."

Banjo's hand paused on the doorknob "Is it a date?"

I shook my head. "Oh no. His dad asked us to do it." But

the tone in his voice had piqued my interest. "Would you be upset if it had been a date?"

To my surprise, he answered easily. "With Rafe? No. Anyone else? Yeah, maybe. Sorry, I know that's shitty, because we aren't official or anything." He tucked a loose strand of hair behind my ear. "I know I don't have the right to be jealous when I can't offer you more than what we're doing right now."

I shrugged. "I can't offer you anything in return either. So whatever we are, I'm all good with it. You date who you want. I'll date who I want. We'll hang out when we can. Maybe I'll try sucking your dick again, but next time, it'll be with the door locked." I grinned.

He pulled me in again and kissed me hard. "I like you, funny girl. Saturday, okay? Hang out with Rafe on Friday, me on Saturday. Deal?"

I brushed my lips over his once more. "Deal."

16

RAFE

*T*he stairs creaked beneath my weight, protesting the way I thundered down them. At the bottom, I dragged my shirt over my head, while simultaneously trying to shove my feet in my shoes. I was late. I'd slept in, and my brain felt like mush. I'd been smoking more than usual, and it was messing with my sleep patterns. I was going to bed later but still had to get up for school. Which meant I was dragging ass through all my classes. I probably needed to cut back a bit. Take a break. Do a vegetable detox. Or something a little more clean and wholesome than avoiding all my problems by getting high.

"You're late. Again."

I ground my teeth together. That right there was why I smoked in the first place. Just one word from him, and my fingers twitched, craving to hold a joint, take a drag, and let the pot do its thing.

Being high was the only way my father was bearable.

The only way my life was bearable.

I pretended I didn't notice him standing by the door in his preppy clothes. He wasn't fooling me. We might have been a little better off than most of the people in Saint View. We lived in one of the nicer neighborhoods. Our house was under a mortgage instead of government-owned. But my father had delusions of grandeur. He dressed like he was from Providence. And on first glimpse, you might have been forgiven for believing the smarmy exterior he showed the world. He dressed nicely. No jeans or baseball caps like most of the other men around here. He always wore fitted pants and button-down shirts. His hair was always artfully slicked back, his beard groomed. But if you looked closer, you'd see his appearance was as phony as his smiles. His shirts were made of cheap fabric. The watch that gleamed on his wrist was a knockoff.

We might have had a little more than most in Saint View. But that didn't make him better. In fact, he was worse. Much worse.

Mom and I were the only ones who ever got to see the real Todd Simmons. The rest of the world didn't know how lucky they were.

"Hey, Mom," I said, sidling up to her in the kitchen and kissing her cheek. "How are you?"

She gave me a worried smile. "Good, but your father is waiting. Here, quick. I made you some breakfast." She pushed a plate toward me, and I plucked the warm toast from it. "Your backpack is by the door. Go, before..."

Before Dad lost his temper. Yeah. I knew the drill.

"Will you be okay today?" I asked. I looked her over, but she looked perfectly put together. Her makeup was flawless, and she was already dressed, despite it still being early and her having nowhere to go.

"I'll be fine. See you tonight."

Reluctantly, I followed my father out the front door and to his car. Expensive, compared to the piece of crap he'd bought for Mom. But Mom wasn't the one with the image to uphold, was she? I slumped into the passenger seat and pulled my backpack onto my lap. Ten minutes to get to school. Ten minutes I'd have to endure with the man, and then I could sneak off and get high before homeroom. Thank God. That detox would have to wait until tomorrow.

Dad started the car, glancing over at me as he got us on the road. "Sit up straight."

I did as I was told, because it was easier than arguing.

"Better. Now listen, about tonight."

I sighed. "I've practiced the speech, Dad. Just like you told me to."

"Good. Has Lacey?"

"How would I know?"

Dad shot me a sharp look. "Haven't you been getting friendly with her? I told you—"

"Yeah, you told me to show her around. I did." Not exactly true, but Lacey had covered for me when my dad has asked about it. I owed her one for that.

Dad's fingers tightened on the steering wheel. "I told you to make friends with her. You know who she is. Who her family are."

Yeah, he'd told me to kiss the rich kid's ass, while Colt had told me to run her out of town. The entire situation just made me want that joint hidden in the bottom of my backpack even more. Colt was my best friend. My brother. He'd been there for me through everything, and if he said Lacey had to go, then I didn't need to question him. He'd have a reason, and if he couldn't tell us what it was, it had to be something huge. He'd been tortured when we'd pressed him about it. It still didn't sit well with me.

But my dad wouldn't take that lying down. And he had

ways of hurting me. Ways that didn't just hurt me, but others, too. And that was something I couldn't handle.

Which left me in an impossible situation.

"What do you want me to do, Dad? I can't make the girl like me."

"You're a good-looking boy, Rafe. You've never had a shortage of cheerleaders throwing themselves at you. Make a little effort, and I'm sure you could have Lacey Knight eating out of your hand. Couldn't you?"

It wasn't really a question, more like a command. I didn't say anything.

I should have just agreed. My silence only pissed him off further. "For fuck's sake," he muttered. "Do I have to spell everything out for you like you're a goddamn fucking toddler? When you get to school today, find her and ask her to be your date tonight."

I snapped my head in his direction. "What? Dad, no. We're already doing the speech together."

"So this is the perfect opportunity. You'll have her alone, away from all the other boys at school."

I just turned away, staring out the window, wishing we were already at school.

"You'll do this, Rafe. I'm not asking. I'm telling."

There was nothing new there. That was how he'd run my entire life. And he never failed to remind me.

He was the boss.

He was the one in charge.

I was just his minion.

17

LACEY

*R*afe caught up to me in the hallway before lunch. I jumped in surprise when he put his hand on my arm and tugged me into the nearest empty classroom.

I raised one eyebrow. "Uh, hi?"

"Hey, sorry. I just..." He glanced through the glass panel of the door and then pulled me away from it.

I folded my arms across my chest. "Did you seriously just drag me in here, only because you're embarrassed to be seen with me out there? What do you want?"

"The dinner thing tonight...did you, uh, practice your speech?"

"Of course. I'd never do something like that unprepared. Question is, did you? And will you even be sober for it. Judging by the smell of your clothes, I'm going to go with, probably not."

"I practiced. And I'll be fine by then."

I doubted it. Rafe wasn't fine at all. His eyes were bloodshot, his clothes disheveled. I softened a little. "Are you okay? You seem...stressed." Which was weird for a guy who'd probably been smoking pot that morning. Wasn't pot supposed to chill you out?

Rafe sat on the edge of a desk and pointed to the spot next to him. "You really mean that, don't you?"

"Mean what?"

"When you asked if I was okay. You act like you actually care about the answer."

"Of course I do."

He just stared at me. "You don't even realize that's weird, do you?"

"It's not weird. Lots of people care how you are, Rafe."

"Name one."

"Me. Jagger." Me again, I added silently. Because I really did. There was an odd sadness behind his eyes, and I had a suspicion his drug use was more of a coping mechanism than a pure desire to get high. Nobody got high before class on a regular basis, just for fun. He intrigued me. This smart boy, who seemed hell-bent on smoking his future away.

He didn't say anything. Just shifted an inch closer until our arms touched. I liked the warmth of him.

"Will you be my date for tonight?" he asked.

I blinked. "Date?"

He grinned. "Yeah, you know. I'll pick you up. We can go together. Maybe I'll bring you a flower."

"I don't really like flowers." My cheeks went hot. I don't know why I said that. It wasn't even true. But he'd caught me off guard.

He waited a moment, then he pushed to his feet. "Shit, it's okay. You don't have to say yes. I just thought—"

I grabbed his hand. We both glanced down at our joint fingers in surprise. "I didn't say no. I'm just wondering what Colt will think of this. Were you planning on telling him that you're defying his 'run me out of school' orders?"

Rafe sighed. "Colt isn't my biggest problem right now."

There it was again. That sadness behind his icy-blue eyes. It drew me in. "What is?"

"Go out with me tonight, and maybe I'll tell you. Come on. These dinners are completely dull. If we're being forced to go, shouldn't we get to have a little fun?"

I wasn't entirely sure what fun was to Rafe. But if we both had to spend our Friday night in a roomful of overly entitled snobs in suits, then I guessed we may as well do it together. "Pick me up at six, then?"

He grinned. "It's a date."

I stared at the hideous green-and-gold uniform in the mirror, twisting left and right, but there wasn't an angle that magically made it any better. I traipsed out into the living room.

Selina's eyes widened. "Oh my."

"I know," I grumped. "It's hideous."

"There's a reason none of the kids at your school wear the uniform. And that right there is it."

We both dissolved into laughter.

"It's good to see you smiling," I said. "And at least you look fantastic."

Selina did a little spin, showing off the magenta dress that clung to her body like a second skin. She'd paired it with tall black heels and a cute, lightweight jacket. Her shiny black clutch was gripped between her fingers, her nails perfectly matching the color of her dress.

"Thank you. It's nice to smile. And to wear something other than sweatpants."

I hadn't actually seen Selina in sweatpants once over the

last few weeks. I doubted she even owned any. But I understood her point. She hadn't worn anything quite as bright and cheerful as she was tonight, either.

"You went all out for this dinner, huh? It's probably going to be boring."

Selina pulled me up from the couch. "Getting to see you speak is never boring, sweetheart. And I needed this. I needed a reason to get back out there. Now, what time is this boy picking you up? I don't know how I feel about this."

"You know, most parents would be pleased when their kid says she's going on a date with the principal's son."

"And if you were talking about the principal of Edgely Academy, I'd be over the moon. But we're talking about Saint View...this boy does have all his teeth, right?"

I snorted on a laugh, and Selina threw me a wink.

"Be nice, okay? Try not to be a total snob."

"I'm not a snob!"

I raised one eyebrow.

"Okay, fine, I am. But only when it comes to you. I just want you to have the very best. And that includes a boyfriend who isn't going to end up in prison before he's twenty-one."

I groaned. This was exactly why I hadn't wanted to introduce her to Banjo. She said these things in jest, but I was ninety-nine percent certain that deep down, she meant them. She hadn't looked impressed when I'd told her she'd have to drive to the dinner alone tonight, because I had a date. Her frown hadn't lessened any when I'd talked Rafe up, telling her how he was top of the junior year. She hadn't gone all-out and put a blanket ban on me dating anyone from Saint View, but if she knew Banjo's brother was a drug dealer, or that Rafe got high before class, she would have a restraining order out before I could blink.

A knock at the door had her raising an eyebrow. "He knocks. I have to admit, I'm surprised."

"Did you expect him just to honk from the gates?"

"I expected him to holler your name like a caveman, actually."

I didn't think she was joking. Shooting her a warning look, I smoothed the ugly uniform, then opened the door, Selina close behind me.

"Hi—" I faltered, surprise catching me off guard when Rafe wasn't alone on the doorstep. "Um, Principal Simmons. Hi."

I shot a 'what the fuck' look at Rafe, who stood behind his father. His face was like a storm cloud, and I was pretty sure I could hear his teeth grinding from across the doormat.

"Good evening, Miss Knight. I hope you don't mind, but I tagged along with my son. I couldn't just sit in the car while he came to collect you. That would have been awfully rude."

He peered past me to Selina. "You must be Lacey's aunt? We spoke on the phone at the beginning of the school year. I'm Todd Simmons. Principal of Saint View High." He gave Selina a charming smile and then added, as if it were an afterthought, "And Rafe's father."

Simmons offered a hand to my aunt and I slipped past them. Rafe and I watched, dumfounded, as my aunt took his hand and beamed at him.

"Todd. Have we met before? You seem familiar."

I doubted my aunt had ever been in the same room as Todd Simmons. It's not like their social circles overlapped. But she had a good poker face. Surely she was as confused as I was about what was going on here.

"We should go," Rafe said without introducing himself or greeting my aunt. "We're going to be late."

Selina frowned at his rudeness, and his father shot him a glare. But Rafe was having none of it. He was on a noticeably short fuse that was about to fizzle out. He threw his hands up and stalked to the car.

I chased after him. "Rafe! Wait!"

I caught up with him as he slid into the driver's seat. I wasn't sure where I was supposed to sit, but Principal Simmons and my aunt were both still chatting in the doorway, so I picked the passenger seat. From there, I could see Rafe's face. He stared straight ahead at his father, his expression ready to turn the man to ash.

"I can't believe him." He swore low under his breath. "He's a fucking toad." Then he swiveled toward me. Pain burned behind his eyes. Suddenly, he slammed his hand down on the door lock, which set off a whirring noise, all the other doors locking in unison. "Put your seat belt on."

He didn't give me time to protest. He turned the key in the ignition, and the engine roared to life. Then we were shooting backward out of the driveway at a speed that churned my stomach.

"Rafe!" I yelped, grabbing for my seat belt.

"Yeah?"

Principal Simmons was running down the driveway after us. His face was red, and he pumped his arms, chasing us down. There was something inherently cartoonish about him. I couldn't help but laugh. The entire situation was ridiculous.

"Drive!"

The corner of Rafe's mouth lifted in a grin. "I knew I liked you for a reason, princess." He threw the car into drive and put his foot down on the accelerator.

I twisted, looking over my shoulder at Principal Simmons and my aunt standing in the middle of the road, mouths hanging open.

My aunt would kill me later, and this likely spelled doom for any sort of friendship Rafe and I could have had. My aunt would never allow it after he fishtailed a car out of our street. In fact, it wouldn't surprise me if she were calling the cops right now to report my kidnapping.

Despite all that, Rafe's casual comment was what I concentrated on. "You like me, huh?"

Rafe grinned. "Maybe."

I maybe liked him, too.

I liked Banjo as well. But I was here, in a car with Rafe, not at all kidnapped, despite what my aunt probably thought. And Banjo and I were just fooling around. We'd both said as much. We weren't a couple, so if I was maybe a little intrigued by Rafe, too, no big deal.

Rafe drove us out of Providence and to the outskirts of Saint View. He slowed as we approached the venue where the dinner was being held. But instead of parking, he gave the building a middle finger salute, put his foot down on the accelerator, and took the winding ocean-front road to the cliffs that overlooked the beach.

I didn't comment. I might have spent time preparing for the speech we were supposed to give, but the allure of Rafe with his guard down was a thousand times more interesting than some stuffy dinner.

At the lookout that sat atop the cliffs, he pulled the car to a stop and got out, slamming the door behind him. I did the same, meeting him at the front of the car. He sucked in deep breaths, hands held to the back of his head, while he stared out over the ocean. The sun was getting low, and a wind whipped around us, chilling me through my flimsy blouse.

"Shit, sorry. I didn't even let you grab your jacket. Here. Take mine." Rafe shrugged out of his school blazer and put it over my shoulders.

"Thanks." I leaned on the hood of the car, the metal beneath my ass still warm from our drive.

It didn't take Rafe long to start talking.

"I can't stand him. How sad is that? I despise the man who helped bring me into this world. If I could push him off this motherfucking cliff, I would." He picked up a stone and hurled it over the edge. It disappeared without a sound. Then he turned to me, gaze full of regret. "Shit, Lacey. That back there was really embarrassing. If you want me to take you home, I will."

"Want to explain instead? Because I'm confused. I thought we were going together. As a date?"

"Yeah, me, too. Then my dad tells me at the last minute that he was coming with me. I didn't know he was going to ambush you and your aunt like that. He's unbelievable."

"Why would he bother? Neither of us are all that interesting."

Rafe sighed. "He's a user. He's been desperate to meet up with your aunt from the minute you started school at Saint View. He probably had some grand notion of all of us arriving together, with your aunt on his arm or something. I don't know. He was insistent I bring you tonight. I'm pretty sure he had this whole thing planned out. Meanwhile, my mother is at home, alone and upset, because he didn't even invite her. He pulls this shit all the time. Treats her like she's his pet or something. He's completely isolated her. She used to have friends once, but not anymore. He'd sulk for days if she tried to see any of them, and eventually it became easier for her to just not see them at all."

I gaped at him. "That's abuse! Now I feel bad for leaving my aunt there with him."

Rafe shook his head. "He's probably charming the pants off her. But he's a snake. Warn her. He's not the man he makes out to be."

I nodded. I felt awful for his poor mother. The thought of the woman being told to stay home so her husband could flirt with someone else...with someone who'd just lost her husband, no less... Bile rose in my throat.

"Sorry your dad is an asshat."

Rafe snorted on a laugh and came to sit on the hood beside me. "Yeah, me, too."

"But you're kind of an asshat, too, you know."

Rafe sighed. "I know. I'm sorry. I shouldn't have asked you out, just to keep my father happy. Dick move. My bad."

I folded my arms over my chest, heat creeping up the back of my neck. This was embarrassing. I'd let myself get excited over Rafe asking me out, thinking he was sincere. I hated that I was now disappointed.

Rafe nudged me with his elbow. "You angry?"

I twisted to look at him. The storm in his expression had died down. "Yeah, I'm angry." But my words had little power behind them. Because there was something about Rafe that just made it impossible to be upset with him. Especially after he'd confided in me about his mother. He reminded me of a kicked puppy I just wanted to take care of. If a puppy could be six foot, gorgeous, with muscles for days thanks to football practice.

"I don't want you to be. Thing is, I wanted to ask you out. Not the way I did. But for real. A proper date. Not to this stupid school thing."

"Don't make up bullshit just to dig yourself out of a hole." I dropped my gaze to my hands. I didn't need his backtracking. He'd been forced into asking me out. That was that. He didn't need to try to make me feel better about it now. I was a big girl. I could take it.

He reached out and took my chin in his hand, tilting my face so I had to face him. "Hey. I'm not lying. That very first day of school? I laid claim on you."

"Excuse me, what? You laid claim on me? What the hell does that mean?" If he was trying to get out of a hole, this wasn't the way to do it.

But he was insistent and wouldn't let me pull away. "It means I was so damn attracted to you, that when Banjo said he had dibs because he'd met you first, I broke our code and said he could go fuck himself."

I rolled my eyes. "How incredibly caveman of you both. Did you ever think to ask what I wanted?"

He inched closer. "Honestly? No. But I'm asking now. What do you want, Lacey?"

My mouth dried.

Rafe chuckled, and the sound rolled over me like hot molasses. Sweet, thick, and delicious.

"Come on, princess. Cat got your tongue? Tell me what you want? Who you want?"

My brain scrambled. "I don't know," I whispered. My heartrate kicked up a notch. He was so close, and he smelled so good. Something inside me yearned to lean in and beg him to kiss me.

His thumb grazed over my lip. "What if I help you make up your mind?"

His mouth was less than an inch from mine, and I could barely breathe with the anticipation.

"Close your eyes, Lacey. Let me help you decide."

As if my brain had completely packed up and left town, my eyes fluttered closed of their own accord. His lips brushed the corner of my mouth, and I gasped at the contact. How such a tiny touch could have such an impact on me, I didn't know. But all of Rafe's touches seemed to affect me like that. The second pass of his lips made mine tingle, and when his mouth finally pressed to mine, I was ready and waiting, dying inside from the anticipation of what his kiss would be like.

His tongue swept across the seam of my lips, urging mine open. His hand held my head in place, not that he needed to. I wasn't going anywhere. I leaned into the kiss, tasting him, exploring him. My hands fell onto his chest, then I gripped his shirt and dragged him closer. My head swam, not quite sure how we'd gotten here, but wanting it more than I wanted air.

We molded together, kissing in the fading light. It felt good. Easy. Natural. Like we'd kissed a hundred times before.

When we pulled apart, we were both panting for breath. But I couldn't turn away. I'd felt that kiss right through my entire body. If he'd looked down, he would have seen my toes curling. If he'd pushed me back on the hood of the car right then and there, I would have gone willingly.

"I didn't expect that," he murmured, his lips over mine once more.

I let out a little laugh. "Yeah, join the club. You're not a bad kisser."

He raised one eyebrow. "Not bad?" He leaned in again, claiming my mouth once more.

This kiss was hard, hot, and fast. I moaned, scrambling to get closer. This kiss was even better than the last. It was explosive. Powerful. Dominant.

My head spun in dizzying, delighted, horny circles.

"How 'bout now?" he asked with a smirk, like he knew exactly how much I'd enjoyed it.

I pulled back and tried to calm my racing libido that yelled dirty suggestions in the back of my mind. Instead, I tilted my head to one side, letting the mood between us become playful. "What's one up from not bad?"

"Amazing?"

"I was thinking more like mind-blowing."

Rafe rested his forehead against mine and groaned. "Don't talk about blowing right now."

I dared at glance at his lap. His school slacks pulled tight over a very impressive erection.

"Don't stare at me like that either, Lacey. I'm trying really hard right now not to think with my dick, but if you keep looking at it, it's going to be real hard not to use it on you."

Heat flared between my thighs, and I pressed them together. Just the thought of him using it on me... Him flipping me around, bending me over the car, lifting up my skirt...I suddenly saw the appeal in being used.

Rafe pushed off the car and stalked a few steps away before turning back to grin at me. "Stop it."

"Stop what? I didn't do anything."

"You didn't need to. Your thoughts are written all over your face."

"Oh yeah?" I challenged. "Let's hear it then, mind reader. What am I thinking?"

"You're thinking about how if I walked over there right now and pushed your knees apart, you'd let me. You'd let me run my hands beneath that skirt, and up your thighs. And how you'd let me kiss you until you begged for more." He cocked his head to one side and studied me with a gaze that made me feel completely naked. "Am I right?"

Aaaand, it was time to change the subject. Because all of

that sounded so good I might be tempted to let him test out his theory. "We're going to be late for the dinner. Assuming we're still going, that is?"

Rafe chuckled, his expression smug. "See? Mind reader."

I grinned. "Come on. I'm serious. We can't just hide up here all night making out." As tempting as that might be. It was no skin off my nose if we didn't go to the dinner. But something told me if Rafe didn't show up, there would be consequences. And I needed a breather to work out how I'd just ended up kissing Rafe Simmons on the hood of his father's car. Dammit, I hadn't even crossed him off my suspect list yet.

"That dinner is the last thing I want to do," Rafe complained. He came back to my side, the mood between us changed.

My heart went out to him. Whatever was going on between him and his dad was obviously bigger than just tonight. On impulse, I picked up his hand and squeezed it. "Come on. Let's just go. He's not going to make a scene in front of all those people. Plus. It's Friday night, and I'll bet there's an open bar..."

He squeezed my fingers back. "I like your thinking."

We got back in the car, and as we drove back down the hill, I couldn't help but shoot him little glances. This might not have been a date, but that didn't mean it had to be a complete waste of an evening. Rafe might have had ulterior motives tonight, but so did I.

"Do you like football?" I asked. "Playing it, I mean?"

Nobody ever called me subtle.

He shrugged. "Honestly? Not really. I only play it as a means to an end."

"How so?"

"If I get a football scholarship, I won't have to rely on my father to pay for college. And the sooner I get out from under his thumb, the better. I can't wait for the day he has no say in my life."

"What about the other guys on the team?"

He shrugged. "Depends who you mean. For some of them, football is their only shot at college. It's their whole life."

"Banjo?"

He nodded. "He lives with his brother. There won't be a ticket out of this town if he doesn't earn it kicking a pigskin."

I felt a bit bad talking about Banjo behind his back, but I pushed my guilt away. This was why I'd come to Saint View. To dig up dirt the police could use. Getting distracted by cute boys was a bonus, not the goal, and I couldn't let it interfere.

"Is the team close?"

"Yeah. We're tight. We won state last year. That binds you."

"I can imagine," I murmured. "Congratulations," I added on as an afterthought.

"You like football?"

I wrinkled up my nose. "My uncle wasn't a fan, and my aunt doesn't like any sport where you get dirty. So I've never had much to do with it. The parties are okay, though," I finished, trying to steer the conversation off me and back to him. I didn't like thinking about my uncle. And how on Superbowl Sunday, we'd order Chinese food and watch old movies instead of watching the game. I didn't really like football parties either, though the last one I went to had turned out to be interesting. At the very least.

Rafe shot me a glance and proved he really could read me like a book. "I owe you an apology about the party the other night. I was high. And being an asshole. Colt...we're tight. I wish I knew what his problem is."

Him and me both.

We pulled into the parking lot of the venue, and Rafe killed the engine, but neither of us moved for a minute.

"I guess we have to go inside, huh? Maybe my father won't put us on detention for the rest of the year if we go in and suck up to all these rich assholes."

I didn't comment on the fact my aunt was one of them. And by association, I was, too. Instead, I got out of the car and pondered Rafe in a different light; tried to imagine him picking me up, carrying me through a fire.

I was too busy gawking at him. I didn't notice the pothole until it was too late. My ankle rolled, and I stumbled forward, trying to find my balance.

"Whoa," Rafe said, catching me before I fell. His hands wrapped around my upper arms, and my chest met his. "You okay?"

I went to assure him I was fine. When something occurred to me. I screwed my face up in pain. "Ow, no. My ankle. I think I've twisted it."

Rafe looked down at the little divot in the road doubtfully.

I tried a different tactic. "Don't worry," I said, overly loudly, "I'll be fine." I took a step forward and stumbled again. This time on purpose.

Rafe caught me again. "Hey. Stop. You're obviously not okay, though how you managed to hurt yourself on such a small hole, I don't know."

"Clumsy," I said through my fake grimaces. I gripped his arm. "It really hurts. Do you think you could help me inside?"

He put his arm around my lower back, and I put mine

around his. My fingers pressed against his spine, and for half a second, I let myself enjoy the contact. Was he seeing that blonde from the party? I could imagine him putting his arm around her like this, and the two of them walking into school or the mall together. And not just because she'd faked a twisted ankle. Jealousy flared. Which was ridiculous. One kiss and a few spilled secrets didn't give me that right.

"Just hop," Rafe said. "There's chairs inside the door."

I gave a half-hearted hop then faked a laugh. "These shoes aren't made for hopping." Which was true. My shoes were the only things I'd been allowed to pick out myself, so I'd chosen a pair of chunky wedge sandals. They weren't exactly appropriate for anything but strutting on flat, level ground.

Rafe stared down at my feet. "Those shoes are so extra. Come here."

And just like that, my not-so-brilliant, spur-of-the-moment plan worked. I sucked in a breath as Rafe scooped me up into his arms and strode toward the door.

Flashes of *that* night burned through my head. Fire. Smoke. Strong arms around me, and my head against a solid chest, embroidered letters beneath my fingers.

Rafe set me down on a chair just inside the door, and I tried to catch my breath.

"Hey, are you okay? You look like you've seen a ghost."

"No, I just...when you picked me up like that, it reminded me of something else."

He frowned. "Something bad, by the expression on your face."

I shook my head. "No, actually. It's all good. You just surprised me." I rotated my ankle around and pointed at it. "I really don't think it's all that bad. Come on, let's go see if your dad and my aunt made it here."

I pushed to my feet, not even bothering to fake a limp. My little performance had done its job. When Rafe had picked me up, I might have had flashbacks to that night. But that had only cemented the realization that it didn't feel right. I didn't fit in Rafe's arms like I had the guy who'd rescued me. It didn't feel the same. It might not have been the solid proof that the police needed. But I trusted my gut instinct. Rafe wasn't the one who'd pulled me out of the fire that night.

A sense of satisfaction, and then anticipation, rolled over me. If Rafe was off my list, next time we hung out, I couldn't see things remaining quite so PG. And that was something to look forward to.

18

BANJO

I sent Rafe three Facebook messages on Saturday morning before the lazy prick woke up.

Banjo: *You up?*

Banjo: *Yo, get up. I need to talk.*

Banjo: *Not going away, asshole. I can see you've read my messages.*

It was that last one that finally got a response.

Rafe: *Fuck off. Not all of us get up before dawn to go surfing.*

Banjo: *Neither did I. I'm still in bed. How was your date with Lacey last night?*

Rafe: *Fine. We did the speech. Played the poor, disadvantaged student to some suits. Well, I did. Lacey already knew half the room. She went home with her aunt.*

Huh. Not what I'd expected at all. But also, very vague. And the fact was, there was one thing I wanted to know, and if I didn't come right out and say it, he probably wouldn't tell me.

Banjo: *Anything happen between you two?*

I stared at my phone and willed a message to pop up. When one didn't, I knew I had my answer.

Banjo: *A kiss?*

Still nothing.

Banjo: *Sex?*

I pounced on my phone when it beeped.

Rafe: *Not sex.*

They'd kissed then. I bit my lip. I'd spent all last night getting drunk, alone in my bedroom, and all I'd been able to think about was the two of them out on a date. I knew Rafe. When he liked a girl, he didn't hold back. I knew he would have been putting the moves on.

Thing was, I couldn't work out if I was jealous...or turned on. I rolled over and buried my face in my pillow. Fuck.

Rafe: *You kissed her, too, huh?*

My thumb hovered over the screen. I never normally thought twice about telling Rafe everything I'd done with girls. Right down to graphic descriptions that earned me brownie points and high fives. But something stopped me this time.

Rafe: *Your silence is just as telling as mine was.*

Banjo: *Yeah.*

Banjo: *I'm taking her out again today. I want to kiss her some more. Just putting it out there.*

Rafe: *Colt will have both our heads if he finds out.*

Banjo: *He'd better not find out then. We cool, though?*

Rafe: *Always.*

Well, that was a relief. I exited out of my conversation with Rafe and started a chat with Lacey.

Banjo: *Morning, beautiful.*

Lacey: *Charmer.*

Banjo: *Beach today? Meet me there at noon?*

Lacey: *Can't wait.*

I couldn't either. I showered quickly, then thundered

down the stairs and into the kitchen. I frowned at the two empty wine glasses on the kitchen counter. Augie had obviously had someone over last night. For business or pleasure, I had no idea. I hoped the latter. I put the two glasses into the sink and filled it with sudsy water.

He came down the stairs only a minute after I did, while I was elbow deep in cleaning up his mess.

"You couldn't spring for a dishwasher? Or at least do your own dishes?" I grumbled.

He clapped me on the shoulder on his way to the refrigerator. "When you come work for me next year, we'll have the money for that stuff. Right now, I'm busting my ass just to pay our rent and buy food."

I sighed. "I told you. I'm not coming to work with you."

Augie laughed, like the notion I wouldn't want to do what he did was ridiculous. "Yeah, well. We'll see about that. I've had a lot of interest in you."

I dropped a knife, and it clattered against the stainless-steel sink. "What? You've been telling people about me?"

He shrugged and pulled out a stool at the counter. "People know who you are. The hotshot football player and all."

I went back to scrubbing. "I'm not going to be here next year, Augie. I'm going to get a scholarship and get the fuck out of this dead-end town. This might be enough for you, but it sure as hell isn't for me."

I shot him a glance over my shoulder, but he didn't even seem upset by the accusation. Probably because it was one I'd made many times before. But I'd been more vocal about it in the last twelve months. Ever since Augie started talking about me working for him once I turned eighteen.

I didn't even want to think about it.

"Do we have a picnic basket somewhere?" I asked, changing the subject.

Augie scoffed. "Why the fuck would we have a picnic basket? Do I look like the type who goes on picnics?"

No. He looked like the type who dealt drugs on the side of his other illegal activities.

"Forget it then," I muttered.

"You taking some cheerleader out on a date? All romantic and shit?"

"She's not a cheerleader. And her name is Lacey."

"The slut who was giving you a blowie last night? Fuck, little bro. You don't take those girls out on picnics. You just get what's between their legs and move on to the next one."

Before I knew it, I was dragging Augie off his stool and had him pinned to the kitchen cupboards. My fingers balled into fists in his shirt. "Don't fucking talk about her like that. She's no slut."

Augie raised one eyebrow, then shoved me away hard. "Who is this chick? Her pussy made of gold?"

I ground my teeth, fighting back the urge to take a swing at him. "I mean it, Augie. Don't."

He waved me off. "Fine, fine. I got better things to do anyway." And then he disappeared through the front door, slamming it behind him with a bang.

I blew out a slow breath, and one by one, unclenched my fingers. I loved my brother. And I knew I owed him a lot. But sometimes, I really fucking hated him, too.

---

*W*e'd picked an awesome day for the beach. The nights were getting colder, but today was unseasonably warm, and girls were out in bikinis. The water was still a steady sixty-five degrees, so with a bit of luck, I'd be able to convince Lacey to go for a swim.

I waited for her at the top of the path that led from the road down to the soft sand of the beach, and grinned when I spotted her convertible, top down, wind blowing through her hair. I jogged over, opening the door for her.

"Hey, you." I grinned. "Have I told you how hot you look driving that car?"

She grabbed a beach bag from the passenger seat and unclipped her seat belt. "No, but you can tell me now."

"Straight out of every teenage boy's dreams."

She wrinkled her nose adorably. "Not sure that's a good thing."

I took the bag from her and shouldered it. "Fine. Straight out of my dreams, then. Better?"

She got out of the car, closing the door behind her. My automatic instinct was to step closer, cage her in, and kiss her. But there were people around, and if we were keeping this on the downlow, kissing her out in the open probably wasn't such a good idea. So instead, I forced myself to step back and give her some room.

I didn't miss the flash of disappointment in her eye. And it had me feeling pretty good about myself. I liked the idea of keeping her waiting. Wanting. It was a pleasurable sort of torture. One I got off on.

My hand brushed hers as we walked down to the sand. I led the way, picking a path through families and groups of friends. "Can you swim?" I asked.

Lacey skirted some seaweed washed up on the shore before she answered. "Swimming is probably the one sport I'm not completely uncoordinated with. I'm not going to win any Olympic medals, but I won't drown."

"Good." I dumped our stuff down on the sand. "Because I want to show you something, but it involves swimming."

She shrugged. "I'm up for it. It's so nice today."

"For more reasons than one."

She nudged me with her elbow. "Smooth talker."

I nudged her back. "Princess."

She inched closer to me. "I kind of like it when you call me that."

"I know. Now get your gear off."

She raised an eyebrow. "Back at you."

I pulled my shirt over my head. The slight breeze coming off the water danced over my skin.

Lacey's gaze dropped from my face and ran across my chest, lingering lower on my abs.

I was getting turned on just from her watching me, so I put my hands on her shoulders and twisted her to face the ocean. "The view is that way. Quit gawking at me."

The elbow I copped that time was harder and straight to my midsection, but I laughed. "I like it when you're feisty."

"And I liked the view I had, thank you very much. But this one is nice, too. I love the ocean."

I started to agree with her, but the words dried on my lips. Lacey pulled her T-shirt off, then went to work on the buttons of her denim skirt. She tugged it down over her hips and ass, leaving her in the tiniest white bikini I'd ever seen. It barely covered her tits.

"Banjo?" She waved a hand in front of my face.

I blinked. Then started packing up our things. "The beach was a terrible idea. Get your stuff. Let's go back to my place."

"What?"

"Seriously. It's either that or I throw you down right here on the sand."

A look of understanding dawned in her eyes and quickly became a full-blown smirk. "Nope. I want to swim."

I groaned as she strutted down into the ocean, her pert ass fucking bitable in that damn bikini. I was an idiot. Seriously dumb. I'd known she probably had a smoking-hot body. I'd held her in my arms that night in the car. I'd seen her in tight clothes at school. But nothing had prepared me for Lacey in a bikini. All I could think about doing was ripping it off her.

She was at the water's edge when I stopped thinking with my dick and let my brain issue the command to follow her. I raced across the sand, leaping over the ankle-deep water and then running through it until I was waist high. A wave, tiny compared to the ones the beach could produce at the right time of day, loomed, and I dove through it, welcoming the cold water. It was deeper on the other side, and I treaded water, watching Lacey's more tentative approach to getting wet.

"Oh my God, it's freezing!" she yelped when a wave splashed over her stomach.

"Come here, then." I reached out a hand and grabbed her, pulling her into my arms. Her skin was pebbled with goosebumps, and her nipples stood out, pressing against the fabric of her swimsuit. I ran my hands up and down her arms, and over her back, my fingers slipping easily beneath the flimsy ties of her top. "I like this bikini," I said into her ear. "Actually, I kind of fucking love it."

She clung to me, wrapping her legs around my waist in the deeper water. With her mouth just below my ear, she whispered, "I thought you might."

Swimming. Concentrate on swimming. We were still within view of the beach. And a lot of kids from school came down here on weekends. Kids from her old school, too. I didn't want to out us. Not until Lacey was ready for that. And not until I'd worked out what the hell Colt's problem was. It was keeping me up at night. I needed him to be on board with this. I didn't want to have to choose between them. Colt was my brother. I'd be forced to choose him over a girl I barely knew. But the thought of letting Lacey go before I'd even really gotten to know her left me feeling oddly empty. She had me kind of smitten. Something I wasn't used to being. It wasn't often I wanted a girl for more than a night. But ever since that first day at her house, something about her captivated me. Every time we'd hung out since, I just fell further and further under her spell. I wanted to spend time with her. Get to know her. Peel back all her layers and dig beneath them to find out why I couldn't get her out of my head. I wanted to know the mundane stuff. Her favorite color. If she liked Mexican food as much as I did. What sort of movies she watched. And then go deeper. I wanted to know what her childhood had been like. If she missed her birth parents. What her dreams were for after high school.

But I was also a guy. And there was a physical aspect to my attraction for her that yelled at me loud and clear. I wanted to plunge my dick between her legs. And having them wrapped around me right now was not helping. She put her arms around my neck, giving me the chance to run my hands up the sides of her body. Over the curve of her hips, over the sides of her tits. Her breath hitched when I flicked a thumb over her taut nipple.

"I like that," she whispered. "But we aren't far from the beach. Someone might see us."

I nodded. I pried her hands from around my neck. "I can fix that. Come on." I started swimming farther out, keeping an eye on the rocks to our right.

"Whoa, wait. Where are we going? There's no lifeguards out here. We probably shouldn't go too deep."

"You'll be okay, I promise. It's not far." I was normally on a board when I came out here, but that was with waves cresting around me. It was almost completely flat today.

She still looked a little doubtful, but she followed me anyway, with sure strokes, powering her through the water. I was a strong swimmer. You had to be when you surfed as much as I did. But my style was nonexistent. Hers was pristine. Born of years of swimming lessons in a fancy indoor pool, I'd bet. Not like me, who'd been tossed into the ocean as a toddler and never really taught proper strokes.

We swam together, and once we were far enough out, I led her toward the rocks.

"See that one there?" I called. "We need to get on it."

She nodded, letting a small wave push her in the right direction. I paddled on the spot behind her, admiring her ass as she climbed carefully onto the rock, water sluicing over the firm cheeks of her behind. Fuck. I couldn't wait to get this girl alone. There were so many things I wanted to do with her. I wanted to explore her body, slowly, carefully, on soft blankets, finding out what she liked until she screamed. And then there was a part of me who wanted her quick and dirty, wherever I could. That was the part of me that yelled the loudest.

I pulled myself up beside her on the rocks and grabbed her hand.

"Wow, I've been coming to this beach all my life, and I had no idea you could get around here."

"Most people don't," I said, leading the way, walking carefully over the rocks, clutching her hand in mine in case she slipped. "Most people are too scared to swim out as far as we did, especially near rocks and away from the lifeguards. It's a bit of a surfer's secret. We've huddled in the caves up here when the surf gets too big to get back to shore."

"That sounds scary."

I shook my head and glanced back at her over my shoulder. "It's the best fun. It's a rush. Everything about surfing is."

"You really love it, huh?"

I shrugged as we approached the mouth of the caves. "It's probably the only good thing my parents ever did for me. I come out here and smell the salt in the air and let the roar of the ocean clear my head. Everything else just falls away. There's no space for problems when you're trying to catch a big wave, you know? It's just me and my board and the water."

We stepped inside and let our eyes adjust to the dimmer light.

She peered around at the large, mostly dry, space. "This is awesome. How far back does it go?"

"It's pretty deep. We can go in farther." I led her far enough that we were out of the wind that whipped the mouth, but I didn't take her so far back we couldn't still see the light of day. "Let's not go any farther than this."

She pouted. "Why? Bats?"

"Might be, but they don't bother me." I gave her a wicked grin. "I just want to be able to see you when I strip you naked."

Lacey sucked in a breath.

I studied her reaction to determine whether she'd actually want me to do that. It was the entire reason I'd brought her here. Really, the cave wasn't all that exciting. But it was private. Away from the squeals of children and school gossips. The surfers wouldn't be around at this time of day. And all I wanted to do was get her out of that wet swimsuit.

I stepped in closer, giving her every chance to stop me. But she didn't. My hand grazed her flat belly, and when she didn't back off, I trailed one finger higher, to the tiny bit of string between the triangles of her top. I pulled it experimentally, letting it snap back against her skin. "Do you want that, princess? Do you want me to get you naked right now?"

She let out a shuddering breath that told me exactly how much she wanted it.

"What if someone comes?"

I shook my head and slid one hand beneath a triangle, cupping her tit. A perfect, high, tight handful. Two fingers found her nipple and squeezed. She whimpered.

"Isn't that part of the fun? Doesn't it turn you on, thinking about being naked in here, my tongue all over your body while someone could walk in at any moment?"

Her breathing became ragged. I took my hand away from her nipple, and instead brought her into my arms, and ran my nose up her neck until my lips brushed over her earlobe. "I'm going to take the way you're pressing against me right now as a yes, princess."

I undid the string at her back and then the one at her neck in quick succession. One flick of my wrist left her standing there in front of me, in nothing but that tiny white thong. I couldn't wait any longer to kiss her. I dipped my head and claimed her mouth. She moaned loudly, telling me exactly how turned on she was. I grabbed two handfuls of her boobs, groping them while our tongues delved deep into each other's mouths. Her hands traced over my skin, brushing water droplets from my shoulders, my pecs, my abs.

Two ties at her hips were all that were keeping me from

seeing her completely naked for the first time. I pulled away from her mouth and stepped back just far enough that I could see her face as I did it.

One string...two...

She moaned as the material fell to the floor.

My dick swelled beneath my swim shorts. Fuck, I could come just staring at her. She was a stunner. Long legs that led to a sweet, completely bare pussy.

"Banjo," she whispered. She reached for me, but I stopped her.

"Wait. I just want to drink you in for a moment."

Pink swept her cheeks. I couldn't stop staring at her. Slowly, I walked in a circle around her, raking my gaze over every inch of her flesh. Once we stood face-to-face again, she bit her lip.

I popped it free from her teeth. "Stop it."

"What?" she whispered.

"You wear your heart on your sleeve, princess. And it makes it real easy to know what you're thinking. So stop it."

"Stop wearing my heart on my sleeve?"

"Stop wondering if I find your body attractive."

"You didn't say anything..."

"I don't need to. I'm going to show you instead."

I dropped my head to her neck and kissed and sucked a trail down her skin to the swells of her breasts. Taking one in my hand, the other in my mouth, I was rewarded with the sweetest "oh," I'd ever heard in my life.

I drew her nipple into my mouth, rolling over it with my tongue, until she grabbed the back of my head, spearing her fingers into my hair.

Then I dropped to my knees and placed a chaste kiss to her belly button, then another to the lower part of her stomach. Her breath hitched, and I kissed her bare mound.

"Fuck, I want you," I murmured. "I'm so hard."

She moaned louder. I loved how she reacted when I got dirty with her. And I could get dirty all day long. I was a pro at it.

I ran my hand up her thighs, urging her legs apart, and glanced up as I took my first taste of her.

Her mouth dropped open, and her eyes widened. "Oh God," she whispered. "Banjo. We can't. What if someone comes in?"

"Then they can walk right back out, because you taste too good to stop."

And she did. Fuck me, nothing had ever tasted sweeter than having my tongue between Lacey Knight's creamy white thighs. I plowed my tongue between her pussy lips, finding her nub and teasing it until her legs shook.

"Get down here," I encouraged. The floor of the cave wasn't particularly comfortable, with only a thin layer of sand covering the rock, but I didn't think either of us cared in that moment. She sat, and for half a second, we just stared at each other.

"I'm not done with you," I warned her. I knew she didn't have much experience, and I was in my element when I was in control. "Sit back. Lean on your hands."

She did. Those gorgeous fucking tits pointed right at me, but I didn't let my gaze linger long. I pushed her knees apart and went right back to sucking her pussy.

Her fingers gripped my hair, pulling it, pushing me away, then dragging me back like she didn't know whether it was all too much or all too good.

I was about to make it so much better.

I shoved two fingers in my mouth, licking them free of sand and salt before I ran them over her center, coating them in her own arousal. And then nudged them inside her.

A full body shiver ran through her. Fuck, she was wet. So wet. I worked her clit with my tongue and let her grind down on my fingers.

Her hips rolled, and she found a rhythm that I matched, working her higher and higher. Her head dropped back, her hair, wet with salty sea water, fell loose down her back, and it was the most beautiful thing I'd ever seen. She was all laid out like some sort of siren. The way she took my fingers made me wish I had a condom. I wanted her to come around my cock. I wanted to feel her pulse and contract around me.

I could be patient.

But she couldn't. Not when she was this close to orgasm.

She reached up to pinch her own nipple, surprising me by the bold move. And then I wondered why. She might not have had much experience. But nothing about Lacey was timid. Hell, she'd gone eye to eye with Colt, and even I wouldn't want to do that. She'd taken Gillian's insults in stride.

I liked her all the more for it.

"Banjo," she moaned.

"I got you, princess. I know what you need." I picked up the pace. Pumping my fingers in and out of her, ignoring my cock that screamed to get in on the action. I sucked her clit again, over and over until she cried out.

"Oh God!"

Her cries echoed around us, bouncing off the walls.

Her pussy clamped down on my fingers, her body spasming with her orgasm. She moaned again, long and loud, and I worked her through it until her hips slowed and her moans became whimpers.

I found her mouth and kissed her. This time, it was slow and sweet, but damn, I so badly wanted to fuck her. She looked up at me through hazy, satisfied eyes. And then laughed.

It was infectious. I grinned back at her. "What?"

She shook her head, sitting up. "I can't believe I just let you do that. I wouldn't have even known if someone had walked in. I kept trying to look over your shoulder and be quiet so we'd hear if people were coming..."

"The only one coming around here was you."

"Smug much?"

I nodded. "Completely. But we should probably get back before the tide gets high or that wind picks up any more."

She stood, picking up her bikini, and I watched as she tied it back on, already planning how I could get it off her again. Maybe I could take her back to my house. Or we could go somewhere and make out in the back of the car. Or even better, in hers, with the top down, since she seemed to get off on public displays.

At the mouth of the cave, she nudged me with her elbow. "Guess what?"

"What?"

"I'm not the only one who has their thoughts written all over their face. And judging by yours, your mind is a dirty place to be." She grinned at me. She leaned in, brushing her lips over mine. "I like it." Then she dove into the water.

Fuck. Maybe she really was a siren. Because I followed her without another thought.

19

LACEY

hat the hell was I doing? That was all I could think of as I swam back to the beach with Banjo right beside me. Who the hell was that girl, brazen enough to let a guy take off her bikini and go down on her, when any number of people could walk in at any minute? That wasn't me. That was something Meredith would do. She'd die when I told her about this.

And when I told her about what I'd done with him during the week...not to mention what I'd done with Rafe...

Damn. Meredith was going to have a stroke. I'd have to make sure there was medical help nearby when I confessed.

But you couldn't keep the smile off my face. Life at Saint View High? Not so shabby. If I ignored all the drama with Gillian and Colt, that was. And their mildly threatening 'suggestions' to leave school.

Whatever.

We made it back to the beach and jogged from the water. I was surprised to find we'd lost almost two hours, between swimming and, well...other things. My stomach roared in protest.

"Whoa. Orgasms give you an appetite, huh?" Banjo joked, flopping down on the sand where we'd left our towels and bags.

I wrapped a towel around myself before sitting next to him. "Apparently. I'm starving."

"Good. Because I brought food."

"You did?" I was surprised. Banjo didn't seem like the type who thought very far ahead. Yet, when he unzipped his backpack, he pulled out sandwiches, drinks, fruit, and cookies. He'd even put in ice packs to keep everything cold. "You packed a picnic? How cute are you?"

He chuckled, the sound deep and delicious. Toe-curling. Just like everything he did. "Glad you think so. My brother gave me a hard time."

"I love it. Your brother obviously doesn't know how to win my heart."

Banjo went quiet. "Is that what I'm doing?"

A familiar voice calling me from down the beach saved me from having to answer Banjo's question. I thanked my lucky stars, because he'd caught me completely off guard, and I had absolutely no idea how to answer him. So instead of ignoring Meredith calling my name, I took the coward's way out and scrambled to my feet, brushing sand from the back of my towel.

Meredith stood just a few feet away, in a one-piece swimsuit that had so many cutouts it showed more skin than my bikini. Owen stood beside her, toned, tall, and handsome in a pair of swim trunks. I knew him from Edgely parties. He was a nice guy. Sweet. Charming. Not at all my type, or Meredith's, though the three of us hung out sometimes. He'd been good to me during my uncle's funeral, but I hadn't heard from him since. I hadn't thought anything of it. It wasn't uncommon for us to go weeks without talking. So I was a little surprised to see him with Meredith, but hey, maybe I'd missed something. I felt like I'd barely spoken to Meredith since I'd started at Saint View.

"Hey, you," I greeted. I gave Meredith a hug and then smiled at Owen. To my surprise, he stepped in for a hug, opening his arms and putting them around me. I hugged him back, a little awkwardly.

I motioned Banjo over. He stood slowly, gaze trained on Meredith and Owen as he strolled across the beach. His lazy gait said he didn't have a care in the world, but something seemed off to me. He had a sudden tension to his shoulders that hadn't been there a moment ago.

"Banjo, did you officially get to meet Meredith and Owen at the wake? I don't think you did, right? Meredith is my best friend."

Meredith leaned in and kissed his cheek. "Good to see you."

Owen stuck his hand out to Banjo. "Owen Waller," he introduced himself.

Banjo looked down at Owen's hand and then back up at his smiling face. I don't think I've ever seen someone move so slowly. He glanced at me, and only then did he take Owen's hand.

Owen eyebrows furrowed, and their handshake was as limp as a wet noodle. Banjo didn't even bother to give his name.

"What are you guys doing down here?" I asked, trying to break the odd tension between the two guys.

"Nothing much," Meredith replied. "Just felt like lapping up the last few days of warm weather. What about you two?"

Flashes of what Banjo and I had done in that cave danced behind my eyes.

Meredith's gaze trained on me like a laser beam.

I blushed. Dammit. She knew me too well. It was like she could see right inside my head.

"Okay." She laughed. "Apparently that's a conversation for later tonight. Call me? I haven't seen you all week."

"We missed you at Jamie's party last night," Owen added. He glanced over at Banjo, his face full of disdain. "I guess you had better things to do."

I frowned. "Not better. Just had a school thing I couldn't get out of."

Owen brightened a little at that. Banjo scowled.

Okay. The vibe between them was uncomfortable, and I wanted to send Owen on his way so I could have the real Banjo back. This growly, scowling version was kind of hot, but I liked it better when he was smiling and joking around. Not to mention kissing me and...well, kissing all parts of me. When Banjo slung his arm around my shoulders in a possessive manner, his gaze never leaving Owen's, I didn't stop him. He kissed the top of my head, and Meredith's eyes nearly popped out. But it was Owen's disgust that got to me. It was time to wrap this up.

"We're on our way out. I'll call you tonight, okay, Mer?"

"You'd better. Actually, we need to discuss your birthday, too. I have ideas."

"I bet you do," I groaned.

"Don't ruin my fun with your birthday-hating attitude, Lacey Knight. You are going to have the most amazing eigh-teenth birthday party anyone has ever seen. Second only to my own. Of course."

I snorted on a laugh. "Of course. I'll see you two later."

I gave Meredith another hug but sidestepped Owen, giving him a wave instead. I grabbed Banjo's hand and led him back to our stuff. Banjo knelt and started packing our stuff into his backpack, along with his wet towel, while I pulled my clothes back on.

"Your birthday is soon?" he asked.

"October fifth."

He glanced up. "No shit? So is mine."

"Birthday twins."

"Guess so." His smile didn't really meet his eyes, though.

I sighed. "Spill it. What's wrong? You look like you've been sucking lemons." *Instead of pussy*, I added silently in my head. Oh my God. What was wrong with me? I'd had a taste and now I had sex on the brain.

"Who's the guy?" Banjo asked.

I shrugged. "No one interesting. Just a guy I know from my old school."

"You went to a girls' school."

I squatted in the sand so we were eye height. "Did you think that meant I never had anything to do with boys at all? We went to lots of Edgely parties."

"Did you have a thing with him?"

I squinted. "A thing?"

"Did you kiss him? Let him touch you?"

I grinned. "The way you just touched me?" There I went again. But audience be damned, I leaned in and kissed him because he was cute when his eyes were glowing green. "Jealous much?"

"Yes," he grumped.

"You weren't jealous about me going out with Rafe last night."

"That's different. It's Rafe."

The tone in his voice caught my attention. "Did Rafe tell you what happened between us?"

He nodded.

"So you know we kissed? And you're okay with it? How

is that any different to me kissing Owen? Not that I did kiss Owen," I rushed to clarify. "I haven't. I'm not interested in him like that."

"I don't know. It just is. Rafe is...different." Banjo ran his hands through his hair and stared out at the ocean, deliberately not meeting my eyes.

"Can I ask you something?" I sat beside him again, nestling into his side. I was relieved when he relaxed a little and put his arm over my shoulders.

He glanced down at me. "I have an idea what you're going to ask, and I'm going to let you ask it. Because it's you. And something about you makes me want to tell you all my secrets."

"Do you like Rafe? As...you know. More than just a friend?"

He bit his lip, and I reached up, brushing my fingers over it. "Safe space, Banjo. No judgement zone."

His gaze flicked over my face, studying my expression, and for once, I was glad I was easy to read. It helped when you were trying to convince someone to share a secret.

"Yeah, sometimes I think I do. I don't know. I'm not gay. If I were, I'd just say it. I don't want you thinking you've been some sort of beard for me. Because dammit, Lacey, I'd go down on you all day long if you let me. And I'm so fucking attracted to you, I'd do you right here on this beach. Screw all these people."

"Sshh, I know. I know. But maybe you'd do that with Rafe, too?"

He snorted on a laugh. "I don't know. I haven't a clue how he'd feel about that. It's not something we've ever discussed. Maybe, whatever it is I feel sometimes when I'm around him is completely one-sided. But to answer your question, no, the idea of getting dirty with Rafe doesn't weird me out."

"It's kind of hot, actually," I admitted.

Banjo rounded on me, kissing me so hard he pushed me back in the sand. "You're perfect, you know that? I can't believe I just admitted all that to you and your only reaction was to say that it was hot."

"Want to know what it's like to kiss him? I could tell you," I teased.

Banjo groaned and pressed his body into mine. "How 'bout we just go back to my place and stop talking about Rafe? I'm sure there's better things our mouths could be doing."

He didn't need to tell me twice. I was up and out of the sand before he was.

LACEY

On Monday morning, I parked my car in the student lot, beside a familiar dark-green sedan. I hadn't heard from Banjo yesterday, and I'd found myself missing him. Which was ridiculous, considering how we'd spent all day Saturday together. We'd gone back to his place after the beach and made out some more, until it started getting dark, and I started worrying that Augie might walk in and bust us again. Banjo had asked me to stay over, but staying over would have inevitably led to sex. And despite how brazen we'd been at the beach, I didn't want to lose my virginity with salt and sand drying in my hair and a constant worry Augie would appear. Plus, Selina would have had kittens.

I'd been too chicken to call Banjo yesterday, even though I'd wanted to. But I didn't want to seem too eager either.

My 'play it cool' plan went out the window when I saw his car before school. I grabbed my books from the passenger seat and practically skipped to Banjo's car, hoping he was still inside, getting one last cigarette in before going into school.

The window rolled down as I approached. I bent over, huge smile pulling at my face. "Hey, handsome."

"Good morning to you, too, princess."

I jumped back.

Augie raised an eyebrow. "Not the brother you were hoping for, I guess, judging by that reaction."

Not even remotely the right brother. Something about Augie set off alarm bells in my head. And when he called me princess, it was nothing like when Banjo did it. Hell, it wasn't even like when Colt said it. When Augie called me princess, it was with barely concealed malice.

"Sorry," I muttered. "I figured Banjo borrowed your car."

"Not today. Just dropped him off since I had some errands to run here."

"Errands, meaning you had some drugs to sell to high school kids?"

Augie's eyes narrowed. "Why? Looking to score, princess?"

"No. Thank you." It was on the tip of my tongue to tell him to quit calling me that, but I knew it would only encourage him. I started to walk away but then I remembered something I needed to ask him. Reluctantly, I turned back.

"Banjo's birthday is coming up."

Augie pulled a cigarette from somewhere in the car and sparked his lighter before answering me. "Yeah. So?"

"It's his eighteenth. Are you planning anything?"

Augie let out a laugh that was laced with sarcasm. "Like what? High tea, with cupcakes and sandwiches cut into tiny triangles? Some sort of debut into society?"

I stared at him. "Like a party, asshole."

"Ooh, she's mouthy. In more ways than one."

Fuck him. "Forget it. I don't know why I bothered asking.

I was just trying to be polite since you're the only family he has. I'll take care of it myself."

I stormed away, grinding my teeth in unison with Augie's laughter.

"You do that. We all know what you're doing."

That stopped me in my tracks. Because as far as I knew, nobody but Meredith and Selina knew what I was doing here. "What the hell does that mean?"

"Slumming it with the poor kids. Ticking something off your bucket list, maybe. But then what? My dumb-ass brother is following you around like some pussy-whipped moron. And you're looking at him with come-get-me eyes. Maybe you think he's even falling for you. But I know him. Right now, he's probably thinking about how you're gonna save him from his miserable small-town life. How you'll be the one to pull him from this piece-of-shit town. Well, good. I hope he uses you to get as far as he can. Because we all know that as soon as you get tired of slumming it, you're going to go running straight back to Providence and those stuck-up pricks from Edgely Academy."

Anger burned in my gut, and my mind whirled, trying to make sense of everything Augie was saying. I tried to sort fact from fiction, but it all blurred into one, until tears pricked the backs of my eyes.

Augie's smile widened.

I wouldn't let him get to me. Without a word, I whirled on my heel and strode toward the school. Augie's laughter followed me.

"Bye bye for now, princess."

he black cloud of Augie's taunts hung over me all day. I was grateful Banjo and I didn't have any classes together apart from music, and I was seriously considering skipping it, just to avoid talking to him about what had happened that morning. I sat in the back of my history class, stabbing a pencil into my notebook while I contemplated Augie's comments.

The intercom crackled to life right in the middle of Mr. Sliden's blow-by-blow account of the Battle of the Somme.

"All football players will be required in the gym for the rest of the day. We'll be conducting a team briefing ahead of this weekend's game."

Beside me, Tate Masters high-fived another football player whose name I'd forgotten, though I recognized his face. Meredith and I had determined he'd been at the bonfire party and crossed him off the suspect list.

"All right, all right, settle down. I know we're all excited to see our boys play this weekend, but right now, we still have three minutes left of class..."

It was a losing battle. The class had erupted into excited chatter about this weekend's game, and the football team were already gathering their things, completely ignoring the teacher's pleas.

"Sorry, sir," Tate called as he sailed out the door. "Coach will have our hides if we're late."

Mr. Sliden just watched Tate go with a small shake of his head. The Untouchables were out in full force today, so it seemed.

Mr. Sliden gave up on his lesson and shooed the rest of us out the door as soon as the bell rang. Through the glass windows, the football team streamed toward the gym, and I decided that it wasn't worth risking a detention for skipping a class Banjo wouldn't be at anyway. Thank you, football.

So I followed the swarm of seniors to the cafeteria and joined the line. I scanned the crowd idly while I waited, my gaze jumping from one table to the next. I spotted Gillian, sitting with her minions. No sign of Colt, though.

"Looking for me?"

I stiffened. Speak of the devil, and he shall appear. Or in my case, think of him. I knew who it was instantly. And he was entirely too close. The back of my neck prickled with awareness, and if I hadn't already had my nose practically pressed against the T-shirt of the boy in front of me, I would have taken a large step forward.

"I don't particularly like looking at you, Colt. So no." I tried to make the words sound as bored as possible, but I heard the tiny wobble in my voice. Dammit! What was it about this guy that messed with my head? With anyone else, I was quick-witted and ready with a comeback. With him, my tongue felt too big for my mouth. And somehow, despite being a big guy, he always managed to catch me by surprise.

"Lies," he said quietly.

I didn't answer him.

"You're still here, princess. Over two weeks now. I give you credit. I didn't think you'd last one day with us here in the ghetto."

I whirled on him and leveled him with a glare. "Why? Because some asshole with a God complex said I don't belong? You think awfully highly of yourself, don't you? I saw your little Instagram post about me. You can tell your girlfriend I don't want whatever imaginary crown the two of you seem to think you have. You can keep it. But I'm not going anywhere. Not until I get what I came for."

I cringed internally as the words poured from my mouth like I'd turned on a faucet. Dammit, Lacey. Shut the hell up.

Colt cocked his head to one side, eyes narrowing. "And what exactly did you come here for? A little wrong-side-of-the-tracks cock? You sick of all your pretty boys and their fancy cars, flashing around their daddy's money? I can give you that."

I shoved him away. "You're disgusting."

He laughed, and my breath hitched at the sound. "Say it like you mean it."

I didn't say anything. For the life of me, I tried. But my mouth refused to form the words.

His grin turned devilish, and dammit if it didn't just make him all the more attractive. His intelligent eyes gleamed, like this little game of cat and mouse entertained him.

I spun back to face the line, startled to find it had progressed without me noticing. I stepped forward, but Colt wouldn't give me an inch. If anything, he moved in closer, until his front pressed against my back. I stilled. Every muscle in my body froze at his touch. Alarm bells went off in my head, and yet, the rest of my body wanted to melt into him like a Goddamn ice cream on a summer day.

His fingers swept the back of my neck, brushing my hair aside. Like they had a mind of their own, my eyes closed.

Behind me, he shifted so his lips brushed my ear. "I'll break you, princess. You and your ivory tower."

A shiver rolled down my spine. But it wasn't one of fear, despite the underlying threat in his words. No. Colt didn't scare me.

What scared me was the fact I wasn't scared at all. What scared me, was the fact his words did nothing but turn me on.

That was a bigger problem than Colt trying to run me out of school. That spoke volumes about how messed up my head was. This boy could threaten to break me, and all I wanted to do was find out how.

I needed air. And I couldn't get that with Colt so close, stealing my oxygen.

I stepped out of line and took one step back so Colt and I were side by side. "Thing is, Colt," I said quietly, my voice as deadly as his was. "You can try, but I'm not breakable."

I walked out of the cafeteria, knowing Colt's eyes watched every step. I hoped like hell I wasn't lying to myself, as well as to him.

LACEY

*S*omething slammed into me from behind, and I hurtled toward the bathroom door. I got my hands up just in time to protect myself from a broken nose. The door swung in, and I caught myself on a tiled wall, three girls crowding in behind me. The distinct click of the door being locked echoed in the silence.

Gillian stood at the front of her pack of she-wolves, quite the alpha, with her shoulders thrown back, her teeth bared. I was surprised there wasn't some sort of mangy dog drool dripping from the corner of her mouth. She certainly looked ready to tear me apart.

"How stupid are you, Lacey?" she snarled. "Truly, I really want to know."

I narrowed my eyes. "While I'm super grateful you're so concerned with my IQ, perhaps it should be yourself—and your minions—who you're worried about? After all, you're the ones who need to hold hands to go to the bathroom. If you'll excuse me..." I went to move past them and was shoved back against the wall. I sighed, like I was completely bored, while my mind ticked over how to get out of here without getting my ass handed to me. I'd never been in any sort of fight before, but I wasn't a wimp. I'd taken boxing classes at the gym once. It had never included more than choreographed kicking and punching routines on a bag. It had been a short-lived endeavor, with Meredith and I both admitting we hated it afterward. I'd never actually had to hit anyone. But I thought I could probably take Gillian, if I had to. I was taller and more solid than the tiny cheerleader. The problem here was Gillian wasn't alone. "Just say what you want to say, and let's be done with this? I've got things to do."

Gillian's face was so red she might explode. "I tried being nice to you."

I interrupted her to laugh. Then I stopped. "Oh. You're serious? You think that was being nice? Sweetie. Wow. No wonder you only have these two as friends." I was being catty, I knew it. And probably not helping the situation, but what else was I supposed to do? Stand here and cower to the self-proclaimed queen? Please. That wasn't my style.

"He doesn't want you. You know that, right? I saw you, just now, practically preening because he whispered a few words in your ear. You molded like a piece of freaking Play Doh. So if you have any self-respect, do yourself a favor and stay away from him. He's been mine since we were freshmen. We've got plans, and a life. We're getting out of here. Together. So you can try to get your claws in him. And hell, maybe he'll let you think you have. Maybe he'll let you think you've won. But just remember who he'll be with at the end of the day. And which of us he'll use, chew up, and spit out." She looked me up and down, hate and jealousy practically streaming out of her pores. "Watch your back, bitch."

I watched them go, standing there, against a grimy high school bathroom wall. And wondered how this had all gotten so messed up, so fast.

LACEY

I should have known something was wrong from the way heads turned the minute I walked into school on Thursday morning. But people whispering about me in the halls of Saint View High wasn't all that unusual. I foolishly determined that Colt and Gillian had put up something about me on Instagram, but when I pulled my phone from my pocket and brought up their account, there was nothing new. The last thing they'd posted was a loved up black-and-white of the two of them in bed.

It was puke-worthy.

I tucked my phone away, grateful at least that I seemed to have dropped off their radar after my moment with Colt in the cafeteria and subsequent showdown with Gillian. All had been quiet on the home front, which was almost worse. I'd spent the entire week walking around in a permanent state of semi-anxiety, wondering if Gillian was going to jump out and throw a punch at me. Or worse, if Colt was going to turn my insides to melted lava with just a single look. Goddamn him.

Instead, it was Jagger who popped out of the doors, tucking her arm into mine. Her hair was a magnificent shade of blue today, and I flicked a strand of it playfully.

"I like this. Suits you."

"Thanks!" she chirped too loudly. She gave me an over-enthusiastic smile.

"What's up with you? How many coffees have you had?"

She waved her hand around in the air. "Oh, who knows. What's your first class? I'll walk you there."

"Ugh, math. I need to stop at my locker first, though."

But Jagger tugged me toward the corridor that led to the math rooms. "Nah, you don't. Carrying all those books is good for upper body strength. You don't go to the gym, do you? So that's even more important for you."

I frowned, pulling my arm from hers. "Maybe so, but my math book is in my locker."

Jagger's smile fell. "Oh. Maybe Mrs. Wiley won't mind if you don't have your book? You could share Rafe's?"

I shoved my hands on my hips. "Or, we could just go to my locker and get it right now. But obviously you don't want me to do that, so how about you tell me why?"

My heart flickered in my chest. Maybe Banjo was decorating it? Guys did that for girls they liked, didn't they? I didn't really know since I'd gone to an all-girls' school before this. My eyes widened when I considered that it might be Rafe doing the decorating. But surely not. I'd kind of been avoiding both of them all week. Which had been easy to do because they were so tied up with football stuff that they'd barely been around. I'd missed them, though. Especially Banjo.

I picked up speed, with Jagger trailing me, biting at her nails. "Lacey, no. Stop."

But it was too late. The crowd seemed to part as I reached my locker.

I sucked in a breath.

It wasn't Banjo. It wasn't some heart-filled cheesy sentiment or decorations on my locker door. It wasn't Rafe either.

It was huge red letters that spelled out a single word.

Murderer.

Red spray paint dripped down the face of the locker while I stared at it in shock.

"What the fuck?" Banjo's angry voice came from behind me.

My fingers trembled.

Rafe's voice joined Banjo's, but it all faded into the crowd.

Murderer.

In a daze, I moved toward the locker and spun the combination. Sticky red paint coated my fingers, and I glanced at it absently, realizing it was the same color and consistency as blood.

The lock popped, and the door sprang open, only to let out an avalanche of papers. Jagger rushed to my side and then dropped to the floor to gather them. She gasped, then looked up at me, her eyes wide.

"What are they?" I asked numbly. They certainly hadn't been there when I'd put my things away yesterday. I closed my eyes. I almost didn't want to know. More threats? Because this had to be Gillian and Colt. Had they stooped to cut out letters from magazines, ransom note style?

She handed me the pile she'd made. "Who is that, Lacey?"

I choked when I focused on the top photo. Of all the things I could have imagined, this wasn't one of them. I leafed through each one, my eyes blurring with tears. "My uncle," I whispered. "They're photos of my uncle."

His headshot from the Providence School for Girls website. I recognized it instantly. But what clogged my throat was the words scrawled across his face in red sharpie.

Liar.

Cheat.

Rapist.

Breath stalled in my lungs. My legs buckled, and Jagger yelped as the floor came up to meet me. Strong arms caught me before I hit the floor, but it felt like crashing down onto cement anyway. Shouts and yells echoed through my ears. It was all I could do to hold on tight and bury my face in the chest of the boy carrying me away from the lies.

"Sssh," he murmured into my hair. "Hold on, Lacey."

I jerked in his arms.

It was the same words someone had said to me when they'd pulled me from the fire.

I stared up into Banjo's green eyes, filled with concern.

It's not him.

And that was all it took for me to erase Banjo from my list of suspects. A gut instinct that roared this wasn't the same. I looked past his shoulder, to Rafe and Jagger, following us. Jagger had her teeth biting so hard into her bottom lip I was surprised she wasn't bleeding. And Rafe's expression held nothing but barely concealed rage. He picked up speed, moving ahead of us to hold open a door, and then we were outside. Fresh air slapped me in the face. I sucked in deep lungfuls, letting it clear my brain and strengthen my frozen muscles.

"Beat it!" Banjo snapped at a handful of spectators in the little courtyard.

Their eyes widened, and they took off, leaving me, Jagger, Rafe, and Banjo alone in the courtyard.

I pushed against his chest. "Put me down."

For a moment, I thought he wasn't going to listen. A fierce protectiveness exuded from him. He seemed ready to argue that he should hold me from now until eternity.

I reached up and cupped the side of his face with one hand. "Banjo, I'm okay. Put me down."

His jaw was locked tight, but ever so slowly, he lowered my feet to the ground until I was standing. The four of us stood in a circle, the three of them staring at me.

"Really, I'm fine. That just…" A lump rose in my throat, and I shook my head when Jagger took a step toward me.

"Who would do that?" Jagger asked quietly.

I scoffed. "You really don't know who? Colt has had it out for me since the day I got here."

Banjo and Rafe both frowned at that.

"I don't know," Rafe said slowly. "It doesn't seem like his style. Gillian, though…"

"Why would they write that on your locker?" Jagger asked. "I thought your uncle died in the fire at Providence."

I shook my head, then looked each one in the eye. I hadn't trusted anyone but Meredith with the real details of my uncle's death. But facing these three now, I knew I could share my secrets with them. "The police haven't released all the details of my uncle's death to the public. He was stabbed first and left for dead. The fire at Providence wasn't an accident, like the media has been reporting. It was deliberately lit to cover up my uncle's murder."

Jagger clapped one hand over her mouth, her eyes going wide. Both boys swore low under their breaths.

"But they don't think you…?" Jagger gasped.

I shrugged. "I'm the only one they've been able to place

at the scene of the crime. They've been asking a lot of questions."

Rafe paced the length of the courtyard, his hand running through his hair. "How the fuck did Gillian and Colt know about this?"

I shrugged. "I'm more concerned in knowing why they wrote those things on the photo of my uncle."

"I can't believe them," Jagger muttered furiously. Her fingers balled into fists. "You should go to the police. This is slander."

"I know. And I will. I just...I just need a minute." My fingers still shook, and a rolling nausea in my gut refused to subside.

"I'll drive you home," Banjo said, linking his fingers through mine. His hands were warm. Comforting.

"Thank you, but I have my car. I'll be fine."

He shook his head. "You're trembling like a leaf. I'm not letting you drive yourself anywhere."

Rafe quit pacing. "Banjo can drive your car, and I'll follow in mine to bring him back. Okay?"

"No, no, you guys don't need to do that. You've got class and football stuff."

But Rafe was determined. "I hate feeling helpless. Let us do this."

Jagger stepped in and hugged me hard. "Let them help you, Lacey. They won't take no for an answer anyway. I'll take care of your locker. And when you come to school tomorrow, it will be like none of this even happened, okay?"

I sniffed into her shoulder and held her tight for a moment. "Thank you," I whispered. I glanced around at each of them. I hadn't expected to come here and make friends. But I realized in that moment, that aside from Meredith, I'd become closer with these three in a few short weeks than I had with any of the people I'd gone to school with for years.

And I wondered how, once all this was over, I'd leave them to go back to my real life. In that moment, I wasn't sure I wanted to.

COLT

I found Gillian laughing with a group of her friends outside the gym. She tossed her long dark hair off her shoulders, and ran her tongue over her lips. She was always doing stuff like that. Dropping her gaze and looking up at me through half-lidded eyes. Trailing her fingers up her side, gathering her skirt so it showed just more leg. Skipping up the stairs ahead of me so I'd get a flash of her panties.

Normally, I lapped it up. Last time she'd flashed her panties at me like that, I'd pulled her behind one of the buildings and taken them off her. After I'd fucked her, I'd pocketed them and let her walk around for the rest of the day in a short skirt with no underwear. Fuck, that had been hot.

But right now, after that scene in the hallway? Gillian's little pink tongue gliding over her gloss coated lips did absolutely nothing but fill me with annoyance.

"Hey, baby," she purred.

Her friends all turned, their eyes wide when they saw it was me. Gillian got off on that shit. That people got nervous around the two of us. Hell, maybe I did, too. I don't know. But it was the last thing on my mind right now. I grabbed Gillian's arm and towed her away without a word to her friends.

"Down boy!" she joked.

Her friends giggled, but as soon as I pulled her into the empty gym, and the door closed behind us, she dropped the act, wrenching her arm from my hand. "What the hell, Colt?"

I let her go, rounding on her instead. "What the fuck was that?" I spat out.

"What?" she asked, all big-eyed, fake innocence.

"Don't give me your bullshit acting. What the hell did you do to Lacey?"

A frown creased the space between her perfect dark eyebrows. "What I did? Don't you mean what *we* did?"

I gaped at her. "We? I just turned up to school. The first fucking thing I see is murderer painted across her locker and the girl hitting the floor in a dead faint."

Gillian rolled her eyes. "Right? So dramatic. And you think I'm an actress. Someone should hand the princess an Oscar for that performance."

I just stared at her. Her mouth was pressed into a hard line. It wasn't attractive. It morphed her features into something cruel. Something ugly. When had that happened? I'd fallen for her the first day of our freshman year. She'd been a fucking goddess, sunshine bouncing off her hair, those perfect legs eating up the quad and moving around the school with a confidence I sure didn't have as a gangly fourteen-year-old. And then she'd smiled at me, and it was like all my Christmases had come at once. I couldn't get enough of her. I'd chased her for months, and when she'd finally caved in, it was everything. Getting to hold her hand. Kiss her. Fuck her. Being with Gillian had catapulted me to the top of the food chain at Saint View High. And I'd loved it. I'd been a nobody in middle school. Always too tall. Too gangly. Musical instead of athletic. But all of that had changed in high school. And Gillian had played a huge part in it.

She cocked her head to one side. "Are you actually upset about this? It went according to plan. There's no way she'll be coming back to school now. Job done. Things can go back to normal."

"Plan? What plan are you even talking about?"

Gillian's eyes narrowed. "You're the one who keeps threatening to run her out of school!"

"Not like this. This isn't what I wanted."

Gillian's expression turned nasty. "You've got to be joking? *Now* you lose your balls? Why did you even put those photos in my bag if you didn't want me to use them?"

"What?" I snapped. "I didn't put any photos in your bag."

She shoved her hands on her hips. "Then who did? They didn't just magically appear there."

I thought that over for a second and then swore under my breath. The frown on Gillian's face smoothed over, and she pressed herself against me, peering up at me with those big blue eyes. "What does it even matter, anyway? She's gone. We both got what we wanted."

"And hurt someone in the process."

Gillian lifted one shoulder. "So? Why do you even care? It's just one dumb girl who thinks she rules the world because she has money."

I grabbed her chin. "I have a reason for not wanting her here. What's yours?"

Gillian's smile widened, but there was something distinctly snake-like about it. "You, of course. You don't think I see how she looks at you?"

That stopped me in my tracks. My grip on her chin loosened.

Gillian's laugh echoed around the silent gym. "Oh my God, you don't even see the way she stares at you, barely concealed lust in her eyes. Like she doesn't secretly hope you're going to throw her down on some cafeteria table and take her virginity right there in front of everyone."

I shook my head. "You're way off base there."

"Am I?" She pushed up onto her toes and brushed her lips across mine. "I don't think I am. And that bitch needs to know her place. This is my senior year. I'm not letting anyone ruin what I've built."

Her fingers found the button on my jeans and popped it open. Her gaze glued to mine, she dropped to her knees. "We're good together, baby. Nobody is going to ruin that. Especially not some uptight princess. You think she'd blow you in the school gym, in the middle of the day?"

Her lips wrapped around my dick, and I sank into her warm wet heat. Fuck. She was right. What did it matter how we got rid of Lacey? All I knew was that I couldn't be around her.

Not then. Not now. Not ever.

LACEY

*R*afe parked at the end of my driveway, engine idling, while Banjo drove my car into the garage. We both got out, and he walked to my side, pulling me into his arms in a tight hug. I held him close, pressing my face into his chest.

"Thank you for driving me home," I mumbled, but he seemed to understand.

He smoothed my hair back from my face and tilted it up to his.

"I hate that your sad eyes are back," he said softly. "I just want to make them go away again."

I smiled, but I knew it didn't reach my eyes. "Just kiss me," I whispered. "That helps."

His mouth brushed over mine, soft and sweet, and I had to fight back a sob and the urge to ask him to stay. Rafe was waiting, and I probably needed some time alone to work out my next move.

Banjo pulled away. "I'll see you tomorrow. But if you need to talk, I'm here. Call me. Night or day."

I kissed his cheek, waved to Rafe at the end of the drive,

and then let myself into the house. From outside, the roar of Rafe's engine came, and I was completely alone again, with just my thoughts for company.

Liar.

Cheat.

Rapist.

I gripped the banister to keep from falling back down the stairs. Anger burned through me, hot and feral. Gillian and Colt could say what they wanted about me. They could shun me. Turn the rest of the students against me. Make me a social outcast. It didn't matter. I had the friendship of the only three people in that school I cared about anyway, so that had backfired right in Colt's and Gillian's faces.

But they'd upped their game today.

It wasn't a game at all anymore.

I refused to let them slander my uncle just to get at me. He was a good man. The best man I'd known. Those things they'd written on his photos were bald-faced lies.

A tear rolled down my cheek.

"Lacey?"

My aunt's voice startled me, and I quickly brushed away my tears.

She descended the stairs, frowning at me. "What are you doing home? School hasn't finished yet."

"I wasn't feeling well," I said limply. "So I came home."

She put her hand to my forehead, and I couldn't help but smile. It was something she'd done to me regularly as a small child, whenever I'd complained of an upset stomach.

"You don't have a fever."

"I think I just need to lie down for a while."

Selina nodded and tucked her arm around mine, leading me back up the stairs toward my bedroom. "Sure, sweetheart."

I blew out a long breath. "I like him. A lot. We've been spending time together and—"

Selina held up a hand. "No, Lacey. It's not happening."

"What?"

Selina's face flushed. "We haven't even spoken about the little stunt you and that other boy from Saint View pulled last week."

I'd been waiting for this. I'd been out most of the weekend and had actively avoided Selina when I had been home. But I guessed there was no avoiding it any longer. "I'm sorry about that. But he was going through a tough time, and I was just trying to be there for a friend." Not that we'd really been friends when Rafe and I had taken off, but we had been by the end of it. Selina didn't need to know any of that.

"Well, his father didn't see it like that. And neither did I. It just looked like some irresponsible decision-making to me, which seems to be happening more and more since you started at that school. Your clothes for one thing."

I glanced down at my tiny skirt and top that showed a sliver of my belly. I'd paired it with my red Converse sneakers, and when I'd studied my reflection in the mirror this morning, I'd thought the outfit was cute. Totally Instagram worthy. But I knew how Selina was seeing me. I could see it written all over her face. It rankled.

"What about my clothes?" I asked, irritated.

"Do I really need to say it?"

I blinked. "Yeah, I guess you do." I never challenged Selina like this, but what I wore was my prerogative. And she didn't get to judge me on it.

She lifted one shoulder. "You look slutty, Lacey. Trashy. And that's not the way we raised you."

I ground my molars together. "Anything else?" I grit out.

Selina ran her hands over her thighs. "Your friend will have to have his own party another time. I'm sure he and your other Saint View friends would be more comfortable at something more low-key."

She wasn't wrong. Hell, I'd had the same thought. But the difference between Selina and I was I wanted to make sure everyone had a good time. She just wanted to make sure they weren't there. At all.

I pushed to my feet. "Are you saying that my friends can't come to my party?"

Selina turned away.

That only got my back up further. "You can't do that."

Her head snapped up. "I don't know who you are right now. You've never been so rude before."

"I'm not being rude! You're sitting there, judging my clothes. My friends. Selina, you're judging me!" Hot tears pricked the backs of my eyes. This was the woman who I thought loved me unconditionally. Right now, her love felt very conditional. That hurt, right down to the depths of my soul.

"I just want things to go back to the way they were," Selina said quietly, but there was a force in her tone that I hadn't heard before. "I don't want you seeing those boys. And I want you to enroll at Edgely for the remainder of the school year."

"No."

Selina shot to her feet. "You won't speak to me like that."

I stood a little taller. I might not have known them long, but Banjo, Rafe, and Jagger had my back today. Jagger was quickly cementing herself in best friend status, right alongside Meredith. While Rafe and Banjo...hell, I didn't know what I was doing with either of them. I liked Rafe. There was something magnetic between us that I wasn't done exploring. And Banjo...the thought of not seeing him again squeezed my heart painfully. They might be kids from the wrong side of the tracks, but that didn't mean they weren't worth standing up for.

"I don't want to fight, or disrespect you," I said softly to my aunt. "But I'm not a little girl anymore. And I have the right to make my own decisions. I hope you can understand that." I was done with his argument. There was no point discussing it further if she couldn't see my point of view and I couldn't see hers. I moved toward the bedroom door. "I'm going out. I need some air."

She let me go, and I was at the front door before she yelled out, "I mean it, Lacey. I won't allow it."

I dug my fingers into the doorknob, yanking the door open before twisting back to stare up at the woman I didn't even recognize right now. "Are you seriously forbidding me to see my friends?"

Her voice was cool, icy even. "If that's what it takes to get you back on track, then yes."

I just shook my head. And then walked out the door. There was nothing else to say.

LACEY

I drove aimlessly for hours until it started getting dark. Often, my vision got blurry with tears, and I pulled over on the side of the road, just sitting there until I was calm enough to drive again. I'd never had a fight with Selina. We'd never had a reason to argue before. I'd always been polite and respectful. Gotten good grades and kept myself out of trouble. In return, she'd always let me do pretty much anything I wanted. But apparently, having friends who didn't have a net worth in the millions was all it took for our house of cards to come tumbling down.

The entire argument had left me completely disillusioned. All I could think now was, did I even know the real Selina? My parents hadn't had money. I knew that. So did I disgust her as much as my new friends seemed to?

With my gas tank dangerously close to empty, I found myself driving around Saint View. I could have gone to Meredith's place and unloaded on her. She would have welcomed me with open arms. But it was Banjo's house I finally stopped at. Augie's car was missing from its spot on the driveway, and I hoped that meant he wasn't home. I wasn't ready to deal with him either. I still hadn't told Banjo about what he'd said. That had all disappeared into insignificance with everything that had happened since.

I glanced up at Colt's bedroom window in the attic of the house next door and jumped when his dark gaze met mine. My heart thumped behind my rib cage. He was so damn beautiful. I'd be lying if I said a part of me didn't want to walk straight up the stairs and let his black gaze devour me. Because that was the way all our interactions left me—feeling completely consumed. Even seething mad, there was always some sort of sexual undercurrent with him that was impossible to ignore.

But instead of giving in to it, I raised one fist into the air, pointing it in his direction, and ever so slowly, raised my middle finger, flipping him off.

I didn't believe Rafe or Banjo for a second when they said this morning's antics hadn't been Colt's style. Hadn't he threatened to break me, just twenty-four hours earlier? He might not have worked alone, but he knew what his bitch of a girlfriend was up to. I had no doubt in my mind that she'd gloated to him, and that they'd sat up there in that bedroom, laughing about how easy it had been to get rid of me.

But he had another think coming. They all did. Him. Gillian. Selina.

Without even waiting to see if Colt responded, I stormed up the path to Banjo's door and bashed my fist into it, praying he'd be home from football practice. Under the rafters of Banjo's roof, I couldn't see Colt anymore, but I'd swear I could feel his anger. I knew he didn't want me anywhere near his friends, and that only made me want Banjo more. Colt could go fuck himself. Everyone who thought they had the right to dictate my life, when I was mere days away from legally being an adult, could go fuck themselves.

Banjo opened the door. "Lacey! Hey..." His gaze darted to my car parked outside his house.

"Colt knows I'm here. I'd apologize, but frankly, I just don't care anymore. So tell me now if you do, and I'll go."

Banjo's gaze didn't falter for a second. Instead, he reached out, grabbed my arm, and dragged me inside, shutting the door behind me. And then I was in his arms, kissing him, melting against him, my anger ebbing away with every slide of his tongue, every touch of his fingers.

"Banjo! What are you doing down there?" Rafe hollered down the stairs.

I pulled out of Banjo's embrace. "Rafe is here?"

He nodded. "We're playing video games. I can get rid of him."

I cocked my head to one side. "It's fine. I'm down for video games, but can we play them while we drink? Because I seriously need to get drunk tonight. It's been a day."

Banjo wiped a tear from my cheek. I hadn't even realized it was there. "Sure we can. Go on up. I'll find something in Augie's stash."

I nodded gratefully and trudged upstairs, pushing open the door to Banjo's little bedroom.

Rafe did a double take at my appearance, but then his eyes narrowed, his gaze raking over my face. He abandoned his controller to the mattress and crossed the small gap between us. "What the fuck happened? Have you been crying all day? Is this about Colt and Gillian?"

I shook my head, but then another sob escaped my chest. I was so over crying but I couldn't seem to stop. The minute Rafe looked at me with kindness and care in his gaze, I dissolved once more.

"It's not them," I moaned miserably. "Well, it is, partially. But I had a huge fight with my aunt, and we never fight. She's the only family I have, and it just feels shitty right now. All of it." I choked out another sob, and Rafe pulled me into his arms, smoothing my hair back with one hand. "Hey, sssh. I've got you, okay?" He kissed my forehead, then glanced over my head. "And Banjo's got enough tequila for several rounds of alcohol poisoning. So that sounds fun, right?"

I snorted. Banjo didn't seem bothered by the fact I was in Rafe's arms. He just looked worried about me.

He held up a full bottle and three little shot glasses. "No lemon, but judging from the expression on your face, you aren't going to care."

He passed me the shot glasses, and I handed Rafe his. We held them while Banjo cracked open the bottle, then poured, the clear liquid sloshing over onto our fingers and dripping onto the carpet.

"Whoa," Rafe said, licking his fingers. "Don't be wasting good alcohol."

Banjo shook his head. "Plenty more where that came from. If Lacey wants to get drunk, we're getting drunk. Yeah?" He looked to Rafe who nodded, and they both turned to me.

I held my shot glass up. "Cheers to shitty days and the hot boys who rescue you from them."

Both guys grinned at that, and the three of us clinked out glasses together before downing them. I grimaced as the liquid burned my chest.

"No good?" Banjo asked.

"Too good." I held up my glass. "Let's go again."

We all took another shot. Pleasant warmth spread out through my limbs, and I wandered around Banjo's bedroom, studying all his possessions. I could feel the guys watching me, their video games apparently abandoned.

I spotted a little Bluetooth speaker on a chest of drawers. "Want to listen to some music?"

Banjo got up and found his phone. "What do you like?"

I shrugged, sitting beside Rafe on the bed. Our legs brushed. "Whatever you want. I'm not fussy."

I smiled as a familiar opening riff played through the speaker. I glanced up at Banjo and bit my lip. "'Sex on Fire'? Really, Banjo? You trying to tell me something?"

A slow, sly smile spread across his face. "Read into my song choice however you want."

Rafe chuckled, and I glanced over at him.

He lifted one shoulder. "Hey, I like this song, too. I'm not saying anything."

I shook my head in amusement. "Fine. Let's play video games then."

The two of them looked at each other.

"What?" I asked.

"Have you ever played before?"

I studied the console. "Uh, no. But you can teach me?"

Banjo sat back down next to me on the bed. "Or you could just tell us what happened with your aunt."

I sighed and stood. "Nope. I'm over it. I just want to get drunk with my friends and forget about Colt and Gillian and Selina and everything else that happened today."

Banjo leaned back on his hands, his gaze warming me all over. Or maybe that was the tequila. I didn't know, but either way, it was a pleasant sensation. It was nice to feel warm and safe, after a day of feeling cold and miserable. Banjo always had that effect on me. He truly was like a ray of sunshine, bottled up in a body made for sin.

"Is that what we are?" Banjo asked quietly. "Friends?"

I nodded. "Of course we are."

"What about us?" Rafe asked. "You and me? Friends, too?"

I glanced between the two of them. They were so different. Banjo with his shaggy blond hair and freckles from the sun. Rafe darker, more serious, but no less hot with his gorgeous eyes that sparkled with intelligence and wit.

"Sure," I said softly.

Rafe shot a look at Banjo. It made me remember the way Banjo had confessed to there being something extra between him and Rafe. Something neither of them had ever explored or even talked about. The way Rafe looked at Banjo in that second had me wondering if Banjo's feelings weren't completely one-sided.

"I've got an idea!" I said, a little too loudly. "Truth or dare."

Rafe groaned, but Banjo bounced on the bed like a puppy dog. "Come on, it'll be fun. I haven't done this since that time we played with Colt, and he dared me to jump off the roof."

Rafe shook his head, but his lips turned up at the corners adorably. "Don't you remember how bad that was? You fucked up your ankle, and Willa had to drive you to the hospital because she thought it was broken. Nothing good comes from this game."

I shrugged. "You've never played with me before."

Rafe's gaze clashed with mine, and something hot and heady passed between us.

"I'm in," he said, voice tight.

I scooted until I was sitting against the wall, legs tucked up beneath me. Banjo made himself comfy at the head of his bed, back leaning against the pillows, while Rafe edged so close to me our arms brushed.

"Truth or dare?" he asked.

I bit my lip. "Dare." My voice came out oddly breathy, like his nearness alone had the ability to physically affect me.

"I dare you to kiss Banjo.""

I raised one eyebrow, surprised. And maybe a little disappointed. Not about there being a kissing dare. I was playing with two teenage guys. Of course these dares were going to get sexual. Hell, I wanted them to. Otherwise, I wouldn't have started the game. Everyone knew party games like this were only played so you could make out with your secret crush. But he'd caught me off guard when he'd said to kiss Banjo, and not him. "You want to sit here and watch me make out with Banjo?"

He grabbed the tequila bottle and took a long, slow swig, his gaze never straying from mine. "To start."

Heat bloomed low in my belly. I wasn't entirely sure what he meant by that, but there was a hidden promise in his words that shot heat straight between my legs. If he meant what I thought he meant, then playing this game had been a very, very good idea. Or perhaps a very dangerous one. Only time would tell. But right now, with my core already throbbing, if felt right.

"Come here, Lacey," Banjo said, his voice deep.

A shiver rolled down my spine. He was lying back against the pillows, hands propped behind his head. I crawled across the bed, watching as his smile grew. It was infectious. And I loved kissing Banjo. I touched my lips to his and then went to pull back, knowing Rafe was watching. But Banjo's hand shot out lightning fast, pressing to the back of my head, holding me in place. His tongue coaxed my lips open, and before I truly realized what was happening, I was falling into the kiss, tugging him close, our lips moving together. We'd kissed a lot, he and I. It was familiar, but still exciting, and the longer it went on, the more I wished the two of us were alone.

When we eventually broke apart, we were both breathless. Banjo threw a smug, shit-eating grin in Rafe's direction. Rafe simply smiled into the bottle then took another swig.

Banjo sat up a little straighter, focusing on me. His gaze hovered on my lips. "Truth or dare, princess."

Truth would have been taking the coward's way out. Everybody knew that. "Dare."

"Kiss Rafe."

I raised an eyebrow. "Really? That's all you two got? You're just going to dare me to kiss each other? You both know I've already done that."

"And more," Banjo said with a laugh.

I shot him a look, but he didn't seem to care.

"Fine," I said to him. I turned in Rafe's direction. His icy-blue eyes watched me, and I suddenly felt like I couldn't breathe. Hadn't this been what I'd been waiting for? Over the last couple weeks, I felt like I'd gained permission to kiss Banjo whenever I wanted, at least if we were alone. But I didn't have that with Rafe. He still felt forbidden. But that didn't stop me from wanting him.

"Gotta stop staring at me like that, princess," Rafe said lazily, "Or someone is going to have to dare me to do a lot more than just kiss you."

I swallowed hard. I leaned in, letting my lips brush by his ear. "You don't need to be dared for that."

It was supposed to come out teasingly, almost a joke, but with a snap of his hand, Rafe dragged me across his lap and laid his mouth over mine. And God, it was good. I closed my eyes, snaked my fingers into his hair, and let his kiss rock me to my very core. Beneath me, his erection stirred, and that put a whole host of new ideas in my head.

When we finally pulled away, I glanced over at Banjo, feeling the tiniest bit guilty, even though he'd been the one to dare me. I expected to see jealousy in his eyes. But all I saw was heat.

"Well, fuck." He pulled a pack of cigarettes from the nightstand and lit one up, not even bothering to crack a window. On the exhale he murmured, "If you two are gonna kiss like that, then I need a smoke. And maybe a cold shower. That was hot."

A tiny laugh escaped me, and I sat back against the wall. "I can't believe I just did that."

"Why?" Rafe asked, motioning for Banjo to pass him a cigarette. "You're young and hot. You should be doing stuff like that all the time."

"Do you?" I asked.

"Make out with girls while my best friend watches? Hasn't happened before, but I'm not against it."

Interesting. I took another shot of tequila. It was really starting to course through my system now. Not only turning me on but loosening my lips. I wouldn't betray Banjo's confidence, no matter how drunk I was.

But that didn't mean I couldn't help things along a bit. I had two seriously hot guys in front of me. Two hot guys who were both a little drunk, and judging from the way they'd just kissed me, plenty horny.

"Rafe. Truth or dare?" I asked.

He took a drag on the cigarette and blew the smoke in my direction. "What do you think?"

"Dare."

"Fine, dare it is. Do your worst, princess." He was so full of arrogance. It was going to be fun to surprise him.

"I dare you to kiss Banjo."

Rafe coughed. "Say what?"

"Kiss Banjo," I repeated. But then I felt bad about pushing him into something he might not want to do. I didn't want that. I just wanted to see if under the guise of a dare, he might do something he'd been secretly thinking about for a while. "Or you can switch to truth," I added on, giving him an out.

He glanced at Banjo. And there it was again. That look. Something that screamed barely concealed attraction. I was sure of it.

He handed me the cigarette. "You good with this?" he asked Banjo.

Banjo grinned. "Are you? I'm a fucking excellent kisser, Rafe. You might just fall in love if you kiss me right now. Lacey can vouch for me."

Rafe shook his head. "Shut up, dickhead. Kiss me then. Blow my mind."

If I hadn't been trying to play it cool, I might have squealed with excitement.

Banjo sat up and shifted across the bed. The two of them stared at each other for a long moment, breaths becoming ragged.

I couldn't do anything but watch.

"Fuck it," Rafe murmured. He leaned in, lips locking with Banjo's.

Banjo was quick to respond. He grabbed Rafe's face and pushed him back until his head hit the wall. It was rougher, harder, all the softness they'd had with me gone out the window while they both tussled for control. They grappled with each other, a violent mess of lips and teeth and tongues.

But then something changed. They found a rhythm.

They went from fighting, to melding to the other. Moving in unison, both giving as much as they got. There was something beautiful about that kiss. Something that got me deep in the feels. Something that told me the two of them had been waiting to do this longer than either would admit.

Banjo groaned, sitting back. Rafe opened his eyes, and both of them turned to me.

"Did you get what you wanted out of that?" Rafe asked, his voice slightly hoarse.

I grinned at them. "Did you? Because that was the hottest kiss I've ever seen."

Something silent passed between them.

Rafe moved in first. "Time for a new game," he whispered, kissing me again with a determination that guided me to the middle of the bed.

Behind me, the mattress shifted, dipping beneath Banjo's weight as he maneuvered in behind me.

My breath quickened. "What game?"

Rafe shifted his mouth to my neck, kissing me there until my eyes fluttered closed and my head dropped back.

Banjo moved to the other side, placing a kiss below my ear. "One where we get you very naked."

My eyes flew open. "We? As in both of you? I can't... Banjo, I..." He knew I was a virgin. There was no way I was going to lose my virginity in a threesome. That was just too much.

But all I saw in Banjo's gaze was solid strength. Safety. Someone I trusted. Some of the butterflies in my belly disappeared.

"Rafe," he said.

Rafe glanced up from my neck, his gaze slightly unfocused.

"Third base," Banjo commanded. "Nothing more. Got it?"

He looked at me, then back to Banjo. "Even if she begs for it?"

Oh my God. I just about melted into a puddle.

Banjo chuckled behind me. "Especially then. Leave her something to dream about."

Oh, there would be no problems there. This was already something right out of a dream. A super-hot dream I never wanted to wake up from.

Rafe leaned in and kissed me again, while Banjo gathered up my hair, kissing the back of my neck and pushing my shirt aside to kiss his way down my shoulder. His fingers trailed down my back, eventually coming to rest at my sides.

"Gotta get you naked, baby," Banjo whispered in my ear. "Trust us. We won't go too far."

"I do," I whispered back.

"Good." Banjo lifted my shirt.

I wished I'd worn nicer underwear, but I hadn't exactly expected to be doing this when I left the house this morning.

Neither boy seemed to care. Rafe's gaze raked over my skin, my chest, my cleavage, before he tilted my mouth up to meet his again. His kisses were drugging, pulling me into him, making me feel more than I'd thought possible. It suddenly didn't seem like a big deal that I had two gorgeous guys kissing me. They were slowly stripping me of my clothes, vowing to make me feel good, but to also go at my pace. Why exactly had I been nervous? Stupid, when what they were promising seemed oh-so-delicious. And just a little bit wicked.

"Have you two done this before?" I asked.

Banjo's fingers rolled over my spine, unsnapping my bra

and drawing the straps off my shoulders. I shivered as he pushed it away, dropping it on the floor. Banjo trailed hot, wet kisses along my skin, while Rafe cupped my breasts, his palms grazing over my nipples. "Have we had a threesome before? That what you asking, princess? Or you asking if we're virgins, too?"

Banjo chuckled. "Definitely not a virgin here."

I shook my head. "I know you guys aren't virgins. Have you had a threesome before?"

Rafe nodded. Behind me, I thought Banjo might have as well.

"Just not together," he said, confirming my thoughts. "Or with other guys."

"Oh. You must think I'm ridiculous...still holding on to my V-card and all..."

Rafe leaned in and kissed me. "We don't think anything. I don't care what you are. Or what you aren't. Want to know a truth?"

I nodded.

"I just want to strip you naked and get between your thighs."

Heat flushed my face.

Banjo shifted to my side and laughed. "You made her blush. Talk dirty some more, she likes it."

"I do not," I protested, though I had no idea why, because we both knew I did.

"Yeah, you do. You love when I tell you exactly what I'm going to do to you. Lie back. Because now I'm gonna kiss you, so you can't squeal while Rafe takes off your panties."

Oh. My. God. The two of them were too much.

But then Banjo's lips were on mine, kissing me hard, pushing me back against the pillows, his fingers pinching and squeezing my nipples. I rubbed my thighs together to ease the sensation building between my legs.

Rafe lifted my skirt, settling it around my midsection, and I gasped as his fingers hooked in my panties, drawing them down my legs in exquisite slowness.

"Fuck, Lacey," he groaned. "You're so gorgeous. I love bare pussy."

I whimpered.

"Get your mouth on it then. Before I do," Banjo said, leaning down to take one of my nipples into his mouth.

But it was Rafe I watched. I had my head elevated on pillows, so I could see them both, but Rafe drew my attention. He watched me relentlessly, never looking away. Inch by inch, he slid down the bed and then placed kisses up and down my thighs. Each one inched closer to where I wanted him, and needy little noises escaped my throat. Like they had a life of their own, my knees fell apart, and Rafe's next kiss landed directly over my core.

"Oh," I moaned, my hips jerking up.

Rafe didn't waste any more time. His tongue plunged between my thighs, opening me up and giving me exactly what I wanted. He licked over my clit, massaging it before flicking lower, pushing its way inside me just a little. Over and over, he did that, while Banjo worked my nipples, and gave me deep kisses that had me yanking his hair, tugging him down, not wanting him to stop. Sensation roared through every limb, every muscle. Banjo at my mouth. Rafe between my thighs. If I'd been a guy, I would have been embarrassed at how quickly the two of them brought me to the edge of orgasm. But they licked and kissed me in tandem, their tongues relentless until I was quivering on the verge.

Rafe's fingers found my entrance and drove inside, filling

the aching void. That was all it took. Sensation coursed through my body, starting from my core and radiating out like bursts of sunbeams. My cries of pleasure were swallowed by Banjo's talented mouth. My thighs clenched as my internal walls clamped down on Rafe's fingers. My hips had a mind of their own, rolling in time with his movements, riding out the orgasm until all I saw was stars.

Rafe's fingers were replaced by soft, slow kisses to my sensitive flesh. Banjo moved back, and I blinked open hazy eyes, my body still floating on a cloud of bliss. Rafe crawled up my body and claimed my mouth. He tasted of my arousal, but I held him to me, kissing him hard, and he responded eagerly, his tongue plunging inside my mouth, owning it.

We moved away, and for a moment, the three of us just stared at each other.

Banjo shook his head and grinned at Rafe. "Didn't expect to be doing that tonight when I asked you to play video games, did you?"

Rafe's smile lit up those butterflies in my belly again.

Banjo stood and went to his drawers, riffled through them, and then tossed a T-shirt at me.

I caught it, then pouted at it. "We didn't...I mean, I did... but you guys..." Heat flushed my face. I didn't know how I'd ended up in this situation. I didn't have the experience to handle it. I sat up, pulling my knees to my chest, suddenly feeling completely exposed and vulnerable.

But Rafe twisted my chin so I had to face him. "Hey, wherever you just went in your head, stop it. Nothing else is happening tonight."

"But..."

"But nothing," Banjo said. "It's late. I'm already naturally gorgeous, but Rafe needs his beauty sleep. You staying, bro?"

Rafe nodded. "Too fucking drunk and horny to drive anywhere."

I bit back a smile. "I should go. Selina will be wondering where I am."

But Banjo shook his head and dropped a kiss onto my shoulder. "No way. You've been drinking, too. No one is driving. Put that shirt on. You're sleeping here."

Rafe lay back on the bed and patted the space next to him. "Lacey sandwich."

They were right. I wasn't ready to talk to Selina anyway. After tonight, I was more determined than ever that any birthday party I had would include all my friends. Especially Banjo and Rafe. If Selina couldn't accept that, then there'd be no party. I'd send her a text, saying I wasn't coming home and then turn my phone off. I didn't want another argument to kill the good mood I'd found here with the guys.

I opened up Banjo's shirt and lifted it over my head. The material was soft, almost to the point of being silky, and it dwarfed my body, covering up my nakedness. Something scratchy brushed over one still sensitive nipple, and I glanced down.

My vision blurred, my brain rejecting the image before I even really got to comprehend it.

SVHF.

Saint View High Football.

I stared up at Banjo, blood draining from my face.

LACEY

"You okay?" Banjo asked. "You look like you've seen a ghost."

I ran my fingers over the embroidered letters, trying to make sense of the swirl of questions this shirt had aroused in me. In all my weeks at school, I hadn't seen anyone wearing a shirt with the letters embroidered like that. This was it. The shirt I'd been searching for. Just not in the place I'd wanted to find it.

"This shirt," I started, voice shaky. I stared into Banjo's eyes and found nothing but the safe place he always offered me. It had been Banjo and me from day one. Despite my body screaming warning signals at me, my brain fought to make coherent sense. It couldn't be him. There was no way. He hadn't known my name before that day at my uncle's funeral. The man at the fire had called me Lacey. This shirt was just setting off emotions in me that made no logical sense.

I sucked in a deep breath. "I need to tell you something."

Banjo sat on the edge of the bed, and Rafe must have

noticed the tone in my voice, because he, too, focused his full attention on me.

"That night of the fire at my old school. The one that was set to cover up my uncle's murder. I was there, too. I got overwhelmed by the smoke and flames."

Despite my earlier gut feeling that neither of these guys was the one who had carried me out, I still watched them carefully, waiting for any sign that I'd made a mistake. But they both just sat quietly, waiting for me to finish. I relaxed a smidgen, believing again that neither of them knew anything.

"Someone carried me out. A man. And he was wearing one of these T-shirts."

Banjo shook his head. "What the hell, Lacey? You don't think it was me?"

I bit my lip. "I don't know what to think. I came to Saint View, only knowing that the letters on the man's shirt stood for Saint View High Football. So yes. I started off thinking it might have been you. It was the same night as the party on the beach. Neither of you went to that."

Rafe raised one eyebrow. "So we're top of your suspect list? Because we own football shirts and didn't go to some party?"

I sighed, wishing I could take another swig from the tequila bottle. Because when he put it like that, it did all sound insane. I fished the list from my purse and passed it to him. "I know. I'm sorry. You weren't the top of the list. You were just on it. But then I got to know you both better and I crossed you off. See? This shirt, it just threw me for a second. I know it's ridiculous. Any number of Saint View students or supporters could have that shirt."

Banjo frowned. "Actually, no. Only players wear these ones. There's no supporters' T-shirts like it."

"So..."

"So whoever killed your uncle is probably on the team," Rafe concluded.

"Fuck." Banjo swore. He took the list from Rafe and eyed it before handing it back to me. "But why?"

I shrugged. "That's what I've been trying to work out. I have no idea. I have no idea about anything. Why would he kill my uncle but then stick around long enough to save me, knowing I might be able to identify him?"

"You didn't see his face?"

I shook my head. "No, there was so much smoke, and I was really out of it. All I know is he was big. And fit enough to lift me from the floor. I was close to unconscious, so I would have been heavy and awkward. All I could focus on was the letters on his shirt."

Banjo flopped down on the bed and squinted at the ceiling. "Okay, this is all too much when I've still got tequila in my blood. I vote we sleep on this and talk about it some more tomorrow."

He snaked an arm around my waist and pulled me down between the two of them. I landed on my side, and Banjo immediately fitted himself to my back, while Rafe and I stared at each other.

I blinked in surprise. "You don't hate me? I lied to you."

"Everybody lies, princess. Some of us are just better at not getting caught."

I glanced at Rafe sharply.

But before I could ponder it too deeply, he ran his hand up my thigh, below the hem of Banjo's shirt, and grinned wickedly at me. "Lost your panties, huh?"

Suddenly, all thoughts of lies, fires, and having feelings for more than one boy flew right out of my head.

*T*he next morning, I woke up in a tangle of arms and legs, pressed between two half-naked boys who'd both somehow lost their shirts and jeans during the night. Everything came rushing back. Messing around with the two of them. Kissing them. Letting them take my clothes off. More than once. Banjo's shirt hadn't lasted long once we were all in bed together. Hands had wandered. Tongues had made me squeal. And still, I'd gotten nothing more than a feel of their chests. They were treating me with kid gloves, refusing to go any further until I was sober. I was pretty sure I'd sworn never to drink again, because even this morning, after two mind-blowing orgasms the night before, I wanted more. Of both of them. I couldn't choose one over the other, and so far, neither had even hinted at making me.

A buzzing noise caught my attention, and I untangled myself, finding Banjo's shirt and my skirt and pulling them on. For the life of me, I couldn't find my panties, but it didn't matter. I needed to go home before school anyway. There was no way I was rocking up at Saint View this morning, reeking of sex with yesterday's clothes on. Wouldn't that have been the scandal. Not that any scandal could possibly be bigger than what had happened yesterday with my locker.

"What are you doing?" Banjo mumbled, blinking blearily at his watch. "It's early. Come back to bed."

I tiptoed over, not wanting to wake Rafe, and kissed Banjo lightly on the lips. "I've got to go home and get changed for school. I'll see you there, okay?"

"Mmm, you better. I've got something to ask you."

I smiled softly. He was so cute. So sweet. He'd taken such good care of me last night, and in the cold, sober light of the morning, I appreciated that. It would have been easy to get carried away. To go all the way with the two of them, and though I'd thought I wanted that, I realized this morning I hadn't been ready for it. Not for both of them. The two of them together were fun, and hot and so damn sexy, but I wanted my first time to be special. I wanted real connection. Not just a good time.

"What do you want to ask me?" I smoothed his tousled hair back.

"I got a room for tonight. In Ridgeback, for after the game. Come watch me? Afterward, you can stay with me if you want."

My heart fluttered. "Just you and me?" I whispered.

He strained up and kissed me. "Just the two of us." He pulled my head down to deepen the kiss, and I was tempted to fall back into bed with him right now, school be damned.

But I couldn't give Colt and Gillian that satisfaction.

"If she's staying with you after the game, she rides there with me," Rafe said without opening his eyes.

I glanced at Banjo. He shrugged and just kissed me again.

"See you at school." Then he rolled over and was sound asleep before I even got to the doorway.

I tiptoed out, checking the hallway for signs of Augie, but it was clear, so I raced down the steps and let myself out the front door. I was relieved to see Augie's car was nowhere in sight, and when I chanced a glance up at Colt's bedroom window, it was empty. It was predawn, so that shouldn't be all that surprising, but I breathed a sigh of relief. Had he noticed my car had been there all night? Surely he had?

"Doesn't matter either way," I said to myself, opening the driver's-side door and tossing my things onto the passenger seat.

Rafe's words about how everyone lied floated back into my head. It was true. I was lying to myself right now, trying to pretend I didn't care whether Colt had noticed or not.

My cell buzzed from within my purse again, and I realized I still hadn't checked the earlier messages that had woken me. I fished the phone out and hit the home button.

"Shit," I whispered, scrolling through what felt like a hundred notifications. Most from Selina. I hadn't told her where I was. I'd meant to send her a text last night, and I'd completely spaced out...via orgasm.

I somehow doubted Selina would accept that as a valid excuse.

Oh, well, I supposed that solved the problem of the party. I'd likely be grounded for my eighteenth instead. Ugh.

The other handful of messages were from Meredith. Given as I was already on my way to face Selina, I hit the little green call button by Meredith's name.

"Where the hell have you been!" she yelled, her voice echoing through the speakers of my car.

I started the engine and pulled out of the driveway with one last look up at Colt's bedroom window.

"Settle down," I complained. "I've got a headache." Or more accurately, a hangover.

"Selina was blowing up my phone last night. And not just mine. My parents' phones, plus everybody from Providence and Edgely she could get a hold of. Nobody knew where you were. We all assumed you were dead in a gutter somewhere! I'll bet Selina had the cops put out a missing person report."

Already short-tempered from lack of sleep and a pounding headache, I had a short fuse. "And this is why we had an argument yesterday. Did anyone think to call any of my friends from Saint View? I don't exactly have a lot of them, so it wouldn't have taken any of you long to find me if you'd bothered."

"Excuse me?" Meredith snapped back in the same tone I'd used with her.

I sighed. I deserved that. She'd been worried, and I'd been bitchy. "Sorry," I said quietly. "You hit a nerve. I didn't mean to be a bitch."

Meredith blew out a breath. "Me neither. I was just worried. I did think to call Banjo, but I didn't know his number or his last name. And I couldn't remember your other friends' names. My bad."

I shook my head, steering through the streets of Saint View. It was quiet on the roads this morning. Nobody was out this early, and the sun was just rising over the beach-side road. I was tempted to stop and soak it in, but that would just be delaying the showdown I needed to have with Selina.

"No, it's my fault. I haven't made any effort to introduce you to them. The only reason you got to meet Banjo was by chance."

"I'd like to meet them," Meredith said, her voice quiet. "Not just because of how hot they sound, either. I miss you. I feel like they've been getting all your time lately."

Guilt swirled my insides. "I know. I'm sorry. I'm going out of town tonight for a football game, but I heard about a party at the beach tomorrow. Do you want to come?"

I changed lanes, taking the road out of Saint View and into Providence. The sun splashed early morning light over the houses that grew bigger with every passing mile.

"Can I bring some of the others? Everyone has been asking about you."

I hesitated for the briefest of moments, but I didn't want to upset Meredith by saying no, even though I wasn't sure it was a good idea. Judging by the way Banjo had been with Owen, I was worried the party would end in disaster. But I did miss Meredith. And it would be a good test. If there were any problems between my old friends and my new ones, we could hash it all out now, before my birthday. That was just smart.

"Okay, sure. I'll even pick you up. How about that?"

Meredith squealed happily, clapping her hands. "I need to go shopping. What does one wear to a Saint View party? Something with easy access?"

I choked on a laugh. "Planning on lowering your ridiculously high standards? You know no one in Saint View has a trust fund, right?"

"If the boys there are good enough for my best friend, then they're good enough for me. Will the football team be there? Maybe we can cross some more names off the list?"

"Yeah, about that. There's been some...developments. But I'll tell you about it on the way to the party tomorrow, okay?"

"Can't wait. Lace?"

"Yeah?"

"I miss you."

I parked the car in the driveway. "Miss you, too. But we'll rectify all that tomorrow, okay?"

"Deal. Tomorrow, we party Saint View style."

---

*S*elina rushed out of the house and into the garage before I'd even managed to turn the engine off. She was a blur of messy hair, satin nightgown, and oddly smudged makeup. She yanked open my car door.

"I'm sorry," I blurted out before she could start yelling.

"Truly. I meant to call, but I was angry, and I lost track of time, and then I fell asleep and—"

"Lacey, get out of that car."

I did. I closed the door behind me and leaned against it. Shit. She was mad. Super mad. I braced myself for the screaming.

She threw her arms around me and burst into tears. "Where have you been? I was so scared. I thought something had happened. That you'd been in a car accident, or worse." She shifted back to arm's length, shaking me slightly. "I was so worried! How could you do that? Right after we lost your uncle. You're all I have, Lacey. You hear me?"

I trembled. Emotion welled up inside me. I hadn't even thought about the fact she might have been truly worried. Or about the fact I was the only family she had. I was a troll. A horrible, ungrateful bitch. The truth of that wormed its way up my throat and lodged there, impossible to swallow. "I'm sorry," I gasped. It was impossible to control the burning behind my eyes. Tears spilled over, running down my cheeks. I made no move to dash them away.

But Selina reached out and did it for me. Then pulled me to her, crushing me with surprisingly strong arms, for how petite she was. "I'm sorry, too. I was awful yesterday. I don't know what came over me. Maybe it's these new anti-anxiety meds I'm on?" She laughed a little. "Can we blame that? Or hormones?"

I smiled through my tears. "Sure."

"What on earth are you wearing? Whose shirt is that?" Her nose wrinkled. Then her gaze landed on the emblem, and her eyes widened. "Is that a Saint View Football shirt?"

"Yes."

"You were with a football player last night? Rafe?"

I nodded.

Selina rubbed at the back of her hand absently. "Okay." She seemed to have difficultly forming the word. "Okay," she said again, more firmly, as if she was convincing herself more than me. She pasted on a smile. "That's okay."

I didn't want there to be any lies between us. "And Banjo."

Her eyes snapped up to meet mine. Her mouth formed a tiny O. "You were with...two football players? From Saint View?" she choked out.

The look on her face would have been hilarious if I hadn't also just really wanted her to accept I had friends at Saint View now. What our relationship was exactly, I didn't have to divulge. Hell, I didn't even know myself. But I wanted her to accept that neither Rafe, Banjo, Jagger, or anyone at Saint View were bad people, just because of their zip code.

"Two football players, from Saint View. Yes."

She nodded slowly, and then to my surprise, she took my hand and led me inside. "That's good," she said eventually, leading me over to the breakfast bar. "Because I wanted to show you something. Wait here."

I did as I was told while she ran upstairs and came back with a corkboard. She placed it down on the kitchen bench and said, "Ta-da," waving her hands over it, looking as pleased as a toddler presenting a painting to her parents.

"What is this?" I peered at the board. There was a floor plan, tacked to the center, and around it, she'd printed photos of all sorts of random things. Costumes, flowers, candles, food. "It's your birthday party," she said proudly.

I shook my head. "Selina, no. I don't want to argue about this again. I meant what I said yesterday. I don't want a party."

Selina grabbed my hand and squeezed it. "No, you said you didn't want a party without your new friends at Saint View. See all those black pins on the dance floor?" She pointed to a cluster of pushpins, piercing the center of the floor plan. "That's all your Providence and Edgely friends."

"And the green ones?" I asked, lightly tapping my finger to the green pins interspersed between the black ones.

"Are your Saint View classmates. Everybody mingling. All happy as clams."

She was missing the point entirely. "Sel, the Saint View kids aren't going to come into Providence, dressed in suits and ballgowns. It's too much."

Selina held up a hand. "That's why it will be a costume party! That will take money out of the equation. No one will be in designer dresses or suits."

I tilted my head. "That's not a bad idea."

"And I booked out Mojitos Beach Bar."

I glanced up in surprise. "The entire restaurant? That's..."

Selina frowned. "Too much?"

I shook my head. "Actually, it's kind of perfect. It's in Saint View, but it's a beautiful building, and the food is great. Nobody can deny that. Plus, they have that huge dance floor and space for a live band."

"Right? That's exactly what I thought. And it overlooks the beach." She squeezed my hand again. "Sweetie, I really am sorry about yesterday. The minute you walked out, I realized you were right. And I started planning all this. I booked the restaurant. Emailed your friends. I just wanted to show you that I understood and listened to what you were saying—"

"Wait, what? You emailed my friends? Who? How?" My computer had a password on it, one Selina had never asked for, though I would have given it to her without complaint. Besides that, even I didn't have the email addresses for more than a handful of people.

"Todd Simmons was very accommodating. He gave me his number during dinner the other week, and when I explained what I wanted to do, he emailed me over all the addresses for the senior class." She clapped her hands together excitedly. "I already got some RSVPs back."

"Selina, no," I whispered. "Isn't that against some sort of privacy laws? You didn't seriously invite the entire senior class? That's more than a hundred kids!" Most of whom I'd never even spoken to. This was not what I had in mind when I'd said I wanted to invite my friends. I'd meant Jagger, Rafe, and Banjo. That's it. Not the entire freaking grade.

Selina flapped her hands around. She was beginning to remind me of a seal. "Plus all your old Providence friends. Their email addresses were easy enough to get from your uncle's laptop. But you'll need to invite the boys from Edgely..." Her voice faded into background chatter, while I panicked over a party I'd never really wanted. The entire senior class, she'd said. Which meant Gillian.

And Colt.

Fuck.

GILLIAN

*M*arcie never had anything intelligent to say, even at the best of times, but today, her incessant chattering irritated me more than normal. I plastered on a fake smile and nodded occasionally, letting out a little laugh every now and then. But the entire time I had my eye on the school gates.

"Earth to Gillian? What's up with you this morning?"

"Hey?" I answered, dragging my attention back to the group.

"What's so interesting about the parking lot that you have to keep staring at it?"

I flicked my hair over my shoulder. "Just waiting for Colt."

Marcie let out a longing sigh. "You two are complete couple goals. You'll get prom queen and king for sure this year."

The other girls all nodded enthusiastically.

"Glad I'll have your vote."

Like it mattered. Sure, I wanted to be prom queen. Didn't everyone? But there were more pressing things on my mind this morning. And one of them had just pulled into the parking lot. "Gotta go, ladies. Colt's here."

I flounced away, strutting across the quad. Eyes turned as I went, just the way I liked it. Girls who wanted to be me. Guys who wanted to be with me. It was nothing new. And I was thoroughly bored of all of it. The only thing in my life I wasn't bored with was him.

"Hey, baby," I purred. I put my hands on his chest, and not for the first time, marveled at how cut he was. I knew exactly what he had beneath that shirt. Defined pecs. Mouthwatering abs. Biceps I could never drag my eye away from when he worked out in his backyard gym. He'd been a good-looking boy, following me around when we'd first started high school. But he'd grown into a man who drew the attention of women wherever he went. At first, it was just the odd woman, a waitress flirting with him while she took our order at a café. Or a random girl at school who had the balls to go up against me. But his response had been the same to each of them. Complete disinterest. For three years, Colt had worn blinkers around other girls. He only saw me.

Until her.

Colt's lips were unresponsive when I pressed up onto my toes and brushed my mouth over his. Normally, he would have grabbed me around the waist, pulled me tight, and put his lips to my neck. He'd whisper something dirty in my ear and drag me into a bathroom for a quickie before home-room. All of that was missing this morning. Kissing him had none of the usual spark. It was like kissing a store mannequin.

"How was your night?" he asked, voice cool. Uninterested.

I tried to ignore it. "Fine. I tried to call you." About a dozen times.

"Yeah, I know. Sorry. I had other things on my mind. I wouldn't have been good company."

I brushed off a demand to know what other things he had on his mind. After our argument yesterday, I had a feeling I wouldn't like the answer. I thought I'd smoothed that all over, but apparently not. Irritation prickled at me. I was his girlfriend. We'd been together for years, and hell, this whole 'run Lacey out of school' thing had been his idea. He was the one who kept saying she couldn't be here, though he refused to tell anyone why. I'd gone along with it because he'd said to.

Because I hated the way he looked at her.

Okay, mostly because of the way he looked at her. Something deep inside me taunted that he'd never focused on me like that. Not even when we'd first began dating.

It didn't matter. I had plans. And those plans included Colt. Not Lacey fucking Knight. Lacey Knight had the money to go and do whatever the hell she wanted after high school. I didn't have such luxuries.

"Was that slut the thing on your mind? Why you were too busy to answer your girlfriend's calls?"

He looked down at me sharply. "Jealousy doesn't suit you, Gillian."

I bristled. "You think it looks good on you either?"

"Who the hell would I be jealous of?"

If he'd asked me that a few weeks ago, I would have said no one. After all, as seniors, we were top of the food chain. But then the princess had showed up. "You were pretty green over Banjo carrying Lacey out of school yesterday."

Colt's eyes narrowed. "Perhaps I was green because I was sick over what you did to her."

Oh, fuck no. He wasn't going to pin this all on me. "I was just doing what you didn't have the balls to do," I hissed.

Colt shook his head. "I don't have time for your shit this morning. Come see me when you're not being a bitch."

"Me?" I screeched.

Colt shot me a look that clearly said I was making a scene. But I suddenly didn't care. He wasn't going to blow me off after everything I'd done for him yesterday.

Everything you did for yourself, a voice whispered in my head. I ignored it. Maybe it benefited me, too, but Colt was the one who'd started the war. I was just a soldier in it.

Colt started to walk away.

Both of us stopped as an engine revved, and Lacey's red sports car pulled into the school lot.

"You've got to be kidding me. She is not seriously going to show her face here today?"

A tiny smile pulled at Colt's lips. "Guess she is."

Anger boiled in my blood. "She's going to be a social pariah. Wait until I tell everyone she invited me to her birthday party. What a loser."

He dragged his eyes away from Lacey climbing out of her car. "I got one, too."

I rolled my eyes. "How tacky. I don't know what she's trying to prove there. Maybe we should throw a party the same night? Completely whitewash her."

Lacey strode up the path. She'd paired a tiny pair of shorts that showed off her legs, with a long-sleeved T-shirt and big hoop earrings. She held her head high, staring Colt down. There wasn't a trace of the mess she'd been yesterday. Without even consciously thinking about it, I stepped up to Colt, putting my arm through his possessively.

"Lacey," he called.

She stopped abruptly, as if he'd surprised her, even though they'd been staring right at each other.

But then her expression hardened. "Not in the mood, Colt. Take your shit elsewhere."

"I'd love to come to your party," he called back, as if she hadn't spoken.

I gaped at him. "Excuse me?"

Lacey's expression was probably a mirror of my own. She looked just as confused as I was.

"I said, I'd love to go to her birthday party. I'm sure Gillian would, too, wouldn't you?"

"No," I said bluntly.

He shrugged. "Your loss."

Lacey's eyes narrowed. "I didn't send that invitation. That was my aunt's misguided attempt at surprising me. Just consider yourselves uninvited."

"Suits me," I quipped. "I wouldn't have come anyway."

But Colt shook his head. "Nope, I've got an invite. I'm going. If you two don't like it, not my problem."

He untangled his arm from mine and without a good-bye, headed in the direction of his homeroom, leaving me and Lacey staring after him.

A mixture of hurt, embarrassment, and anger, not to mention the need to save face, had me turning on Lacey. "I don't know what you're playing at, but it won't work."

Lacey rolled her eyes. "I meant it. My aunt invited the entire senior class. It's not some ploy to steal your boyfriend. Come. Don't come. I honestly don't care. I just want to have a good time with my friends. You know what those are, don't you? People who actually genuinely like you?" She glanced in the direction Colt had walked off in. Then said snidely. "Or perhaps you don't."

Her words cut straight through me. They were too close to the truth. I had no real female friends. Sure, I had acquaintances, like Marcie and the other cheerleaders. But could I call them up in the middle of the night if I was stranded somewhere? Would they even answer? I somehow doubted it. And I couldn't blame them, because would I get out of bed for them?

No.

Colt was all I had, but now even he seemed to be slipping away. I'd felt the gap between us widening, and yet I was powerless to do anything about it. Yesterday should have brought us closer. He'd left those photos in my bag. I'd thought I was doing what he wanted, and yet it had somehow turned into this. Him walking off, and Lacey Knight smirking at me like she'd won.

I spun on my heel. She might have won this battle, but she wouldn't win the war. If Colt was the prize, I'd fight to the very end.

LACEY

*T*he drive to Ridgeview after school took almost two hours, but being in a confined space with Rafe made the time go all too fast. He'd picked me up from the end of my driveway, and I'd jumped in his car before Selina could notice he wasn't Jagger. We might have made up that morning, and the party might be full steam ahead, but I doubted she would have been happy about me spending the night with Banjo. It was probably too soon to push that button. Plus, I was a mess of nerves about the whole thing, I didn't need anything else to worry about. I was excited to watch the guys play football. I'd been to a few Edgely games, but since I had no interest in any of the guys there, I'd barely paid attention. Instead, I'd listened to Meredith's gossip and drank the booze she'd snuck in. But tonight, I was anxiously excited about what was to come after the game. Spending the night alone with Banjo had my palms sweating with anticipation. I'd stopped at a pharmacy and grabbed a packet of condoms on my way home from school, wanting to be prepared. And I was wearing my nicest underwear set.

I jiggled my leg impatiently, finding it difficult to concentrate. Rafe kept shooting little glances at me, and eventually, he reached over and put his hand on my thigh. "Stop. You're making the whole car shake."

His fingers were warm on my skin and I liked it. It was somehow grounding, yet at the same time, I wished his hands were a little higher. I'd been thinking about sex all day and was horny as hell. It didn't help I was now in a confined space with a guy I was super attracted to. Just the memory of what he'd done to me last night made me press my thighs together.

"What are you so worked up about? It's just a game. You're like a ball of nervous energy."

I shook my head. "I'm fine."

He glanced over at me. "You're worried about tonight? With Banjo? I'm driving home after the game. You can always come with me."

"It's not that. I want to stay with him."

"You going to give up that V-card?"

It could have so easily sounded like a prying question. Or it could have been laced with jealousy, especially after last night. But from him, it was just a question.

"I want to. I like him. A lot."

Rafe squeezed my leg. "He likes you, too."

"He said that?"

"Doesn't need to. I know him."

I let out a breath I hadn't realized I'd been holding. Then studied his profile. He wasn't wearing his glasses today, switching them out for contacts, ready for the game. He looked different but no less handsome.

"I can't stop thinking about last night," I admitted out of the blue.

He grinned at me. "Me neither, babe."

"Is it weird then? That I'm sitting here in a car with you, talking about having sex with someone else?"

Yes, I answered my own question. It was totally weird.

But Rafe just shrugged. "Not weird for me. We aren't there yet, you and I. We had some fun last night, but if you'll recall, we stopped because it didn't feel right to go further. Not for your first time. Not saying I won't be getting hard tonight, thinking about you and B, getting down and dirty, but I know he'll take care of you. Our time will come."

A shiver rolled through me at the promise in his words. I reached over and stroked my fingers down the back of his neck. "You're kind of amazing, you know that?"

"That's what you said last night, too." He wiggled his eyebrows playfully, but then he groaned. "We need to stop talking about last night. I can't play with a hard-on."

I glanced down at his lap and, sure enough, his erection strained against the loose material of his shorts. I trailed my finger from the back of his neck, over his shoulder, and then dropped my hand to his thigh. I walked my fingers toward the bulge beneath his shorts.

"Lacey..." he warned.

"What?" I asked, all fake innocence. I rubbed my hand over him. He was hard as a rock. "That looks painful."

"It is." He laughed. "And you aren't helping."

I glanced around. The highway was two lanes, but it was fairly empty. Just a few cars ahead of us, and a quick glance in the side mirrors told me there was one car, way behind. I moved my fingers to the waistband of his sports shorts and reached inside, pulling the end of the drawstring that held the silky material over his hips. "You've got good concentration, right?" I teased. I slid my hand lower. "You can still drive, if I want to do this?"

I snuck my fingers beneath the elastic and ran my palm

down the lower part of his abs. Smooth, tight muscle contracted beneath my fingertips.

He fought back a grin. "Whatcha gonna do now, princess? Feeling bold?"

So bold. And so turned on. I circled my fingers around the base of his cock, battling his shorts and underwear with my other hand. "Lift up," I urged, and he did. I tugged his clothes down his legs, him helping things with one hand, the other on the wheel. His cock jutted out. Thick and hard.

I sucked in a breath.

"Like what you see, princess?"

I nodded. I ran my hand over his erection, stroking the soft velvet of skin over stone. I kept an eye on his driving, but he seemed to be doing okay, keeping his eyes on the road, even while I worked him.

The road was straight. No one was around. And Rafe had done so much more to me last night. I desperately wanted to repay the favor. And to see him unravel. He was so cool and calm. But there was something I could do that would change that.

I leaned over, ducking my head beneath his arm, and wrapped my lips around his erection.

"Oh fuck." He dropped one had to the back of my head. The other gripped the wheel so tight his knuckles cracked. I ran my tongue up his length, popping him out of my mouth at the top.

"You okay?" I asked.

"So okay," he groaned. "Don't stop. I won't kill us. Swear."

I laughed, but my head was still in his lap, and I wanted to get him back in my mouth. I pressed down over him again, taking him as far as I could before sliding back up. Rafe kept the pressure on the back of my head light, but the longer I sucked him, the more his hips shifted. Each time, I took him a little deeper.

"Hell, Lacey. You're killing me."

"Concentrate," I murmured between slides of my tongue.

I gripped his dick and used my mouth and hand in tandem, picking up the pace. A throb started up at my core. This was all sorts of wrong, and yet I loved it. I almost wanted another car to drive past us and see what we were doing. Hell, I almost wanted to tell him to pull over so I could ride him on the side of the road. Anything to get a bit of relief for the ache between my legs. But I didn't. Despite the arousal curling through every cell of my body, I wanted this to be about him. The way it had been about me last night.

Rafe's fingers twisted in my hair and pulled ever so slightly. Just enough to feel good rather than painful, and I moaned around his cock.

"Fuck, baby. I need to come."

Moisture beaded at the top of his dick, and I rolled my tongue over it, taking him deep again. His thighs clenched.

"Lacey!" he yelled.

His cock kicked, spurting hot liquid down the back of my throat. It took me by surprise, but I swallowed hard, wanting to finish what I'd started. And wanting to hear him call my name like that, over and over, because it was the sexiest thing ever. I kept licking and sucking, swallowing him down, while he ran his fingers through my hair, called me baby, and told me how amazing I was.

Eventually, I moved away, and our gazes clashed for the briefest of moments. "Was it okay?" I asked, though I had a good idea it was.

Rafe laughed, then twisted his head to me. "Are you

kidding? You sucked me off while I was driving to a football game. This is the best day ever. Best blow job ever. You're fucking amazing. Kiss me. Quick."

I grinned and leaned in, planting my lips on his before he pulled away to concentrate on the road. "Glad you liked it."

"I liked it a lot," he said, tugging his shorts back up. "And you finished, or rather, I finished, just in time, because we're here."

I hadn't been through Ridgeback often. It looked like a similar sort of place to Saint View. Perhaps a tiny bit on the more affluent side, if the cars around us in the parking lot were anything to go by. It was already filling up, mostly with Ridgeback supporters, wearing maroon and gold. Groups of teens and families were lining up early to get the best seats. Rafe grabbed his gear from the trunk and locked up before coming around to my side. He dropped his bag at my feet. We faced each other, secretive little smiles playing across our lips. He stepped in, pinning me against the car. Too close to be just friendly.

"I heard your coach on the intercom today. He said he'd sideline anyone who was late," I whispered, glancing over at the line of people, wondering if any of them were from Saint View.

He shrugged. "Coach also said we couldn't have sex before a game... I apparently don't follow rules well."

I laughed. "We didn't have sex."

"Only barely." He leaned in and brushed his lips over mine.

I pushed him away. "Go, or you'll get sidelined. I came to watch you play."

"You came to have sex with Banjo," he drawled, but he did it with a grin.

I slapped him on the arm, then he trotted off toward the players entrance. He blew me a kiss from the entranceway, then disappeared inside.

I bit my lip, unable to wipe the grin from my face. I waited until he was out of sight, then headed for the spectators' line. My phone buzzed, and I got it out, skimming the text from Jagger that let me know where to meet her.

The door on the nearest car swung open, and I dug my heels into the gravel to stop myself from running smack into it. "Hey! Watch—"

Gillian stepped out of the car, fully dressed in her cheerleader's uniform, hair brushed into a high ponytail. The rest of the doors opened, other cheerleaders spilling out. Shit. I hadn't realized we had an audience. Maybe she hadn't noticed.

"Slumming it with Rafe Simmons, huh, princess? Guess you aren't better than the rest of us after all."

She shut the car door, the slam making me jump. She clucked her tongue and walked away, her minions following her.

Great. Whether we wanted to or not, Rafe and I had just outed ourselves.

29

LACEY

*A*t halftime, Jagger made her way back through the crowd, plonked down beside me, and passed me my popcorn and drink. She took a long swallow of her soda before she spoke. "Sorry I was so long. The line was epic."

"No problem. I'm not that hungry, anyway." I was too nervous to eat. I'd played it cool during the game, cheering for our team as a whole, but not Banjo or Rafe individually. It wasn't as if I was anyone's girlfriend. Calling out their names would only draw attention to myself. We were winning by a mile, so cheering was really just a distraction from the fact the game was half done, and I was mere hours away from being alone in a hotel room with a very delicious boy.

"I heard something interesting in the line," Jagger said, her voice full of fake nonchalance.

Even still, I played dumb. "Oh?" I shoved a bunch of popcorn in my mouth and watched the cheerleaders prancing around on the football field.

"Mmm," Jagger said.

Her gaze was burning the entire left side of my body. I was sure I was blushing.

"Apparently you and Rafe were making out in the parking lot."

Well, shit. News certainly traveled fast, didn't it? I twisted to face her, letting out a long sigh. "Are you mad?"

She raised one eyebrow. "Why would I be mad?"

"Because he's your ex? Most girls would be mad. I probably would be."

"Nuh. Not me. Not when it's Rafe. And you. I love you both. And don't forget, I broke up with him. I just want him to be happy. But, I want you to be happy, too. Do you know what you're getting in for with him?"

I shrugged. "I'm not really in anything. We aren't a couple."

"Then what are you?"

A guy and a girl with an incredible attraction? Friends who go down on each other? Hell, I couldn't say that. "I don't know," I said truthfully. "Casual. I guess."

"You sleep with him?"

"No."

"But you want to?"

There was no point lying about it. "Yes."

She nodded. "Okay then."

"That's it?"

"We can compare notes afterward, if you want?"

I dissolved into giggles. "Maybe not."

"Didn't think so. Oh, look, second half is starting. Go Saints!"

I echoed her war cries until the end-of-game buzzer sounded, and all the Saints crew jumped to their feet, clapping and stamping as our guys ran from the field. Banjo and Rafe both pulled their helmets off, fist pumping the air with the other guys. Seemingly in unison, they both looked to me. I ducked my head before Jagger could catch on. I liked Jagger a lot. And I trusted her. But I didn't know how to explain what was going on with Banjo, Rafe, and me. So until I did have a label for it, until one became more serious than the other, it seemed like a good idea to keep the entire thing on the downlow. We tramped down from the bleachers, shoulder to shoulder with hundreds of other fans. It was cold tonight, and I was glad I'd brought a jacket and scarf. The wind was picking up, and I was grateful to have the extra layers.

Jagger and I stood by the players' entrance with a smaller crowd of people who waited for the them to get changed. Aaron, the guy Jagger had been dancing with at the party, was the first one out. He trotted straight over to us, his gaze plastered to my friend.

She squealed and threw her arms around him. "You were so good! One win down!"

"Many more to go. Hey, Lacey." He smiled warmly at me.

I waved back. I liked the two of them together. Jagger hadn't said much about him but judging from the way she snuggled into his side, his thick arm resting around her shoulders, they'd been hanging out. Pure happiness radiated from her.

"You need a lift home?" she asked.

I gave her a hug. "No, I'll let you two be alone. See you at the beach party tomorrow?"

"Yes! Can't wait!"

"Me neither.

I watched the two of them walk across the parking lot to Aaron's car and waved as they joined the swarm leaving the fields.

"Bye, Lacey," a deep voice said in my ear.

Rafe. He was freshly showered, his hair still wet and slicked back. Banjo stood just behind him. There was a promise and anticipation in his eyes, a raw hunger that curled my toes.

I dragged my gaze back to Rafe's. A tiny bit of me was disappointed he wasn't coming back to the hotel with us. But like he'd said earlier, our time would come. And I couldn't wait.

"Bye," I said. I stepped in and wrapped my arms around him in what was supposed to be a goodbye hug. But somehow it went on for an indecently long time and ended with him groaning as he pulled away.

He tossed a look back over his shoulder at Banjo. "Be good to our girl."

My heart thumped. Our girl. Was that what I was? Warmth kindled inside me when Banjo nodded.

Banjo and I walked toward Augie's car, anticipation thick between us. I glanced into the back seat as I got in, remembering what we'd done last time we were on it.

We closed the doors, letting the electricity build around us in the silence. My heart raced.

"Damn, I want to pounce on you so bad right now. I'm so tempted to say screw the hotel and just throw you into that back seat." He grinned over at me. "But I want to do this right. And there's something I need to talk to you about first."

A tendril of worry curled around my heart as his expression went serious.

"Okay." I pulled my bag onto my lap. It was really just an oversized purse, but it had been big enough to shove in some extra clothes, my phone charger, and, of course, the little packet of condoms I was suddenly unsure I needed. "Is everything okay?" Had Rafe told him what I'd done on the drive there? Did that mean Banjo had changed his mind about the two of us? I would be crushed if it did.

He reached over and put his warm hand to the back of my neck. "Between you and me? Yeah, babe. We're great. But after what you told us last night about your uncle and the fire, I did some digging."

My fingers strangled the straps of my purse. "And you found something?"

"I checked out the last four guys on your list. Three easily told me where they were that night. Marco was visiting his grandmother at a nursing home, and I called and asked for the sign-in record. He checks out.

"Perry and Lucian were away together dirt biking for the weekend. Their families are old friends, and his sister confirmed it when I asked her at school today."

I frowned. "The only other person on the list was Aaron. But there's no way it could have been him."

"What makes you say that?" Banjo slowed for a traffic light. "He's a big guy. He could easily have lifted you off that floor and got you out."

That was true. But... "He's with Jagger."

Banjo made a noncommittal sound in the back of his throat. The light went green, and he put his foot down on the gas.

"You don't seriously think it could have been him?"

Banjo shrugged. "I'm not going to rule him out because he's dating your friend."

I sighed. "I really kind of wish I hadn't started any of this, you know?" I let my head drop back against the head-rest. "It's draining. And a constant source of anxiety."

Banjo's fingers rubbed into the tight muscles of my neck. "Did you tell your aunt about the photos?"

"God, no. She'd be devastated. She couldn't take something like that."

Banjo bit his lip like he wanted to say more.

"What?" I asked.

"The things that were written on those photos..."

Liar. Cheat. Rapist.

"Were blatant lies," I snapped.

"Are you sure?"

My mouth dropped open, and I shifted away from his touch. "Of course I'm sure. My uncle was a good man. He took me in when my parents disappeared. He was well respected. Well liked. You didn't know him, Banjo! He was the kind of guy who would give a homeless person his shoes."

Banjo pulled the car up in front of the hotel, shut off the engine, then twisted in his seat. He grabbed my hand, and reluctantly, I let him. This was not how I'd envisioned this night going. We were supposed to be making out right now. Falling all over each other on the way up to our room.

"Please, Lacey. Listen to me. I believe you. I really do. I didn't know your uncle at all. But I do know something about people not always being what they seem. Everyone has secrets. Some darker than others. And most of the time, the people who love them most are the last to know."

He looked away, staring out through the windshield. A muscled ticked in his jaw.

"Are we still talking about my uncle?" I asked quietly.

He forced his gaze back to mine. "Just food for thought." He leaned in and kissed me softly. "Is this really what we want to be talking about tonight?"

It was a blatant attempt to change the subject, but I let him. If he hadn't, I would have. I didn't want to consider that my uncle, a man I'd loved, who'd always been there for me, could be anything other than what he seemed on the outside.

So instead of questioning Banjo about what he was hiding, I kissed him back. And then I followed him into a hotel.

The inside was nothing fancy. The bored receptionist thrust a key into Banjo's hand, pointing toward a set of stairs that led to the second floor. The walls were an ugly salmon pink, though the paint was fresh, and occasional potted ferns spruced up the otherwise dull hallway. There were no electronic locks on the doors like every other hotel I'd ever stayed in. This one still used a traditional brass key that only turned after Banjo jiggled it around. He opened the door, and we wandered in, taking in the small room.

"I know it's not what you're used to—"

I shushed him. "I don't need a fancy room. Just you."

He placed one finger beneath my chin and tilted it up. "You've got me."

Something in his gaze made me think he meant it for longer than just one night. My heart squeezed. The butter-flies in my belly disappeared. When he laid his lips on mine any worry I might have been holding on to—about my uncle, about the secrets Banjo kept, about Rafe, or Jagger, or my aunt—they all flew out of my head. All that mattered was Banjo and the way I felt when I was around him.

I dropped my bag to the floor and kissed him back; soft, slow, and sweet.

"Want to take a bath? This room is supposed to have a huge one."

"Really?" I walked away from him, pushing open the only

other door in the room. "Oh wow." The en suite wasn't huge, but it had obviously been renovated recently, because it didn't match the rest of the room at all. The white tiles were clean and new, and a corner spa bath took up half the space. Banjo squeezed in behind me, leaning across to turn the faucet on.

"How hot do you like it?" He grinned, cranking up the hot water. "If last night was anything to go by, you like it steamy."

I nudged him playfully. "I know you just had a shower, but you're getting in with me, right?"

His gaze caught mine, and it was as hot as the steam rising from the water. "I was hoping you'd say that."

I crossed the space between us and gripped the hem of his long-sleeved T-shirt. He lifted his arms as I hoisted it up his torso, exposing the muscles of his stomach one by one, followed by his pecs. I trailed my fingers over him as he reciprocated, taking my jacket from my shoulders and pulling my shirt over my head. I shimmied out of my jeans and enjoyed his sudden intake of breath when he caught sight of me in my underwear.

"Thank you, Victoria's Secret," Banjo murmured.

The black lace bra pushed my breasts high, giving me cleavage for days. The panties were little more than a scrap of fabric, barely covering me.

"I almost don't want to take those off you," he said without looking me in the eye.

"I kind of feel the same about those sweatpants." They sat low on his hips, showing off the V of muscle that ran either side. "Girls have a thing for gray sweatpants, you know."

He cut the flow of water to the nearly full bath. "So we're just going to stand here and admire each other only half naked? That somehow seems like a good thing and a letdown all at once."

I giggled. "Nope. There's other things I want to do more." I rubbed my hand suggestively over his semi-hard cock before tugging the drawstring on his sweatpants.

"Tell me." His voice dropped an octave, hitting me right between my thighs.

"You remember that first day we met? At my house? I wanted to sleep with you then. It drove me mental, thinking about it, wondering what it would have been like with you. What it would have been like to lose my virginity to a one-night stand." I shoved his sweatpants over his hips and ass. "I'm glad we never got to do it."

The sweatpants dropped to the floor, and he stepped out of them, crowding in on me. "What's changed since then? Got feelings for me, princess?" he husked out, watching me intently.

Breath stalled in my lungs. My initial instinct was to play it cool. Laugh it off. Say I just liked the anticipation. But the words that came out were anything but. "I like you," I whispered, suddenly realizing how deep my emotions ran. "A lot. So yeah, Banjo. Yeah. I've got feelings for you. A lot of them."

His mouth crashed down on mine, hot and hard. I lifted up onto my toes, wrapped my arms around his broad shoulders, and kissed him back just as hard, putting every single one of my feelings into the kiss, making sure he felt them all. His fingers gripped my hips, and then I was hoisted into his arms. My legs acted on autopilot, circling his narrow waist, his erection pressing to the lace of my underwear.

Without breaking the kiss, he stepped over the edge of the bath and sank down into the deep, warm water, submerging us both to mid-chest height.

"My bra," I gasped out on a laugh. It was completely soaked through, as were my panties.

"You won't be needing it for the rest of the night anyway," he said, lips against my neck. He undid the clasp, and slid it off, dumping it over the side of the bathtub in a wet pile on the floor. He leaned back, taking my tits in his hands and squeezing them gently. "So perfect," he whispered. His fingers found my nipples, and for a maddeningly long time, he teased me. Tweaking them, rolling them, lifting me out of the water so he could suck them. He licked the water droplets from my cleavage, his tongue swirling patterns across my damp flesh. "Stand up," he whispered.

I did as I was told, expecting to feel a chill over my wet skin, but then he sat forward, onto his knees, and pulled the soaking wet lace from around my hips. His eyes were level with my pussy, and suddenly, I was anything but chilled. I was so hot I was ready to self-combust.

"Sit back on the edge," he encouraged.

I did, and then with a wicked grin, he said, "Now open your legs."

A moan escaped me.

He moved through the water, fitting himself between my thighs that had no problem obeying his commands. They'd fallen right apart, as if this was an everyday occurrence.

A thrill raced through me. If I made this thing with Banjo official, this *could* happen every day. All our nights could be like this. Filled with his hands on my body, mine on his.

His tongue found my center, and it only took him moments to work me into a frenzy. I leaned back on the wall, my legs trembling with the power of an orgasm barreling down on me.

"Banjo," I panted.

He suddenly stood, water pouring down his long, lean, tight body in tiny rivers.

I whimpered in need, needing him to get over the edge.

"Not yet," he said, stepping from the bath.

His words were full of promise, and I followed him without another thought. He picked up a towel, drying me off, walking me backward into the bedroom until my calves hit the bed and I fell back. He opened his overnight bag, taking a row of condoms from the top. He ripped one off and threw the rest onto the bed.

I tracked his movements with an eagle eye. My breath hitched as he ripped the top off the silver foil package, pulling out the condom. His fingers wrapped around his cock, and I trembled all over at the sight of him pumping himself.

God, that was hot.

He rolled the condom over his length in seconds, like he'd done it a million times before. And maybe he had. But I didn't care. He was here with me right now, and that was all that mattered. *He* was all that mattered. Him and me, and what we were about to do. I wanted it. I wanted him.

My heart clenched with an emotion I didn't want to name. I was falling for him. There was no doubt about it. I didn't want to get my heart broken, but Banjo had always made me feel like I was the one in the driver's seat. I was the one who called the shots. With Banjo, I could have it all. Him. Rafe. Whatever the hell I wanted.

And if I couldn't get it by myself, he'd have my back.

"Kiss me," I whispered, my throat clogging with emotion.

He crawled over me, fitting his cock at my entrance and resting his weight on his forearms. His gaze burned mine, and instead of blurting out my feelings, I strained up to kiss him.

His lips stole my whimpers as he notched at my entrance. "You okay?" he whispered.

I nodded. And I was. I was a nervous ball of excitement and anticipation, but I was ready. I'd never been more ready in my life. "I want to do this," I whispered, running my hand down the side of his face. "With you."

Emotion flickered in his eyes, and then he pushed inside me, filling the ache deep within that cried out for him. My hips lifted. There was no pain. The sensation was foreign, but I wanted him so much, it wasn't unpleasant. He stilled, letting me adjust to his size, groaning into my mouth.

"Fuck, princess. You're so tight. This is going to kill me slowly."

Him and me both. I pressed up against him, encouraging him to move. He did. He slid in and out, rocking his body in a slow, sensual rhythm that had me aching for more. On instinct, I moved with him, running my fingers down his back, dropping kisses on his lips, his cheeks, his neck, his chest. Every inch of him I could reach. Our hips rolled in time, me meeting his thrusts, each one building me back to the edge I'd found in the bathroom.

"Banjo," I moaned.

He reached between us, finding my nub and working it slowly, in time with his dick. I couldn't stop looking at him. Drinking him in. This beautiful boy who had made this moment everything I could have ever wanted it to be.

This boy I could fall in love with.

Our gazes locked, and sensation roared through me. It spiraled from between my legs, arcing its way through my torso, across my chest, down my arms. I cried out my pleasure, sparks dancing behind my eyes as my orgasm overtook me.

Banjo shuddered above me. His hips pumped faster, taking us both higher until he put his lips to my neck and let out a groan of pleasure, finding his own release.

With Banjo murmuring nonsense words in my ear, I fell back down to earth. He was heavy on top of me, both of us sweaty and sated, but instead of pushing him away, I wrapped my legs around him, holding him close.

"You're perfect, you know that?" he said, kissing my shoulder.

"We are," I corrected. "We're perfect."

In that moment, I believed it.

30

LACEY

*T*he next morning, I woke up warm, cozy, and wrapped around Banjo. There wasn't any other place in the world I wanted to be but right there in his arms. My limbs were heavy with relaxation, my breathing slow. His arm slung across my naked torso drew my attention. I traced over the smattering of freckles on his skin, winding my fingers from his wrist, up his forearms, and along his biceps.

"Morning, princess," he mumbled without opening his eyes. "What time is it?"

"Late," I whispered back. "We need to get up and check out."

His arm tightened around me. "And if I just wanted to stay here all day?"

"The hotel might have a problem with that. And my aunt would probably come looking for me."

"She thinks you're at Jagger's. She'll never find you, and then I can keep you."

My heart clenched. He painted a pretty picture with those words. A day of lying around, naked with the boy who'd taken my virginity in such a perfect fashion was truly tempting. But I knew Banjo wouldn't have the cash to pay for another night in this hotel, even if it was cheap. And I wouldn't embarrass him by paying for it myself. Plus, I'd only just smoothed things over with Selina. I didn't want to risk ruining it again.

I kissed his shoulder, then wriggled out from his grasp, searching the floor for wherever I'd dropped my bag.

Banjo shifted over onto his side, propping his head up with his hand. The sheets rode low on his hips, barely covering his erection. "You sore?" he asked, watching me pull on clothes.

I shrugged. "Only a tiny bit."

A frown creased his forehead at that, and he looked so adorably worried that I put one knee on the mattress and leaned across him to kiss it away. "You didn't hurt me. Last night was great."

His hand grabbed the back of my neck, and he deepened the kiss.

I batted him away. "Stop it, before I fall back into bed with you. Come on, get up."

"Already up," he drawled, cocky smirk back in place on his tanned face. "Want to come see?"

I rolled my eyes. "Not what I meant, and you know it."

He grinned, then jumped out of bed, erection jutting out from his hips. I stopped what I was doing, just to watch him.

He made a show of checking the time. "Still got ten minutes 'til checkout..."

I threw his T-shirt at him. Because if he didn't cover up soon, I'd be tempted to take him up on that offer.

Banjo got dressed in record time, and we did a quick scout around the room, making sure we hadn't forgotten anything. He opened the door and waited for me before pulling it closed behind us. I shifted my bag onto my shoulder, and when Banjo put his arm around me, you couldn't wipe the smile off my face.

"Thank you for last night," I said quietly.

He dropped a kiss on my upturned face.

"Well, well, isn't this interesting? The princess and the court jester, doing the walk of shame."

I stopped and spun around at the familiar voice that came from behind us.

Banjo glanced over his shoulder and groaned. "What do you want, Gillian?"

Gillian carried a duffle bag, last night's cheerleader's uniform poking out of the open zipper. My Banjo bubble popped. I hadn't even considered there might have been other kids from school staying at the same hotel. But of course there would have been. It was a long drive back to Saint View, and the game had ended late. There'd probably been a party. The Saint View kids wouldn't have thought twice about crashing. Or hell, maybe they'd had their own, elsewhere in the hotel. I hadn't even considered it. I'd been too caught up in what I'd been planning to do with Banjo.

She widened her eyes, all fake innocence. "I don't want anything. Just merely tucking this away for future reference. See you two back in Saint View." She shot me a triumphant look, like she'd won something over me. Then turned on her heel and flounced down the stairs, disappearing out of sight.

"Hey," Banjo said, putting his hands on my arms and twisting so I faced him. "You're trembling. What's wrong?"

I glanced down at my hands. They were balled into fists, and he was right. I trembled head to toe.

"I'm going after her." I still hadn't had it out with her over what she'd done to me at school.

Jagger had managed to get the worst of the spray paint from my locker, but it had left an ugly red smear that looked like blood. I was so sick of Gillian's shit, and this weekend, she'd seen me kissing not only Rafe outside his car, but leaving a hotel room wrapped up in Banjo's arms. I may as well have just given her a can of accelerant to throw on my burning body. This would be all over school by the time we got down to Banjo's car if I didn't do something about it. I took off after her.

Banjo caught me around the waist before I'd taken three steps. "Hey, chill. As much as I'd love to see you and Gillian in a catfight, that isn't happening on my watch. Let her go. She isn't worth it."

"She's going to tell everyone. About you and me. And Rafe. She'll tell Colt."

Banjo shook his head. "Let her."

I sighed and pushed away from him, heading down the stairs, but no longer intent on chasing down Gillian. Banjo chattered beside me about the game, as if he'd instantly forgotten about her. But I hadn't forgotten. And I knew it would only be a matter of time until the entire thing blew up in my face.

---

*B*anjo dropped me home, and I spent the rest of the afternoon alternating between moping over whatever Gillian's plan for exposing me would be. And girlish squeals as I replayed the previous night with Banjo. Meredith called me right in the middle of my inner turmoil.

"What time are you picking me up?" she asked without saying hello.

"For what?"

"The Saint View beach party? Remember? You said you'd give me a ride?"

"Oh, yeah. That."

"Oh no. No, no, no. Why do you sound like you'd rather eat your own eyeballs than go to a party tonight?"

"One. Ew. Two. Do we have to go? I'm not in the mood to be around people."

"Oh. Okay then."

Guilt ebbed at my conscience. I'd promised to spend some time with Meredith. And introduce her to my Saint View friends. I missed her. And I really did want to somehow combine the two sides of my life. That was never going to happen if I sat at home on a Saturday night, licking my wounds and waiting for Gillian to destroy me. It wasn't in my nature to be so easily defeated.

"I'll pick you up at eight."

"Yay!" Meredith yelled. "Owen is coming, too. He's meeting us there after his polo match or something."

I rolled my eyes. I should have known. "Did you invite anyone else I should know about?"

"Nope! Just the two of us. See you at eight!"

I hung up and flopped back on my bed. It was already mostly dark outside, and if I was picking her up in less than two hours, I needed to get ready. So I pulled up Spotify, connected my phone to the Bluetooth speakers in my bedroom, and put on a Chainsmokers album to get me in a party mood. I wished I had something to drink. It would have been easy enough to sneak downstairs and steal a bottle of something from the fully stocked bar my uncle had kept. But thinking about going to his den, where he'd spent so much of his time, just saddened me. The den had a smell to it that I'd always associated with him, and I didn't want to remember how much that smell had always comforted me.

Or worse, find it no longer smelled like him at all. That would be unbearable.

Plus, I was driving, so drinking wasn't a good idea. Instead, I got up and made myself get dressed, knowing I'd feel better once I was actually out. I wasn't going to hide in my bedroom because Gillian was a bitch. By the time I picked up Meredith, my mood was a thousand percent better.

She climbed into the passenger seat and threw her arms around me. We hugged awkwardly across the gearshift.

"It's been forever!" she declared.

It hadn't even been weeks, but admittedly, that was weird for us. For years, we'd seen each other every day. We'd spent each school day together and then hung out all weekend, in between my music practices. A twinge of guilt flickered when I thought about my music. This was supposed to be my year. And then my uncle had died. I'd started at Saint View. Lost my head, and maybe my heart to a boy. Maybe more than one boy. Started some sort of war with another. And music had been pushed to the back burner. There was just too much going on. Banjo and I hadn't even started our music assignment, and the recital wasn't that far away. It was already October, and the end of the year wouldn't be far behind. I vowed to talk to him about it tonight and nail down a time to practice.

"So tell me what's been happening at Edgely? Anything new and exciting? Is everyone losing their minds, suddenly being in a co-ed school?"

"What do you think?"

"I'd be surprised if someone isn't pregnant already."

Meredith checked her reflection in the little mirror on the back of the sun visor. "Rumor mill says it's Calia Jankins.

She's been mysteriously absent after hooking up with Leyton Cowley."

"No way? She was as prim and proper as they come in Providence."

"Just goes to show, you never really know a person..."

For some reason, I thought of Colt. I barely knew him at all, and yet, somehow, he was never far from my mind. It irked me I still didn't know why he hated me so much.

"And what about your Saint View posse? You and Banjo seemed pretty tight at the beach the other day."

I chewed my lip, trying to stop the smile spreading across my face.

Meredith knew me too well and pounced. "Girl! You went there, didn't you?"

I shrugged. "Might have."

"And? Don't hold out on me, I want all the details."

Happiness bubbled through me until I felt lighter than air, and I spilled all the dirty secrets of my night with Banjo, while my best friend hooted and hollered from the passenger seat. It made the drive to the beach pass quickly, and Meredith was still fanning herself as we pulled into the gravel parking lot.

"Well, now I'm even more determined to get me a Saint View boy tonight. I want someone to throw me down on the bed and do it rough and dirty."

"I'm sure if you lead with that, you can have any guy here you want." I laughed at the idea of walking up to a random stranger and telling him she wanted to be thrown onto a bed and taken roughly. Thing is, I wouldn't put it past her. She'd do it, without batting an eyelid.

"Lead on, sister."

We picked our way over the sandy path that led down to the beach through the sand dunes. Darkness had completely fallen while we'd been driving here, and we both flicked our phone flashlights on in order to make sure we didn't trip over dried seaweed. But once we hit the beach, the glow from several bonfires cast a pleasant glow, and we both shoved our phones in our pockets.

Meredith hooked her arm through mine, and we giggled together, wandering around the crowd looking for familiar faces. Or for faces Meredith might want to know intimately before the night was through. I searched the crowd for Banjo or Rafe but couldn't see either of them. In fact, it was an oddly small turnout for a beach party. I hadn't seen a single guy from the football team. I spotted Jagger sitting with some friends and towed Meredith in her direction. I introduced them quickly, and to my surprise, Meredith threw her arms around Jagger. Jagger glanced at me over Meredith's shoulder, a 'what the hell?' look on her face.

"Thank you for looking after my girl. I already adore you for that," Meredith gushed.

At that, Jagger shrugged and hugged her back. But then they both turned to me.

Jagger smiled. "She's been a handful. But I kind of like her."

"And she kinda likes you, too," I quipped.

"Aww, group hug!" Meredith called, pulling both of us in.

When we moved away, Meredith's eye caught on something over my shoulder. "Okay, don't look, but who is that hottie sitting across from the bonfire?"

Of course, Jagger and I both turned around.

"My God!" Meredith hissed, "don't you know the meaning of the word 'don't'?"

Jagger laughed but grabbed Meredith's hand. "Trenton Parks. Come on, I'll introduce you. You coming, Lacey?"

I shook my head. "I'm going to get us some drinks. I'll be back."

Jagger nodded, and I knew she'd take good care of Meredith for a few minutes. Judging from the way her and Trenton were ogling each other, by the time I got back, they'd have their tongues down each other's throats anyway.

I cast an eye around the beach, settling on a smaller group huddled in a circle, and determined that was where the keg was. I made a beeline in that direction, dry sand squishing between my toes with every step. I still couldn't see Banjo anywhere, so I shot him off a quick text. I stopped when the little bubble appeared, signaling he was typing a message, and waited for his reply. It came back almost immediately.

Banjo: *Sorry, babe, Coach called a last-minute meeting. The entire team is here. Cheerleaders, too. Call you in the morning.*

Disappointment deflated my good mood. That meant I'd come out tonight for nothing. I'd wanted Meredith to get to know my friends, and two out of three now weren't coming. But one glance back at Meredith and Jagger, and I realized it didn't matter. The two of them chatted up a storm with Trenton, all three laughing with the glow of the fire on their faces. Meredith sat closer to Trenton than any stranger needed to sit to another. Unless they were hoping said stranger would lean in for a kiss.

I didn't know Trenton at all, and I'd have to ask Jagger about him later, but for now, Meredith and Jagger both looked happy. That pleased me. It was the beginning of my two worlds coming together.

"Lacey," a voice called to my left.

I peered into the darkness of another beach path. I had to wait a few moments for the guy to move into the firelight, but when he did, I realized it was only Owen.

"Hey." He smiled at me.

"Hey, yourself. You made it."

"Thanks for the invite."

I didn't mention I hadn't actually invited him. That was beside the point now anyway. Plus, it was nice to see him. I still knew so few kids at Saint View, and they all had their cliques. With mine being mostly AWOL, it didn't hurt to have an extra person to hang out with. "I was just going to the keg to get drinks. Come with?"

He nodded eagerly, then threw an arm over my shoulder, squeezing me. "So how have you been? It's so good to see you without your bodyguard."

"Bodyguard?" I frowned. "Oh. You mean Banjo?"

Owen wrinkled his nose. "Is that his real name?"

"Yes."

He raised an eyebrow.

I bristled. "What exactly is wrong with his name?"

Owen must have heard the tone in my voice because he smiled widely, shaking his head. "Nothing, nothing. It's just unusual. Let's get those drinks."

I led the way to the keg, and Owen held out plastic cups while I filled them. We moved back to the fire, and I took an overflowing cup from him, taking a large gulp. Fizzy beer filled my mouth. He handed a cup to Meredith, and I gave an extra one to Jagger. They were both still deep in conversation with Trenton, so Owen and I sat beside them, and I let him dominate the conversation with his polo stories.

The fire flicked up orange, blue, and green flames. They were magnetic, stealing my attention, though Owen didn't seem to mind. After a while, I stopped pretending to listen. The flames drew me in, pulling me closer, calling to me. The heat became uncomfortable, and instinct yelled to move back, but I stubbornly refused. Was this what my uncle had felt, lying on the floor while the flames destroyed everything around him? Had he been conscious while they'd inched closer? Or had he died the moment the knife had entered his body? Sharp pain splintered through me at the thought of him bleeding out, maybe begging for his life, while his murderer lit a fire around him.

"Whoa, Lacey. Get back."

I blinked, Owen's face coming back into focus. He grabbed my wrist, a little too sharply, and examined it. "Are you burned?"

I pulled my hand away. "I'm fine!" I said too loudly, shaking myself out of my own head. But that only served to spin my vision in dizzying circles. I moved back to the edge of the group, letting the cool night air blow over me. My skin felt chapped and raw from the heat of the flames, like I'd been sunbathing on the beach at the high point of the day.

At some point, Owen handed me another beer, and we tapped our plastic cups together. I giggled when beer sloshed over onto the sand.

"Oops," I laughed. I glanced around. "Where did Jagger and Meredith go?" They weren't sitting beside me anymore.

He looked at me a little strangely. "Jagger went to make a phone call. And Meredith went off with that Trenton guy. She said she'd find her own way home. Remember?"

I didn't remember at all, but I had been lost in the flames for a while and hadn't really been paying attention. I shrugged.

"Are you okay?" Owen asked, tilting my head in his direction.

My vision blurred for a moment before he came into focus. "Yeah, sure. I'm fine. I think I just—oh shit." My stomach lurched.

Owen's concern amped up. "What? What's wrong?"

I jerked my head toward the fire. On the other side, a pair of dark eyes watched me, his usual frown marring his beautiful face.

Owen frowned. "You know that guy?"

"Yeah, I know him." Sort of. Did anyone really know Colt? Surely there was someone he let in. Maybe he poured all his secrets out to her Gillian while he was dick deep inside her. Heat flushed my body, and my head spun. I didn't want to think about him dick deep in anyone.

Except me.

Not that that would ever happen, especially not after the stunt he'd pulled with my locker during the week.

"Why is he staring at me?" I whispered to Owen. At least I thought I'd whispered. It sounded kind of loud. "He's such a creep."

"I don't know. I'm going to tell him to back off. I don't like that he's making you uncomfortable."

Owen went to stand, but I grabbed his hand and pulled him back down.

"No. Don't. I'm a big girl. I'm perfectly capable of fighting my own battles. And Colt and I are overdue to have a conversation about this." A sudden surge of determination had me pushing to my feet, wobbling slightly. How had two beers gone to my head so quickly? Even still, if I was going to have it out with Colt, I'd need Dutch courage. I plucked Owen's drink from his hands. "I need to borrow this. You don't mind, right? Go find Meredith. Or hey! You could find a nice Saint View girl to chat up! I'll find you when I'm done, okay?"

Owen shook his head. "Lacey, no, I—"

"Didn't you hear what she said?" Colt's voice was dangerously low.

It sent goosebumps rippling across my skin. When had he moved in so close?

"She said she wants to talk to me. So unless you want me to lay you out flat on the sand, I suggest you sit your scrawny ass down and shut the fuck up."

I bit my lip, gaze darting between Owen and Colt.

A giggle escaped me. "Well, that escalated quickly."

Colt sighed and wrapped his hand around my arm, tugging me away from the fire. His grip didn't exactly hurt, but it was no nonsense.

It didn't feel like when Owen had gripped my wrist.

Unlike with Owen, I didn't try to back away from Colt.

I wanted to go with him. I liked the way his hold spoke of dominance and possession. With my inhibitions lowered by the alcohol, jealousy flashed through me, hot and searing. He was unfairly beautiful. And something deep within me yearned to unravel him. Get beneath his skin and find out what made him tick. He'd erected walls around himself, but what was on the inside intrigued me.

We reached the water's edge, and I squealed as it lapped at my feet. The light from the fires barely made a dent in the darkness, but when Colt rounded on me, I felt more than saw the anger in his expression.

"What the fuck are you doing here?"

"Public beach. And you aren't my father. So back off." I was all talk. I still made no move to pull my hand from his grip. Pathetic. Why didn't I just swoon at his feet already? I tried to stand a little straighter and looked him in the eye. I took another sip of my stolen beer.

The cup flew from my hand, splashing all over me.

"What the fuck, Colt!" I yelled.

He let go of me, and I lifted my top to wipe sticky beer from my face.

"Why did you do that?"

He moved in, until he completely invaded my space. "Because, princess, you're drunk off your ass."

I shook my head, but that only made it spin more. "I've had two beers. I'm not drunk."

Colt's expression darkened. "You sure about that? Two beers shouldn't have you wobbling all over this beach and practically falling in that bonfire."

"I didn't fall in the bonfire. And what do you care anyway? Why are we even down here? Where's your girlfriend?"

He let out a short, mocking laugh.

Anger rolled through me. "You know what, Colt? I'm the one who doesn't care. About any of it. I thought I wanted to talk to you, and hash out whatever your problem is, but now I realize the problem isn't something I might have done. It's just you."

"You really don't remember, do you?" He cocked his head to one side.

I threw my hands up in frustration. "Remember what? The way you painted murderer across my locker? The way you wrote cheat, liar, and..." I couldn't say the other thing he'd written on my uncle's photos. "I remember all those things." My throat grew tight. "Why? Did you and Gillian sit around one night, thinking up the cruelest possible way to hurt me? Because if so, you win. You fucking win, Colt. Happy?"

Colt's black gaze pinned me to the spot. Ever so slowly, he raised one hand, running it down the side of my face. "No, princess. I'm not happy. Not happy at all."

My breath hitched. He was so close. Close enough for his breath to mist over my lips. The stillness between us became an agony I couldn't bear. I didn't dare move. My head screamed to shove him back. To get away from him. And yet, my body wouldn't obey. He was just like the fire. I couldn't look away, even though he had the ability to burn me alive. His lips ghosted over mine, the touch so light I thought I'd imagined it before his lips moved to my ear.

"Every word on those photos is true, princess. Every. Single. One."

My eyes flew open, and my palm connected with his cheek in a stinging slap. "You're a liar." I seethed.

"You're naïve," he threw back, voice laced with venom. "Wake up, princess. The man you thought your uncle was doesn't fucking exist. He never did. You put him on a pedestal. He was never a hero. He's the bad guy in this fucked-up fairytale."

"No." I shook my head. "You are. And I'm done with your shit. I'm leaving." I stumbled away, pulling my keys from the bag slung across my shoulder.

Colt plucked them from my hand with deft fingers. "You're not driving anywhere. Not like that."

My gaze narrowed on him. "Give me my keys."

"No."

I lunged for them. He sidestepped, and when his body wasn't there to take the impact, I stumbled. Unable to catch my balance, my knees hit the sand in the shallows, saltwater spraying all over me. Cold water seeped through my jeans, soaking me up to my thighs.

Colt just stared at me, lip curled in disgust.

I pushed to my feet, ignoring the freezing chill, the wind whipping around my now soaked clothes. "Give them to me."

Colt shook his head, like I was the most pathetic person he'd ever laid eyes on. He drew his arm back, and then with one last look in my direction, threw my keys into the ocean.

"No!" I waded in, knowing it was pointless. I spun around to glare at him. "What am I supposed to do now?"

He shrugged like he didn't have a care in the world. Like this entire drama had nothing to do with him. "Not my problem."

I stared out at the ocean. The water was freezing. Tears pricked the backs of my eyes. I splashed from the water and stopped in front of him. "I hate you," I yelled, storming past him. I didn't go back in the direction of the fires. I didn't want to see anyone. I just wanted to get away. Far away, from Colt. From Saint View. From the lies and the confusion. I didn't know what the hell I was doing, thinking I could come here and find my uncle's murderer. I'd found nothing. Done nothing but fall into Colt's web of lies. I ran up the beach, taking another path back to the road, and began the long walk home.

Colt's dark gaze followed me, until the darkness swallowed me whole.

31

LACEY

I stumbled down the beach road, barely feeling the uneven ground beneath my feet. It was nothing compared to the hurt Colt's lies and accusations had caused.

The wind whipped, chilling me to the bone. Wet denim chaffed my thighs, and my head spun miserably until I had to double over, retching into the gutter. Exhaustion weakened my legs. And finally, I let the tears roll down my face. They weren't just for what had happened with Colt. But for my uncle, and the fact he was gone too soon. For the fact people were trying to smear his name through the mud. For me. And for Selina who had to live without him.

"Lacey!"

I looked up wearily.

Owen's worried face poked out the driver's side window of his Aston Martin. "Jesus, fuck," he swore.

I hadn't even heard his engine. He got out, slamming the car door behind him.

He crouched in the gutter beside me, his expression morphing into anger. "I'll kill that guy. Did he hurt you?"

I shook my head. Not physically anyway. "I just want to go home," I whispered.

Owen nodded and helped me into the passenger side. I curled up in a ball, my wet clothes soaking his seats, but he didn't seem to mind.

Without me asking, he cranked up the heat. "I'm going to take you home. It's all going to be okay."

It wouldn't, but what was the point in telling him? There was no need to drag him down to my level of misery. We wound through the outer streets of Saint View, and I clutched at my rolling stomach.

"Oh God, Owen. Pull over, I'm going to be—" I slammed my finger on the window button and just barely got my head out of the car before I was sick again.

Owen cringed as I sat back against the seat.

"Sorry," I whispered. "I'll pay for your car to be washed tomorrow."

Owen handed me a little packet of Kleenex from the glovebox. "I'm not worried about that. I'm worried about you. How much did you have to drink tonight?"

I racked my brain trying to remember. "Two? Three? I think?" But that couldn't be right. I'd never gotten sick off three watered-down beers.

Owen's molars ground so hard I could hear it over the white noise of the heater. "He's a dead man," he muttered. Then he looked over at me. "I think he drugged you, Lace."

I blinked. "What?"

"That guy. He must have put something in your drink."

Anger and confusion swirled within my cloudy head. When had Colt even been near my drink, apart from when he was knocking it out of my hand? But all that came out of my mouth was a pathetic, "I hate him."

Owen's fingers gripped the wheel so tight his knuckles

went white. I concentrated on that. Owen was here, looking after me. I was warm again. Safe, and on my way home, where I could collapse into my bed and sleep for the rest of the weekend. I wouldn't think about Colt for another second.

Not until I'd had some sleep.

Then, when I was fully rested, and whatever drug he'd given me had left my system, I'd plan my revenge. I didn't care how petty this thing between us had been. He'd crossed the line. He'd crossed it when he and Gillian defaced my locker and defamed my uncle. And he'd left the line for dead when he'd drugged me tonight. What the hell had he been planning? A shiver rolled down my spine. If he was capable of drugging me, then I doubted there weren't other lines he'd be willing to walk over.

Owen pulled into my driveway and cut the engine. He got out quickly, running around to my side to help me out.

"Where's your keys?" he whispered.

"Bottom of the ocean."

"Spare?"

"Oh! Yes! There is one. In a fake rock somewhere..."

Owen searched around in the darkness of the garden while I slumped against the doorframe.

"My aunt is going to kill me," I said quietly.

"Not if she doesn't find out." Owen came back, triumphant with a key in his hand. He shoved it in the lock, and it turned easily. Beeping on the other side greeted us, and I fumbled with the code.

We both breathed a sigh of relief when the warning beeps stopped without setting off the alarm. Owen got beneath my arm again, supporting me. My legs barely worked.

"Where's your bedroom?"

I pointed to the stairs, and he half-dragged me up them.

"That's my room," I said, words coming out a little slurred.

Owen tucked us away inside, locking the door behind him.

"Thank you," I whispered. "I don't know what I would have done if you hadn't found me tonight. I probably would have had to sleep in that gutter. Or worse, call my aunt."

Owen's squeezed my arm. "Anytime."

I pressed up onto my toes and kissed his cheek. "You're blushing." I laughed when I pulled away. "That's cute."

I wandered over to my dresser and opened it, but Owen nudged me out of the way.

"I'll get it." He tugged open the drawer, lifting out a nightshirt as I wandered to the big bay windows and looked out into the dark night.

I fumbled with the button on my soaking jeans, dragged them down my legs, then stepped out of them. Owen brought over the shirt he'd found for me, putting it down on the window seat. Then his fingers gripped the bottom of my T-shirt and hauled it over my head.

"Thank you," I whispered. My arms felt like lead. My mouth thick as cotton. I reached for the nightshirt, but Owen stepped in close behind me. Before I realized what was happening, he undid my bra.

I clutched the bra to my breasts. "Owen!" I snapped.

"I've got my eyes closed. But you can't sleep in this underwear. It's drenched. Take it off."

He was right. I needed to get completely changed. I glanced over my shoulder and saw he had his gaze diverted toward the wall. I dropped the bra and picked up the night-shirt, pulling it on over my head. I waited until it was draped over my thighs before changing my panties. When I was done, I glanced back at Owen who was still facing the wall. I instantly felt bad.

"Sorry for snapping at you," I murmured.

"It's not a problem. That's what friends do, right? You snap, I let it roll off me." He pushed the blankets back and patted the bed with a smile. "Get in. You'll feel better in the morning."

I slid between the sheets and I swear nothing had ever felt as good. He covered me up and smoothed back my hair, the rhythmic movement so amazing that I instantly closed my eyes. Sleep tried to take me hard. It was as if every muscle in my body just gave up the fight. I sank into the mattress like a complete dead weight, drowning in the blackness.

Through dreamlike fog, hands skated over my chilled thighs, lifting my nightshirt to run over my belly and trying to dip beneath the elastic of my panties. I groaned, shifting away from the unwanted, crawling touch, confused as to whether it was real or in my head. I lashed out, but nothing connected with my flailing limbs. Nausea rose in my belly with the movement, but I was too groggy to do anything but whimper into the pillow. The hands wouldn't leave me alone. They followed me through the blackness, marring my body. It was a relief when sound cut through my sleep and drug-riddled brain, and the hands disappeared. I blinked in the low light of my bedroom, barely able to make out a shape at the window.

"Owen?" Why was he still here? Taking phone calls in my bedroom? A heavy uncomfortableness settled over me. I wanted to tell him to leave. That I appreciated his help, but I didn't want him here anymore. I tried to keep my eyes open, fearing the hands that moved in the darkness.

But sleep caught me once more, and this time, I didn't

dream. I fell into the black abyss, which looked startlingly like Colt's eyes.

32

LACEY

I slept for most of Sunday. Selina eventually let herself into my room, with a tray of dry toast and flat ginger ale, and sat on the end of the bed. To her credit, she hadn't given me a hard time for being hungover. She'd just kissed my forehead, and I'd gone back to sleep. The toast and soda were still on my bedside table when I'd woken up at dawn this morning. My stomach had still been queasy, but I'd choked down the cold, stale toast. I felt marginally better after getting up for a shower. I'd had hangovers before, but never one like that. Owen's comments about being drugged drifted through my mind, and the more I thought about it, the more I thought maybe he was right. There were black spots in my memory, and I'd never felt so out of sorts with my own body.

School didn't help my mood any. And the black cloud that had rolled in on Saturday night with Colt, hung around all week. I was frustrated with myself, and with the lack of progress I'd made since coming here. I was no closer to finding the man who'd rescued me from the fire. All I'd managed to do, with Banjo's and Rafe's help, was provide alibis for the entire football team. Banjo still swore that only team members had those shirts, but with no leads to follow, I was at a dead end and wondering what I was still doing here.

Banjo, Rafe, and Jagger. That was it. I was staying for my friend and the two boys I didn't want to lose.

And for Colt.

Because, damn him, he was never far from my mind. Only now, when I thought of him, anger surged through my blood. What he'd done couldn't go unchecked. And if I tucked tail and ran back to Providence, he would have won. That was the single thought that kept me turning up at school each day. I'd been approaching this entire thing wrong. I knew nothing about him, and yet he seemed to know so much about me. I needed to know more so I could use his weaknesses against him.

Rafe caught me in the quad one morning. He leaned in and gave me a kiss on the cheek that likely didn't look at all platonic. Or maybe it was just me who noticed the way his lips lingered, his nose brushing my neck as he inhaled, while goosebumps exploded over my skin.

"Eighteen this weekend, princess. How are the party plans coming along?" He leaned back against the brick wall beside me, close enough our pinkies could touch.

I shrugged. "Truthfully? I've let Selina, Jagger, and Meredith take over. All I had to do was organize myself a costume."

"Did you pick one?"

I nodded, a small smile pulling at my lips. From the minute Selina had mentioned costumes, I'd known exactly what I wanted to go as. "I'm not telling you, though. It'll be a surprise."

Rafe folded his arms across his broad chest. "Come on, tell me. I can't wait until Saturday to know."

The bell rang, and I winked at him. "Gotta go to class. See you later."

I had music class next, which I was both looking forward to, and dreading at the same time. When I got there, Miss Halten was nowhere to be seen, her desk empty. The rest of the class stood around talking in small groups, except for Gillian, who was on Colt's lap while they played tonsil hockey. Gross, but it allowed me to slip into the seat beside Banjo without them noticing me.

I immediately relaxed in his presence and let my gaze drift over his handsome features.

"I missed you," he whispered. "I've barely seen you all week."

I nodded. I'd been keeping a pretty low profile. Going straight home after school to work with my tutor who was disappointed with my progress and attention. He was threatening to tattle to Selina. I didn't want that to happen. She'd been so happy for the last few days, buzzing around, coordinating the restaurant chef and the decorator who was turning this birthday party into something next-level outrageous. I didn't want to put a downer on her good mood in any way.

"Rafe said you won't tell him what you're wearing to your party."

"That happened just two minutes ago. How did you even see him in that time?"

He held up his phone. "We have this thing called instant messaging? You should try it." He nudged me playfully. "So, you going to tell me what your costume is?"

I shook my head. "Nope."

"How are we supposed to couple dress if I don't know what you're going as?"

I bit my lip. "Is that what we are? A couple? Where does Rafe fit into that?"

Banjo shrugged. He picked up a pencil and tapped it absently on the desk in a rhythm that sounded vaguely familiar. "I don't know. Do we have to label it? All I know is I had a great weekend with you. And I can't wait to do it again. When? This weekend? I can do that thing you like with my tongue, and —"

I shushed him as the teacher walked in and cleared her throat, glaring in our direction. Heat flushed my cheeks. If she'd heard that, I'd die. Though I supposed she'd heard, and probably seen worse, after teaching a bunch of horny teenagers day in and day out. Especially with Colt and Gillian in her class. The two of them had no shame. If I turned around, I wouldn't be at all surprised if he had his hand up her skirt.

Not that I was jealous. I wasn't. He was hot, but he was an asshole, and he could go suck a bag of dicks.

Miss Halten spent part of the lesson discussing harmonies, and then thankfully, let us work on our performance pieces. Banjo and I needed the time desperately, and we worked well together, searching for a piece we could both shine in. Admittedly, there was some flirting and a little under-the-desk touching, but I mostly managed to keep us on task until the bell rang. We traipsed out of class, and he pulled me into his arms. Before I could protest, he dropped a kiss on my lips.

"See you at lunch, okay?"

I nodded, and kissed him back, my lips lingering on his, then we headed in opposite directions. Me to the English block, him to woodwork.

The girl's bathroom was on the way, and I ducked in quickly to make sure my clothes were straight and my makeup wasn't smudged from Banjo's kisses.

I pushed the door open, and a hand on the middle of my back propelled me forward. I spun around and glared at Gillian. She locked the bathroom door behind her.

"Your moves are getting predictable, Gillian. Just you and me today? No girl posse in tow?"

Gillian rolled her eyes. "You're so fucking dramatic."

"You probably would be, too, if you'd just been shoved into the bathroom."

"Get over it. I just wanted to talk to you."

Well, that was rich. "Why?"

"Honestly?"

"Do you actually know what that means?" I snarked. "You didn't when you wrote those bullshit lies about my uncle."

She flapped her hand about impatiently, like I was boring her. "Okay, sure, I stuffed them in your locker and spray painted the door."

"This isn't news to me."

"Look, I feel a tiny bit bad about that, okay? So I'm trying to do you a favor. How 'bout you shut up for five seconds and let me talk?"

I narrowed my eyes and went to push past her, makeup be damned. I didn't want to be in an enclosed space with Gillian. I didn't trust myself not to swing a punch at her. "I don't need your favors."

She shoved me back. "Actually, princess, I think this time you do. I can't just sit back and watch this anymore. It's too pathetic. Honestly, every time I look at you, I just want to weep for the shame of the situation you can't even see."

I threw my hands up in the air. "So enlighten me, then.

What is it that the queen bitch of Saint View High knows that I don't?"

"Not just me. Everybody who's anybody can see it. It's been entertaining, but I'm bored now, and I think the fireworks that are about to go off will be so much more fun. For me. Of course. Not so much for you. So listen up. Whatever you think you have with Banjo and Rafe? You're wrong."

"You don't know anything about it, Gillian. Mind your own business."

"Oh, but this is my business. And I do know about it. Everything about it. You think I haven't noticed you slutting it up with the two of them? Making out with Rafe one day, doing a walk of shame with Banjo the next? Juiciest gossip I've ever had the pleasure of holding on to."

"If it's so juicy, why haven't you told the entire school, then?" I'd been waiting for it. But she had no proof, so if she wanted to tell everyone I was with two guys at once, let her. I was sure Saint View High had its fair share of bed-hopping.

She cocked her head to one side. "It's always good to have an ace up your sleeve. And your dirty little secret is mine. But I do want to warn you. You can't trust them."

I snorted. "Rich, coming from you. You're so snake-like I can practically see your fangs."

Gillian actually looked somewhat pleased with that analogy, even though it hadn't been meant as a compliment. She raised one shoulder in a shrug. "Don't believe me. But I know for a fact that Colt forbade them to date you. And nobody goes against Colt."

I choked on a snort of laughter. "It's like you actually believe he's some sort of god."

"He is around here."

"Then why was I kissing Rafe before the game on Friday? Why did I spend all of Friday night in Banjo's bed?

Maybe Colt isn't the one with the God-like power around here. If I can get Banjo and Rafe to go against his ridiculous fucking rules, maybe I'm the one with the power?"

Gillian's smile widened, and she burst into laughter. "Power of the pussy, huh? If you truly believe that, then you're more deluded and under their spell than I realized. If that's the case, I simply feel sorry for you. I suggest you take your pretty little ass back to where you came from, while you still have your reputation somewhat intact. Because I promise, you hang around here much longer, there'll be no reputation to salvage. Those boys will rip the meat from your bones and spit you out when you're done. You've no idea what you've walked into."

Ice flushed through my veins at the barely concealed threat in her voice.

Gillian smirked and dusted off her palms on her skirt. "My work here is done. See you at your party, princess. It's going to be a hell of a night."

33

LACEY

*J*agger zipped me up and gasped as I spun in a little circle.

Meredith, sitting on my bed behind her clapped her hands and bounced on the mattress. "You look amazing!"

I studied myself in the mirror. The long gold-and-white dress fell right to the floor, the bodice fitted, the skirt billowing out extravagantly. Tiny, shimmering beads were stitched into the fabric, gleaming from every angle. Meredith had curled my hair earlier, and now it fell down my back in soft waves, below an intricate golden crown that sat atop my head.

"It's not too much?" I asked, mainly aiming the question at Jagger, because nothing was ever too much for Meredith.

She shook her head. "No way. It's perfect. Those boys won't know what hit them."

My smile faltered.

Jagger shook her head, her hand waving in my face. "No. No, no, no. You stop that right now, Lacey Knight. You should know better than to listen to Gillian. I can't believe for one second you believed her bullshit."

Meredith frowned from her spot on the bed. I'd filled them both in about what Gillian had said, and both had been livid. "I swear, she'd better not show her face at the party tonight. Or I will not be held accountable for my actions."

I smiled at them. "I know, I know. I'm not going to let it get to me. I swear."

Something outside the window caught Jagger's attention, and she pulled the gauzy curtains aside to peer out. When she turned back, she winked at me. "Good, because Banjo just got here. And he looks mighty fine."

I squealed and rushed over. Sure enough, Banjo leaned on the side of his brother's car, grinning up at me. My mouth dried at the sight of him in a *Top Gun* flight suit, complete with Aviators. He beckoned me to come downstairs.

I gave the girls a hug each. "I'll see you there, okay?"

They shooed me out the door. They were both being picked up from my place by their dates—Aaron and Owen.

"We're going to have the best night," Meredith squealed.

I hadn't been at all excited about this party, but now as I descended the stairs to meet Banjo, excitement started swirling around my belly. Selina stood at the bottom of the staircase, snapping photos on her phone, tears misting in her eyes. She caught me by the shoulders when I reached the door.

"I can't believe you're eighteen," she breathed. "I swear it was just the other day we opened this door and found you on the step with your social worker. You looked up at me with those big eyes, and my heart broke into a million pieces. I fell in love with you right then and there, you know? And I've never stopped. Not for a moment. And now you're all grown-up."

A lump rose in my throat. "Thanks, Mom."

Selina pulled away, blinking at me in surprise. "You've never called me that."

"Is it okay? It's just you're the only mom I really remember. You're the one who has always been there for me. And I don't want to regret not telling you that, the way I do with Uncle Lawson. I wished I'd called him Dad. Because that's how I think of him."

Selina's eyes went glassy. "He would have loved that. But he already knew. He was your dad, even if you never actually said it. He knew."

A sob burst from my throat, and Selina and I launched ourselves at each other, holding tight until my sobs became hiccups.

I pulled back, wiping my fingers beneath my eyes. "I'm ruining my makeup. And Banjo is waiting for me."

Selina shooed me out the door on her way upstairs, no doubt headed to her own makeup mirror to fix the mess we'd made of her eyeliner. I let the fresh night air wash away the last of my sorrow over my uncle. Tonight wasn't the time for that. Tonight was about celebrating. It wasn't just me turning eighteen.

I rounded the path that led to our driveway, and the moment I saw Banjo, it was like my feet had a mind of their own. I ran the last few steps and threw myself into his arms. He caught me effortlessly and lowered his lips to mine, soft and sweet.

"You look smoking," he whispered, fingers tightening around my lower back. "Happy birthday, baby. Here." He placed a thin rectangular present in my hands, wrapped impeccably, with a silver bow.

I didn't have to ask to know he'd wrapped it himself. The perfect wrapping job was somehow reminiscent of the tidy way he kept his house. It was all very Banjo, and all at complete odds with the laid-back surfer vibe he showed off to the world. I knew him. The real him. The one he hid from the rest of the world.

I pulled off the ribbon and peeled back the edges of the paper. I gasped.

Banjo knew me, too. So well.

A beautiful pile of personalized sheet music lay beneath the wrapping. My name was in a gold foil font across the top, and the lines were blank, just waiting for me to fill in with my songs. It was beautiful and personal and had me on the verge of choking up again.

"I know I've made our music study sessions more about making out than writing songs."

I snorted. "Understatement of the century."

"But I know how talented you are. And I promise, as part of this present, I'm going to stop distracting you and start supporting you to get your songs down. And eventually out into the world."

"Some distraction might be okay. I'm not a nun."

Banjo wriggled his eyebrows at me suggestively.

I slapped his chest but then leaned in to kiss the sting. "Thank you. It's beautiful. I love it. And also, happy birthday!" I grinned back at him. "Ready for your present?"

His eyes raked over my curves, heating my blood. "The only present I want is to fuck you while you're wearing that dress."

I laughed. "Okay, maybe that can be a present for later.

But here." I thrust a bag into his hand, waiting eagerly as he opened it.

He pulled out a frame and studied the print inside. "This is our beach!" he hollered. "I surf right there." He pointed to a spot on the print just before the ocean met the sand.

"I found a local photographer."

Banjo grinned. "I love it."

An overwhelming rush of feelings came over me, as I realized there was nothing that made me happier than the pure joy on his face. That look, and knowing I put it there, was everything. He had so little. No parents to celebrate this day. A brother who didn't seem to care. Banjo had been my rock from the minute I'd laid eyes on him. Always there to put a smile on my face when everything else felt dark. From that first moment, at my uncle's wake. To him finding me after I fled from Colt at the football party. To him taking my virginity. Gillian was wrong. She didn't know Banjo like I did. He wouldn't hurt me.

I stared up into his green eyes and whispered words I hadn't planned to say. "I love you, Banjo."

For the longest moment, he didn't say anything. Then his mouth crashed down on mine, stealing my breath. Our tongues danced, while our fingers grabbed at each other, pulling closer, needing, wanting.

A car engine and a shout from behind broke us apart.

"Get a room already!" Aaron yelled from the driver's seat of his car that now idled behind Banjo's.

Owen pulled in moments later, and Meredith and Jagger joined us on the driveway.

Meredith did a twirl in her ballerina costume. "Let's get this party started!"

We all piled into our respective cars, and we followed

the convoy into Saint View, in a cloud of happy chatter and building excitement.

It would be hours later before I realized Banjo had never said I love you back.

———

*R*afe was waiting at the front of the restaurant when Banjo and I arrived, a small present bag clutched in his fingers.

Banjo kissed my temple. "I'll wait for you in the lobby, okay?" He strode away, tucking his keys into the pocket of his flight suit.

I smiled at Rafe, then ran a finger up his bare arm. "Aren't you cold?" I asked. He'd picked a Roman gladiator's costume, which showed off a lot more skin than Banjo's flight suit. Rafe's left his muscled calves bare, and the top half was sleeveless. Not that I minded the view. Rafe's biceps popped. I was glad he didn't seem to feel the cold.

He leaned in, kissing my cheek, making me shiver. "Happy birthday, Lacey."

"Thank you."

He handed me the little bag, and from inside, I produced a tiny velvet box. I glanced up at him curiously and then popped it open.

"Oh wow," I murmured. Gently, I touched a finger to the delicate gold chain with a music note hanging from the center. "It's beautiful."

"As are you. Here, let me put it on for you."

He pulled the chain from the box, and I lifted my hair, turning around so he could fasten the clasp at the back. The music note sat just above my cleavage, inches from my heart. I loved it.

"You Saint View boys are good at presents."

"We're good at partying, too. You ready to do this?"

Other kids from school were streaming in, as well as some from Edgely and Providence. There were calls of happy birthday from some of them, but it was clear to me others didn't even know who I was, and they were solely here to party.

"Ready."

"I'll see you inside then. I'll let you and Banjo have your moment of glory." He was gone before I could protest.

Banjo was waiting just inside the lobby, gazing around at the gathering crowd. I slipped my hand inside his.

"This place is fancy for Saint View."

"Wait 'til you see inside these doors. I hope you're prepared for next-level, over-the-top ridiculousness. Because I'm sure Selina, Meredith, and Jagger went all out."

"You haven't seen it?"

I shook my head. "They wouldn't let me. It's supposed to be a surprise."

He put his hand on the heavy wooden door. "Let's get surprised then."

I lifted my skirt slightly so I wouldn't trip, and entered the room, Banjo close behind me.

"Ladies and gentlemen, the birthday boy and girl have arrived!" someone yelled.

The entire room turned in our direction, a huge cheer going up that took me by surprise.

"Holy shit." Banjo laughed, waving one hand at the people milling below.

We'd entered on a dais of sorts, with stairs leading down to the main part of the room. I could see everything from our higher vantage point. It was grander than I'd expected.

Fairy lights twinkled everywhere, fresh flowers sat on tables, and the dance floor already heaved with bodies. Smoke machines gave a romantic, fantasy vibe. The football team rushed us, and Banjo was swept up, then dragged down onto the dance floor. I backed out of the fray and cast my eye over the beautiful room. Everyone lost interest and went back to dancing.

Everybody but one.

Colt stared at me from the very center of the dance floor. Bodies writhed around him, the lights dim, the music thumping, but in my head, it was like there was a spotlight shining down on him. His gorgeous eyes drifted over my body, and it somehow felt like he was right there in front of me, touching me, mapping my curves with his hands instead of his gaze. Each touch, each caress, lit up a fire in my body.

He'd come as a prince. Navy-blue suit with royal sashes and badges. A sword at his hip. And a crown, strikingly similar to my own, perched on his head.

He didn't move from his spot. And I didn't move from mine. The two of us stayed locked in some sort of mental battle, neither of us willing to look away. He was the prince to my princess. I couldn't have picked a better costume if he'd been my boyfriend and we were couple dressing.

Anger surged. I hated him. I didn't want him here. The only thing that had stopped me from removing his name from the guest list was he was Banjo's best friend, and this was his night, too. I'd thought I'd just be able to ignore Colt, but how could I? He'd done it just to play mind games with me. He'd known it would throw me off. Or maybe he thought it was funny. It wasn't. I ground my molars together. It didn't matter how his eyes on me made me want to part the sea of people and go to him. The pull was so strong, it would have been easier to just give in. Throw myself at his mercy. Beg him to kiss me. Fuck me. Just so I could stop wondering what it would be like.

It was Colt who turned away first.

I'd won.

But somehow it didn't feel like winning.

I forced my feet to move and circled the room, being the gracious host, chatting with people both from my old life and from the new. I sipped the punch, accepted birthday presents, and laughed politely when appropriate. I snatched a few moments here and there with Banjo, but he was Mr. Popularity, too, getting dragged into conversations or onto the dance floor. I spotted Rafe every now and then, his eyes burning with desire each time, and I promised myself I'd get some alone time with him before the night was through. I hadn't been alone with him since last weekend, on the way to the football game, and it had been much too long. I missed his kisses. His heart. I just wanted some time for the two of us, away from prying, judging eyes.

Owen caught up with me by the bar and pulled me aside, out of earshot of the bartenders and those waiting for drinks. "Damn, Lacey. You're stunning in that dress. Why a princess?"

I shrugged. "Long story. Listen, I've been meaning to call you."

Owen visibly perked up, obviously pleased by that.

I cringed internally. I was beginning to think that Owen might have a crush on me, and I didn't want to encourage it. He was a nice guy, and I was appreciative of his help last weekend. But that was as far as it went for me. There was no attraction from my end. Not like I had with Banjo or Rafe.

Or Colt.

I forced myself to stop subconsciously searching the room for the guys and focus on Owen. "I just wanted to say thank you. I have a lot of black spots from the other night, but I remember you helped me. I'm grateful."

He squeezed my upper arm, then let his fingers trail down my skin. "You're welcome. You know I'm here for you, right? Anytime."

I forced myself to smile.

"Maybe we can go out somewhere during the week? Just you and me."

My eyes widened. "Oh. Um, like a date?"

Owen nodded. "Exactly like that."

He stepped in closer, and I fought the urge to take a huge step back. It wasn't exactly that he disgusted me. He'd been kind to me. I didn't want to hurt his feelings. But if he invaded my bubble any farther, I wouldn't be as polite.

"Um." Shit. There was no way around this other than to just be honest. "I'm sorry. But no. I just don't feel that way about you."

Surprise widened his eyes, but then he laughed. "Wow. Okay. Well, that's never happened before."

His laugh didn't quite sound sincere, but I laughed, too, feeling awkward.

"I'm sorry."

"Why are you sorry, babe?" With the worst possible timing, Rafe swooped in behind me, fitting his chest to my back and wrapping his arms around my middle. He kissed my cheek.

Owen scowled at him. "Not your business."

Rafe loosened his grip, moving me to stand at his side. But his attention was all on Owen. "Excuse me? Anything to do with Lacey is my business. Who the hell are you?"

Owen looked to me. "Seriously? Who is this?"

I sighed. "Owen, I'll talk to you later, okay?"

Owen shook his head and stalked off. Rafe smirked.

"You didn't have to do that," I complained, slightly irritated.

"The guy was hitting on you. I heard every word. You didn't like it."

"Or you were jealous?"

He shook his head. "Don't get jealous over small dick pricks like him. And anyway, I wanted to show you something."

He guided me into the shadows and pushed me up against the wall, kissing me slowly, his tongue invading my mouth and my senses until I forgot all about hurting Owen's feelings. I snaked my hands into Rafe's hair.

"Tonight?" I whispered, pulling back from him, breathless and needy, heat coiling between my legs. "Come home with me tonight."

He touched his forehead to mine. "I want to, baby. I do. What about Banjo?"

"Both of you," I whispered boldly. "It's my birthday, after all."

He gave me a wicked grin. "Indeed it is, princess. And birthday girls always come first."

I went to kiss him again, but he dodged my advances, and instead, caught my hand. "First, though, Banjo and I have a surprise for you."

I raised one eyebrow, then leaned in, pressing against him seductively. "Is it the sort of surprise where we're naked? Alone? In a room, and I take your—"

"Jesus, stop," Rafe said, voice dark and verging on pained. "Or I won't be able to get through this." He towed me up onto the stage, grabbing Banjo from a conversation with one of his football friends. "It's time," he said.

Banjo nodded and followed us up the stairs. He positioned me in the center of the stage and made a motion to someone at the back of the room. A spotlight lit us up, bathing us in bright, yellow light. I blinked a few times to adjust my eyes, while Rafe went to a microphone and tapped it, checking to see if it was on.

Someone cut the music and upped the house lights, so I could see each and every face in the crowd.

Apart from Colt. I couldn't see him anywhere.

"Good evening, everyone," Rafe began, drawing the attention of the last few people in the room. "For those who don't know us, I'm Rafe, and this is Banjo."

Banjo stepped forward and gave a wave, before Rafe continued.

"We've gotten very close with Lacey since she came to Saint View..."

I jerked my head in his direction. Close was an understatement. But there were only a few titters from the crowd. At least most people were mature enough to take it at face value.

"...and we wanted to do something special to mark her eighteenth birthday."

I glanced in Banjo's direction, and he grinned.

"You'll love it," he whispered.

Rafe signaled to someone at the back of the room again, and a screen dropped down behind us.

"Turn around," Banjo said in my ear. "Happy birthday."

My cheeks flamed beneath the makeup, but I turned around, squeezing Banjo's hand in the process. On the screen, 'Happy Birthday, Lacey' flashed up, and an annoyingly jovial, upbeat song played.

"Here's a little trip down memory lane," Banjo's voice said on the video.

I groaned good naturedly as a photo of me at age five, just after I'd come to live at Lawson and Selina's flashed up on the screen. The next image was a more recent photo. The dreaded braces years. I winced as the room chuckled with laughter. But it was in good fun. There were photos of Meredith and me in our matching school uniforms. Me, Lawson, and Selina on a family picnic. Me playing on stage at a Providence recital during my junior year. Then a handful of selfies Jagger had dragged me into, plus one she must have secretly taken, of me, Rafe, and Banjo all huddled together after the football game.

The video ended, and everybody clapped. I turned back to face the room of people smiling up at me. My aunt was in the front row with Meredith and Jagger not far behind her.

Then, across the room, Colt caught my eye. He reclined against a pillar, casual, and with a smirk aimed my way. Him the cocky prince, me the haughty princess. Our outfits a pair in a way we'd never be. Like before, our gazes collided and held, fierce electricity slamming between us.

A loud moan ripped through the sound system.

The crowd gasped, and a familiar voice said, *"Fuck, Lacey. You're so gorgeous. I love bare pussy."*

Hoots and hollers erupted. I spun around.

The world around me tipped upside down. Because right there on a huge screen, for everybody I knew to see, was my worst nightmare. One I couldn't wake up from. It just kept playing.

My naked body. Laid out on Banjo's bed, legs spread, while I panted in need, waiting for Rafe and Banjo to pleasure me.

"Get your mouth on it then. Before I do."

On the screen, Rafe went to work between my thighs, while Banjo kissed me and I moaned like I was a porn star. I held Rafe's head, grinding against him while he went down on me.

Blackness dodged the edges of my vision, and yet I couldn't look away.

"Turn that off!" someone yelled, but it faded into the laughter and the catcalls from the rest of the room.

"Lacey!" someone shouted, but I'd gone numb all over as shock rolled through my system.

Banjo shook me. "Lacey!"

That woke me up. My gaze focused in on his face. His beautiful green eyes that I loved. And then I drew back my arm and slapped him hard across the face.

My palm stung. Banjo's expression morphed into shock.

"Lacey..." he said quietly. He didn't even lift a hand to his cheek, though the outline of my fingers appeared almost instantly.

I felt little satisfaction in it, though.

"You taped us?" I hissed. "How could you!"

"Lacey, I—"

I held up a hand. "Shut up. Don't even bother."

Banjo backed off a step, only for Rafe to take his place.

I shot him down with a single look. "Don't tell me you didn't know what he was doing. You're an asshole."

Hurt and betrayal washed over me like a tidal wave, ready to drag me down and drown me in its depths. And in that moment, I might have let it.

I'd trusted them. And they'd betrayed me. In the worst possible way. In a way I couldn't come back from. It was fine for them. Society didn't treat men the same way they treated women. They'd be local legends. The Saint View slum dogs who'd had a threesome with the society princess. And I'd be the slut who'd been stupid enough to let two boys film her at her most vulnerable.

Bile rose in my mouth. I fled the stage, running for the door.

"Lacey!" Meredith yelled, my aunt and Jagger right behind her.

I shook off Meredith's touch, face burning with shame. I couldn't even look at my aunt. Couldn't bear the thought of the woman who I'd just called Mom for the first time seeing me like that. Shame rolled through me, mixed with a healthy dose of hate. In one sick, twisted move, they'd ruined everything I'd spent the last thirteen years building with Selina. Just one glance at her horrified face told me she'd never look at me the same. And I couldn't blame her. I'd embarrassed her in front of everybody we knew. It would be minutes before the entire episode was online, and then we'd never live it down.

"Just leave me alone," I begged them, choking on my tears. "Please. Just leave me alone." I ran for the door again, bursting outside. The frigid wind whipped around me, and the waves roared. They smashed onto the beach, calling me in their direction, promising to drown out the laughter still bellowing behind me. I hit the sand stumbling, kicking off my shoes.

The smell of smoke filled my nostrils. The glowing red end of a cigarette broke the darkness, but I was practically on top of the person before I realized who it was. I dimly took in her sparkling dress and spiked heels.

"I warned you," Gillian said into the night air. Then she laughed cruelly. "Stupid bitch. You didn't really think they'd love you back, did you? They're broken, princess. All three of them. They've lived through shit upbringings and traumas you know nothing about. They can't love you. Not even if they wanted to."

Her laugher took my breath away and replaced it with a stabbing pain.

She'd been right. She'd warned me. I hadn't listened.

And I'd paid the price.

Gillian's laughter was the last thing I heard as I ran blindly down the beach and into the darkness.

34

LACEY

I ran until my lungs burned. Until the lights from the party disappeared. Until the people shouting my name were drowned out by the ocean. And then I sank down onto the sand, still cold and wet from the high tide, and cried. Great heaving sobs that jerked my entire body. I hadn't grabbed my coat, and the wind whipped around my bare skin.

It had all been lies. Devious little lies, one stacked on top of the other. Each one so tiny I hadn't noticed them all building up until they came crashing down on top of me. Each one splintered my skin, ripping it, tearing it like tiny shards of falling glass from a shattered window. But it was my heart that was broken. I had feelings for Rafe, and he'd thrown them in my face. And Banjo...I couldn't breathe when I thought about how just hours ago, I'd stood in his arms and told him I was in love with him.

I loved him.

But he loved Colt.

I should have known when he'd told me he thought of Colt as his brother. He'd told me he owed Colt everything.

Colt had declared a war on me from the very first day of school. And yet I'd thought Banjo and Rafe would go against that? I was an idiot. A stupid, foolish girl who'd listened to the lies of boys.

At least Colt had never lied. A bitter laugh fell from my lips. How ironic, the one I hated the most, was the only one who'd been truthful this entire time. He'd said I was breakable.

He'd been right.

"Lacey," a voice said in the darkness. He sat down beside me in the sand. "God, there you are. Are you okay?"

I didn't have the strength to run away anymore. Didn't have the strength left to fight. It had all gone to shit. "No," I whispered to Owen. A sob bubbled up my throat. "No, I'm really not."

He put his arm around my shoulders and pulled me tight. I burrowed against his chest, letting the warmth of him thaw my frozen body, drawing comfort from being held.

He dropped a kiss on my head and rubbed my chilled arms with his palms. "Sssh," he whispered. "It's all going to be okay."

But it wasn't. He didn't know that. I couldn't stop crying. My tears soaked his thin shirt, sobs racking my entire body until I was exhausted and weak. Logically, I knew I was crashing after the spike of adrenaline, but there was no stopping it. Owen was a safe place. He'd gotten me home from this beach once before, and I instinctively knew he'd do it again.

"Thank you for coming after me," I whispered. "I don't know what I'd do without you."

Owen grasped my chin and tilted my face up to look at him. He used his thumbs to wipe the tears from my cheeks. "I'm always here for you. Always."

I closed my eyes, trying to ward off a fresh round of tears, but it was impossible. They seeped between my eyelashes, running down my cheeks again. Owen kissed my temple, then my cheek, the edge of my mouth, chasing tears.

His lips landed on mine.

I didn't move. I was spent. Emotionally and physically drained. His kisses grew bolder, pressing against my mouth, running his tongue over my unresponsive lips, urging me to open.

"Come on, baby," he murmured. "I know how to make you feel better."

His voice snapped me out of my trance. I shoved him. "Owen, stop."

It was as if I hadn't spoken. He came right back in, harder this time, taking what he wanted. There was nothing gentle about this kiss. It was demanding. Hard. Unfeeling.

His fingers wrapped around my upper arms, holding me in place while he assaulted my mouth. Nausea rolled my stomach, and I shoved him away again.

"Owen! I said, stop! I told you before, I don't feel that way about you."

His fingers still bit into my skin, but he reared back.

"You stupid bitch," he hissed. "You give it up for the Saint View trash, but not for me? I've got hired help who earn more than those fuckboys will ever earn in their lives."

I struggled with his grip on me. "Maybe so, but that doesn't make you better than them. And it sure as shit doesn't determine who I sleep with. Let go!"

The back of his hand cracked across my face, taking me by surprise. Sharp pain exploded in my cheekbone, and the force of the impact had my head snapping to the left. I cried out at the pain, covering my cheek with my hand. My eyes watered as I slowly brought my gaze back to his.

I jerked away at the expression on his face. It was cold. Hard. Furious.

For the first time that night, a new emotion crept in.

Fear.

This wasn't the Owen I knew. This wasn't the Owen who had rescued me from the beach last weekend after Colt had thrown my keys into the ocean. This wasn't the boy who had cared for me and helped me into bed.

"Is that how you like it?" he sneered. "Do those Saint View boys rough you up before they plunge their cocks inside you?" He yanked my hand and rubbed it over his straining erection.

I tried to pull away, but he yanked my arm so hard my shoulder jolted in pain.

"I know what you do for them, slut. The whole fucking world just saw it. You do it for them. You can do it for me. At least I can afford to pay you."

He grabbed the spaghetti strap on my dress and shoved it down my shoulder. The material bit into my skin, and I cried out when he squeezed my breast.

"Owen, stop!" I yelled.

But he was no longer listening.

I fought to get away from him, scrambling backward across the sand, but he caught me easily, cracking his hand across my face again.

The metallic taste of blood filled my mouth, and I moaned in pain.

"Oh, that's how they get you to moan like that, huh?"

Another backhand had my eye swelling.

I opened my mouth to scream, but he clapped one meaty hand over my lips, pushing the back of my head down into the sand with force.

"Now now," he whispered, running his nose up my neck

and to my ear. "No need for that. Hold still, and I'll have you screaming in pleasure. If I move my hand, are you going to scream? Shake your head like a good girl."

I shook my head.

He moved his hand.

"Fuck you," I screamed in his face. "Hel—"

I only got half the word out when his fist slammed into my stomach. My whole body locked up. I'd never felt pain like that before. It spread out like a wildfire from my midsection, stealing my breath. Another blow across the face had me curling into a ball, instinctively trying to protect my head. I squeezed my eyes closed. There was no fighting him off. He was too big. Too strong. His fists rained pain all over my body, while he swore at me, called me a slut and a whore.

He didn't let up. Not for a moment. His rage and his fury were all directed solely at me.

My mind drifted. The pain lessened. And as I floated in and out of the fading blackness, my only thought was I'd trusted all the wrong people. Banjo. Rafe. Owen. They'd all betrayed me.

But this wouldn't be my downfall. They might have won this battle. But this was a war.

If I lived through this, I'd be their princess no longer.

I'd be their fucking queen.

And they'd bow to me. Whether they liked it or not.

To be continued...

Preorder book 2— Dangerous Little Secrets (Coming September 24th, 2020)

Preorder book 3— Twisted Little Truths (Coming December 28th, 2020)

*W*ant more of Banjo and Rafe? Yeah, I did too! So I wrote them a steamy little bonus scene that takes place the morning after their almost threesome with Lacey. Download it from the bonus material section of my website https://www. ellethorpe.com/deviouslittleliarsbonus

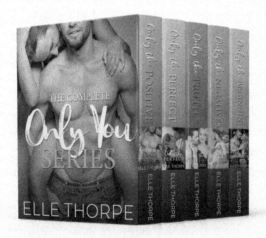
"Reese, stop! I have HIV."

The words exploded from his lips like a cannon blast,

halting me in my tracks. The silence was deafening as I slowly turned around.

"What?" I honestly wasn't sure I'd heard him correctly.

He shook his head, one hand gripping the back of his neck. He took a step towards me. "There's a chance I have HIV. A good chance. I've had direct exposure and I'm being tested for it."

My hand flew to my mouth as my heart skipped a beat. HIV? As in AIDS?

He grimaced, his features twisting, his hurt clearly evident on his face. "And that's why I didn't want to tell anyone. I didn't want to see that look of disgust. Especially not from you."

I dropped my hand, shame creeping over me. I wasn't disgusted, but shock rolled through me like a wave, making my movements sluggish. How was I supposed to react?

"Don't worry, you can't catch it from kissing, or from anything else we've done. You're safe."

All the heat and passion between us had disappeared, and where moments before his voice had been sweet, he now sounded sharp and sarcastic. He shook his head and jogged over to his horse.

My feet were rooted to the spot. I wasn't responding the right way. I didn't need his body language to confirm that. But my brain seemed to be disconnected from my body. I had no idea how to make it move, or make it talk. No idea how to make it do anything that would salvage this situation, so we could go back to making out. I touched my fingertips to my lips.

His face was blank when he turned back to face me.

"You see now why we had to stop? I told you it had nothing to do with you. Do you believe me now? I couldn't stay away from you. So maybe you could do me a favour and stay away from me."

For this month only, the boxset is on sale for $5.99. Save over $10, off the regular price of all five books. Tap here to learn more.

ALSO BY ELLE THORPE

The Only You series (complete)

*Only the Positive (Only You, #1) - Reese and Low.

*Only the Perfect (Only You, #2) - Jamison.

*Only the Truth - (Only You, bonus novella) - Bree.

*Only the Negatives (Only You, #3) - Gemma.

*Only the Beginning (Only You, #4) - Bianca and Riley.

*Only You boxset

*All of Him - A single dad anthology, featuring Only the Lies. Only the Lies is a bonus, Only You novella.

Dirty Cowboy series (complete)

*Talk Dirty, Cowboy (Dirty Cowboy, #1)

*Ride Dirty, Cowboy (Dirty Cowboy, #2)

*Sexy Dirty Cowboy (Dirty Cowboy, #3)

*25 Reasons to Hate Christmas and Cowboys (a Dirty Cowboy bonus novella, set before Talk Dirty, Cowboy but can be read as a standalone, holiday romance)

Saint View High series (coming July-December 2020)

*Devious Little Liars (Saint View High, #1)

*Dangerous Little Secrets (Saint View High, #2)

*Twisted Little Truths (Saint View High, #3)

Buck Cowboys series (coming early 2021)

*Buck You! (Buck Cowboys, #1)

*TBA (Buck Cowboys, #2)

*TBA (Buck Cowboys, #3)

Add your email address here to be the first to know when new books are available!

www.ellethorpe.com/newsletter

Join Elle Thorpe's readers group on Facebook!

www.facebook.com/groups/ellethorpesdramallamas

ACKNOWLEDGMENTS

I hope you enjoyed the first book in the Saint View High series. What a wild ride it's been, getting inside these characters heads and digging out all their secrets. There's so much more to come over the next two books. Believe me when I say, you ain't see nothin' yet.

A huge thank you to all my readers, new and old. To the ones who have been here all along - I still pinch myself that you keep coming back. Thank you! And to the newbies, welcome aboard! Come hang out with us in my facebook group!

Thank you to Jolie Vines, Zoe Ashwood, Emmy Ellis and Karen Hrdlicka who make up my stellar editing team. And an extra thanks to Jo and Zoe for being my author besties too! Thank you to Sara Massery for the chats, sprints and graphic design advice. Not to mention for the push to try a new genre. Thank you to Shellie, Lissanne and Dana for your early feedback.

And as always, a huge thank you to my family. To Jira, Thomas, Flick, and Heidi. You four are the loves of my life and I couldn't do any of this without you.

Love, Elle x

ABOUT THE AUTHOR

Elle Thorpe lives on the sunny east coast of Australia. When she's not writing stories full of kissing, she's a wife and mummy to three tiny humans. She's also official ball thrower to one slobbery dog named Rollo. Yes, she named a female dog after a dirty hot character on Vikings. Don't judge her. Elle is a complete and utter fangirl at heart, obsessing over The Walking Dead and Outlander to an unhealthy degree. But she wouldn't change a thing.

You can find her on Facebook or Instagram(@ellethorpe-books or hit the links below!) or at her website www. ellethorpe.com. If you love Elle's work, please consider joining her Facebook fan group, Elle Thorpe's Drama Llamas or joining her newsletter here. www. ellethorpe.com/newsletter

- facebook.com/ellethorpebooks
- instagram.com/ellethorpebooks
- goodreads.com/ellethorpe
- pinterest.com/ellethorpebooks

CPSIA information can be obtained
at www.ICGtesting.com
Printed in the USA
BVHW082154010822
643541BV00002B/114

We can start to become who we want to be, and live the life we want to live.

Letting go of our attachment to our inner processes enables us to identify fear and face it. When we realise it that our emotions are a part of us, but they are not us, we can detach from them, and observe them when they rise up inside us. We no longer become defined by our anger, or our sadness, or by the things that frighten us. When we are able to observe our fear of the dark from a distance, we find ourselves able to no longer be afraid of the dark. When we no longer hold on to the emotions that manipulate us, and release them into the air as if they were doves, we can choose to be in charge of how we feel, how we think and how we act. We are no longer at the mercy of those things, those entities, who gain from being able to 'push our buttons'.

Letting go enables us to resist the charms of the ad execs and find contentment where we are, with who we are and with what we've got. Letting go allows us to recognise and feel grateful for all the blessings in our life. Letting go allows us to be our own authentic selves, and not the products of our past, or the desires of others, or the influences of things. Letting go allows us to reduce our suffering, and take ownership of our lives, our behaviour and our identities.

When we let go of our yearning to be anything other than who we are, we find ourselves sated, satisfied. We are no longer hungry for completion from the false icons of materialism.

When we let go of the internal tensions that cause us to be triggered by external influences – our attachment to pride and ego, of who we think we are 'supposed' to be, or desperate need to be right all the time – we can take ownership of our pure, unadulterated selves. We move closer to our id, our intrinsic identity, and when this happens extenuating circumstances cease to exist.

The big person is not the angry person, the fighter, the boaster, the bully or the abuser. The big person is the calm equanimous person, the one unswayed by taunts or attacks on their pride and ego, calm in the face of adversity, interested only in praise or criticism as tools for improvement, not in need of the approval of others, and not controlled by wants, status, things and people.

There is no conflict, no pressure and pain, no tug of war if you let go of the rope. Only equanimity, peace, contentment and love.

But letting go can be one of the hardest things we will ever do, and is a practice that must be entered into for life. And once we learn to let go, the lightness and brightness of life will be waiting for us.

In order to let go, we must first find the thing that we are holding on to. It is this attachment that causes the suffering, as the Buddha identified those thousands of years ago. When we feel embarrassed it is our attachment to pride that is causing us hurt. When we feel undermined it is our attachment to our ego that is causing us hurt. When we feel anxious, lost or in emotional pain, somewhere within ourselves there is an attachment that is causing us hurt.

When we feel stuck, as if we are being denied the rich rewards of life that we feel we truly deserve, somewhere there is an attachment that is posing as an obstacle in our path. By exploring ourselves we can find the thing that we need to let go of, and find a way around the blockage. Perhaps it's a fear we need to overcome, perhaps it's a skill that we need to learn, or perhaps it's a stubbornness that we must release in order to do get past this obstacle.

We can let go of internal attachments to those things that are not truly us – our biases, our inability to deal with our emotional states, the things that haunt us from the past which have now become part of who we perceive ourselves to be. And when we let go of these things it allows us to jettison parts of our identity which no longer serve us, or which are holding us back, in order that we can reinvent ourselves and move forward. And we become less burdened, more agile, bright and lighter in the process.

Where once we were thought we were a person who was afraid of public speaking, we no longer identify with that anxiety and find ourselves equipped to become the person who wows the crowd by learning what it takes to become an amazing orator. Where once we were the person who was bad with numbers, we can instead become someone who can push through that mental roadblock, go back to college to learn maths and reverse that part of us that we hid behind. Where once we were someone who couldn't leave the house because a past mugging left us terrified of the street, we are now the person who sees that mask for what it is, and choose to distance themselves from it, denying the muggers that continued control over them years after the event by reclaiming the streets for themselves.

When we learn to let go, we decide which forces can exert any power over us. Do we let the snide comments of others ruin our days, or do we see their comments more a reflection of them than of us? Do we let rainy weather spoil our morning, or do we choose to remember that above the clouds the sun is shining? Do we decide to rid ourselves of the things that no longer serve us, as comfortable and familiar as they are, and do we take a chance and step into the unknown?

Do we have the drink we crave now, or decide to wait until later, to see if we can? And when we see that we can, do we choose to feel empowered that we've rested a little control from the bottle? Or do we really identify as someone who cannot resist?

Do we let go of our perception of who we think we are, in order to find the person we can be?

It's in our nature to find comfort in the familiar, and when we are enduring an extended period of sorrow, it is this sorrow that becomes familiar. It becomes a part of us, of our identity, and like the innocent party in an abusive relationship we cannot leave, because the sorrow is all we know. We are stuck in our rut, enclosed and captive, but it is home and we know what to expect. Our depression, anxiety and sadness become our friends, and as much as we wish we weren't here, we don't wish to be anywhere else.

When offered a chance at freedom from this prison of our own making, we become defensive, finding excuses and reasons to stay inside our cell. Our sense of identity, our pride and our ego are all so attached to our hurt and our weakness and failure that we don't want to be anywhere else. This is, after all, who we are.

At least, that's what we've convinced ourselves.

Of course we have visions of the perfect life. Daydreams of dancing along pristine beaches next to crystal seas, hand-in-hand with our loved one, enjoying all the blessings that life has to offer. But dreams and visions are all they are. We are comfortable with what we know, and not knowing any different we find it hard to believe that anything better is possible. We become so stuck in this pattern of belief and disbelief, so blinkered to what could be, that we find security and solace in what is. When opportunities for a better reality arrive, we bat them away angrily. When doors open in front of us, we step back and find justification for not striding forward into the lives, and the identities, that could be.

We have become institutionalised in our grief. It has become a mask that we have hidden ourselves behind for so long, that we have forgotten it's just a mask, and not our real identity. But we can take it off, we can discard it, we can choose to stop it controlling us anymore. We don't have to identify with our failings. We can choose to identify with something else instead.

Good things don't happen to me, we think, so what's the point in trying? I don't deserve happiness and success. What if it doesn't work out? All that time and effort would have been for nothing. How embarrassing. What will people think? The shame of trying and failing seem so much greater than the satisfaction of simply trying.

Because good things like that don't happen to people like me.

But all we're doing is finding excuses to stay safely wrapped inside the comfort blanket of unhappiness. It's what we know, it's part of our identity and we are attached to its cosy familiarity. And it's this that keeps us warm and safe as it drags us down into the darkest, murkiest depths. We cling to our sadness, and turn our backs on joy. After all, one is certain and the other merely a maybe.

But attachment is suffering, and in those three words we find the biggest truth about human dissatisfaction and unhappiness. Indeed, this is one of the most powerful truths in the universe and, in a nutshell, reveals the problem and solution to the human condition. It is the things we are attached to that cause us to suffer, that cause us pain, and which become obstacles not just to our happiness and contentment, but to the material rewards we seek, the dreams we dare to dream, and the lives we've always wished for.

It is attachment that keeps us deprived of the joy and contentment that we seek. It is attachment that causes wars, that is responsible for famine, that prevents mankind from curing disease, that leads to inequality and destitution, that leads to fear and crime and all social ills. It is attachment that prevents mankind from reaching out beyond the confines of this planet and exploring the stars. Attachment to pride and ego will drown us as surely as bricks in our pockets, dragging us to the bottom of the sea. If we could simply let go, we could float to the surface, and up to the sky, and up to the stars, and be free.

It is attachment that is causing our unhappiness.

So often when our pride or our ego is hurt, we blame the outside world, the influences beyond our control, but if we were to look within ourselves with a level of clear self-awareness and objectivity, we would understand that it is our attachment that is truly causing us this pain.

When we feel pain, by seeking out the source of that hurt within we can let go of aspects of ourselves that don't serve us, or at least choose which attachments we are prepared to endure the pain for, and which we are prepared to release our grasp on. When we become bitter because life doesn't reward us as we think it should, is it because we have become so attached to an aspect of our identity that our ego has become hurt? When we trip and nearly fall, to the amusement of others, it is their giggles or our attachment to pride that is causes us painful embarrassment? When we reject peace and agreement and instead choose conflict in order to make some point or other, it is our pride stabbing us repeatedly in the back. We must stand our ground, we tell ourselves, we must, we must, even though the ground is giving way beneath us.

When a loved one passes away, it is not their passing that hurts us, but our attachment – our love – that hurts us. Indeed, when we fall in love, we say that we accept the risk of this pain, because the joy of love is so intoxicating and fulfilling that we are prepared to face those consequences. We are prepared to endure the inevitable heartbreak of bereavement and grief, because that is the price of love. And it is worth it.

But attachment can hurt us in other ways. When we have a bad hair day it is our attachment to our self-image, and ultimately our ego, that is hurt. And when we can't have that thing we want, it is the attachment to lack and the sense of dissatisfaction that causes us pain. Unable to gain the status that we believe material objects provide us – unable to prove ourselves to be worthy in the shallow surface world – we find ourselves hurt, making excuses and looking for someone or something to blame.

When we find ourselves so attached to the opinions of others, as we are increasingly encouraged to do in the social media consumerist shallow surface world of the west, we become paralysed, unable to enact the great joys that we loved as a child because we worry what people might think. That same attachment to the values and opinions of others prevents us from taking steps to realise our dreams, to fulfil our potential, to take the strides we see others doing, when instead we find we don't have the courage, because we are afraid of what people might think.

This attachment to the validation and permissions of others strangles us, becoming tighter and tighter like a snake tightening its grip around our neck with every breath we take. Eventually, that pressure to keep up with the Joneses, to live up to ideals that are not our own, to gain the respect of our peers who are too busy themselves wondering what other people think, it wears us down.

Rather than being validated we become violated, our sense of self in tatters because nobody cares, because we've worked so hard for the attention and the approval, and it never came. Our attachment to these strange ideals that are so alien to us, of wanting to be a part of a community that doesn't reflect who we truly are, of pretending to be someone we are not, has left us confused and unsure of our identity. We don't know who we are any more, or what we really want, or what holds any value for us.

But what's worse, all of that effort, all of that emotional energy was spent attempting to attain things that don't matter.

It doesn't matter what car you drive. All that matters is that you turn up when you need to. It doesn't matter who made the jacket you're wearing or what restaurant you eat at. All that matters is that you're clothed and fed. It doesn't matter how many bedrooms your house has, as long as you have a roof over your head. None of it matters.

It doesn't matter that you lost the argument. It doesn't matter that your neighbour has a bigger TV than you. It doesn't matter that someone hurt you. It doesn't matter if the world knows you did the kind deed, only that the kind deed was done. It doesn't matter what people think about your clothes, your status symbols, that you would hug a tree or dance in the rain if only you could summon the courage.

All that matters is that you are able to let this all go, because that is where you will find your freedom and reward and yourself. No longer tethered, no longer under the thumb of your past or your status or your fears or your insecurities, you can let go of the things that are holding you down, and spread your wings and fly.

When we have no attachment – or at least learn the discipline of letting go – we find ourselves filled not so much with pain or hurt or resentment or bitterness, but with peace and contentment and maybe even joy. When we can let go of thoughts of personal injustice and the disempowering anxieties of those things that we cling to, we are free to pause and appreciate everything that we have.

When we let go of the anger, the fear, and the other negative emotions that control us, soak up our capacity and misdirect our attention, we find ourselves free to look around and appreciate how rich and beautiful our lives and our world are. Rather than looking for the next thing, or to have the last word, prove a point, get revenge or feed our addiction to the petty rewards of the surface world and perpetuate our constant state of dissatisfaction, want and lack, we find ourselves instead experiencing a state of peace, forgiveness, contentment and happiness. Our capacity is not taken up with the trifles of the material world, but we are able to contemplate greater things, find enjoyment and riches beyond our dreams in the motion of a blade of grass in the wind, or the clarity of a raindrop on the velvet petal of a rose, or the smile of a stranger, or in the sense of satisfaction that comes from helping another even in the smallest way.

There is happiness in the chirping of the cricket in the grass. Magic in the sound of the wind in the trees. There are explosions of experience in our senses of taste, touch, feel, sight and sound. Even the smallest bubble from the mouth of a goldfish can contain a lifetime of happiness.

But beyond finding joy in the mundane minutiae of everyday life, the ability to let go can put us at an advantage in all the worlds that we wish to inhabit. Conflicts are avoided and mastered because our egos are no longer attached to the notion of winning at all costs, and we can choose which battles to forgo and which are worth the effort. We can skip trivialities that otherwise would have become sticking points and obsessions, and learn to recognise which ideas are holding us back simply because we can't let go of them. We can choose to strategically disconnect from our ego and from our sense of self, to find the best way to tackle any obstacle or problem, and then take the action required to make it work. And we do so without complaint, without frustration or annoyance, and only with the great satisfaction that comes with knowing that we are on the path of freedom.

Letting go offers us new avenues, new chances for contentment and new worlds of riches we hadn't previously even considered because we were too busy holding on to the familiar, the regular, but ultimately the thing that was causing us pain and preventing us from advancing. By letting go of the good, or the thing that we perceived to be important, but which was simply superficial, we open the doors to a bigger, richer world, with more to offer.

Our dogma and the blind allegiances to religions, flags, nations and political parties become cages that keep us trapped, preventing us from to progressing to a better world. Our stubborn attachment to principles and notions, our unwillingness to forgive and our points of pride keep us stuck in a world that suffocates our potential for greatness. And the walls are getting closer. How liberating to let go of that loyalty to our ego's follies in order to contemplate what lies beyond – the ideas, the people, the opportunity to think freely, to see reality for ourselves, rather than through the values that have been prescribed to us.

We can only be free when we release our attachment to that which holds us back.

Like a ship moored in the harbour, unable to fulfil our purpose on the high seas until the ropes are released, we can never truly see what life can offer us – and what we can offer it – while we are attached to notions, feelings, pride, identity and ego.

The idea that "people like us don't do things like that" keeps us boxed in, our shoulders hunched due to the confinement of our cells, our backs aching, and our shoulders bruised from the burdens that we carry. But by letting go, we say, "people like me do whatever we want" and we are liberated, emancipated, and free to discover our new worlds, and our new selves. Free to see through fresh eyes. Free to explore new lands, ideas, sensations and to dream new dreams. Free to exercise the responsibility that comes with great power.

Letting go of these cages releases our resistance to life. When we stop fighting and start playing, there's nowhere we can't go, nothing we can't learn, nobody we can't be. When we let go of our fear, our anger and hatred and bitterness and resentment fall away too. We are children again, playing wide-eyed and full of wonder as if it's our first visit to the seaside.

There is a universe of ideas and opportunities out there, and the things we are attached to are stopping us from exploring it. The ideas that we hold dear, the stubbornness of our identities, the cages of our ascribed morals. The newspapers we read, the people we spend time with, the values we've never challenged, are all recognised now as walls that have kept us away from being our biggest, best, happiest selves.

Letting go is the most powerful thing we can do. Letting go releases visions of ourselves and our lives into reality. Letting go dismisses the traumas and upsets of the past and opens the doorway to the future. Letting go allows anger and sorrow to drift away, releases the resistance to the work that must be done, and under its wings hide the two gifts of forgiveness and healing.

Letting go of who you are allows you to be who you could be. You, but without the trappings of what others had in mind for you, without the shackles of approval and permission, without the burdens of expectation. Letting go is your key to shape your world into whatever form you wish, to giving yourself enough room to make dreams come true, and to build a better future for yourself, and for the world. Let go today and be born anew tomorrow.

But more than this, when we learn to let go of the past, and of the future, we can relish this moment, right now. We can see the abundance around us, and see that we want for nothing. By letting go of wants, desires, and the things that keep us in a sense of dissatisfaction and lack, we suddenly find that we have everything we could ever need, and usually most of the things we want, too.

When we stop to breathe deeply, and in doing so release all our tension and attachment, we find this moment. When we focus on the sensation of the air on our skin, or the feeling of our feet on the floor, or what our fingers feel like as we move them back and forth, we release everything that we hold on to, everything that holds on to us, and it all drifts away like a feather on the breeze. We experience nothing but the sensation of being and our own awareness.

In this moment, right now, the past and the future meet. We see the inevitable decay of shallow material desires and understand that their real worth is magnitudes smaller than we once believed. And we start to be able to put value on the things that count – the sensation of breathing deeply, of the feeling of moving our arms, our bodies, the connection with the floor on which we stand, and the ethereal threads that connect us to every point and every person in the universe.

Letting go of biases, of beliefs, of all the things we've been taught to think, of the desire for approval and validation from others, enables us to find ourselves in the middle of our universe. A drop in an ocean of thought, part of an infinite continuum of being.

Finally, we see ourselves without the adornments of want and lack. Finally, we see ourselves through the sensations of our senses, of our connection to this place in time and space. We see ourselves as part of a vast expanse where money is meaningless, where status means nothing, where just our basic essence spreads out in all directions. Infinite. Immaculate. Divine.

There is no fear here, just being. There is no judgement here, just awareness. Now we know what it means to just be.

And when we bring ourselves back to this shallow world, of contracts and laws, of fashion and stuff, of laundry and goods and services, our perspective is broadened. We can rise above everything, because we know we can do anything.

Let go of fear and no obstacle is unworthy of an attempt to overcome it. Let go of fear, and no goal is unworthy of an attempt to reach it. Let go of fear, and we can be who we want to be, because nothing else matters.

And if that is true, then let's be someone good, someone great, someone with the life we've always wanted. The life we deserve, that we're capable of, that we have no reason not to have.

My eyes, which had seen all, came back,
Back to the white chrysanthemums.

— Kougi Isshō

Chapter 20
Lorenzo With The Vase

"Yesterday is but today's memory, and tomorrow is today's dream." – Khalil Gibran

This must be the place, thought Genaro as he looked up at the villa. But the shutters were closed and now at the end of summer the wind was blowing leaves that were piling in the doorways. He hesitated for a moment, before stepping through the gate and proceeding up to the front door. It looked as if it hadn't been opened in years.

When no-one answered his knocks, he searched around the house, hoping for a gap in the shutters, so that he might catch a glimpse of... it. But inside all was dark.

As he completed his circuit around the grand villa, he heard the sound of sweeping, and turning the corner came face to face with an old gardener, trying in vain to clear the leaves that were blowing around faster than he could collect them up.

He introduced himself as Genaro, a porcelain expert and restorer from the University of Naples. He had been travelling for a long time, in the hope of meeting a man who was known only as Lorenzo With The Vase. And in doing so, he had hoped to see the article which gave him his name – a pristine example of an ancient Chinese vase that stood taller than a man. It was thought to be the last of its type, considered by many to be priceless, and considered by others to be a myth.

The gardener paused for a moment, and leaned against his broom. From time to time people still turned up in the village, looking for the villa with the wonderful vase, and he would take great pleasure in recounting the tragic tale. Of course, these days the visitors were less frequent as the story began to fall out of memory, but from time to time he still got the opportunity to recount the sad story of his old boss, Lorenzo With The Vase.

Lorenzo With The Vase had lived in this once impressive villa for many years, a ruthless capitalist and trader, he had spent his whole life amassing riches for the sole purpose of purchasing a mythological Chinese vase that he had heard about as a child, in a story that immediately captured his attention.

Lorenzo With The Vase talked about this ambition so much that it was a wonder anyone in the world didn't know about his goal. Until one day it was a goal no more, and he had made enough money through his business activities to fund a voyage to the other side of the world. He was gone for months, and when the village had nearly forgotten all about him, whispers started circling that he was on his way home.

And then one day he arrived, and in tow was a huge wooden box, carried slower than a funeral cortège on the back of a cart. A few days later the whole village was invited to a grand unveiling at the villa, and Lorenzo With The Vase revealed his grand purchase to his friends and neighbours. Standing on a plinth in the grand entrance hall of his villa it was a sight to behold. At least seven feet tall, with a glaze that captured all the colours of the rainbow, the white vase was decorated in pale blue scenes that seemed to describe the entire history of China. Emperors, battles, animals and landscapes covered the ample sides of this beautiful, delicate piece of porcelain.

For years it was all the industrialist ever talked about, and before long he was given his new moniker by the people of the village as a term of endearment. They meant no harm by it, and enjoyed hearing his stories about his journey to China to seek out and return with this lifelong object of obsession. Lorenzo With The Vase even began to refer to himself by his new name – it became a good way to introduce his story to anyone who hadn't heard it yet.

One day, some years later, Lorenzo With The Vase was admiring his wonderful acquisition when, on a gust of wind and with a flap of feathers, a large crow flew into the villa through an open window, and came to perch atop the rim of the delicate ornament. His heart skipped a beat as the giant vase shifted slightly on its plinth.

Grabbing a mop that was leaning against the wall he attempted to gently shoo away the crow. But each time it flapped just a few feet into the air before coming down to perch once again on the rim of the vase. And each time the vase swayed just a little bit more.

After some waving of the mop, and some lunging at the crow, the bird eventually took flight, and leaving several black feathers behind exited out the window from which it had come. But in all the commotion the unthinkable happened.

The vase swayed this way. And then it swayed that way. Back and forth it went, swaying and twisting on the plinth. In slow motion it came down, turning as it fell, and as its belly hit the hard marble floor it shattered into thousands of pieces, which spilled in every direction.

Genaro gasped. The gardener had been leaping around as he recounted the tale, re-enacting the battle with the crow with his own broom, leaves flying in all about him, and now he paused, resting again against his broom as he regained his breath. He returned to his story.

Lorenzo With The Vase was a broken man. In that instant his own name had turned from a celebration If a life goal, to a constant reminder of this tragedy. He wept as he tore a curtain from the window, and collecting up all the pieces he wrapped them in the fabric and slung it over his shoulder.

The last the gardener ever saw of Lorenzo With The Vase was that day, as he skulked from the village weeping, his makeshift sack over his back, his cries echoing around the square.

Genaro couldn't believe his bad luck. He had travelled all this way for nothing, and as he left the villa behind him and walked through the square in the direction of the train station, he wished he'd stayed in Naples. But just when he thought it had been a wasted trip something caught his eye. Looking down, among the dry leaves and dust in the gutter something gleamed white and blue. Picking it up and turning it over in his hand he immediately recognised the Chinese porcelain. Lorenzo With The Vase must have dropped it from his pack on his way out of town, he thought, as he put it in his pocket.

A few hundred yards down the road, Genaro's eye was caught by another gleaming piece of porcelain, beckoning at him from the dirt. And every hundred yards or so he found another and then another. Eventually, the trail of broken porcelain led him to the next village, to the door of an old antique shop.

Genaro showed the antiquarian the broken pieces, and the shopkeeper told him how, some years earlier, Lorenzo With The Vase had come into his shop. He had pleaded, distraught and in tears, with the shopkeeper. He begged him to fix his vase, but the shop keeper couldn't help him, and sobbing, Lorenzo With The Vase had left.

The shopkeeper pointed Genaro in the direction the weeping man had gone, and he set off that way. Sure enough, every now and then he would find another piece of porcelain to show him the path Lorenzo With The Vase had taken on his mission to find help. From village to village and shop to shop, Genaro heard the same story. A sorrowful man calling himself Lorenzo With The Vase, carrying a tattered cloth full of broken pieces of porcelain asking for help. In some of the stories the distraught man's own name even seemed to cause him pain, and in all of the stories, he was sent on his way to seek help elsewhere.

As the days and the weeks and the months went onwards, and Genaro kept following the trail of broken pieces, and eventually he had gathered enough to fit some of them together. In the dim light of whichever lodging rooms he was staying that night, he would sit with glue and a magnifying glass, attempting to marry some of the pieces he had collected. And then the next day the quest would begin again.

Nearly a year had passed, and the trail of broken china was inching Genaro closer to his beloved home of Naples. He travelled with a small cart now, carrying growing pieces of repaired vase gently lest they break again, and it was beginning to take the shape of the thing he had initially travelled so far and for so long to glimpse in the first place.

After days of following his porcelain trail he would spend the nights lovingly restoring and repairing, aligning the jagged edges of pottery, putting to use his many years of training as a restorer. And then one night in lodgings, after many more long days, he sighed to himself as he looked up at a beautiful, almost fully-restored vase, standing at least seven feet tall, with just a few jagged edges. Would he ever see it completed, he wondered?

If he kept following the trail as he had done for these many months, it would only be a matter of days until he had finally restored this beautiful piece of Chinese artistry. He couldn't wait to finish his adventure, to return home victorious. He yearned to be back in his study at the university, surrounded by his precious pots and jugs.

The next day he continued the journey, collecting and following shards of blue and white, and again it led to an antique shop. But this time the story was different. The antiquarian spoke of a tired looking man who had come into his shop just hours earlier, muttering something about being Lorenzo With The Vase, and holding in his hand a few small pieces of porcelain. The antiquarian wasn't sure what this clearly deranged individual wanted, but he pointed him towards Naples University. There is a man there called Genaro who might be able to help.

Genaro rushed as fast as he dared with his delicate cargo in tow. His home town appeared in the distance as he came over the hill, and he could just make out the roof of his University. Finally, he arrived, and as he wheeled the delicate vase through its beloved corridors, he saw a man waiting outside his office.

The exhausted man looked up and smiled as Genaro brought the enormous, nearly perfect vase to rest in front of him. The old man surveyed the porcelain, its smooth surface hiding any signs of being shattered into all those pieces. He gently ran his hand across its surface until he came to rest at a small jagged hole in the pot.

Reaching into his pocket, he produced the final piece of broken porcelain and handed it to Genaro. Fetching his glue, the restorer put it seamlessly in place. And the Vase was complete, perfect once more.

For what must have been the best part of an hour, the two men gazed upon the impressive vase in silence. Drinking in its curves, its delicate decoration, the way its glaze caught the light. Eventually the old man smiled at the academic, shook his hand and turned, walking towards the exit. Only now he didn't seem so old any more, a spring in his step betrayed a fresh energy that Genaro hadn't noticed before.

Stunned that he would simply walk away after being reunited with his beloved artefact, the restorer was lost for words as he called after him.

"Wait," he shouted. And then, not really sure what else to say, called out "I'm Genaro."

Without turning around, and pushing open the door as he stepped into the sunlight, the old man replied:

"I'm Lorenzo."

Blown from the west,
Fallen leaves gather,
In the east.

— Yosa Buson

Chapter 21
The Unanswerable Question

"Out of nowhere the mind comes forth."
– The Diamond Sutra

Why do you do what you do? Why do you walk the path you walk? Is it to reach your destination? Is it to find the pot of gold that waits for you? Or do you walk the path for its own sake? What's your intention? What is the purpose of your actions? What are your expectations?

Expectations are strange things. They are imaginings of things that might be, that could be, that perhaps should be. Such is their nature that more often than not they lead to disappointment rather than delight. When they are met there is no sense of surprise because we had already imagined what that would be like – that is what expectations are. But when they are not met, we find ourselves saddened, let down, aggrieved or somehow set adrift and generally dissatisfied with the outcome.

It is only on rare occasions that we find expectations exceeded, the odds of which are so slim that the surprise and happiness it brings are as unusual as a Dodo egg. Are the odds worth it?

Expectations arise when our intention is based on the outcome and not the act itself. Acts of altruism become selfish, acts of creation become commercial, and acts of work become a chore. Pay me. Reward me. Show me the money. Celebrate my significance.

When we donate our millions for a new library to be built in our name, do we do it because we want people to read books, or do we do it because we want people to know we gave them a library? When we make a song and dance out of giving to charity, or supporting a worthwhile cause, who is the real benefactor?

But what of the act itself? When you're focused on the outcome, your energy is wrapped up in the expectation. The act suffers. When you're just there for the money you're not interested in doing a good job. When you're just focused on the destination, miles of beautiful journey pass you by unnoticed.

When we focus our minds on the reward the act becomes inauthentic, and we sacrifice where we are, who we are, and what we have right now for what we might gain in the future. And because, as we know, expectations rarely deliver, we have ultimately given away our happiness only to find ourselves disappointed later.

Yes, goals are important, they motivate us and give us something to work towards. But often the action and the goal don't align. Philanthropy for the sake of being a philanthropist is inauthentic and doomed to hollow failure. Philanthropy to help others, though, is sure to succeed. Creating art to make money is not creating art. Creating art for the work itself truly is.

You don't become a world class sprinter by focusing on the finish line, but by learning how to sprint. By passionately committing to the doing, and doing in this moment, authenticity and success cannot be far away. Indeed, the doing becomes the success, the reward in itself. We get to do "the thing".

When we focus solely on the goal, we lose our passion and our drive when we realise how far away our goal really is, and our authenticity evaporates. We pay the price in our integrity and the quality of our work.

The true artist creates because they feel the possibilities in every brush stroke. The true philanthropist gives when no-one is looking, and no-one will ever know. The truly compassionate and empathic will help and help and help, and when they get no thanks in return they will help and help some more.

"Love is something you give, not something you receive," says Naval Ravikant.

Better to be kind and be taken advantage of, than to ever be mean.

Better to give without expectation and understand that the only reward may be to be seen as a source to those who take, than to deprive the world of what we have to offer. When we are the source, the rewards will come in other ways than those we might expect, but they will come.

When we let go of the reward and focus on what's important, the work we do becomes more valuable, and holds more meaning for us. When we put all our effort into this moment, the job at hand, the task and our connection with it, we have a chance at brilliance. We are tuning in to our infinite continuum of being.

When the reward is not important, any reward that does — and surely will — find us, will always delight. We can never be disappointed when the prize is unexpected. And when no reward arrives our heart never breaks because we have already been rewarded by the work that we've done, and the satisfaction that comes from doing something to best of our ability.

Our prize will come when we know that we've made someone else's day a little easier. It will come from knowing the quality of our work has been recognised. When we have given the small amount that we can, which to another is a fortune.

It will come when we feel cleansed of negativity, and inspired to do more, to help more, create more. And when our intention is the work itself – and when the intention of others is the work itself – the world will experience the lush growth of spring, the rivers will be cleansed, and the healing will begin. That will be our reward, and we will be richer than we could have possibly imagined.

Yet this all seems paradoxical. If we act without expectation, without an idea of reward, what if our actions are for nothing? What if we never get anywhere good?

When questions like this come into our mind, we must stop to remember that life is a Koan. First described by the Zen Buddhists, a Koan is a paradoxical puzzle which often is impossible to answer. What is the sound of one hand clapping?

But the purpose of a Koan is not to figure out the answer, but in the contemplation of the question. And so it is with life. We are not here to find out the meaning of life, the universe and everything, but to contemplate the question. When we try to find an answer, we will only be disappointed, because whatever we find – perhaps 42 – is not the answer we were expecting, but a disappointment.

The answer, instead, comes from the contemplation of the question. The dance, the action, the intent, and not the reward that comes from it. The meaning of it all comes from the way in which we have freed ourselves from all the delusions and the rules and the judgements and the opinions of others and of ourselves, and followed our hearts and lost ourselves in the task.

When we have no expectations, when we aim for no rewards, the task becomes our purpose, we become masters of the dance. And when we become lost in our purpose – in our doing – we are found by those who appreciate our commitment to the process, and appreciate how we have sought to free ourselves from the shackles of conformity.

By doing things not because we are expected to, not because it is the done thing, or because that's just what people like us do, but instead because we want to, because we are driven to and because we find meaning in the act of doing it, we discover light and treasure. Every step we take brightens the skies, and clears a path for others to follow.

Our energy becomes attractive, addictive, and contagious. Our own fire ignites the fire of others without itself becoming dimmed. And the world begins to resonate and shine and shimmer.

We can have whatever we want as long as we lose ourselves in the process, as long as we act authentically with our intent in the act and not in the reward. Let go of expectation and avoid disappointment. Let go of expectation and avoid failure.

Just be, and do, and ignite your world. And then step back and appreciate your canvas.

Let's all adore
In the same well of clouds
This one moon

–   Tagami Kikusha-Ni

Chapter 22
Which Way Home?

"There is the path of fear and the path of love. Which will you follow?" – Jack Kornfield

Every day we are faced with the choice of two paths. Both lead in roughly the same direction, but one is littered with potholes and boulders and the going is treacherous, while the other is smooth and easy to traverse, the going quick and pleasant.

One of these paths is lined with flowers and golden temples, and as we progress along it the flowers bloom ever more vibrantly, their perfume becoming sweeter and more intoxicating the further we go. Each golden temple that we pass is more magnificent and shines brighter than the last, and each step we take is so cushioned and enchanting it's as if the very ground itself is propelling us along. Birds sing and circle above us, the air is warm and fresh, and our way is lit with the beautiful dappled light of dawn.

The other path is lined with the detritus of everyone who has gone before. Rubbish and litter block our way, and we are faced with hazards that threaten to trip us up with every step. The way is littered with the ruins of great institutions that sought to do good work, their smouldering remains lying testament to follies of fear and its destructive power.

On one of these paths we find fellow travellers, and together we help each other along, share stories of our dreams and what we hope to achieve, and we offer and receive encouragement. We travel quickly together, and the path we leave behind us is smoother, clearer and more inviting for the next travellers who will follow in our footstep.

On this path we are cheered along by the breeze and the trees, and the animals that live in their branches. We feel buoyed by the possibility not just of reaching our destination, but of the joys and adventures that we will experience along the way. The weakest among us benefit from the combined strength of the group, and grow stronger, faster and more confident. The path lifts them up as it does for all who walk this way, they are energised and healed by the warmth this route offers them.

On the path of love, we find opportunities for growth, we find excitement and new things to interest us, we embrace our differences and find ways to use our unique experiences to enrich the lives of others just as our lives are enriched by theirs. We stand on each other's shoulder to reach the highest, most delicious fruit.

On the path of love we celebrate possibilities, differences, and the opportunity to help each other. Together we learn that anything is possible, as we reach for the stars and bring into reality the things that we had merely dreamed of just days earlier.

Walking the path of fear is a very different experience. Here we find danger in anything that's strange and unusual, and find ourselves steeling against conflict and attack from those different to us. Anyone who looks different, lives a different lifestyle, has a different culture, different tastes, a different language or who thinks differently to us is not just a danger, but is the enemy.

On the path of fear we find ourselves hating anyone who threatens our identity by offering us something we haven't experienced before. We put up walls around us, as we dodge the imaginary bullets and arrows that we think are whizzing around our heads, and try not to fall into the potholes or trip over the carrion that litter the path.

There is some unity to be found here, but only among the equally bitter, angry, fearful and hostile. If we don't fall in line with these people, we fall into conflict with them. Everything represents a risk, a danger to be avoided. Everything could harm us and will if we let our defences down.

We build our walls higher, and protect the space within them as if it were sacred ground. We call it freedom, but we're building a prison for ourselves, and in all this time we haven't moved down the path at all. Instead we've forgotten where we were going, and we find ourselves lost, in a place where the earth is scorched, and the sky is filled with smoke.

On the path of fear, we hoard our riches because there isn't enough to go around, and we know that it will all be stolen from us. On the path of love there is enough for everybody and we are happy to share, knowing that doing so will enrich our lives even more.

On the path of fear all gates are closed, and the fog is so thick we can't see further than a few inches in any direction, terrified of what danger lurks in the mist. On the path of love, we can see for a thousand miles in each direction, and what we see are beauty, opportunity, and friends that we can work with to build something wonderful. Friends who will help us on the journey to realise our dreams.

On the path of love we find happiness in the laughter of children, and the success of others. We find contentment in what we've got, abundance at every turn. We find happiness growing within us, not because of where we are or what we've got, but because that's who we are. And this happiness radiates outward, adding colour and bright sunshine to the already opulent landscape.

On the path of fear the success and happiness of others reinforces our failure and misery. We are never content because we always want more, and ultimately never have enough. We find we are relying on the outside world to deliver happiness, and it never does. It's dark here. Unwelcoming. And no matter how hard we work we never seem to get any further along the path. We sit, in our self-built cages cursing everyone outside the walls for our misfortune, when it was us all along, that put us here.

Struck by a
Raindrop, snail
Closes up.

— Yosa Buson

Chapter 23
Be Who You Could Be

"Everything around you that you call life was made up by people that were no smarter than you, and you can change it." **– Steve Jobs**

What we focus on expands, yet we revel in the rumination of that which irks us, or causes us discomfort, or even worse, pain. And in doing so these things grow so big that they dominate the horizon, eventually blocking out all the sunlight and plunging us into darkness.

And in the pitch black it becomes impossible to see the abundance of beauty that surrounds us in every moment, in every place, in every corner of our universe and beyond. Yet if we were to focus the same amount of our energy on the good in our lives, we would find ourselves walking beneath hundred-foot tall sunflowers, eating the sweetest fruits and carried along on the most magical birdsong.

But the glee with which we darken our skies gives the kind of instant satisfaction that comes from eating yet another slice of cake. And while we revel in each slice that we shovel into out sticky mouths, we are oblivious to the deterioration of our health, of our growing waistbands, our rotting teeth and of the wasps that are circling our heads constantly, ready to sting us if they don't get a taste of our sugar.

251

And this predisposition to focus on and give voice to those things that we find unpleasant, or to seek out conflict instead of peace, or to defend those things precious to our ego at the expense of our happiness, makes our light grow dim. And in the pitch black, the flowers that surround us wilt, the seeds struggle to germinate, and the land grows dry and cracked.

Instead we become hooked on our misfortune, on the things that make our lives inadequate and unsatisfactory, on the things we dislike, and we find ourselves unable to stop sharing this with the world. These things become part of our identities, we become associated with that bad thing that happened to us, with the thing that poisons us, we become the victim, or the angry person, or the hard to please person, or the joyless person.

Yet each time we share a hardship with the world, we double it. Each time we sit woebegone with our misfortune, with increase the power that it holds over us. Each time we find ourselves unable to be happy due to that thing which happened to us, or paralysed from taking action because of some condition, or state, or circumstance, or incident, we are increasing the burden upon us, the stress within us, manifesting our unhappiness, and all because we are resisting freedom. We are resisting happiness.

What if you could just get on with it, without these things holding you back? What if you could overcome those fears to step outside the front door, and take back ownership of your life. What if you could acknowledge those things that irk you, or which have harmed you, and lay them to rest in the past so you could get on with the important work of building your future, today?

Inside us, somewhere, we have the answers to every question we will ever need to ask. We have the potential to realise our dreams, and to own our lives, to be the versions of us we would be if we could just stretch our wings, unfurl our petals, and flourish. We can do and be anything we wish.

But in the shade of those things that we ruminate on – the things we dislike, the traumas, the bad luck, the anxiety, the fear and the worry – in the darkness of the things that we have allowed to grow far beyond their true size, the answers that we need are impossible to find. The solutions to living the life we want and being the person that we want to be are lost in the darkness.

All it takes is for us to allow a little brightness in for us to find our way again. Only by giving energy to the good things in our life, can we let those answers grow. Only by letting the blinding light of gratitude shine on us, can we see the way forward, the solutions and the route we need to travel. By acknowledging how abundant our lives already are, and dismissing any thoughts of dissatisfaction we can invite more of the same. In that light we will see our world transformed, and in that light we will see ourselves – strong, tall, free, young, and smiling.

"There will come an answer," said The Beatles. "Let it be."

Let your problems be. Let your traumas be. Let your fears be. Take a breath. A deep, revitalising breath. Breathe out. Let it be. All of it.

It's time to focus on everything you have, right now. It's time to be grateful for everything you've achieved. It's time to seek out the things in your everyday that bring you happiness. Look around you now, enjoy the architecture, the sunshine, the murmuration of starlings in the sky, the feeling of your bare feet on the soft carpet, the sounds of far off music playing in a house nearby, the curtains moving in the breeze from the open window, the smell of coffee brewing on the stove, the textures of the world around you, the design of your favourite things, the feeling of a good conversation with a close friend, your morning shower, of nodding off into glorious sleep after a hard day, of that first taste of ice cream at the beach.

It's time to acknowledge the hardships, thank them for what why've taught you, and to get on with what you need to do. Get it done, and it will be done. Deal with the boring jobs, have the difficult conversations, tackle the difficult questions. But ruminate on them and they will prevail and grow until they block out the light. So, let them be. Just get it done, and focus yourself on the smallest and the biggest sources of pleasure in the world.

Your favourite song on the radio. Learning that a good friend has received some good fortune. The satisfaction of a job well done. The cheery greeting of your dog when you get home. The pleasure of art. The satisfaction of a good deed.

Give the good things in your life the energy they need to grow and become towering beacons of joy and strength. Those other things, the things that once blocked out the light, deal with them as if they are trifles. Put them to bed. Let them rest.

Take a deep breath. A deep revitalising breath. Breathe out. Because you have important work to do, and you won't be able to any of it if your time and capacity is filled with worries and distraction. You won't be able to do any of it if your energy is spent making mountains out of molehills, and conjuring up storms in teacups, or fixating on the past.

Because you have goals to set, ambitions to realise, and confidence to grow. Because you're about to step out of your comfort zone and do something that you never thought you could. You're going to achieve something that you thought "someone like you" could ever achieve. Something that you thought could only be achieved by someone else. Someone better than you. More talented than you. More disciplined than you. Stronger.

And how do you know that you'll be able to do it?

Because everything that has been achieved by mankind has been achieved by people. Human beings. You are a human being.

Human beings have built bridges and dug tunnels over and under the sea, to bring nations closer together. They have engineered machines that can peer inside the human body and create pictures of our internal organs. Human beings have created machines that can travel at fantastical speeds through space, have built impossibly tall buildings that reach into far into the sky, and have created works of art that have astounded and challenged and amazed.

Human beings have cured illnesses, helped those less fortunate to heal themselves, to find a purpose and a place in society. They have welcomed the outcast, shared knowledge, and grown gardens in the desert where weary travellers have found rest and nourishment.

You are a human being

As human beings we often look at those who do amazing things as if they're a different species to the rest of us. Somehow, even though we are made of the same stuff, they are different, superior, something we could never be.

But the gap between where they are and where we are has been created by a difference in attitudes and perspectives. So often we think that where we are is a reflection of what we're worth or what we're capable of. We think that "people like us don't do things like that."

But in asking the question "what makes those other people so special?" we have to remind ourselves that we already have all the answers we could need. Once we push our ego and our pride and our excuses to the side, we know what it takes to become like them. We know how we are equipped and where we need to do extra work and gain extra experience and knowledge.

If we want to become a doctor, we know that we don't yet have the skills and the knowledge, and the prerequisite qualifications to realise that dream. But we have the skills to find out what we would need to do to become a doctor. And we have the skills to take the steps needed to work towards it. And with each step we fill in the gaps, and we gain the experience, the knowledge, the skills and the qualifications, to realise that ambition.

We have the answers we need to take us where we want to go.

If we want to build rockets to the moon, we can either find the gaps in our knowledge and seek to fill them and become a rocket scientist. Or perhaps we could approach it from a different angle. Could we hire rocket scientists to build the rocket for us? Could we travel to the moon metaphorically, in art, in literature, in imagination?

There are steps we can take, and all we need to do to start moving in the right direction is to look inside ourselves. Look inside and see what we're capable of, and what we're not capable of – yet – and start taking the steps to realise our dream.

But in order to do this, we must push past the conditioning that says it's too difficult, it's too hard, that people like us don't do things like, that it's impossible.

As long as you think it's impossible it will always remain impossible.

If they had thought it was impossible, Orville and Wilbur Wright would have stuck to building bicycles rather than flying machines, and they would never have got off the ground in Kitty Hawk in 1903. If she had thought it was impossible, Elizabeth Garrett Anderson would have abandoned her efforts to become the first female doctor in Britain. But despite being turned away by every university in the country, she looked elsewhere and eventually obtained her qualification in France in 1865. If he thought it was impossible, Yuri Gagarin wouldn't have climbed into his Vostok spacecraft in 1961, to be become the first human to safely orbit the Earth.

In order for us to realise our dreams, we must first understand that the thing we aspire to isn't simply a dream, but something possible. We must have the belief that it can be achieved, and when something can be achieved it becomes doable. And by becoming aware of the tools we are already armed with, and where the gaps lie, the possibility exists that we can make it a reality.

Ordinary people do extraordinary things. And they do them not simply by fantasizing, or by blindly assuming that it cannot be done, but by seeking the information required to do it. And armed with that knowledge ordinary people can do the things that make dreams come true.

But dreams don't come true by sitting still. Dreams don't come true when we find ourselves paralysed by fear. Dreams come true by doing something. Taking a step outside your front door, outside your comfort zone. Dreams come true by recognising your patterns and breaking them.

As family relationship expert Jessie Potter famously said: "If you always do what you've always done, you'll always get what you've always gotten."

The things you've always done, those practices, those ways of thinking and ways of seeing, they've brought you here, to where you are now. But if you've been here for a while, and you're feeling stuck, it's because those same practices, processes, patterns and thoughts can take you no further.

If you could brush aside the excuses, becoming aware of where you stop and your ego begins, you would be armed with the self-awareness to see where your gaps are. You'd be able to discover which patterns you need to change to reach those dreams, and which dreams come at too high a cost and which are within reach.

The dream of being an astronaut may seem appealing, but the commitment involved, the years of study, relentless training, time away from your family, and the mortal danger may be a price too far. Or it may not be.

The dream of owning your own home may seem impossible. But when you start exploring the options, the true costs, the different methods of ownership, of looking at other types of property in other places, you might find it very possible.

Even the dream of being confident, capable and unafraid may seem impossible. But by imagining what that looks like, and what steps you would need to become that version of you – how you would need to behave, hold yourself, go about your business – it may seem quite doable.

Dreams become possible when we believe them to be, and they can become doable when we find out what it would take to make it a reality. All that we need to do when we arrive at this point is take the decision to do it or not. And if we decide to do it, we simply must.

When we set a course, take the consistent action required to achieve it, and leave the rest to time, any mountain can be climbed, any garden can be planted, and any target can be met. As long as we're prepared to get uncomfortable.

Uncomfortable means making the effort. It means staying up a little later, stretching our horizons a little wider, and opening ourselves to new ways of seeing. It means going further than we've ever been before, embracing new responsibilities, and facing new unknowns with the courage to make it through to the other side. It means embarking on a journey to that will change the shape of our life, our world, and the universe that radiates out from us in every direction backward and forward in time.

Uncomfortable means doing things differently to the way we've always done them, being different to the person we've always been, and daring to step out from the hiding place of our comfort zone.

It means finding our fear and pushing past it, finding our limits and going beyond them, acknowledging our story and rewriting it. By seeing what we're capable of, and making the impossible possible, we know that we are not limited by our old paradigms but free to do whatever we want to do, go wherever we want to go, and be whoever we want to be.

Our fear shows us where to go. Letting go shows us how to get there.

The butterfly –
What are the dreams that make him
Flutter his wings?

\-   Kaga no Chiyo

Chapter 24
All Time is in This Moment

"Let us never know what old age is. Let us know the happiness time brings, not count the years." –
Ausonius

Everything is distilled into this moment. Everything. Right here, right now, you are the nucleus of everything that has been, everything that will be, and everything that could be. It exists within you in as much certainty as the oak tree lives within the acorn. The ethereal threads that connect us to everyone, everything, every notion and every time, not only connect us but they act as conduits the transfer all of those things into a single place. A singularity where everything exists at once, in all its states, with all its facets visible, depending on how you wish to observe it.

You are the singularity. You are the single point of infinity.

Everything that will ever exist is condensed within you, at your very centre, waiting to be observed, explored, experienced. This dense cluster of realities offers a glimpse of infinity, and only by looking deep into yourself will you get the opportunity to see those things that swirl in its dense, infinite core. Only by looking deep within yourself will you get the opportunity to go anywhere that you can imagine, see things beyond description, understand the unlimited potential of that you have within you. That you've always had within you.

"Below the threshold of consciousness everything was seething with life" said Jung.

The profiteers of control, who have kept us distracted by matters of the surface world, who have hijacked our thinking with television news, soap operas and small-minded trivialities, who have used a notion of god to keep the workforce subservient for hundreds of years, need us to think alike, act alike and be alike. It is important that the system keeps feeding itself, and feeding off unique souls who should be amorphous but instead find themselves categorised, standardised, pigeon-holed and tribalized.

We willingly hand ourselves over to the profiteers of control so we can be kept, hoodwinked, for meagre rewards. But if we were to break free, our rewards would be infinite, and the power our masters hold over us would be lost. The profiteers of control need our compliance, and they trick us into believing that we need to give it to them.

But within us the dense cluster of our entire universe waits patiently to be awakened, to be found, so that we might finally understand that this is all for us. All of it. The pain and the suffering, the heartbreak and the sorrows all serve to guide us to our unlimited potential. All the lessons that we learn, everything we see, everything we do, every thought we have, and every thought we don't, all are telling us to look a little bit closer. Every experience of joy, every ounce of happiness, every sensation, every taste, every moment of love, are asking us to look. Look below the surface. It's all there. Waiting to meet us.

As we skip along the surface, sometimes we glimpse what lies beneath and don't even realise it. Sometimes we take a moment to look and glimpse the cornucopia of existence and our world expands before us. Occasionally a soul goes their entire life and doesn't see it at all.

But when it registers, when we understand the power that we have, to control our universe, everything changes. We are the singularity. The profiteers of control lose their grasp on us and we are no longer cattle feeding at the trough waiting to be milked. We can do anything, be anything, go anywhere, transcend everything.

When we read poetry we step into other worlds. When we create art, we bring feelings into being. When we build, when we explore, when we help, when we pause to look, we cease being consumers and instead become the ultimate creators of our own reality.

In a moment we can choose to be still and breathe, and detach ourselves from one place to move to another. We can find flow states in exercise and movement that launch us from one world to another. We can transcend the grip of the surface world and explore the surface of the moon, if we wish, or climb among the petals of a sunflower, or transport ourselves into the rhythms of music that hasn't even been performed yet. We just need to decide to do so.

The entirety of existence is within you at this very moment. At your core you have the power to change history, shape the future, realise dreams, and imagine your own reality. You can light this world with infinite love, or explore a new world on the head of pin. You can stop time, speed it up, or step outside it altogether. Your power is unlimited – you simply need to harness it.

This omnipotence has saved the sanity of prisoners of war and conscience who, despite having their physical freedom stolen from them have enjoyed the infinite freedom of their minds. It has helped Olympic athletes run their best races before they've even stepped foot on the track. It has enabled sculptors to see their finished masterpieces hiding within giant slabs of stone, before they've even picked up their chisel. And it has enabled millions of amorphous souls like us to envision a better reality for themselves and others, to believe that it's possible, and to take the action to make it so.

Your ethereal threads all come together in a single point within you. It is here, if you look closely enough, you'll find your unrealised power waiting to be unleashed to change your universe. Here lies the courage to be different, to take risks, to be the person you want to be, and to start building the thing that others may call a ridiculous flight of fancy today, but will stare at in amazement in a year, or two, or ten.

That idea, that spark, that itch, that feeling. Those things that hurt, or irritate, or urge you forward. These messages that you're fighting to understand, or simply fighting, they're telling you something. They're telling you that you need to look closely, and think for yourself, because all the while you hand over responsibility for your life and your future to the system and the profiteers of control, your own infinite strength goes unrealised.

And like the acorn that falls on the rocky ground with the oak still inside it, or the boy who pulls the duvet up around his ears for just another hour of sleep while the most beautiful sunrise knocks on his window, you will never see the reality that sleeps undisturbed within you. You will find comfort in the patterns that have brought you this far, but will take you no further. You will begin to petrify and stagnate, becoming a stone monument to who you could have been.

Tomorrow you can continue to simply be a consumer, or you can start to build something instead. You can snooze or you can move. You can look and listen and recognise all the messages that are shouting at you from within you and from all around you, or you can fall back on your regular patterns. The world is yours, if you want it. You can have anything, if you'll take it. You can change everything, if you can just let go of where you are and step into the light of what could be.

You are swaddled, but all you need to do to break free is find the energy and the inspiration that exists within you, and follow the instructions. You have everything you need, you have all the answers, you just need to make that decision. And when you do the kaleidoscope will take a turn, the light will shift, and everything will begin to look very different.

The shift will start to happen almost straight away, and soon you'll be looking back wondering if any of it really happened at all. And having come this far, you'll wonder how much further you can go, if you just look a little closer and a little deeper.

You are the singularity. The entirety of existence lies within you. You can follow the ethereal threads outwards, or you can follow them inwards. And when you come to the point where they all converge, you'll be faced with the question that you need to answer. A question that holds your potential and your future in its fingers. All you have to do is answer it.

Now what?

The snow of yesterday,
That fell like cherry blossom,
Is water once again.

-     Gozan

Chapter 25
The Walls of Pride

"All is revealed to those who choose to look." –
unknown

The two warring tribes had fought for generations.
Countless lives had been lost over millennia and the
earth was so soaked with blood that the trees grew with
red leaves and bark. But both tribes were dying out for
other reasons. The one because their land was arid, and
they faced extinction from famine, unable to germinate
the mountains of seeds that remained from their last
successful crops years before. The other faced
extinction because their land was flooded, and each
year more of their crops rotted in the waterlogged soil
before they could be harvested. This season the last of
their seeds had been lost, rotten in the sodden soil
before they could grow.

The beliefs of each tribe rested on the ancient teachings
of their founding fathers and the laws of their elders.
Written in holy texts, each believed that their god was
the only god, and that there could only be one god. In
order that their beliefs be protected both tribes built a
great wall around their lands to keep heretics and
heathens out, and to protect them from the others.

One tribe, whose god was Yeewah, would distract
themselves from their hunger by reciting stories from
their book of texts. The stories were teachings about

how to live a good life, how to remain on the path of righteousness, and how only by following these teachings was the survival of the tribe and its place in heaven certain. The stories taught that those non-believers outside the walls were to be feared, to be fought, and that they threatened everything their civilisation stood for. Those outsiders were the devil.

The other tribe, whose god was Yaaweh, would also distract themselves from their hunger by sharing stories from their book. These stories, written by their forefathers many years ago, told of demons in strange robes, with strange skin, who stood to destroy everything they had built. These evil doers – everyone outside the walls of their tribe – would destroy them if they were not destroyed first. They were to be feared, cast out, and avoided at all cost.

Anyone who was not within the walls of the tribe was different. With different looks. And different ways. And different ideas. And different values. And a different god. And different is dangerous. A threat. The devil. The occult.

On one side of the wall the water continued to rise relentlessly, ruining everything it touched, while on the other side the earth turned to crimson dust, choking and blinding those who walked upon it.

Unable to find solutions to their problems, the people of the two tribes would share stories about the demons outside the walls. And rather than try to face their extinction, they would engage in bloody battles with those others – the non-believers on the other side of the wall – who threatened their way of life.

One morning a young girl, hungry, tired and confused by the attitude of the adults who seemed uninterested in facing the real problems of their people, left home on a journey of discovery. She had grown tired of the stories of the holy texts, and rather than being told about life from the perspective of the elders, she decided to find out about the world for herself. Such activities were strictly forbidden, but desperation and curiosity got the better of her, and she slipped out the house into the pre-dawn darkness, before her parents awoke.

The sun was high in the sky by the time she reached the wall, and her eyes were sore from all the dust that her walking had kicked up. She had never seen the wall for herself, but had her stories about it. She never imagined that it could be so high, and she struggled to see the top of it. She used her hand to shade her eyes from the fearsome sunlight that blazed down on the dusty land of her people.

She knew of the dangers that lay beyond. The demons, the "others" that threatened her family and her way of life. But she wanted to see for herself. She wanted to know what was on the other side. So she began to climb.

The sweat was dripping off her forehead, and her arms and legs hurt from the effort, but looking down at the ground from where she'd come, she knew that she couldn't turn back now. Her parents, she thought, would be looking for her now, gripped with panic about their missing daughter. But she knew she had to see what was really on the other side of the Great Wall that kept her people safe, and kept the enemy out.

Finally her climb was over, and as she pulled herself on to the top of the wall, she paused to sit with her legs dangling over the edge as she surveyed what lay on the other side. The waters stretched for as far as she could see, with just a few hilltops protruding through the waters, with hastily built houses stacked upon them in haphazard arrangements that stretched precariously skyward. Ramshackle rafts bobbed around on the waters below, as people just like her parents – only with different clothes and a different skin colour – traversed from one hilltop to another.

"Hello."

She turned her head in surprise at the greeting, and saw a young boy, about her own age, sitting on top of the wall, surveying the parched land of her people.

"Where have you come from?" She asked the little boy.

He turned and pointed to one of the hilltops sticking out of the water.

"I live just down there. I'm not supposed to be here. Our laws prevent it. And I'm not supposed to talk to people like you. You're different to us. You're demons."

The little girl shrugged.

"You're demons too. Your ideas are wrong and dangerous. You will kill us if we don't kill you first."

The two children sat in silence for a moment, their legs dangling over the edge of the wall. Finally, the boy broke the silence.

"Why is it so dry on your side of the wall?"

The little girl looked back at where she had come from and thought for a moment, before finally speaking.

"Because of the wall, no water reaches our land, and the earth is so dry our seeds won't grow. Our people are dying out and it's all because of people like you, different people with different ways and different ideas, who live on the other side of the wall," she explained. "Why is it so wet on your side of the wall?"

The boy explained: "Because of the wall our water has nowhere to go, and all our crops are rotting in the earth. And it's because of people like you, who are different and have different ways and different ideas, who live on the other side of the wall, who we need to protect ourselves from. People just like us."

Again, the two children sat in silence, this time for much longer. They contemplated everything they'd been told about the wall, and the people who lived on the other side of it. They thought about the demons they'd been told about who threatened the existence of their people, and they thought about the flooded lands and the arid soils that were starving their people to death.

They contemplated how they were just the same as each other, despite their differences.

Eventually the little boy spoke.

"Maybe if there wasn't a wall, your land wouldn't be so dry, and our land wouldn't be so wet. Maybe if there wasn't a wall, we would both be saved, and our problems would be solved."

The little girl replied with glee: "If there wasn't a wall, maybe we could be one tribe instead of two, and we could work together to solve all our problems, instead of fighting and building walls to hide behind. Maybe we should knock the wall down."

Both children, excited by the idea that they had solved all the problems their respective peoples faced, rushed to climb back down the wall and tell their parents what they had seen and what they had discovered. They hurried home, eager to share their ideas, that simply by tearing down the wall between their two tribes and bringing their peoples together, their ways of life would be saved, and that they could live as one, with lush lands and a bright future.

But when they returned to their homes their parents scolded them for going off without telling anybody. When they tried to explain what they had seen and learned, their parents were enraged that they had gone against the teachings of their people, that they had committed terrible sins by speaking with the enemy, by breaking the laws of the land and by contemplating ideas of their own.

The more the children tried to explain their idea for saving everyone's lives, to tell what they had seen, and explain the logic of their plan to bring down the wall, the more the adults – blinded by their own beliefs, biases and teachings – refused to listen.

Hundreds of years later, when the two peoples were just a distant memory, the great wall began to crack and shake, until finally its bricks gave way and it came crashing down. The waters of the flooded land burst forth upon the desert land, and what was once parched and dry become wet and fertile, and what had been submerged arose once more. Soon, seeds began to germinate, and within a few short years the lands of the two peoples were verdant and lush and seething with life. Birds and animals feasted on the fruits and made the trees their home, and sang out across the forests and the grasslands.

After they've fallen,
Their image remains in the mind –
Those peonies.

– Yosa Buson

Chapter 26
Why?

"He who has a why to live for, can endure any how." –
Friedrich Nietzsche.

What do you want? I'm sure the answer comes quite easily, but the chances are, that's not what you really want. These superficial wants hide something much more profound, and often something much more attainable than you think.

Do you want lots of money? Or do you want security, to be free of the stress of debt, and to be able to provide for your loved ones with enough left over for a life with some luxury?

Do you want to be slim? Or are you just unhappy with the way you look when you see yourself in the mirror? Or perhaps you want to be healthy enough to see you children grow into adults.

Want to live in an exotic country? Or perhaps you just don't want to be here, in this location, any more.

Knowing what we really want is one of the hardest things any human has to figure out. It is so closely linked to our sense of identity, of purpose – who we are and why we're here – that it can be a seemingly unfathomable question.

But if you keep asking yourself 'why', then you can eventually discover your 'what', and in that what is the solution to any problem. It can be brutal, it can offer comfort, or it can send you in a completely new direction, but once you know your why your perspective will be changed.

If we aren't happy with a situation, and understand that this feeling of discontent rises from within us and reflects some unknown thing about ourselves, rather than there being a problem with the situation, we can start to ask ourselves why. As each answer presents itself, we ask it why, and keep asking as we leap from turtle to turtle, all the way down.

Eventually we come to an actionable point where we can stop asking because we have our answer. It may reveal an uncomfortable bias about ourselves, it may reveal a genuine problem with our situation, it may reveal the limits of our tolerance. It may reveal preconceived notions that need to be removed, or it may reveal a truth about just what it would take in order for us to feel satisfied.

When you have your why, you have a target. Something to work towards. And that is a luxury that can help to move us forward, to define the action, the something new that will get us unstuck, and challenge us to take the steps necessary to go from our current level of ordinary to the next level of extraordinary.

It is from here that we can start to realise our dreams. Our why provides the foundations upon which we can start to build something that may not benefit us today, and maybe not even tomorrow, but which – in ten years' time – we will be truly thankful that we started building today. It might be a global empire, it might be a body of artworks, it might be a rose garden. Whatever we decide it should be, with time it can and will become extraordinary.

When we know our why we can summon the belief and the determination to make our what happen. We can put aside any doubts, and embrace the fear that has stopped us taking action in the past, because it is trumped by our why. Our why gives us the courage to step into the arena, to step into the spotlight, and put it all to the test. And when we fail, our why will give us the courage to get up and do it again. And again. And again.

It is our why that will enable us to face the ridicule and the critics, whose harsh words simply reveal their own fears rather than our own inadequacies. It is our why that will keep us going late into the night, when we're exhausted, our eyes are sore, and we just want to sleep, but ten more minutes now will put us a few more steps ahead tomorrow.

Our why will stop us procrastinating. It will enable us to endure the most mind-numbing and soul-destroying circumstances because we are working for a higher cause. Our why will become a forcefield against any slings and arrows that would cut down a person without one. Our why is the thing that will prove us right in the long run, long after everyone else has given up and gone home.

Having that motivation is a blessing. It is the reason to keep going, to step out onto the tightrope and brave the winds as the crowds below hold their breath. Some will wish you make it safely to the other side; some will hope that you come tumbling down as each gust of wind causes the rope under your feet to sway wildly from side to side. But you know that this says more about them than it does about you. You've got work to do, and your sights are set firmly on the other side.

Those who are lost, and left dreaming without any direction, are lacking their why. Their ultimate reason, which will keep them working towards their goal tirelessly, never growing bored, always turning up, always putting in the hours and the effort. It is the people who have found their why that realise their dreams. Not those who criticise them for trying. Not those who look on with bitterness and resentment, cursing their bad luck. Not those who see the success of others as a symbol of their own failure.

And often the journey begins with a small step. Just one tentative step, like a baby learning to walk. And then another step. And then another. And before long the road behind you stretches for a thousand miles, and it's lined with golden temples, impossibly tall flowers and trees, the birds swoop overhead, and you're joined on your adventure by a million well-wishers all beckoning you forward, willing you toward the thing you've worked so hard for.

That thing, which you've dreamed of so much, believed was possible, pictured in your mind's eye, is soon within reach. You've endured the hows, the blisters on your feet from walking the long journey, the boring days, the late nights, the side jobs, the arguments, the naysayers, and when you get there it will feel like coming home.

So, what do you really want? Is it a million dollars? Is it a big house? Is it a super yacht? Or is it security? Respect? Comfort and to be somewhere else? What will it take to get there, and what are you prepared to do to make the journey?

Keep asking why and you'll find the answers you're looking for. Keeping pushing aside your ego and your excuses, and you'll see how far you've come and how far you still have to go. Keep seeking out and breaking your patterns, introducing new behaviours and new actions that can launch you forward, and you will grow and so will your world along with you.

Winter seclusion,
Listening, that evening,
To the rain in the mountain.

—   Kobayashi Issa

CHAPTER 27
Why Not?

"Some men see things as they are, and ask why. I dream of things that never were, and ask why not." –
Robert Kennedy

Those people out there with the life you want, they're not stupid – but neither are you. In fact, there are people out there with lives you are quite envious of, who are probably not as clever as you – not nearly as clever as you – but still, they've managed to get what you haven't.

It may be that they got lucky, although we know that luck is really an illusion. Maybe they were born into it, in which case that's wonderful for them. Or it may be that they were chosen by someone, some generous benefactor, who saw what they had to offer and decided to bestow upon them this amazing life.

Or more likely than this, they probably value themselves more highly than you do, they probably think themselves worthy of success, and they are probably prepared to do things that you aren't. It could be that they have realised that their fears are imaginary, and that being afraid of what people think is the perfect way to make people think poorly of you.

It could be that instead of being frightened of risk, they're excited by opportunity. It could be that instead of spending the evenings drinking beer or watching TV, their reading books, finding out how things work, and experimenting with new ideas.

It could be that they stopped their pride getting in the way of their ambitions and dreams. Or it could be that they know what they want, and you don't.

Whatever they're doing, you're probably thinking "I could do that". But, you're not. Chances are they've been doing it for quite a while, while you haven't, and they are benefitting from the results of the two magic ingredients – action, and time.

It is only through action that our potential reveals itself, as does our life, and ourselves. We know who we are not by what we think, what ideas we have, or what we believe our values to be, but by the actions we take. And we make ourselves and our universe manifest in the process.

Our universe reflects our actions, which are a direct result of our inner processes. And it's only by taking action that we can change our current situation. And let's be clear, we are always taking action – even when we sleep. And it either serves us, or it hurts us.

You may think that you're taking action every day, yet you never seem to progress. Slogging away at the coalface yet no sign of any diamonds in the darkness. It's your everyday actions, those patterns that are repeated time after time, the ones that have got you this far, but which are keeping you stuck here, that need to be changed. Those traits, which you have been loyal to all this time, but which now it's time to say goodbye to and replace with new behaviours, new actions and new patterns. Maybe they gave you a leg up once upon a time, or maybe they didn't, but it's time to move on, to improve and clear out the old to make way for the new.

They may be the smallest things – a different route to work in the morning, and different breakfast ritual, or replacing the morning newspaper with a thought-provoking book. Or it may be time to say goodbye to that superstitious ritual that has never served you – crossing on the stairs, avoiding the number thirteen, walking under ladders. These behaviours which have either got you this far, or have done nothing for you at all, and are now taking up space in your day.

Time to find new actions and patterns. Time to try being a different person. Someone who's brave. Not afraid to ask questions. Not afraid to do the thing that will raise eyebrows. Not afraid to step into the arena. Someone who doesn't care what people think, and understands that these social contracts, these norms, these unspoken rules and agreements, they're designed to keep us here, and we must break them if we wish to go further. We must find our own rules if we wish to go to the places we dream of.

These new actions will accumulate into something huge. A glass of water before bed can be a small part of a new life. Getting off the bus a stop early to fit a brisk walk and thinking time into your day could be the birthplace of new ideas. Turning off the television and reading a book could be the start of a new you.

We are always taking action, but it is intent that drives change. And beneficial action done with intent, with no regard for the passing of time, builds empires, dreams, and a new universe that stretches out from you in all directions. Who do you want to be tomorrow?

Because that's the question. That's the opportunity. The choice that you now face.

Do you want to be the you that hides behind a fearful persona, worrying about rocking the boat, about those plastic traumas that have held you back? Or do you want to be the you that takes ownership of that baggage and takes back the power that it holds over you in order that you can grasp tomorrow with two hands. Tomorrow is a new day, and you can be whoever you want, just as long as you take action. Just as long as you do something.

So do something. Anything. And do it now.

Snail
Bit by bit ascend!
Mount Fuji.

—   Kobayahsi Issa

296

Chapter 28
"Grow! Grow!"

***"Once you make a decision, the universe conspires to make it happen." –* Ralph Waldo Emerson**

A blade of grass has a single purpose, and that is to grow. In the Kabbala tradition it is said that above each blade are angels, beseeching it to fulfil its purpose. "Grow, grow" cry the angels, pleading with it to be everything it can be.

The angels urge it to live to the fullest of its potential, to feel the wind and dance with it, to look upwards and reach out towards the sun, to grow full and lush, be all that it can be, and to extract from life everything that is there for it to enjoy.

We are surrounded by colours and textures. From the softest wools and the smoothest cottons to the coarsest stones, all painted a spectrum of shades for us to behold and to feel. The sounds of the world echo around us – the wind rustles the leaves in the trees as it makes them shimmer and sway, the rain taps us on the shoulder asking that we take notice.

There is a music to life that is always playing, a poetry with rhythmical stanzas in every lap of the sea against the shore, every beat of the woodpecker's beak against thee tree and every beat of the hearts in our chest. Light illuminates the stage upon which we perform and the ethereal threads that reach out in every direction connecting us to everything and everyone that is, was and will be vibrate like the strings of a violin to accompany us as we make sense of this universe we find ourselves at the centre of.

We have legs for dancing, feet for running, arms for waving and hands for creating. We have mind for the creation of new worlds and new adventures. There are ski slopes to swoosh down, oceans to swim in, autumn leaves to kick through, bicycles to be ridden, and puddles to be splashed in. There are sunsets to drift off with, dreams to be dreamed about, fantasy lands to be explored, and wonders to behold and be wondered about.

Each of us is uniquely capable of fulfilling a unique potential. Some of us have the passion for sport, others the aptitude for art. Some wish to build, some wish to save, others wish to write. From each our own perspective through which to experience life, the world, and all it has to offer, so long as we choose to make it our own.

We only get one opportunity to dance this dance, so why would we wish to sit this one out. And it is our dance – when we try to dance that of another we simply trip over our own feet. So, dance to your own rhythm, sing your own tune and make dance floor your own.

With our unique potential there is nothing we can't do if we want to. No experience we cannot enjoy, no dream we cannot dream, no flavour, smell, sound that we cannot enjoy.

If you could look up and see them, what would the angels be saying to you?

The oak tree stirs,
For the moment just a dream,
Within the acorn.

About the Author

Chris Brock is a writer, photographer and journalist who was born in the South East of England, where he has lived and worked for most of his life.

After moving to New York to work in publishing for a spell following the attacks on the Twin Towers, he returned to London to explore a variety of creative avenues, becoming an authority in communications.

He has spent time working as a van driver, a carer for people with disabilities, in banking, in kitchens, and in television. His writings explore the world we can see, those we can't and how to make the most of the short time we have in this existence.

This is his third book.

To read more of this work visit: www.chrisbrock.uk and www.dothethinghavethepower.com

Further Reading

Do The Thing, Have The Power: Overcome Self-Doubt and Build a Life You Love.

Build a better life from the inside out, with simple steps to changing your mindset and perspective in order to change your world. With examples from the author's own life, you will learn to own your life, master it – and love it.

Outpost: Collected Writings Volume 1

A collection of the author's essays focused on the topic of finding ourselves and our purpose, and realising out true potential. It explores the idea that we are spiritual beings existing in a material realm, but there is more going on if we choose to look a little closer.

47036058R00181

Printed in Poland
by Amazon Fulfillment
Poland Sp. z o.o., Wrocław